THE
RELENTLESS
HERO

HERO IN PARADISE SERIES

BonzaiMoon Books LLC
Houston, Texas
www.bonzaimoonbooks.com

Angel Vane has been entertaining readers with her brand of crime thrillers for women. Now you can get one of her novellas for FREE, you just need to go to the link and tell her where to send it:

GET MY FREE SHORT STORY NOW
https://BookHip.com/SFTKRK

Prologue

The door of the black SUV opened.

Tubeec Hirad stepped out, then glanced up at the Global Exchange Building. Slipping the cell phone into the inner pocket of his tailored Armani suit, he dodged a group of young aspiring corporate types as he made his way to the revolving doors.

The call had gone as he'd expected. Tubeec marveled at the unwillingness to take his threats seriously. He had a reputation for never bluffing, yet time and again, he was forced to exact a toll on unsuspecting targets because their loved ones refused to comply with his demands.

Passing through the modern chrome lobby, Tubeec waved to the security guards who'd grown accustomed to seeing him enter and exit the building at various hours over the past two months.

"Good afternoon, Mr. Henderson." The guards greeted him. They believed he was Mitchell Henderson, as his security badge indicated.

Just another hard-working investment banker with the private equity firm housed on five floors of the building.

Stepping into the crowded chrome elevator, Tubeec reached past a woman dressed in a short mini skirt and pressed the button for the sixth floor. She recoiled, her eyes locked on his scarred hand. She didn't turn to look at him. A pity. She would have been surprised to see that he was still a relatively handsome man. The fire had ravished over eighty percent of his body, but his disfigured skin was mostly hidden underneath his expensive suit.

As the elevator stopped on each floor, ushering workers on and off, Tubeec inhaled the flowery stench of the woman's perfume. He regarded her flat ass in the tight skirt. She had a pretty face, but her body would do nothing to arouse anything more than mild interest in him.

The computerized voice announced "sixth floor."

"Excuse me," Tubeec said, brushing past the young woman, glancing at her breasts as he exited the elevator. She gave him a seductive smile, no doubt relieved that his face wasn't as grotesque as his hand. Another day, Tubeec would have made her pay for her relief, making her wish she'd never laid eyes on him. Today, he had more pressing business.

Alone in the hallway, he proceeded to the stairwell and took the stairs, two at a time, up the four flights to the tenth floor. Maneuvering through thick plastic covering the open doorway, Tubeec walked into the construction zone, a large, empty space.

Fading late afternoon sunlight stretched across the floor from the box windows lining the walls. The Global Exchange building had been the right choice, although Tubeec had been skeptical at first. Utilizing the space currently being renovated for the Deputy President of Kenya, Kipsang Rono, was risky. Tubeec had taken advantage of the delay in construction as the government shifted focus to the political primaries that would begin in the next few months.

His dark wingtip shoes, powdered with the dust of construction debris, were silent against the concrete floor. The thirteen men were oblivious to his approach, lost in the thunderous cacophony of preparation for their roles in the final stages of his plan. The militants had posed as businessmen, entering the building dressed in expensive business suits similar to his own. Each held a suitcase containing a change of clothes and the equipment and weapons they'd need to complete the delicate operations.

Snippets of conversation reached Tubeec's ears. The trained killers bragged about last week's conquest. Each man insisted he'd pleasured the innocent teen girl the best as if the necessary sacrifice had brought her any pleasure. Tubeec felt no guilt for his part in the gang rape of the young woman. She was a means to an end. A way to control the boy and make him do what Tubeec needed.

As he passed each member of his specially assembled team, a hush fell across the large room. Movement ceased as the men engaged in a synchronized salute, then took an at-ease stance waiting for a sign from him. Tubeec scrutinized them. Each man had been chosen not only because of superb skills but also because of the discretion shown in numerous operations in the past.

But this wasn't a typical operation.

In fact, it was one of the most complex assignments Tubeec had ever orchestrated. A brazen endeavor he couldn't resist. Targeting one of the richest and most powerful families in Africa could cost him his freedom.

Originally, he'd had no plans to complicate this mission, preferring instead to keep things simple. The universe had other ideas, presenting him with an opportunity to kill two birds with one stone, as the saying went.

Completing the inspection of the men, Tubeec stalked toward an empty corner of the room to a window that overlooked the Tribal Museum and Irungu Center across the street. He could feel the eyes of the men tracking him as they resumed preparation for the job.

Tubeec wiped the sweat from his face. The rough texture of his scarred hand against the only smooth skin on his body was a welcomed reminder of the past. Today was the anniversary of the worst day of his life. The day he'd been transformed from a scientist into one of the most dangerous men in Africa.

Some said he was insanely treacherous and unpredictable. Others whispered that he had no soul and had never felt remorse for the atrocities he'd performed.

They were wrong. His soul had died ten years ago today, January 13th, when he watched his twin sons hacked to death with machetes and his wife gang raped by government-sanctioned soldiers. He'd tried to beat them away from his family, but his efforts were futile. The soldiers bound him to a nearby tree, sprayed his body with gasoline, and tossed a match onto the brush underneath his feet. Squirming and screaming as the fire climbed up his body, he'd somehow managed to free himself. Howling his anguish, he'd staggered and stumbled toward his wife and twin sons, left to die in a nearby field. His wounded screams pierced the still air as he gathered their mutilated bodies in his arms.

In his grief, he'd become a monster.

Making others suffer as much as he'd suffered became his addiction, his reason for living. Until he was reunited with his family again, he would kill and destroy. Never would anyone make him feel helpless and afraid. Instead, he would be the one to wield fear as a weapon, daring anyone to try to hurt him again.

The success of this mission would give him what he most desired—revenge. The power to destroy those who'd destroyed the life he'd had before.

"Cangrejos!" Tubeec commanded, his voice echoing through the room.

Frantic footsteps thundered across the concrete floor, stopping mere feet behind him.

Tubeec turned and glared at his second in command, a loyal foot soldier he'd rescued from a Panamanian mafia hit a few years ago.

"Who's on the strike team?" Tubeec asked.

"Yasir, Bashiir, Liban, and Zahi," Cangrejos responded, his arms clasped behind his back as he stared at the ground, not meeting Tubeec's eyes. "They are equipped and ready."

"Bombers?"

Cangrejos said, "Dalmar, Harbi, Xirsi and Suleymaan."

"Were the explosives created to my specifications?" Tubeec asked.

"Yes, sir. Bombers will be deployed to the designated areas inside the Tribal Museum on your command."

"Who's left?" Tubeec asked, although he already knew the answer.

"Rahim, Assad, Geesi, and Nadifa. They will accompany you into the Irungu Center. I will personally serve as the lookout and drive the truck once the mission is complete, as you requested," Cangrejos said.

"Are all of the targets still inside the building?" Tubeec asked.

Cangrejos confirmed, "Yes, we have visuals of Wangari Irungu, Isaac Gatobu, Grace Kadenge, and Mena Nix. All four targets are in the building and expected to remain there until five o'clock."

"And the flower delivery truck?" Tubeec asked.

"Left the shop two minutes ago and will be arriving in ten minutes." Cangrejos' answer came.

Pleased, Tubeec said, "Wrap up the preparations."

Cangrejos nodded, then turned and rejoined the rest of the militia, issuing final instructions to the team.

In a matter of minutes, terror and destruction would be unleashed onto an unsuspecting group of presumably innocent people at the Tribal Museum in downtown Nairobi. No one would expect another attack so soon. Three days ago, a suicide bomber had disrupted a private fundraising dinner for President Noah Thairu on the museum rooftop. His source within the police department confirmed that no group had claimed responsibility.

Tubeec knew that no group would.

The suicide bomber hadn't been trying to kill the beloved Kenyan president. The attack had been part of Tubeec's complex plan to observe and assess the Kenyan police's response to terrorism. Critical information that had allowed him to finalize the plans for today's mission.

Tubeec surveyed the men, now standing at attention in a straight line dressed in green trousers and long-sleeve green shirts. Ammunition belts crossed their chests. Black scarves hid noses and mouths of the men as they stared into the distance, dark paint smeared under intense eyes.

After changing into the green shirt and trousers, Tubeec put on the black combat boots that rested against the wall. He reached into his pocket and squinted as he pulled out his black scarf. Tying it around his head, he lifted the fabric over his nose and mouth, then glanced at his watch.

A surge of energy spiked in the air.

At his cue, the men sprinted to the back wall, grabbing the M4 Carbine assault rifles.

Tubeec would remain unarmed.

He never thought of his own safety.
Why protect a life that wasn't worth living?
They waited for his signal.
Tubeec's words were almost a whisper.
"Let's go."

Chapter One

"Is this the part where I'm supposed to carry you across the threshold?" Julian Montgomery asked, gliding the two oversized suitcases down the hallway.

Mena Nix turned, her eyes wide. She mouthed "no" in his direction then placed the cell phone back to her ear as she headed toward the dark gray steel door at the end of the corridor.

Julian couldn't help but smile as he followed Mena toward the condo they'd been sharing for the past six months, a two-bedroom, one and a half bath, property in one of Nairobi's newest high rise complexes. He would've pinched himself if his hands weren't already full. Readjusting the duffel bag on his left shoulder and the smaller backpack on his right, Julian brought the roller bags to a stop. He leaned against one of the overweight bags, stuffed with Mena's impulse purchases from their trip to Florida for the holidays.

His eyes drifted up the length of her body, from the strappy heels tapping on the lacquered, distressed concrete floor to the skin-tight jeans covering her muscular legs as her hips swiveled seductively with each step. The lacy edge of her thong peeking through the opening between her halter top and the band of her jeans teased him, causing his cock to stir. He settled on watching her round, tight ass and wished his hands were gripping that instead of the handles of the two suitcases.

Mena stopped in front of their door, 12C, and faced him. Rolling her eyes, she whispered, "Do not encourage her."

Julian smiled at the crinkled frown forming in between Mena's eyebrows. The sensual furrow ratcheted her sex appeal toward the top of the charts. Despite what his father believed, Julian had no regrets about leaving behind his life in St. Basil to follow Mena to Kenya for her fellowship at the Tribal Museum.

Julian barely recognized himself anymore. Long gone was the guilt-ridden man who'd exiled himself for the mistakes of his past, living alone and miserable on a yacht in the marina of one of the most beautiful islands in the world. The life he'd had wasn't worth much before he'd met Mena. Because of her, he'd been able to move beyond the pain of his past.

"Yes, Mother. We are at the condo now," Mena said, her voice echoing in the hallway.

A smile played at the corners of his mouth as he watched her bend over to pick up the newspaper resting against the bottom of the door.

"The flight was fine. We both slept most of the way," Mena continued, fumbling through her purse for the key card.

Would he ever get used to how beautiful she was?

Her deep brown skin was a hint darker after a few days basking on the beach. Visions of Mena in her string bikini laying on top of him as the ocean waves crashed over them brought a flush of heat to his face. The trip to Miami had been a whim, his feeble attempt to make up for the disappointment of the trip she'd dubbed "Holidays with the Parents." It had been more like "A Jacked-up Jacksonville Christmas," but he didn't want to think about the miserable, failed attempt to introduce Mena to his father. In fact, he'd be perfectly fine if Mena never met the bastard at all.

He should have talked her out of the plan when she'd first presented it to him, but how could he say no to the woman who owned his heart? He hadn't wanted to let her down, but a part of him knew he was delaying the inevitable. Any Christmas dinner that included Julian and his father in the same room was bound to be a disaster. It was for the best that neither of his parents showed up.

Despite Julian's best efforts, he hadn't been able to salvage the dampened holiday spirit until he suggested spending New Year's Eve in South Beach.

"Yes, I know you love Julian," Mena said, finding the key card and waving it at him with a big smile. "He's pretty alright with me, too."

"Just alright?" Julian asked, grabbing Mena's hand and pressing his lips against her open palm. The tantalizing scent of sandalwood and orange seduced him, sending a jolt of excitement through his body.

"More than alright, babe," Mena whispered. Opening the door with the key card, Mena held wide for Julian to enter. As he pulled the roller bags into the spacious foyer of the condo, Mena slapped him on the butt, giggling as he passed in front of her.

Twenty-one hours of air travel had both of them horny as rabbits. In a few minutes, he planned to have her naked in his arms.

"No, you are not hearing wedding bells!" Mena screeched, stepping out of her heels and walking past him.

Julian studied the luggage, lining it neatly against the living room wall as he struggled to swallow past the sudden dryness in his throat. His back muscles tightened as he slowly removed the duffel bag and backpack from his shoulders and placed them against the floor.

"It's way too soon for bells to be ringing. But, if that changes, you'll be the first to know, I promise. I gotta go. Love you, bye," Mena said, tossing the cell phone onto the round ottoman before free-falling back onto the caramel-hued leather couch.

"Can you believe her?" Mena said, closing her eyes and exhaling slowly. "She just met you, and she's already trying to force us down the aisle. Why can't she stay out of it?"

The subject of marriage was an IED that he had no plans of stepping on. Despite the tugging at his heart, Julian knew he had to take things slow with Mena. She'd gone through a bad marriage and an even worse divorce. Both of which he couldn't seem to get her to open up about. He couldn't blame her for being wary about entering into the institution of matrimony again. Mena would come around eventually, but until then, he needed to keep a wrap on his hopes for their future.

Julian stepped away from the luggage and walked over to Mena, leaning down to kiss her soft lips. "Nothing wrong with your mom wanting you to settle down with a handsome ex-Navy SEAL, you know. But we'll have plenty of time to focus on that in the future. No need to rush into things."

"Exactly. I'm so glad we're on the same page. Just because we're in no hurry to get hitched doesn't mean we're not madly, passionately in love with each other," Mena said, placing her hands on the sides of his face and pulling him close to her. His lips found hers again, indulging in a hot kiss that aroused all of his senses. Her sweet mouth was like candy, and he couldn't get enough of her.

Mena broke the hypnotic spell of the kiss far too soon for Julian's liking.

"You hungry?" Mena asked as her stomach growled.

Julian laughed. "Only for you, but I guess I should feed you before I ravish your body."

"A snack would be good. I have a feeling you aren't going to get much sleep tonight," Mena teased, biting her bottom lip.

Reluctantly, Julian pulled away and headed into the kitchen. Opening the drawer, he lifted a stack of take-out menus and placed them on the counter. "What's your pleasure?"

"Pizza, maybe? Something with lots of carbs," Mena said as she scooted off the couch and headed toward the luggage.

Julian watched her rummage through one of the bags, his eyes locked on the backpack nearby. He should have taken it into the bedroom and placed it in the closet out of her sight. After the "why rush marriage" talk, he didn't want her to find what was hidden inside.

"Why can't people let us be happy like we are? What's the big deal about getting married anyway? I've done that, and believe me, it's not the fairytale that you dream about growing up," Mena said, digging an arm deeper into the suitcase as she maneuvered the contents around.

"Not always," Julian said, thinking about his parent's marriage and then about Dawn and Broman. The love between both couples was evident, but there was enough dysfunction in those relationships to make anyone hesitate about getting married. But now that he'd found

Mena, he wanted everything with her—marriage, kids, dog, white picket fence.

"There are people who have good marriages. Take Omar and Charlie, for instance. Perfect love, perfect marriage, the type any couple would kill to have. But are they the exception? Is that a realistic expectation for the rest of us?" Mena asked, moving to the other luggage. Unzipping it, Mena let the contents fall out, and she began rooting through the clothes and shoes inside.

Julian rubbed the knot tightening in his shoulder. "Every couple is unique. Comparing us to any other couple is pointless. We don't need to be like anybody else."

"True, but it's good to have role models. Did you know Omar and Charlie dated for years before they got engaged? Like five or six years! You and I haven't been together for a full year yet. There's so much that we still need to learn about each other," Mena continued.

"What's wrong with learning and exploring more about each other while we're husband and wife? Do we really need to wait until we hit some arbitrary length of time as a couple before we get married?" Julian asked, a hint of edge to his tone.

Mena paused, looking up at him with a raised eyebrow.

Damn, he wished he'd kept his mouth shut. He wondered what she thought of his outburst. Was she surprised? Concerned? She had to know how he felt about her. He would do whatever she needed him to do, even if that meant putting aside his own desires for their future.

"Just saying, you know, hypothetically speaking. I'm not in a rush for you to slap a ball and chain on me," Julian said, slipping his cell phone from his pocket.

"Oh, really? Don't want to give up your bachelor card for me?" Mena asked, pressing her hands against her hips as she stared up at him.

"I'd give up everything for you. You wouldn't need to ask. But, marriage is a big step and not one we have to think about right now. Pepperoni and bell peppers?" Julian asked.

"What?" Mena stammered.

Julian responded, "On your pizza? Just pepperoni and bell peppers, right?"

Mena nodded, a smile curving at her lips. "Yeah, that's what I want."

Julian placed the delivery order, then walked over and grabbed his backpack from the floor.

"Wait, I think I may have put something in there," Mena said, reaching for the backpack.

"What are you looking for?" Julian asked, keeping it out of her reach.

"The receipt for the mask Wangari bought me," Mena said. "I got an email saying it was ready when we were in Jacksonville and printed it out at my mom's house."

"Why don't you print another copy?" Julian asked, remembering how he'd had to babysit the team of artisans hired by Wangari Irungu, the Director of the Tribal Museum. The pretentious artists had damn near taken over their condo between Thanksgiving and the week before Christmas, visiting six times to evaluate the décor and proposed placement to get inspiration for the commissioned artwork, a welcome to Africa gift from Mena's boss.

"Because I'm hungry and horny, and I don't feel like going back downstairs to the business center to use the printer," Mena leaned forward and grabbed the bottom of the backpack, pulling it toward her. "Wangari was so kind to commission a one-of-a-kind mask for me. I don't want it sitting in the gallery one more day, which is why I need you to pick it up Monday morning."

"Monday?" Julian asked, frowning, taking a step toward the backpack. He watched as Mena unzipped the bag, reaching her hand inside.

"The gallery is closed this weekend for a private event. Monday is the earliest I can get it," Mena explained, lifting his belongings out of the backpack one by one. A hitch caught in his throat as he took another step toward her. He had to do something. Now before it was too late. It was only a matter of minutes before she found the box.

Mena turned the backpack over. Julian scrambled forward as he watched his belongings, littering the floor around her. Squatting next to Mena, Julian extended his leg, blocking her view of the robin egg blue box.

"I'll get it on Tuesday. I don't want to miss your presentation," Julian said. He sat across from Mena, absently rearranging the contents of his backpack, hoping to bide his time until he could sneak the box into his pocket.

"You're not going to miss my presentation because you are going to get to the gallery first thing when it opens. That will give you plenty of time to pick up the mask and bring it back to the condo before heading to the museum," Mena said, straining her head to see around him.

"I don't know. I think that may cut things to close. Don't you?" Julian asked, stretching forward to conceal his attempt to grab the box. Fumbling it in his hand, Julian held on tight as he stood up and walked toward the kitchen island.

Mena leaned over as she looked up at him. "What are you hiding over there?"

Julian licked his lips slowly. He gripped the box in his left hand, tucking his arm behind his back to shield it from Mena's view. He wasn't ready for her to see what was inside, but he'd be hard-pressed to avoid it now. "Wouldn't you like to know."

"I have ways of getting the information out of you," Mena said, rising from the floor. She walked over, stopping inches from him, then slipped a finger along the inside of his waistband. Her soft touch triggered his arousal. Julian took a deep breath as he watched Mena's hands move slowly toward the button of his jeans, pushing it through the hole as she rested a hand against his abs.

"You're not being fair," Julian said. As much as he liked this game, there was no way he wanted her to find what was inside the box. It was too soon. He didn't want to do anything to freak her out or cause her to shut down emotionally. He wanted things to go back to normal first. The synchronized cadence of domestic bliss they shared as they built their life together in Nairobi without any stress or strain.

"Life ain't fair," Mena said, reaching inside his boxer briefs and wrapping a hand around his cock.

Julian let out a low moan as the backpack slipped from his arm.

In a quick motion, Mena tugged at his left arm and slipped the box from his grasp, then rushed across the living room, cackling with laughter.

Panic struck Julian as he lunged for her, stumbling over the ottoman and falling to the ground.

"Mena, wait, don't— "

"What's this?" Mena asked, holding the Tiffany's box tied neatly with a white ribbon.

Julian slumped onto the couch, staring back at her. "Open it and see."

"We said we weren't exchanging Christmas gifts. We agreed that we would give each other the gift of togetherness, nothing more," Mena said, a challenge in her tone.

"It's not a Christmas gift ..." Julian said.

"Then what is it?" Mena asked.

"Open it."

"Not until you tell me what's inside," Mena said, her voice hitting a higher octave.

"Calm down," Julian said, a wave of sadness washing over him. "It's not an engagement ring."

Not this time.

Mena plopped down onto the couch next to him, a hint of excitement glinting in her eyes as she peeled the ribbon off the box slowly then opened the lid.

Gasping, her hand flew to her mouth as she looked inside the box.

He couldn't have dreamed of a better reaction. The emotion etched across her face was pure elation and unconditional love.

Julian wrapped his arms around her, nuzzling his lips against her neck. "It's a charm bracelet. Each year, I'll give you a new charm to add to it. Something to remind you of me ... of us."

Mena fingered the single heart-shaped charm attached to the rose gold thick chain. "It's engraved. J & M. Julian and Mena."

"I could have done something cheesy and put 4ever underneath," Julian said, lifting up four fingers. "But thought I might lose you if I did."

Turning to face him, Mena said, "You could never lose me. This is stunning. I can't believe you got this for me. It's so beautiful."

"Just like you. May I?"

"Please," Mena said, holding out her wrist.

Julian secured it onto her arm. "Now, every time you look at this bracelet, it will be a reminder of how I feel about you."

"I love this, and I love you, Julian."

Julian pressed his lips against hers, his heart about to burst.

"And I love you, Mena."

Chapter Two

Thunder rumbled as Julian glanced up at the ominous storm clouds. Shadows from The Hub, a massive, open-air shopping mecca in Karen, an affluent suburb of Nairobi, loomed behind him. The overcast sky cast an eerie darkness onto the street. Stepping closer to the crosswalk, Julian pressed the button to cross then glanced at his watch.

Ten a.m.

Mena's first lecture at the Tribal Museum started in one hour.

She'd barricaded herself in the condo all weekend since their return, putting the finishing touches on her presentation. Julian had watched her in awe, amazed by her easy conversational style and breadth of knowledge on the Ghanian artist being showcased. He could almost recite the presentation by heart with her. Mena expected him to be there, and he wanted to be in the room to support her on this big day.

The rain had caused extra traffic and delays and now it looked like he wouldn't make it after all.

A gridlock of cars on the road crawled past him.

The steady drizzle of rain turned into a heavy downpour as he waited for the crosswalk signal to change. Tugging at the hood on his rain jacket, Julian glanced at the walk signal, pausing as several cars proceeded through the red light before making his way across the street to the Emershan Smith Gallery.

Stepping toward the glass door, Julian pulled it open and entered. He pushed the hood from his head and tried to minimize the amount of water pooling onto the hardwood.

"May I help you?" A woman asked, walking toward him. She glanced at the wet area, expanding around his feet with disdain, then motioned for another worker who appeared with a cloth to wipe the floor.

"I'm here to pick up a piece for Mena Nix," Julian said.

The woman's eyes grew wide. "The mask commissioned by Wangari Irungu?"

"Yes, that's the one," Julian said, glancing around the gallery. Dozens of customers milled about the space perusing the paintings and sculptures.

"Give me a moment to get it prepared for you," the woman said, giving him a warm smile. "Please feel free to look around and see if any other pieces are to your liking."

Julian nodded, then walked over to a small nook where a series of tall ebony sculptures were arranged in a circle on a pedestal. Slipping a finger under the tag on the shortest one, a male figure with a protruding belly, Julian almost choked at the high five-figure price tag.

A soft vibration fluttered against his leg. Julian reached into his pocket, grabbing the cell phone as he looked out the window at the rain pelting the ground.

"Hey, Kendrick," Julian said, balancing the phone between his ear and his shoulder.

"Happy New Year, my friend. How were your holidays?" Detective Kendrick Caillouet asked, a hint of curiosity in his tone. The St. Basil Police Department detective was Julian's closest friend and the one who'd tried to talk him out of going back to Florida for his first holiday with Mena. He should have listened to his friend.

"Pretty much what you predicted," Julian mumbled.

"That bad?" Kendrick asked. "Sorry to hear that. How are you and Mena?"

"We're good. I made up for things by taking her to South Beach for

New Year's Eve. That helped her to forget about the disaster that Christmas turned out to be," Julian said, even though he wasn't sure Mena had forgotten her disappointment over not meeting his father.

"Well, at least you had someone to share the holidays with. My bad luck in love has dragged into the New Year, despite all my efforts to turn the corner. I swear women don't want the good guys. Until I do something edgy, I'm not going to get the girl," Kendrick said, glumly.

"Don't give up. You'll meet the woman of your dreams before you know it," Julian said, hoping to encourage his perpetually single friend.

"From your lips to God's ears," Kendrick said. "But I didn't call to drag you into my pity party."

"You have an update on Dumay's case?" Julian asked. Priscilla Dumay, the former owner of the Genesis Gallery, a museum for ethnographic art in St. Basil, had led a sophisticated organization that stole embryos scheduled for destruction from cryobanks. After genetically modifying the embryonic DNA, Dumay kidnapped women and forced them to be surrogates for the designer babies she sold for top dollar to infertile desperate couples.

"Evidence keeps piling up on Dumay. There's no way she'll be able to wiggle out of this, despite all of her attorneys' stall tactics. But trying to get Tufa has been close to impossible," Kendrick said.

"Seems Dumay did everything to protect her brother. The surrogates weren't able to finger him as one of the doctors that monitored the pregnancies?" Julian asked.

"Not one of them remembered him being involved. They were all sedated for the embryo transfers and I'm guessing that's how Dumay used his services. Just no way to prove it."

"Damn," Julian muttered under his breath. The thought of Dr. Quentin Tufa not paying for his role in the crimes wasn't sitting well with him but wasn't much he could do from thousands of miles away.

"Adam Russell is still claiming to have damning evidence against Dumay and Tufa, but his lawyers are playing hardball trying to negotiate complete immunity for him before he hands anything over. PIIB has placed him in witness protection while they negotiate the terms. With Adam, you and Mena, and the surrogates, Priscilla Dumay will get convicted and likely serve the rest of their lives in Tiverton," Kendrick said.

"No better place for them," Julian said. Dubbed hell in paradise, Tiverton Prison was a maximum-security facility located on a remote island in the Palmchat Islands chain.

A hand brushed against Julian's arm. He turned to see the gallery attendant holding a clipboard with various papers attached.

Julian said, "Thanks for the update. Keep me posted if anything changes."

Slipping the phone back into his pocket, Julian reached for the clipboard.

"Just a couple of release forms for you to sign, Mr. Nix," the woman said.

Julian almost laughed out loud at the absurdity of her assumption but caught himself. Her label for him wasn't too far from the truth. Mena was by far the breadwinner in the relationship, supporting them with her stipend from the fellowship. Julian contributed where he could by dipping into his savings, but it wasn't exactly fifty-fifty.

"I'll be back for the forms in a few minutes," the woman added, then disappeared around the corner. Scanning the documents, Julian lifted the pen. After signing by the x on each page, he glanced up to see where the woman had disappeared.

A flush of adrenaline raced through his body.

Chapter Three

Squinting, Julian couldn't stop staring at the woman less than fifteen feet away from him.

Tall and statuesque, her ebony flawless face was crowned by a curly mane of shoulder-length jet black hair. She leaned over and studied a carved settee placed in the corner adjacent to the nook.

Their eyes met, and Julian was catapulted back to the darkest time in his life. The pain and guilt over Broman's condition had gutted him, leaving him broken and alone until she'd shown up on his yacht. She'd been through her own hell, having survived a maniac only to struggle with how to reintegrate back into her life. They'd found solace in each other until she'd sneaked off in the middle of the night. He'd known he wouldn't see her again. The next morning, he'd set sail for St. Basil with two boxes of Saltines and a bottle of vodka on board.

Julian swallowed, his heart skipping a beat as he walked toward her.

Sunny Tate. She hadn't changed one bit in all of these years.

"Hey."

Sunny looked away for a split second. "Hey."

"This is ... awkward," Julian admitted.

"Wasn't it always between us," Sunny said.

Julian raised an eyebrow, unsettled by her assessment of their past. "No, but maybe it should have been?"

Sunny gave a reluctant smile. "That would have kept us out of trouble."

"And what fun would that have been?" Julian asked.

"None. No regrets, right?"

"No regrets," Julian agreed.

Going through basic training with Broman and Sunny by his side had been his entire world. Those carefree early days in the Navy when they were too young and self-absorbed to be concerned with anything other than becoming sailors felt like a lifetime ago. The competitiveness and drive to be the best fueled them as they pushed each other to be faster, stronger, and smarter. They'd each achieved the success they'd wanted: he and Broman had become SEALs, and Sunny realized her dream of being one of the few female pilots assigned to special operations.

"What are you doing in Nairobi?" Julian asked.

"Can you believe I live here?" Sunny asked.

"No." Tension wafted between them as Julian shook his head. "Why the hell would you move here? After everything that happened."

Sunny held up a hand. "I've made peace with all of that. Some pain you can't keep carrying around with you. The irony of coming back to this place, and finding happiness was liberating. Now, I live in a beautiful city with amazing people. I have a thriving business in private security, and I still pilot chartered flights for the execs in between. I have a good life here."

He should have been convinced by her optimism, the positivity in her new outlook on life, but he wasn't. The Sunny Tate he knew was more than capable of overcoming any obstacle. But he found it strange that she decided to make Africa her home.

Crossing her arms, she seemed to be wilting under his intense gaze. Julian softened a bit, not wanting to make her feel uncomfortable after all these years. She had a right to deal with her demons how she saw fit, and she'd obviously moved past them all. Just as he had moved past his ... with Mena's help.

"I'm happy for you," Julian said, breaking the silence between them.

"Whatever Montgomery. I know you think I'm bonkers, but I can promise you I'm not," Sunny said, punching him in the arm and daring him to deny it. The Sunny he remembered, in all her full glory, resurrected in that one action.

He wouldn't insult her. She knew him too well.

"Enough about me. What brings you to Kenya?" Sunny asked, a suspicious look in her gaze.

Julian stiffened. "I'm not on a mission if that's what you're thinking."

Four years ago, Sunny had come close to convincing him not to walk away from the SEALs. To honor his best friend by continuing the pursuit of making a difference in the world by eradicating it of terrorists. In the end, Julian couldn't imagine serving in the military without Broman by his side. They'd spent their entire Naval career in the same boat crews and later assigned to the same SEAL team. They were swim buddies, watching each other's backs on every mission. How could he do that with someone else?

He'd walked away from the SEALs and from the Navy, with everyone's understanding that his last mission had been too much to overcome. Sunny was like the rest, oblivious to the truth of what really happened in Central Sulawesi.

She had no clue what he'd done. And she, more than anyone else, would have the right to hate him if she found out the truth.

Sunny asked, "Why are you here?"

Julian hesitated, not sure how to respond to her question.

Sunny's eyes narrowed, her head tilting as she scrutinized his face. "You're here because of a woman, aren't you?"

It was Julian's turn to look away. He didn't want to hurt Sunny. He didn't know if telling her about Mena would.

A man dressed in a rumpled business suit brushed against Julian's arm as he angled for a better position to examine a painting on the wall near the settee.

Stepping closer to Sunny and out of the man's way, Julian decided to be honest. No matter what had happened between him and Sunny through the years, she was still one of his oldest friends. "My girlfriend works at the Tribal Museum."

"And you're here to visit her," Sunny said, her smile not quite reaching her eyes.

"I moved here with her. We'll be in Nairobi for another year and a half. After that, it'll depend on where her next job is," Julian explained.

"Wow. Montgomery is following a woman around the world for her career. Never would have imagined that. What kind of work are you doing?" Sunny asked.

Julian bristled, not wanting to answer her question.

As if divinely inspired, the gallery worker motioned for him as the package containing Mena's mask was brought out from a room in the back.

Julian looked back at Sunny. "I gotta go. My mask is ready."

"No problem," Sunny said. Reaching into the back pocket of her shorts, she handed him a business card. "We really should catch up when you're not too busy. You can buy me a vodka tonic."

Julian took the card and read it.

Tactical and Intelligence Defense Executive Services (TIDES). Sunny Tate. Owner.

Below the names were two phone numbers. A local Kenyan number and the Atlanta cell phone number Julian still knew by heart.

"Bye, Montgomery," Sunny said, walking away. Heart pounding in his chest, he watched her walk out of the gallery. Sunny raised her umbrella and crossed the street to The Hub, disappearing from his sight.

An uneasiness settled within him. He had a feeling this wouldn't be his last encounter with Sunny Tate.

"Mr. Nix, your mask is ready," the woman said, behind him.

Julian rolled his eyes, checking his watch once again.

11:05 a.m.

Damn. He was too late. The lecture had already begun.

Chapter Four

Crossing the wide exhibit hall toward the last sculpture, Mena stopped near the center and gazed at the audience. Hundreds of guests—dignitaries, senior executives of the African business elite, and a hodgepodge of political who's who of Kenyan government—stared back at her. Riveting was the word that came to mind as she thought about the presentation she'd been giving over the past hour.

Wangari Irungu, director of the Tribal Museum, had the forethought and vision to expand the focus of the museum to showcase temporary exhibits of art from internationally acclaimed African artists. The exhibit hall itself was a masterpiece of design, perfectly complementing the very first showcase of three dynamic sculptures by the Ghanian artist, El Anatsui.

"This last piece by Anatsui is a prime example of his philosophy that sculpture should be malleable, flexible, conforming to space, and not rigid. The form has taken on different shapes in each installation, proving the dynamic nature of his work and embodying a view that art should suggest and not dictate," Mena explained. A soft murmur rippled through the air as the crowd nodded in approval and understanding.

Pointing to the sculpture, Mena described the materials used and the composition. She'd practiced her presentation dozens of times over the weekend in preparation for the opening lecture. She scanned the faces of the crowd, recognizing a few of the other conservators at the gallery. Isaac Gatobu sat in the aisle seat on the second row, his scrutiny was palpable. The meticulous conservator scribbled notes. Mena had no doubt he planned to provide feedback, constructive of course, to her in front of the entire team. He hadn't hidden his displeasure with her selection to lead the lecture and considered it almost sacrilegious to let an American teach Africans about the prominent work by a renowned African artist.

Wangari had ignored his complaints and maintained her decision, encouraging Mena and educating her about the cultural differences regarding presenting in Africa compared to what Mena was used to from her training in American institutions.

Sitting next to Isaac was Grace Kadenge, a mediocre conservator and aspiring socialite of the Nairobi fashion scene. Grace was a smart woman but didn't apply herself as much as Mena thought she should, preferring instead to work on her social media presence to attain the fame she desired.

Mena's eyes drifted to the front row, where Wangari sat next to her husband, the Director of Public Prosecutions, Okeyo Lagat. Their hands intertwined, Okeyo whispered into Wangari's ear. As a sensual smile spread across her lips, she nodded, then nudged him to pay attention to the presentation.

Mena felt a twinge of envy, scanning the room once again for Julian. He still hadn't arrived. Why had she pushed him to pick up the mask this morning? With the horrendous traffic and rain, she should have known he wouldn't make it to the museum in time.

"The transformation of these common and simple materials into a complex lattice tapestry of a massive scale is the hallmark of Anatsui's work, making him one of the most impressive African artists of our time," Mena said, ending the formal portion of her presentation.

Applause erupted in the hall, sending a jolt of adrenaline through her body. She'd nailed the lecture, despite what Isaac would probably say later. He never missed an opportunity to criticize her in some way or another. She almost found it laughable now, his need to tear her down to assuage the threat he thought she represented. She wasn't the first fellowship recipient he'd had to work with since the museum opened, and she wouldn't be the last. She couldn't understand why he disliked her. For some reason, Isaac had decided she was unworthy of the fellowship and the experience of working at the Tribal Museum. Mena had become resigned to suffering through his ridicule and derisiveness for another eighteen months.

Beaming, Mena gave a short nod to the crowd. The applause grew louder, and she raised a hand to quiet the room.

As she stepped behind the podium, her eyes were drawn to a man in the back. Mena looked away, then stared back at the lone figure standing at the door.

It couldn't be him. Could it?

Was she imagining him, or was he really staring at her?

Dizziness overwhelmed her. Mena took a sip of water, trying to regain her composure. She still had a Q&A session to facilitate. She couldn't be distracted by his presence.

Swallowing past the lump in her throat, Mena focused her attention on the crowd and fielded questions.

Ten minutes passed, then twenty. He was still at the back of the room, watching her. She tried to relax, but it was impossible.

"Any other questions?" Mena asked after a silence settled in the air. Scanning the room for any raised hands, Mena saw none. She nodded and then announced Wangari Irungu to come forward for closing comments.

Stepping to the side, Mena looked toward the back of the room again.

He was gone.

Her eyes darted across to the doors, and the side walls.

There was no sign of him anywhere.

Mena inhaled deeply, hoping he'd been a figment of her imagination. The last thing she needed was a ghost from her past intruding on her present. Smoothing a strand of her dark hair behind her ear, she tried to calm her frazzled nerves. She was overreacting. There was no way he would cross the Atlantic to find her. What would be the point? They had nothing to say to each other. She didn't know who that guy was, but he couldn't be—

"Mena, is that right?" Wangari asked.

Mena sputtered, not aware of what Wangari referred to. Taking a guess, she decided to agree with her boss and gave a confident nod.

Mena forced herself to focus.

"Now, for those of you who purchased the lunch with the lecture, please follow our intern into the reception hallway to be escorted to the private dining area. I truly hope you enjoyed our lecture on the work of El Anatsui and hope to see you again for future lectures. Good afternoon," Wangari concluded.

The director slipped an arm around Mena's shoulders as the crowd meandered out of the exhibit hall.

"Great job today. You were excellent. The passion in your voice for this work captivated the audience, and that's exactly why I knew you'd be perfect for the presentation," Wangari said.

Mena nodded, her eyes searching the crowd for Julian again. He'd missed the entire lecture.

"What's wrong? I thought you'd be a little happier about how today went," Wangari said.

Mena tried to smile, but she wasn't fooling her boss and friend. "I'm a bit distracted right now."

Mena slumped down in a chair across from the podium.

Wangari took the seat next to her. "Distracted about what? And don't tell me nothing. We've grown too close for you to keep things from me. Especially since it's obvious something is bothering you. What is it? How can I help?"

"You're going to strangle me," Mena said, shaking her head.

"Is this about the errand you sent Julian on this morning?" Wangari asked, raising an eyebrow. "I get that he's your own personal hero, but you couldn't possibly believe he would make it back to the museum in time to see your lecture."

"Are you trying to make me feel worse?" Mena mumbled, covering her face in her hands.

"I'm trying to make you see reason," Wangari said, yanking one of Mena's hands from her face. "If that's not it, then what is it?"

"Things got weird for us after we came back from Florida. We're usually so comfortable with each other, but having him meet my mother probably wasn't the best thing," Mena said, thinking about her mother's incessant prodding about marriage in Mena's future with Julian.

"Families can be tough. The only advice I can give is to try to keep them out of your relationship. Do you think my family wanted me to marry a divorced man twenty years older than me with three teenage kids? They still don't approve of him, even though he's one of the most powerful men in Kenyan politics. I face that challenge every day, but my love for him makes fighting any obstacle worth it," Wangari said.

"My problem is the opposite. My Mom loves Julian. They instantly took to each other, and I swear it's like they're kindred spirits or something. Now she has it in her head that we need to get married, and she's dropping not so subtle hints every time I talk to her," Mena said, rubbing the ache building in the back of her skull.

"You don't see marriage in your future with Julian? I must admit, I'm surprised. Seems like an obvious next step for the two of you ..."

"Yes, but much later on. Not when we've been together for less than a year," Mena said, shaking her head. "I've been married before, and I'm not in a hurry to go down that road again. I don't know why we need to rush to the next step."

"I'm guessing Julian doesn't feel the same way," Wangari said.

"I'm not sure how he feels. I thought we were on the same page about waiting, but then he started questioning why we had to wait. I was stunned. I didn't know if he was playing devil's advocate or giving me a glimpse into his real feelings. He dropped the subject as quickly as he brought it up," Mena said.

"And you don't want to bring the topic back up in case he does want marriage now," Wangari said.

"Right. But he has to be okay with where we are now. He went to Tiffany's and bought this for me," Mena said, holding out her wrist. The rose gold charm bracelet sparkled under the lights of the exhibit hall as the single heart-shaped charm rested against the back of her hand.

"Stunning. Is that engraved?" Wangari asked.

Mena nodded. "It's our initials. I think Julian gave me this as a sign of his commitment instead of freaking me out with an engagement ring."

"Sounds like he knows you well," Wangari said. "Anyone can see that he'd move heaven and earth for you, Mena. I don't think you have anything to worry about."

"I hope so. I don't want to do anything that would change how he feels about me," Mena said.

Wangari patted her on the arm, then stood. "Stop worrying. You and Julian will get pass this. Are you coming to lunch?"

"I'll be there in a second. Just want a moment to get myself together," Mena said.

"Don't take too long. I'm sure Isaac is already trying to steal your spotlight." Wangari gave Mena's hand a quick squeeze, then exited the hall.

Looking around the room, Mena relaxed into the still emptiness of the massive space. Three of the most impressive sculptures she'd ever seen hung against the front walls, the stars of her lecture on full display. El Anatsui had made beautiful works of art from materials that had been discarded. Creating hope out of despair, he forced the world to see the materials from a different perspective.

Was she supposed to do that?

See marriage in a new way. Redefine the challenges and embrace a way to overcome her reservations with holy matrimony?

Her cell phone buzzed in her hand. Swiping the screen, she saw a number she never expected to see. Accessing the text, she read the message.

Need to see you ...

Mena took a deep breath, trying to contain her anger. He hadn't been a figment of her imagination looming in the back of the exhibit hall. What the hell was he doing here? And why did he think she would *ever* agree to see him?

Chapter Five

Pushing through the growing crowd of tourists milling about inside the octagonal-shaped main lobby, Julian side-stepped a family with triplets as they excitedly approached a massive Massai warrior mask near the middle of the room. He glanced down at the pamphlet in his hand: *Transforming Simple to Complex: A Lecture on the Sculptures of El Anatsui* presented by Mena Nix, Conservator and Fellow of the Tribal Museum.

Flipping the paper over in his hand, he stared at the glossy professional photograph of Mena above her bio, which was impressive, to say the least.

Nothing would have been better than watching her, thoughtfully moving between the massive sculptures hanging from the walls, explaining the nature and concepts that made the acclaimed work of El Anatsui unique. He would have watched the crowd hanging on her every word, responding as if on cue to her quips and dramatic pauses.

If he had been there.

"The lecture ended ten minutes ago. If you have a ticket to the VIP luncheon, I can escort you to where it is located," explained a woman with a short afro and kind eyes.

Folding the pamphlet, Julian stuffed it into his back pocket and headed toward the exhibit hall where the lecture had occurred.

Julian inhaled sharply. Knowing that Mena would be pissed that he hadn't made it in time to see her lecture. The last thing he needed was to cause more tension between them. His unexpected questions about marriage had already introduced uneasiness into their relationship.

Zigzagging through the crowd of museum patrons flooding the wide expanse of the museum lobby, he darted toward the entrance to the lecture hall. Hordes of guests dressed in expensive business suits roamed outside the room, the buzz of excited discussions filling the air. He searched the crowd for her face. Awkwardness settled within him as several minutes passed. He couldn't stand here all day, but he was reluctant to leave. Perhaps she'd already left, and he'd missed the opportunity to see her.

Taking a wide arc around the crowd, Julian slipped along the wall and stepped into the exhibit hall.

"You missed it," Mena said, a frown etched into her forehead as she jerked her purse open and stuffed her cell phone inside.

Julian tensed. He'd expected her anger. But, he still wasn't prepared for the ire wafting from her. "I'm sorry. Traffic was bad, but I got the mask. It looks good on the wall behind the couch."

"Wait a minute." Mena's dark eyes bored holes through him. "Instead of dropping the mask off and getting over here as fast as you could, you took the time to hang it on the wall?"

Julian's mind went blank. Words eluded him as a sliver of panic danced across his skin. He'd been in tight spots before. He'd been cornered behind enemy lines, talking his way out of danger with terrorists. He'd been interrogated about rogue actions by the best naval lawyers, maneuvering through their questions without a hint of worry. But Mena's question stopped him in his tracks. What the fuck had he been thinking? He didn't know. Maybe he'd hoped having the mask hanging on the wall when she got home would make up for him missing her lecture?

"You thought that was more important to me than being here as I gave the most important presentation of my career. Julian ... for a smart guy, you missed it this time," Mena said, crossing her arms over her chest.

"I know," Julian said, stepping toward her. "But you didn't need me here. You knew that presentation inside and out. I know you knocked it out the park."

"You're right. I did. Maybe I didn't need you here, but damn it, I wanted to look in the crowd and see your face. Your face was the only one I kept searching for, and you weren't here," Mena said, pressing a finger into his chest.

The touch sent a jolt of desire through him, and he had to stifle the smile that would push her over the edge. As mad as she was, with that one touch, he felt every ounce of her love for him. Enough to give him confidence that this was just a speed bump on their relationship road. They were finally getting a chance to argue and have conflicts like a normal couple, without the threat of danger looming around every corner.

Despite himself, Julian was enjoying this argument.

"I'm here now," Julian said, reducing the space between them to mere inches. Mena didn't step away. Her eyes never left his, locked in a defiant stare as she kept up her steely resolve.

Julian leaned down and brushed his lips against her cheek, then turned to kiss her other cheek before pressing his mouth against hers. Mena didn't pull away, allowing him to part her lips with his tongue and taste the sweetness of her. The kiss lingered, growing more passionate. Their bodies remained separated by a gap that radiated magnetic attraction and desire. The small chasm between them fueled the intensity of the kiss. A feverish crescendo welled within him, sending his body temperature through the roof as his lips blazed across hers.

Julian fought the urge to pull her into his arms, knowing she'd resist him. Her anger was as evident in that kiss as her love. Stepping back, Julian adopted a sheepish smile. "You forgive me?"

Mena closed her eyes, her chest heaving from the exertion of resisting him. He could feel the inner tug-of-war she must be going through—the disappointment of his absence clashing with the excitement of having him here ... finally.

Opening her eyes, she unfolded her arms.

"No," Mena said, then stepped around him and walked out of the room.

No?

Julian looked through the glass ceiling at the angry thunderheads swirling in the charcoal sky. Dragging a hand down his face, he turned to watch Mena addressing a group of VIP guests. Her demeanor changed as she wowed them, then led them down the hallway without a backward glance at him.

Julian slumped down into one of the empty chairs and grabbed his cell phone from his pocket.

Dialing the number, he placed the phone to his ear.

"How'd you know I'd still be up? Do you realize it's 3 a.m. here?" Kendrick asked, sounding wide awake.

"Whatever, didn't you just call me an hour ago?" Julian asked.

"Two hours. What's up?" Kendrick asked.

"I blew it. Mena's pissed," Julian said.

"So you listened to my pity party earlier, and now I have to listen to yours? I'm not crying for you, man. Whatever it is, you and Mena will get past it," Kendrick said.

"I missed her big lecture this morning," Julian started.

"That's the straw, but not what broke the camel's back. What's going on?"

"Weird ass conversation where we kind of talked around the idea of marriage. I feel like we've been out of sync since then," Julian admitted.

"Aren't you glad I talked you out of buying that engagement ring?" Kendrick asked.

"Yeah, I am. I got her a charm bracelet instead. She loved it, but I could tell she was relieved it wasn't anything more serious," Julian said.

"And you don't like that, do you?"

"No. So what do I do now?" Julian asked, leaning back in the chair.

"How about get a job," Kendrick said.

"What? How is that even related?" Julian asked.

"You have too much time on your hands. You need something else to focus on other than Mena, so you don't drive that woman straight out of your life. Sure, that IT gig she tried to set you up with wasn't a good fit, but there's got to be something you could do," Kendrick said.

Julian reached into his pocket and pulled out the card. Flipping it in his hand, he saw Sunny's name and number.

"Maybe you're right," Julian said, tucking the card back into his pocket.

"About you? I'm always right."

Chapter Six

Julian clutched the glass door, pausing to read the name in stark white sticker letters on the grimy surface: Tactical and Intelligence Defense Executive Services. The offices were in a warehouse district, toward the end of a long row of businesses in a strip center, tucked away from prying eyes. Julian pulled the door open. The tinkling chimes of bells slapping against the door filled the air as he walked into the waiting room. A small coffee table sat to the left in front of two worn and ragged leather couches. Magazines littered the surface, topped by a TIDES coffee mug with brown stains around the rim.

Two days had passed since Mena's lecture and things still weren't back to normal. Mena was tense and distracted, which she blamed on her work. Wangari had given Mena a new time sensitive assignment and she'd been working long hours at the museum. She was anxious to prove her laser techniques would work on the piece of art where other conservation techniques had failed.

Julian wasn't so sure that Mena's sour mood was because of stress. The elephant in the room was their unfinished discussion about marriage. He should have told her how he felt, but now it was too late. Bringing it up again would only introduce more strain into their relationship. He knew where she stood on the topic, so why bother.

All of this had convinced Julian that Kendrick was right about him. He couldn't sit around wallowing in thoughts about not being able to marry Mena. Tactically analyzing their relationship to formulate a strategy to weaken her defenses against marriage was futile. She wasn't a mission to complete. She was the woman he loved.

He tried to tell himself that these ebbs and flows were normal in a relationship. Having differences of opinions was normal. He had to suck it up and get over it.

But to do that, he'd need a distraction.

One Sunny Tate could provide.

Julian walked to the counter and tapped the old fashioned bell. A round of sharp rings filled the air and Julian heard rustling and movement behind the cream colored wall in front of him. Leaning on the wood grained surface, he twirled Sunny Tate's business card in his hand, hoping she would help him.

The door behind the counter flung open and an Italian with a lopsided grin emerged, arms crossed over his chest.

"What the fuck are you doing in Nairobi?"

Julian frowned, instantly recognizing Enzo Vinci. Enzo had bombed out of basic training, unable to keep up with the rigorous physical feats required to become a sailor. A scrawny kid from the Bronx, he'd joined the Navy to bulk up and stop the neighborhood bullies from punking him every chance they got. But he didn't have the stamina or mental strength to make it back then. He'd gone home after four weeks and Julian hadn't heard anything about him since. The man standing before Julian had come a long way from those days.

"I could ask you the same thing." Walking around the corner, Julian shook Enzo's hand.

"What? Are we acquaintances now? What's with the fucking handshake? Come here!" Enzo said, wrapping his arms around Julian in a tight hug. "You looking good, Jules. Life been treating you well, I see."

Julian shrugged. "You working for Sunny?"

Enzo nodded. "For the past two years. Best gig I've ever had and the money is fucking phenomenal!"

"Enzo Vinci as private security. Never would have believed it.

When did you grow a pair of balls?" Julian asked, slapping Enzo on the shoulder.

"Trying to get into the Navy kicked my ass. I was embarrassed when I couldn't cut it and decided to follow my old man's advice and go to college. I bulked up, hooked up with the girls, got a degree in Kinesiology but never could get rid of that pesky desire to be a hero, you know. Can you believe I decided to try my hand at the military again? Glutton for punishment, I guess. Joined the marines, made it through basic, but it was rough. I pulled out of that after two years, but I was stationed in Africa and fell in love with this fucking place. Decided not to go back to the Bronx and bounced around. Spent some time in Johannesburg and Lagos before deciding to settle in Nairobi. What brings you here?" Enzo asked, beckoning for him to sit on the couch.

Julian followed Enzo into the waiting room and eased down onto the arm of the sofa. "My girlfriend."

"Hot damn! You caught the same bug I did. What do they say? Once you go black, you never go back?" Enzo roared with laughter.

Julian cringed. The fact that he and Mena were an interracial couple had never registered as being important. They were so much more than their respective ethnicities.

"How long you been here?" Enzo asked.

"About six months," Julian said, reflecting on his days running around taking care of various errands for Mena. When he finished his "honey do" list, he'd lounge on the couch and try to learn Swahili from watching television and news shows. A maid came to clean every week and the only real fun he had without Mena was haggling with the vendors at the local outdoor market during his weekly grocery runs.

Damn, who the fuck had he turned into?

Julian continued, "And I'll be here for another eighteen months. Thought it was about time I got a job."

"We'd be damn lucky to have you. This is a good operation and you already know Sunny. She's tough, but she's fair, spreading the work around so we all get paid well. She should be here—"

The chimes filled the air and Julian turned to look toward the door.

Sunny walked in wearing camouflage leggings, a black tank top and combat boots. Her hair was braided in rows, hanging down her back.

"I honestly didn't expect to see you again," Sunny said, wrapping an arm around his neck and hugging him tight. "Just in time for happy hour. Hope you brought your wallet. I need that vodka tonic right about now."

Not exactly what Julian had in mind, but maybe a shot or four would make Sunny open to hiring him temporarily. "Is there a bar nearby?"

"Ten minute drive away," Sunny said, grabbing Julian's hand. She turned and looked back at Enzo. "Make yourself useful and pick up the equipment I ordered for the job you and Hakeem are doing Friday night. Where is Hakeem, anyway?"

"Probably somewhere getting laid," Enzo laughed.

"Find him and tell him to get his ass over here tonight for the debrief or I'm taking him off this gig. This is a high profile dinner for the political elite in Kenya, protecting one of the richest families in the country. If either one of you messes this up for me, you could screw us out of future work and I'm not having that. Got it?" Sunny asked.

"Yes ma'am," Enzo said, then saluted Sunny. "If I can't find Hakeem though, maybe Julian wouldn't mind stepping in and working the dinner with me. I bet he looks good in a monkey suit."

"Montgomery?" Sunny asked, pushing Enzo toward the door. Squeezing Julian's hand, she leaned against him. "Is that why you're here. You want to work for me?"

"Depends. Would you hire me?" Julian asked.

Looping an arm in his, Sunny said, "No drinks for this discussion. Let's go in my office."

Julian followed her through the open door behind the counter and down a single hallway lined with smaller offices until they reached the end of the hall. Sunny swiped a card and opened the last door, stepping to the side to allow Julian space to enter.

Inside, the room was a tactical haven with live video feeds displayed across three monitors to the left of the desk, which was equipped with an oversized computer monitor and keyboard. A portable computer server sat in the corner of the room, next to a rack of AR-15 assault rifles and a bullet proof vest.

Sunny sat down, propped her feet up on the desk and leaned back in the chair.

"Not bad," Julian said, dropping down in the modern, ergonomic chair across from Sunny. Her office was in stark contrast to the dilapidated furnishings of the front waiting room—modern and new, contemporary and trendy, with African violets planted in baskets placed around the room. Julian mimicked her move, leaning back in the chair and propping his feet on her desk.

He stared at her, the sensual smirk spreading across her face as she watched him, trying to read his thoughts like she'd always tried to do in the past. She hadn't changed one bit—a sprinkle of southern charm, a dash of overt sexuality and an ego as big as the state of Georgia. For as much as he saw that reminded him of the past, there was a new confidence and refined exquisite nature that she possessed now, likely growing out of time and life experiences.

"Do you remember that weekend I flew home with you and Broman to Jacksonville? We drove over to Sarasota and hung out at that beautiful beach with gorgeous fine white sand. It was hot as hell outside, but that sand stayed cool to the touch," Sunny said.

"Siesta Key," Julian said, faint memories of the weekend emerging in his mind. It had been a difficult one for him, for many reasons, but he'd managed to stick it out and enjoy himself despite the circumstances.

"We had good times back then," Sunny said, her smile fading into one more contemplative. "We were so close, like family."

Julian laughed, "Not exactly like ... family."

"I didn't mean like sister and brother or anything like that," Sunny said. "But we trusted each other."

"Until we didn't," Julian reminded her.

"Even still, we managed to work past all of that. At the end of the day, there was no doubt that we had each others' backs," Sunny said.

Julian didn't want to relive that moment, but it was hard not to when he was sitting across from Sunny. The Navy had sent her, the best special ops pilot, to fly through enemy fire and pluck him and

Broman from the field near their camp in Central Sulawesi. The rescue had been dangerous, with El Mago's gang hot on his heels blasting gunfire at him and the helo. But Sunny had gotten the job done, like they all knew she would.

"It was hard for me seeing both of you like that. Broman was bleeding out. You passed out before we could get you in the helo. I thought you were dead the whole time I was flying. The only thing I kept thinking was get back to base. Over and over. Get back to base. Dodging bullets, rising and dropping, doing shit I never should have been doing in a helicopter to get y'all out of there, even though in my heart I thought it wouldn't matter what I was doing," Sunny said.

"But it did matter."

"Broman survived and so did you," Sunny said, biting her lower lip. She looked away and he could feel himself back in that hospital, waking up to find her head laying on his chest, gripping his hand as she slept. For two days, she'd stayed by his bedside, trading shifts with his mother and leaving only to grab a bite to eat or to use the restroom. He had no doubt that knowing they were with him, praying and willing him to live was one of the reasons he'd pulled through.

"Dawn had Broman moved to a coma research hospital in the Aerie Islands. Some hotshot doctor is going to take over his case," Julian said, rubbing a hand down his face.

"Is the new doctor more ... optimistic than the doctors in Florida?" Sunny asked, studying her nails.

"Dawn thinks so. She says the chance of him waking up is less than five percent, but after hearing that he'd never wake up for so long, it's good to have hope," Julian said. Broman had improved to a minimally conscious state. On rare occasions, his body would engage in purposeful movements, eyes tracking a target or fingers moving. It was a big leap from the state Broman had been in, but Julian wasn't getting his hopes up about Broman regaining consciousness.

"Sometimes all we have is hope, right? So, tell me why you want to work for me?" Sunny asked.

Julian raked a hand through his hair. "I need a distraction, something to do while Mena is out pursuing her career at the museum."

"You're not working?" Sunny asked, raising an eyebrow. "Is this Mena woman your sugar mama? You a kept man, Montgomery?"

Julian detected a hint of annoyance beneath Sunny's teasing. Talking to Sunny about his relationship with Mena was not a road he wanted to go down.

"Are you going to help me out or not?" Julian asked, trying to disarm Sunny's verbal attack with his killer smile.

"Do you want to know what you're asking for?" Sunny said, growing more serious than Julian had expected.

"Tell me about the work."

"There's a fine line between private security and hired special operatives and we walk that tight rope every day. The work my guys do is dangerous ... on a good day. There's the search and rescue of kidnap victims held for ransom, recovery of classified information for businesses, supervised escorting of top secret items, and the occasional run in with terrorist groups for unauthorized trespassing through their territory. I don't think your girl is going to want you doing this type of job. Can't you go be an IT rep somewhere?"

"And die of boredom. Come on, Sunny, you know that's not me. I get the risks. I need to be where the action is," Julian said, then dropped his legs from the desk and leaned toward her. "I can see it in your eyes. You know you want me on your team. Won't take me long to make your motley crew look like a JROTC."

Sunny scoffed. "Not with that flabby stomach. I'd have to whip you back into shape with some intense daily workouts. And don't think you'd come in here and run the show. I'm the boss and you'll follow my protocols or get kicked out on your ass. None of that going rogue bullshit you like to do. You're not always the smartest operative in the room."

"Does that mean I'm hired?" Julian asked.

"When have I ever been able to resist you?"

Chapter Seven

"Damn it, Omar! Can we have one, just one, conversation where you're not lecturing me about screwing things up with Julian?" Mena asked, stomping through the deserted lobby of the high-rise condominium. Why had she thought calling her best friend would be a good idea? These days, he was never on her side, playing devil's advocate and trying to make her see the situation from all points of view when all she wanted was for him to listen and commiserate with her in all her glorious misery.

"If you were acting like a sane woman and not some bizarro version of yourself, then I wouldn't need to!" Omar screamed back at her.

Another late night. At least she was home before 11 p.m. this time. Mena waved at the three guards at the security station, then pressed her key card against the side panel of the glass partition separating the lobby from the elevators leading to the private residences. A guard with a visible assault rifle stood watch, ensuring that no one piggybacked through the opening. The condo was known for its militant security measures, one of its primary selling points. Kidnappings of wealthy Kenyans and ex-pats was a real threat.

Mena smiled at the guard, who nodded back at her, then proceeded to the elevator. Pressing the square button, she glanced down at the charm bracelet on her wrist. The symbol of Julian's love for her. A constant and calming presence even when she was still angry with him.

"Why is it so wrong for me to be upset that he missed my lecture?" Mena asked.

"No one is saying that your feelings are wrong. What is wrong is for you to still be pissed about it two days later. Let it go!" Omar implored.

Mena had tried to let go of her anger, but her nerves were shot from the unwanted text messages she'd been receiving over the past two days. No way she was telling Omar about that. He'd blow a gasket. Actually, he'd be on the next flight to Nairobi to take care of the annoying pest himself.

Deep down, Mena knew she wasn't being fair to Julian. Her loving boyfriend was the easiest punching bag for her frustrations. She'd figure out a way to deal with the texts without telling Omar and definitely without telling Julian.

Omar continued, "All you're doing is making yourself miserable. This bad mood is probably because sticking to your principles is causing you to miss out on the D you're used to getting on the regular."

Mena's mouth dropped open as she stumbled into the elevator.

"Trust me, I learned a long time ago that withholding sex from Charlie hurts me more than it hurts him, so I don't do that shit anymore. Now what you need to do is go home and forgive your man between the sheets. I promise you'll feel better about everything after he makes you holler," Omar said.

Mena groaned as a sly stirring ached between her legs. She and Julian hadn't made love since they'd returned from Florida. Spending the holidays in Jacksonville had been Mena's bright idea, but now she regretted suggesting that they spend the holidays with their parents. The trip had been a disaster, and her dear mother had planted the seed of marriage in Julian's head.

Why hadn't she gone to Zanzibar as Julian had proposed? Things would still be good between them, and she would have been getting her daily, and sometimes twice, dose of the man she'd fallen in love with.

Mena pressed the button for the twelfth floor and leaned against the elevator wall. Sighing, she whispered, "I hate it when you're right."

"No, you don't. That's why you call me. Really, love, you are not acting like yourself at all, and I think I know why," Omar said.

"Enlighten me," Mena said glumly. She didn't know if she could handle another scathing analysis of her psyche from Omar right now.

"Even though you have a lot going on, I know that the trial is wreaking havoc on your life … probably at a subconscious level. Having to come back here in a few months and testify against the woman you considered a mentor for trying to kill you would stress anybody out. That's why you're overreacting to this thing with Julian and your mom," Omar explained.

Mena took a deep breath. Not a bad theory. The texts had pushed thoughts of testifying against her former boss from her mind. But, it was in her best interest to let her best friend think he was right.

"What do you want? A gold star for being right about me?" Mena asked.

"Honey, please. You know I go platinum and diamond only. Now, I gotta get to work. On this side of the world, the day is just starting," Omar said.

Mena exchanged goodbyes with her friend, and then slipped the phone into her purse. Stepping out of the elevator onto the twelfth floor, she frowned at the stench of burnt food in the air. Mena followed the horrific scent, growing in intensity, all the way to her door.

Pulse racing, she pressed the key card against the panel and pushed the door open. A wave of gray smoke billowed into her face, almost choking her. Her eyes darted across the living room to the dining room nook, where the windows were perched open at a slight angle, allowing the stench and smoke to escape to the outside.

Closing the door behind her, Mena stopped and listened for Julian, but she didn't hear any sounds. On the island, she found the source of the culinary mayhem. A crusted blackened gooey substance still smoking in a stainless steel pot. Mena couldn't fathom what the dish should have been.

Next to the pot was a folder with a logo of a peach pierced by a trident and a tidal wave curving around the perimeter of the fruit. Below the logo was Tactical and Intelligence Defense Executive

Services. Mena coughed as she ran a finger along the edge of the folder, curious about the contents.

"You're home ... early."

Mena jumped, startled, and turned. In an instant, she felt dizzy, but not from the smoke. Her heartbeat thudded in her chest as her eyes feasted on Julian as if for the first time. His presence filled the room, large and imposing. His muscular chest bare as he rubbed remnants of food from his neck and arms. His smoldering, soulful brown eyes rested on her, hesitation in his glance as he waited for her to make the next move.

Suddenly self-conscious, Mena tugged at the collar of her dress shirt and leaned back against the kitchen island. "Yes, I am, wise guy."

"Don't get me wrong. It's nice to see your face before midnight. Is the restoration going okay?" Julian asked, taking a step toward her.

A flurry of sensations rocketed through her body as he reduced the space between them.

Mena waved a hand through the dissipating smoke. "Yeah, it is. Finally got a breakthrough on the settings I needed to use, and it's starting to work. Remember my co-worker, Isaac, who I told you about. He wasn't too pleased that I actually started making progress on the piece after struggling for the past two days."

"Need me to beat him up for you?" Julian asked, a hint of mischief in his eyes as he took another step toward her.

Mena erupted in laughter. "No, that won't be necessary."

"Well, just know it's an option that's always on the table," Julian said.

"I'll keep that in mind. So, what kind of culinary experiment went wrong here?" Mena asked, jerking her thumb back toward the smoldering pot.

"I was trying to surprise you by recreating your mom's shrimp and grits. She walked me through the recipe over the phone—"

"My mother gave you her coveted grits recipe? I don't even know that one," Mena said.

"She was trying to help me get out the dog house," Julian said, closing the gap between them. His arm brushed against hers as he leaned on the island next to her. "I thought if I could make your favorite dish, you'd finally forgive me. So, she gave me the recipe with a few conditions."

"Which were?"

"Don't write anything down and don't tell anyone, not even you, the secret ingredients ... or she'd Lorena Bobbit me," Julian said, biting his bottom lip as he looked over at her.

"Really? My mother spent years perfecting that recipe. If she was walking you through it, how did it end up like ... this?" Mena asked, enjoying the sight of Julian struggling with not being good at something.

"Got distracted by a phone call. I swear I only stepped away for ten minutes," Julian said.

"A call from T.I.D.E.S.?" Mena asked, her curiosity piqued as she slid the folder toward him.

Julian hesitated for a split second, then took a deep breath. "I got a job."

"A job?" Mena asked, not surprised Julian had finally found work that would meet his interests. It was only a matter of time before he ran out of ways to entertain himself while she went to work every day.

"Private security. The company is owned by one of my old Navy buddies," Julian said.

Mena flipped the folder open and scanned the forms inside. "Is that Sunny Tate?" She asked, pointing to the name on the letterhead of the employment offer memo.

Julian nodded.

"Will it be dangerous?" Mena asked.

"Could be," Julian said.

Again, not surprised. Her attempts to get Julian to take a safe job in the IT field had been met with disinterest and resistance. She knew a part of Julian craved being in situations where he could save the day, be the hero, and make a difference in people's lives. It was one of the reasons she'd fallen in love with him, and she couldn't expect him to change now.

"Promise you'll be careful," Mena said.

"Only if you promise you'll forgive me for missing your lecture," Julian said.

Mena turned to face him. "I'm not mad at you anymore. I miss you. I miss us."

She trailed her hand against the chiseled muscles of his chest, running her fingers down until she stopped just south of his navel. The unmistakable movement beneath Julian's sweatpants was exactly the response she'd been hoping for. Slipping her hand beneath the band, Mena caressed the shaft of his cock as it grew harder and lengthened in her hand.

"I want you," Mena whispered.

Julian let out a low moan as he dipped his head toward her. His penetrating gaze held her in place as he brought his lips tantalizing close to hers.

"You have me," Julian whispered back.

Chapter Eight

Mena whistled under her breath as she swiped her badge against the panel of the main museum door and entered, nodding at the morning security guard. She liked entering through the museum, using the skywalk to cross over to the Irungu Center. Seeing the amazing works of art always lifted her spirits, but not as much as an intense night of lovemaking with Julian could. Her body still ached from last night's sexual gymnastics. Mena made a mental note to not miss her lunchtime yoga classes. She had to keep her flexibility up.

Getting back on track wasn't the only thing lifting her spirits. Twenty-four hours had passed since she'd received the last text message. Maybe the annoying pest had finally realized she wasn't going to meet with him now or ever. With everything going on, the last thing she wanted was to be paranoid about coming face to face with her past. Despite her amazing mood this morning, trepidation lingered.

What if he showed up at the museum again?

What would she do?

Stepping through the empty lobby, Mena walked past the exhibit hall, where the Anatsui sculptures hung from the ceiling. As she headed toward the skywalk, her heels echoed on the granite floors. The morning sunrays blinded her as she walked through the glass-enclosed tunnel and into the Irungu Center. Taking the elevator to the top floor, she headed toward the room affectionately called the bullpen, where the conservators worked tirelessly restoring masks, sculptures, ceramics, and textiles reflecting the beauty and majesty of African tribal artistic expression.

Sliding the door open, Mena clenched her jaw as she prepared for another tense day with her co-workers.

Grace and Isaac were already at work and engaged in another epic debate. Mena didn't want to know what this one was about. She tucked her head and walked past them, hoping they wouldn't drag her into their bickering again. She wanted nothing more than to lose herself in her work, the delicate painstaking process of cleaning a 16th-century ivory bracelet with intricate figures and latticework carved into the surface. Wangari had entrusted the priceless piece into her care, expecting her laser conservation techniques to succeed where the other more traditional approaches had failed. She'd been working fifteen-hour days trying to complete the restoration in time for next week's exhibit opening.

Isaac shook his head. "Your excitement over the guy who turned you into a side piece, then dropped you without warning, is making every feminist around the globe cringe in disgust."

Mena kept her head down, hoping they wouldn't notice her entrance, and headed toward the back of the room to her workstation.

"They wouldn't cringe if they saw Hakeem Underwood or his package. Plus, Hakeem never led me on. He made it clear he didn't want anything serious, and I was fine with that," Grace insisted.

"Liar. You thought you'd be the exception to his rule, so you let him use you like a sex toy until he found another," Isaac said.

"Stop being dramatic. He didn't break things off with me because he found another girl. His work takes him on dangerous missions, and he didn't want me to be the target of al-Harakat or some other crazy rebel group because of him. Now that Wangari's father has hired TIDES as part of the family's personal security detail, he might be assigned to guard the Irungu Center, which would give me the perfect opportunity to make him regret his decision to push me away," Grace said.

Mena looked up, suddenly interested in the conversation. "Grace, did you say TIDES?"

"Yes, check your email. Bodyguards from TIDES are going to be assigned to the museum and Irungu Center as we get closer to the primaries in April. With all the political connections Wangari's family has, her father is ramping up security to prevent an attack or kidnapping to further some political gain," Grace said.

"TIDES is a private security firm for the rich and famous. When kidnappings or corporate espionage occurs, wealthy Kenyans reach out to special ops security firms like TIDES to protect their interests by any means necessary, including tactics the police would never do," Isaac explained.

"Julian got a job working with TIDES," Mena said, an uneasiness settling within her. Julian had told Mena his new work could be dangerous, but she wasn't expecting it to be anything like what Grace and Isaac were describing. Any work that would bring Julian into the crosshairs of terrorists and rebel factions was not something she wanted him involved in anymore. "He said the company is owned by one of his old Navy buddies."

"He's ex-military, right?" Isaac asked. "Makes sense that he'd work for an outfit like TIDES."

"Old Navy buddy?" Grace shrieked. "Did Julian really say that about Sunny Tate?"

"Yeah, why is that a big deal?" Mena asked, walking toward Grace's desk.

Grace's fingers flew across her keyboard as she accessed her social media accounts online. Mena's eyes blurred as Grace scrolled through her friends' list, then stopped on one small logo—the same trident-speared peach with a wave curving over it that Mena had seen on Julian's folder last night. Grace clicked on the link.

"This is your man's old Navy buddy," Grace said, clicking on a picture, then magnifying it to fill the entire screen.

Sucking in a breath, Mena stared at the old Navy buddy—Sunny Tate. The woman was stunning, with dark skin, sparkling brown eyes, and a smile that had to be worth millions. She could have easily been a model on the runways of Paris and Milan, yet her bio stated that she was a retired naval special ops pilot, owner of TIDES, ATL native and self-proclaimed fashionista.

"She's gorgeous," Isaac whispered, stepping between Grace and Mena to get a better view.

Blood boiling, Mena couldn't stop watching the monitor as Grace continued to scroll through Sunny Tate's social media page. Pictures flew by in a blur. Why hadn't Julian told her that the owner of TIDES was a breathtakingly beautiful woman from his past? Perhaps he hadn't thought it was important, and maybe it wasn't. Why should she make a big deal about a pretty woman who'd served in the Navy with him? There was no reason for her to freak out—

"Looks like there's more to the story of Julian and Sunny," Isaac said, pointing at the screen.

Staring back at her was a young Julian Montgomery with an arm wrapped around Sunny Tate, dressed in a scantily clad bikini, on the beach in what looked like Destin, Florida to Mena.

Despite the warning bells clanging in her head, Mena couldn't help but take stock. Sunny was curvy and voluptuous and infinitely more attractive than she was. A spasm of panic shot through Mena.

Reaching over Grace, Mena grabbed the mouse and magnified the photo. On the left of Sunny, a light-skinned black man with short dreadlocks and a sweet smile also had an arm wrapped around her, leaning his head on her shoulder. But Sunny's arms were locked around Julian's waist, her head inches from his as she was caught mid laughter for the photo.

"The post says 'Hanging out with my favorite boys' and tags Julian Montgomery and Broman Garrison," Isaac recited.

Mena felt dizzy. Julian and Broman with Sunny Tate. Sunny and Julian looked close, intimate in the photo while Broman looked like a third wheel. Had Sunny and Julian been a couple back then? Why would Julian think about working with his ex without giving her some kind of warning or heads up?

Grace quickly pressed the close button on the website, jarring Mena from her thoughts.

"Enough of that. No need to think about Julian working with Sunny. If you ask me, that charm bracelet says everything you need to know about where his heart lies," Grace said, probably trying to encourage her out of the funk settling over her.

"I agree with Grace. A ten thousand dollar charm bracelet from Tiffany's should be more than enough to make you feel secure, even with a gorgeous woman like Sunny Tate around," Isaac added.

Mena glanced down at her bracelet, flipping the heart-shaped charm over to stare at the engraved J and M on the surface. Normally, staring at her bracelet made her feel overwhelmed with love, but today the jewelry struggled to work its magic.

"There really should be a lot more working going on in here," Wangari said, a playful hint in her rebuke as she walked into the room.

"We're working," Grace said, fumbling to grab a mask resting on the corner of her desk.

Wangari gave her a skeptical glance, then said, "I received clearance to extend a special invitation to some of my staff for an event occurring at the museum. How would the three of you like to attend a special, private dinner being held tomorrow night to raise money for President Thairu's re-election campaign?"

Starting in April, voters would head to the polls to choose candidates for the dozens of political parties across Kenya. Mena had noticed the buzz building across the city. There were still concerns, despite the peaceful state President Thairu had ushered in over the past four years, that violence could occur at polling stations around the country as rival parties and tribes clashed.

"You know, I'm in. I'm a huge supporter of the President," Grace said. "I need to figure out who I'm going to bring as my plus one."

"Who says you get a plus one? I was barely able to secure seats for the three of you, considering the background checks and profiles needed for all the invited guests," Wangari said.

"Grace can have my seat. Thank you for the kind invitation, but I will pass," Isaac said.

Mena remembered Isaac complaining about President Thairu in one of his spirited debates with Grace months ago. She figured he didn't want to attend a fundraiser for a leader he didn't support.

"Mena, how about you? Are you and Julian available?" Wangari asked. Mena couldn't help but notice Grace pout as Wangari offered Isaac's seat to her.

Mena wasn't sure what Julian would think about attending a Kenyan political fundraising event, but she wasn't about to say no to her boss's invitation. "Of course, we'd be happy to."

Chapter Nine

Julian smirked, as one by one, the members of the TIDES team dropped from the bar, unable to do another pull up. So much for him being out of shape. Dangling low, he looked over at Sunny, who was the last one hanging on with him and banged out four more wide-grip pull-ups. Sunny completed three then dropped to the ground. Just for good measure, Julian did one last set of four before he dismounted, landing with a thud on the soft grass.

"Damn! I can't believe you were able to do that," Enzo said, rubbing his arms. He'd been the first to tap out on the last exercise of the session. They'd started the morning with a 13.1-mile run, then followed with a half-mile swim before launching into sit-ups and finally to the pull-ups.

Julian felt good, showing up his new teammates on his first workout with them. They were strong, but none of them had gone through the rigorous SEAL training he'd endured for seven years.

"Looks like we snagged a good one," Azalea Newton said, stretching forward to shake Julian's hand.

"So much for the bugger being rusty," Simon Newton said, rolling his eyes. Simon was the crankier, lesser-half of Azalea, who preferred to be called Zale. The couple hailed from Australia, and had both worked in special forces, but never been allowed on the same team. Growing disgruntled with the separation from each other, they'd decided to leave the military and work for a private security firm where they could do the work they loved together.

Before dawn, as the TIDES crew ran a half marathon, Julian had been an unwitting captive audience to their boring-ass story of falling in love. He'd gotten a brief respite from small talk during the swim, which he'd finished second in the pack, right behind Travis Glaze, the self-proclaimed intelligence officer of TIDES.

"Glaze was my Julian Montgomery until I got the real Julian Montgomery," said Sunny after introducing them. "Like you, he can track just about anybody down and is a whiz at hacking cell phones and computers."

Glaze had shaken his hand, looking at him with awe. Julian figured Sunny had regaled him with wild stories of their time in the Navy together.

Resting on the side of the lake, Julian and Glaze were shortly joined by Taye Babalola, a six-foot-five Nigerian. A behemoth of a man, he was the other pilot on the team.

"What was Sunny like back then, when you were in special ops?" Taye had asked.

"A lot nicer than she is now," Julian had joked, but there was truth in his words. "About the same, really. It's amazing how much people can change and still be the same."

"She's taught me so much about flying and how to get out of dangerous situations. I know the Navy was sad to lose someone with her skills," Taye continued.

Julian nodded, but the truth was ... for every great Broman Garrison, Sunny Tate, and Julian Montgomery, there were dozens more that were just as good, just as fast and just as brilliant. The Navy had an endless supply of excellent operatives because they weren't found. They were made.

"Let's go! Time to get the sit-ups started," Sunny had called out after the last team member, Shiloh Dayan, emerged from the water.

Shiloh was the quiet one of the group, observing but not engaging in much of the conversation. Julian noticed a reluctance in everything she did as if she was overthinking her every move. Hesitation could get her killed in a special ops mission. She had been a part of the Israeli Defense Forces and decided to leave to get more action, which Julian wasn't quite sure she was ready for. Shiloh had finished last in every part of the training.

"Minimum of fifty, superstar level at seventy-five. Sit-ups, then pull-ups. Go!" Hakeem Underwood had called out to the team.

From what Julian could tell, Hakeem was Sunny's second-in-command, assisting her in leading the team. He had a boisterous, comedic personality that didn't seem to get in the way of him getting the job done. Lagging behind with Shiloh, he'd been assigned to make sure she wasn't alone as the rest of the team proceeded through the exercises.

Julian had banged out seventy-five sit-ups, then ran over to start his pull-ups. He'd missed the competitive nature of working out with a team. The drive to be better than the rest had been instilled in him from his Navy training. Being last meant being dead, and he wasn't keen on dying any time soon.

Not since Mena had come into his life.

Hakeem jogged over with a notepad, then clapped his hands.

"Good job this morning," Hakeem said, a sly smile on his face. "I'm sure there's no surprise here, but our new team member, Julian Montgomery, won the training today by a landslide."

Julian laughed, then said, "So what do I win?"

"Bragging rights are all we give out, but I guess that's not enough for a decorated Navy SEAL. Should we make you a star out of grass?" Simon said.

"I got enough stars. Don't need anymore," Julian responded, not appreciating the Aussie's tone.

"You were impressive out there," Shiloh said, walking over to him. "Really showed that we could be doing a lot better."

Julian smiled at the diminutive woman. "As long as you know you're giving your best, that's all that matters."

"Bullshit! My goal is to beat all of you," Sunny said.

"But now that Julian is here, you've come in second, our fearless leader," Hakeem said, playfully punching Sunny in the arm. She beamed back at him, and Julian wondered about the closeness between them.

"Did I get third?" Simon asked.

"Not this time. That honor went to your wife. Good job, Zale. Your time in the swim gave you the edge over your hubby," Hakeem said.

"Yes!" Zale said, jumping around in a circle. "I beat you, babe!"

"What's next?" Julian asked as the team meandered around the wide-open grassy knoll, trying to recover from the brutal workout.

"Nothing, you get to go home. I'll call you if something pops up," Sunny said.

Hakeem rested an arm around Sunny's neck and glanced at Julian. "How about you let Julian take my place at that fancy fundraising dinner tomorrow night?"

"Why would I do that?" Sunny asked. "He just got here."

"Hell, I think he proved today that he can jump in and outperform all of us. Just like all the stories you told me about him," Hakeem said.

"Just the good stuff, I hope," Julian added, wondering what exactly Sunny had shared with Hakeem.

"Mostly good," Hakeem said, breaking into laughter.

"And what will you do with your night off if I make the swap," Sunny asked.

"What I always do, find some trouble to get into," Hakeem winked and kissed Sunny on the temple. "What do you say?"

"Montgomery? Ready to jump into action this fast?" Sunny looked at him, eyebrow raised. "It's a formal black-tie event to raise money for the campaign of the current president, Noah Thairu, hosted by our clients."

"Yeah, Sunny hit it big when Timothy Irungu hired TIDES to supplement his security detail. There've been some anomalies in his team, and he wants us to assess the guys he's hired. He's worried about an attack on his family with the primaries coming up in April. Wouldn't be unusual for al-Harakat or one of the other tribes to try to take out Thairu's supporters," Hakeem explained.

"And who is Timothy Irungu?" Julian asked as Enzo jogged over, joining their conversation. As a SEAL, he'd had more than his fair share of run-ins with the jihadist terrorist group, al-Harakat. But he wasn't up on the social elite of Kenya.

"Only one of the richest motherfuckers in Kenya. He owns a huge horticultural empire. You know what that is, don't you? Horticulture. It's like fancy-ass gardening, growing all kinds of flowers plus fruit and vegetable farming. But mostly flowers in his case. They're one of the largest exporters of flowers to Europe. The family is worth billions," Enzo said.

"He has one heir, a daughter named Wangari, who he is extremely protective of. You and Enzo would be there as her personal bodyguards," Sunny added.

"Which is ridiculous. Wangari's husband is the Director of Public Prosecutions, kinda like the Attorney General in the U.S. Secret service will be protecting him. Not sure why Timmy wants extra coverage for her," Enzo said.

"Simple. Tim Irungu never wanted his daughter to marry Okeyo Lagat, and he doesn't trust the guy," Hakeem said.

Julian rubbed the back of his neck, his head spinning with the sudden influx of information about Kenyan politics and social elites.

"Look. Job is simple. Protect Tim Irungu's daughter. That's all you have to remember. What do you say?" Sunny asked.

Julian raised an eyebrow. He was going to be assigned to protect Mena's boss. Mena had told him that Wangari was from a rich family, but she'd never mentioned that the Director of the Tribal Museum was one of Africa's one percent.

With Mena likely to be working late on Wangari's special assignment, Julian didn't have anything better to do. Now was as good a time as any to do his first assignment with the TIDES team.

Julian said, "Count me in."

Chapter Ten

Standing in the center of the ballroom, Mena watched in awe as African dignitaries, business elite, and celebrities milled about networking and clinking glasses. The energy was palpable in the air, an excitement and decadence that only slightly distracted her from the disappointment of Julian not being by her side, sharing in this extravagant experience with her.

"Now, that is Yosef Soyinka," Grace said, pausing to tip her glass toward a medium height man, impeccably dressed in a tailored suit. He wore wire-rimmed glasses and had a kind smile as he talked to two women dressed in severe business suits. "He is the owner of several vessels and is the primary shipper of choice for Wangari's family to transport their flowers to Europe. He's worth high eight figures, buys art like candy, and definitely is worth an introduction."

"Go ahead. I think I'll sit this one out," Mena said, ignoring Grace's protests as she turned to walk toward the ice sculptures adorning tables along the ballroom wall. Her head was spinning from the whirlwind of introductions Grace had subjected her to throughout the evening. Mena was barely able to keep up as she kept her eyes trained on the door, waiting for Wangari's arrival. The night before, she'd bubbled with excitement as she told Julian about being invited to this prestigious dinner only to find out he couldn't be her plus one.

"I need a drink," Mena mumbled under her breath. If Omar were here, he'd have a haughty quip and a glass of Hennessy to help shake her out of this funk.

"Perhaps this will do?"

Mena glanced to her left and saw the outstretched, tuxedo-clad arm of ... Norman Gale? Could it really be him? The shining star of conservation that had burned out and faded into oblivion in recent years. What was he doing in Kenya?

"I know you," Mena said, taking the flute of champagne from his hand.

"Do you?" Norman asked, raising an eyebrow as a hint of a smile played on his lips. He was taller and thinner than she remembered. The expensive tuxedo gifted him with a stateliness that suited him well.

"I was in grad school when you gave a riveting lecture on the future of conservation in the art world," Mena said.

"Lasers." Norman nodded.

"I changed my studies the next week, going all-in on laser conservation," Mena said.

"Seems like that worked out well for you, Miss ...?" Norman asked.

"Mena Nix, the current recipient of the Fellowship at the Tribal Museum. I'm a guest of Wangari Irungu," Mena explained.

He extended his hand, which Mena shook.

"Norman Gale. And congratulations to you, Mena. It appears we have two things in common. I work for Ms. Irungu as well," Norman said.

"We have a dubious third thing in common, which maybe I shouldn't even mention," Mena said, rolling her eyes.

"Now, my interest is piqued. Tell me," Norman said, taking a sip of his champagne. His eyes glimmered with excitement as he waited for her to speak.

Mena took a deep breath. She wasn't sure she should have brought the subject up, but it was too late to backtrack now.

"After you left the Genesis Gallery in St. Basil, I was hired to take over the conservation department," Mena said, scrunching up her nose.

"Genesis Gallery?" Norman asked.

Lowering the champagne flute from his lips, he absently reached for the table. The crystal tipped in his hand, almost spilling the contents across the tablecloth, before he rested it on the surface.

"We both had the displeasure of working for Priscilla Dumay," Mena said.

"Priscilla Dumay?" Norman frowned.

"Yes, you know, the diabolical gallery owner turned designer baby-selling criminal," Mena said, with a nervous laugh.

The color drained from Norman's face as he looked away. Turning back toward Mena, his lips pressed into a tight line, Norman nodded, then said, "If you'll excuse me."

Before Mena could process the change, Norman had darted away from her into the crowd to greet other guests.

Why the hell had she brought up the Genesis Gallery?

She remembered Priscilla clearly saying that Norman had left the gallery on terms that were not amicable. Obviously, he didn't want to talk about Priscilla Dumay, and after what the woman put Mena through, neither did she.

Mena groaned, lamenting her social and professional faux pas. She tipped the crystal flute to her lips, then paused, arrested by a tingling dancing across her bare skin.

The air in the room had shifted, charged with a presence she would know anywhere. Turning, Mena saw Wangari entering with her husband, Okeyo Lagat, the Director of Public Prosecution. Two serious-looking bodyguards dressed in dark navy suits and sunglasses cleared the way through the crowd as Wangari and her husband proceeded to the center table.

Mena couldn't take her eyes off the lead bodyguard. Commanding and confident, he scanned the room, assessing the exits and the guests for threats.

She clutched the glass tightly in her hand as a smile played at the corner of her lips. Taking a sip of champagne, Mena tried to disguise her interest, turning slightly to watch the lead bodyguard. Heart pounding in her chest, she strained to see his face more clearly.

It was Julian.

Devastatingly handsome and oozing a magnetic sensuality, Julian controlled the space, getting Wangari and Okeyo settled before stepping back to allow other guests to greet them.

As if drawn by an imperceptible discernment, Julian turned his head in her direction. Behind the dark sunglasses, she knew he was watching her. Mena took another sip of champagne, then tipped her head toward him. He returned the gesture, sending a flurry of butterflies through her body.

Closing her eyes, Mena took a deep breath, trying to calm the desire roaring within her. Thoughts of pulling him into a side room and making love to him with the tinkling of glasses and murmur of polite, elitist conversations in the ballroom as a backdrop to their moans flooded her mind. If she could get close enough to him, Mena knew Julian would never resist the suggestion or her.

Mena opened her eyes again.

Julian and the other bodyguard were gone.

Mena jerked her head around, glancing toward the table where Wangari and Okeyo sat.

He wasn't there.

A hostess walked around the room, tapping a metal triangle. The chime filled the air, signaling that it was time to be seated at the tables, which had cost a staggering donation of ten million Kenyan shillings to President Thairu's campaign.

Mena executed a slow pirouette, scanning and scrutinizing the crowd for Julian. It was as if he'd disappeared. Julian had explained that if he was doing his job correctly, she wouldn't know he was in the same room with her. Was he watching her now as she searched for him? A game of hide and seek? Mena seriously contemplated going on a hunt of her own—

"I can't believe this," Grace said, her mouth dropping open.

Mena forced herself to focus on Grace. "What is it?"

"The President is seated at our table with Wangari," Grace said, her tone bubbling with undisguised glee. "President Thairu will be having dinner with us tonight."

"What?" Mena asked, shocked as she glanced at the man greeting Okeyo Lagat near their table. "That's the President of Kenya?"

She'd seen him on television a few times, but not enough to commit his face to memory. Wangari had kept that little detail to herself. If Mena had known she'd be dining with the President tonight, she would have brushed up on her Kenyan history. The last thing she wanted was to look like an uninformed American, oblivious to what was going on in the world outside of U.S. interests. She'd only paid attention to the more salacious stories about corruption in the Kenyan government and political clashes. Fights between tribes with different ideologies and views toward the future of the country were not exactly the topics she wanted to bring up with the President.

Mena hesitated. Her mind raced with jumbled thoughts as she prepared to meet the leader of the country.

"I'm never going to forget this for as long as I live," Grace shrieked as they approached the table. "How many people get to say that they've met the President of their country? And I will be sitting with him sharing a meal. Thairu should be a lock for re-election as long as Kipsang Rono doesn't decide to run against him."

"Isn't Rono the vice president?" Mena asked.

"Deputy President," Grace corrected, wagging a playful finger at Mena. "And yes, he is currently, but the union was strategic and has been tenuous at best over the past four years. The only man who can give Thairu a real challenge for the presidency is Rono and rumor has it that's exactly what Rono plans to do."

"I suppose that's why Thairu is trying to solidify his base of wealthy supporters at this fundraiser," Mena said.

"Exactly, and we must do everything we can to keep scum like Rono from becoming the president of Kenya," Grace said.

"Welcome, ladies," Wangari said, giving them a warm smile. "President Thairu, I'd like to introduce you to two of the talented art conservators at the museum. Grace Kadenge has been with the museum since it's opening and has restored most of the Maasai warrior art pieces. Mena Nix is this year's recipient of the prestigious fellowship and brings a wealth of knowledge on cutting edge laser restoration techniques."

"Very pleased to meet both of you," President Thairu said, reaching out to shake Grace's hand. Then he turned to Mena and gave her a practiced smile.

"It's a pleasure to meet you," Mena said, as she shook the President's hand.

Chapter Eleven

"That's her?" Enzo asked, lowering the dark sunglasses to peer at the table where Wangari Irungu, President Thairu, and their guests were seated.

Standing in a nook near the front of the ballroom, hidden from view by the guests, Julian removed his sunglasses as he leaned against the wall.

"That's her," Julian said, his tone wistful. Mena was seated next to President Thairu. Julian should have been by her side tonight, instead of babysitting the Irungu Flower Princess and her DPP husband. Mena was stunning in a cream-colored strapless column gown. She was one of the most beautiful women in the room. He'd watched men appraise her as the cocktail hour ended and wanted to rip their eyeballs from the sockets.

"Damn! That is one sexy lady. No disrespect my friend, but how'd you snag her?" Enzo asked.

Good question.

"I'm a lucky guy," Julian responded, readjusting his earpiece.

Now that the President was in the building, Kenyan Secret Service had taken over. He and Enzo had been commanded to stay out of the way.

Not that Julian cared.

Having a break from protecting Wangari and her husband gave him the perfect opportunity to watch Mena for the rest of the night. The quick exchange and acknowledgment of each other as she sipped her champagne had sent a jolt of electricity through him. He wondered if she could feel his eyes on her now? Was she thinking about him as she shook the President's hand?

"TIDES to perimeter delta exit." The command emanated from Julian's earbuds.

"Damn it. They're moving us again. We're going to miss all the fancy entertainment. Fucking bastards. Let's go." Leaving the nook, Enzo headed down the service hallway. Dubbed the delta exit, the emergency stairwell at the end of the hallway led down to the loading dock.

If shit hit the fan and all preferred exit routes were blocked, the president would be ushered through the delta exist as a last resort. Shepherded down three flights of stairs, the President would be ushered into an unmarked van waiting in the loading dock of the museum. Julian and Enzo would remain in the hallway to fight off anyone hoping to hurt the Kenyan leader.

Julian stole one last glance at Mena. Her smile was effervescent as she engaged in conversation with the people at her table. This was the last time he'd miss out on being by her side for an important event. Turning, he followed Enzo, proceeding along the passageway that ran parallel to the ballroom.

"Secret Service is doing our job for us. No way they'll need the delta exit. You think I'm gonna complain that I'm getting paid to sit on my ass? Nope, I'm going to take a fucking nap," Enzo said, chuckling as he plopped into the orange plastic chair lined against the wall near the door to the emergency stairwell.

Julian slid into the chair next to Enzo, disappointed. Not because he was eager to protect Wangari Irungu or her husband. He wasn't. What he wanted was a front-row seat to stare at Mena tonight as she enjoyed her first fundraising dinner with the top echelon of Kenya's social and political scene. Instead, he was in a dingy gray passageway listening to Enzo sleep. Not exactly how he wanted to spend the evening.

Hours later, Julian finally heard a command through his earpiece. He glanced at Enzo, slumped in the chair next to him snoring.

"Enzo, wake up," Julian said. "The President has left the building. They want us to take over security in the ballroom."

Enzo said, "Yeah, now the fuckers need us. Let's go."

Julian followed Enzo back to the nook in the corner of the ballroom.

"What's next?" Julian asked.

"Primary focus is on Ms. Irungu and her husband, but of course, they want us to keep an eye out for the remaining guests as well," Enzo explained, then glanced down at a lambskin card he'd pulled from the inner pocket of his jacket. "Looks like everyone will be moving out to the rooftop garden to enjoy a live band and more cocktails with a dessert sampler."

Enzo extended the card toward him, and Julian took it, scanning the schedule of events for the evening.

"Let's get this over with," Julian said and folded the card, placing it in his jacket pocket.

"I got a better idea," Enzo said, with a hint of mischief. "How about I escort Ms. Irungu and her hubby to the rooftop so you can get a moment to say hi to your lady."

"That's the best idea you've had all night," Julian said.

"You're welcome, bitch," Enzo said, resting a hand against the gun hidden in his waistband as he exited the nook.

Julian watched Enzo approaching the center table where Wangari and Okeyo still sat. Mena engaged in polite conversation with two other guests, but he could tell she was stalling. She wanted a moment alone with him as much as he did. Stepping out into the ballroom, Julian turned toward Mena. A waiter carrying a tray of hors d'oeuvres slammed into Julian, sending the tray crashing to the floor.

"Watch where you're going, buddy," Julian said, reaching a hand out to help. The waiter recoiled from his grasp, staring back at Julian. Fear clouded the man's eyes as he mumbled quick apologies. He was young, probably barely eighteen, and obviously contrite about the mistake he'd made. His white waiter's jacket and black pants were about two sizes too big for his skinny frame, making him look more disheveled than the other polished waiters working that evening.

Julian kept his eyes on the waiter as the kid backed away slowly toward the corner of the room. Resting a hand on his Beretta, Julian felt the hair on his skin rise as he watched the kid waiter being berated by one of the head caterers. Damn shame the kid was getting yelled at for a simple mistake. Turning away from that scene, he headed toward Mena, who stood next to the oversized table.

"Is this against protocol?" she asked.

Julian's body ached from the close proximity of Mena. A sliver of distance separated them, triggering a longing within him to reach out and wrap his arm around her. A move he couldn't do in front of this crowd. She was an Irungu Family guest, and tonight, he was just the help. A trained and paid servant of Wangari Irungu.

"It is most definitely against protocol for a beautiful woman to distract me from my security duties," Julian responded as they followed the rest of the guests toward the doors leading to the rooftop garden. They slowed their pace, allowing the other guests to pass them.

"I hear you're a bit of a rebel. A rule breaker," Mena said.

"Only when inspired," Julian responded, turning to check for any unusual activity. His eyes scanned the crowd even as he focused on Mena. "And you are as good as inspiration can get."

"Glad to hear that," Mena whispered. "Try to meet me outside near the bushes in the corner. I'll be waiting."

Julian watched as Mena was beckoned by the woman she'd been hanging out with for most of the night. The sight of her tight ass in the white dress stirred a fierce desire that would need to be alleviated … soon.

Thirty minutes later, Julian had secured the empty ballroom and reported the "all clear" to Enzo through the wireless communication packs they wore underneath the dark suits.

"All clear outside," Enzo responded.

Julian slipped his dark sunglasses into the inner pocket of his jacket, then headed toward the marble ivory steps of the ballroom leading out onto the rooftop garden.

Stepping out into the night, Julian immediately saw Mena. She stood alone, sipping a glass of wine as she looked over the edge of the building toward the twinkling lights of the Nairobi skyline.

Tucked away behind a series of artistic box bushes next to a crystal pedestal with overflowing forget-me-nots, she was hidden from view of the other guests. Tendrils of her hair danced softly in the breeze against her skin. She rubbed her arms absently.

In the distance, the crowd huddled on the designated dance floor, an area surrounded by velvet ropes, swaying and dancing to the music from the six-person live band. Cocktail tables dotted the rest of the rooftop, with groups of guests lingering around each of them, drinking and talking.

Walking up behind Mena, Julian slipped his arms around her and kissed her softly on the neck.

"I missed you tonight," Mena said.

"Me too," Julian murmured. He inhaled slowly, delighted by the scent of sandalwood and orange wafting from her skin. His hands slid down the length of her dress, caressing her hips. Julian wanted to pause time right then and there, never leaving this moment.

Mena gripped the wine glass tighter, lacing her fingers around the stem. Julian noticed a shift in the air, a seriousness infecting her mood.

"What are you thinking right now?" Julian asked.

Mena shrugged, then sighed. "You ever think about how we met? If Ella hadn't kidnapped me and if I wasn't with you when her dead body was found, I doubt we would have spent enough time together to fall in love. Kind of feels wrong to be so happy when we were brought together from tragedy. Makes me wonder if we're on borrowed time ..."

Mena faced him. Julian looked down into her beautiful eyes. He wasn't sure what had brought on this somber mood, but he was glad she was opening up to him. Instead of pretending everything was fine like she probably wanted to, she was sharing her honest feelings.

Julian shrugged and admitted, "I've been living on borrowed time since my SEAL team was massacred. I don't deserve any of this—"

"Don't say that," Mena interrupted, placing a finger against his lips. "Your actions back then were heroic. You risked your life trying to save your team. It's not about doing the perfect thing or never making a mistake. Julian, you are always willing to put your own life on the line to save others. That's why you deserve all the happiness that you have right now."

"So why don't you think you deserve this happiness?" Julian asked. He could see the worry in her eyes, but he couldn't understand what drove her fears. He knew she'd gone through a bad divorce, and maybe that experience made her anxious about their future. But Julian would never let anything break them apart. He'd fight whoever and whatever to be with Mena.

"I don't know," Mena said, shaking her head. "I'm not sure why I even brought it up."

"I'm glad you did. We're no different than any other couple. We're going to have our fair share of fights, disagreements, challenges, and obstacles. But, you know what?" Julian asked.

Mena looked up at him, her eyes filled with hope. "What?"

"We're strong enough to overcome them all. Nothing is going to break us up. I won't let it. So, don't worry, okay," Julian said.

"Even if I'm not sure I want to get married again?" Mena whispered. "Would you still want to be in a relationship with me?"

"Is that what this is about?" Julian asked, a heaviness seeping into his bones.

Mena looked away.

"Excuse me. Would you like champagne?" The frumpy, kid waiter interrupted. Julian detected a slight tremble in the boy's voice and glanced over his shoulder. An older waiter stood on the other side of the garden, watching and scrutinizing the kid's every move. A thin sheen of sweat coated the boy's face.

"No, we're good," Julian said, waving the waiter away.

The boy nodded, then looked down, eyes darting before he stepped toward the red carpet leading to the dance floor. His steps were cautious and hesitant.

Julian tensed, his eyes locked on the kid's movements as he approached the dancing guests. A stilted, stiff gait. Head turned left, right, then left again. The arms of his oversized white jacket damp with sweat.

Only the arms damp with sweat?

Something wasn't right.

"What's wrong?" Mena asked, worry in her eyes.

"Stay here," Julian said slowly, eyes trained on the waiter inching closer to a crowd of guests near the dance floor. "Do not move."

Turning from the ledge, Julian raced into the crowd.

Chapter Twelve

Adrenaline spiking through his veins, Julian pushed his legs harder, zipping through the crowd. Grabbing the kid waiter's arm, he jerked him back, sending the tray of champagne flutes falling to the ground with a loud crash.

Crystal shards decimated against the ground as the liquid sprayed across guests standing nearby. Gasps and screams erupted through the night air as all eyes darted to Julian and the kid.

He held on tighter as the kid waiter jerked and writhed, but kept his movements still and cautious. He didn't want to ignite the disaster he was trying to prevent. The kid waiter started to wiggle within his grip, easing out of the oversized white jacket with his free arm to try to get away.

Someone in the crowd shrieked. "Oh my God!!! He's got a bomb!!!"

Panic swelled through the crowd.

"He's a suicide bomber!"

"We're all going to die!"

The Irungu family security guards in the crowd brought out their weapons, some training them on the kid waiter and Julian, while others tried to corral the crowd from panicking and trampling back toward the ballroom. They all knew the risks too well. Any sudden movement could detonate the bomb before any of them had a chance to diffuse the situation.

Julian turned the kid waiter toward him. The fear in his eyes was palpable. He'd seen that haunted look before.

Two security guards stepped closer to Julian, but he held up a hand, stopping their movement.

The cries and screams grew to a crescendo as the other guards slowly started to direct the crowd toward a concrete stairwell near the furthest end of the courtyard.

Julian stole a quick glance behind him. Mena stood where he'd left her near the crystal pedestal overflowing forget-me-nots. Defiant, refusing to leave him and join the others to seek safety. She had a clear path to the French doors that led into the ballroom, but she hadn't tried to escape. As long as he was out here, he knew she would be too.

The kid waiter jerked against Julian's grasp. Julian took a step toward him, tightening his hand on the kid's skinny arm. He watched the boy's hand moving toward his pants pocket, fumbling as he pulled out a small detonator.

One push of the button would end the life of every person on the rooftop.

"Did they force you to do this?" Julian asked, keeping his voice steady and calm.

The kid waiter's eyes grew wide, tears welling, as he stared back at Julian. Releasing the boy's arm, Julian raised his hands in the air.

"Did they kidnap you?" Julian asked.

The kid waiter nodded, adjusting the detonator in his hands, closing his fingers around the small object.

"Tell me what happened?" Julian asked.

The boy shook his head, eyes darting through the crowd as sweat rolled down the side of his face.

"I'm not going to hurt you," Julian said, taking another step back to give the kid waiter more space. If he could get the kid to talk, it would give all of them much needed time. If he was lucky, he might be able to convince the kid there was another way out for him. One that didn't end with blowing up himself and the hundred guests on the rooftop. "Tell me what they did to you."

The kid waiter took a deep breath, his eyes locked on Julian's.

"It's okay. You can talk about it."

The kid waiter began slowly.

"They took me and my sisters. They wanted me to go into the city for a mission, but I refused. I didn't want to leave my two little sisters alone with them. I've seen what they do to women and young girls. My sisters are ten and thirteen years old, but that wouldn't stop them from violating them. I was afraid of what they would do to my sisters if I left to do a mission for them," the kid waiter said, through choked sobs.

"What happened after that?" Julian lowered his arms, his mind whirling with the harrowing story he knew was coming. He'd witnessed similar acts on his missions in Africa, gathering intelligence against al-Harakat.

"They raped Bishara. She was barely a teenager and they raped her right in front of me. They told me I could have saved her from that pain if I had done the first mission. Then they asked me if I wanted to save my youngest sister. I could save her if I would agree to do a mission for them. A mission that would not only free my sisters but would send me to the happiest place I could imagine," the kid waiter said, his tears slowing as he loosened, then tightened his fingers around the detonator.

"Heaven," Julian said, familiar with the rhetoric used by terrorists like al-Harakat to convince young kids to sacrifice their lives.

The kid waiter nodded slowly.

In the periphery, Julian could see the guests toward the furthest end of the rooftop. The size of the crowd wasn't getting smaller. His eyes darted toward the exit stairwell. Something prevented Enzo from opening the door. Three men worked feverishly with Enzo, trying different tactics, but none seem to be working. Julian figured the terrorists had sealed the exits to ensure maximum damage from the suicide bomb.

A hush fell over the crowd as the kid waiter continued to speak.

"I had to save my sisters from any more pain. I couldn't let them continue to rape them. They promised me that if I do this, they would set them free. I don't want to kill these people. I tried to take the bomb off, but it is tied onto me. I tried to blow myself up before I got here, but they had someone watching me. Following me. He pointed his big gun at me and told me to go inside, serve the people, and make their last night happy. Then after dinner, when everyone was on the rooftop dancing, I was supposed to press this red button." The kid waiter held his hand high, thumb poised on the button that seemed to glow against the night sky.

A round of gasps floated through the air from the guests, as some wailed.

"You don't have to do that. I promise, I can help you if you let me. What's your name?" Julian asked.

"Uhuru," the kid waiter said.

"Uhuru. I'm Julian."

"I wish we were meeting under different circumstances Mr. Julian," Uhuru said.

"So do I."

Uhuru continued, "The bad men with guns told me that if I didn't complete the mission, they would do horrible things to my sisters instead of setting them free. I don't want to do this, but what other choice do I have?"

Julian had spent weeks working with explosive specialists in Nigeria, part of small bomb-disposal units, trained to disarm improvised explosive devices. It had been years since he'd watched the specialists do their work, studying their moves and methods from afar as his SEAL team guarded the perimeters from surprise terrorist attacks. Right now, those memories were all he had to save this kid and the rest of the guests on the rooftop.

"You can choose to let me help you save yourself and all these innocent people." Julian said.

"I don't want to kill people. Please, if you can help me not kill people. I want a chance to be free of this burden," Uhuru said, fresh tears falling down his cheeks.

"Then that's what I'll do," Julian responded, then turned toward the crowd of guests collectively holding their breaths near a corner of the courtyard. Enzo and the other security guards were working to unhinge the exit door. "Anybody have scissors? I need scissors!"

A woman in a long emerald green gown emerged from the crowd, digging in her purse as she walked confidently toward him.

"Here, I have these," the woman said, handing Julian a pair of embroidery scissors. Flipping the small object in his hands, Julian tested the sharpness against the tip of his thumb, happy to feel the sharp prick. The scissors were the perfect size to make the delicate snips needed to free Uhuru.

Turning back to the boy, he said, "We're going to sit down right here, next to each other, slowly. Then I'm going to get you out of this vest."

The boy nodded and lowered his body in unison with Julian until he was sitting on the soft grass of the courtyard, his hand still clutching the detonator with the red button.

"Lay that down carefully by your side," Julian said, motioning to the detonator, "then lie flat on your back."

Enzo rushed over to Julian. "We need to get these people off the fucking rooftop now! Can't get the stairwell door open. It's jammed from the inside."

Julian would rather try to get the vest removed without an audience of screaming, scared guests. The only other option was the delta exit they'd guarded before.

"Send some of the other security guards to check the ballroom. If it's clear, take the guests inside and get them down to the loading dock through the delta exit," Julian directed. "And avoid the windows. Stick to the inner walls, single file."

"The motherfuckers are probably watching, aren't they? Waiting to see fucking fireworks," Enzo whispered.

"And if they don't, they could remotely detonate," Julian said, turning to look back at Enzo. Concern creased his friend's face.

"You got this?" Enzo asked, nodding down at the suicide vest.

"Yeah, I got it. Get these people out of here and to safety," Julian responded with more confidence than he felt.

Sirens filled the air as the police grew nearer. No doubt many of the guests had sent texts and made calls to alert the authorities. But the local police wouldn't be able to do what he could. He had to make sure

Uhuru didn't become another victim of the terrible violence terrorists inflicted on the innocent.

"On it. Don't you fucking die up here, you hear me," Enzo said, then walked briskly back to a group of four other men, relaying the directions.

Julian looked up and saw Mena staring back at him, her dark eyes wide with fear, concern and ... love. She stood like an ethereal vision, watching over him as he tried to save this teenager's life. He needed her to go with the others, not wait for him on the rooftop. He needed to know she was safe.

"Mena," Julian said.

She took a step toward him, but he held up a hand, warning her not to come any closer.

"I'm not leaving you," Mena said, her voice unwavering in its determination.

"Yes, you are. When the bodyguards over there start to take the guests out, you need to be the first one out of here," Julian said.

"I can't go ... not without you," Mena shook her head.

"You have to. You're too beautiful, too distracting to me right now."

Mena laughed. "I can't believe you're trying to joke at a moment like this."

"You trust me?" Julian asked.

The guests were moving now slowly past Uhuru and filing through the French doors, exiting the rooftop.

"Of course I do," Mena said.

"Then I'll meet you downstairs," Julian responded.

Mena took a deep breath, hesitating as the guests continued to exit the courtyard. He needed her to be safe and not wait for him. But would she walk away from him knowing that his life was in danger? If the situation was reversed, he knew there was no way he'd leave her side.

"Please," Julian whispered.

Mena looked toward the sky, then turned and walked away, blending in with the last of the crowd of other guests leaving the rooftop.

"God bless you, sir! God bless you for saving us," a man said as he passed Julian and Uhuru.

He wasn't blessed yet.

As soon as the last guest had cleared the rooftop, Julian brought his attention back to Uhuru. The boy was still, his breathing ragged despite the peaceful look in his eyes trained on the scissors in Julian's hands.

Reaching for an edge of the fabric, Julian made the first cut.

Chapter Thirteen

Cheers roared into the night as Julian, escorted by a dozen military and police officers, emerged from the loading dock in the alley behind the Tribal Museum and Irungu Center. Many of the guests had remained, standing behind barricades set up by the Nairobi police department. Uhuru trembled uncontrollably in Julian's embrace. After cutting the fabric strategically, Julian removed the vest without disturbing any of the wires. As he carried the kid down three flights of stairs to the first floor of the Tribal Museum, the military bomb experts rushed past him, heading to the rooftop.

Julian was shocked he'd pulled it off. Memories of the steps he'd watched the Nigerian explosive specialists perform hundreds of times had slammed into his head, guiding his actions. In reality, the truth was his special ops training had kicked in, instinctively, and took over. He'd practiced for years how to handle situations more difficult than this one. The thoughts, the actions, the decisions were as familiar and easy as breathing for him. This time, he'd been able to free a teenage boy from the heinous mission that al-Harakat or some other terrorist faction wanted him to do—killing prominent Nairobi business and social elite.

Two EMTs rushed toward him, extracting Uhuru from his arms.

The kid looked back at Julian, relief, and gratitude in his eyes as he was led away. Julian's shoulders slumped, the weight of the evening crashing over him. He needed to find Mena. She could have died tonight if he hadn't been on that rooftop. If he hadn't noticed the signs.

Turning toward the guests crowded behind the police barricade, Julian took a step then stopped. Nine soldiers dressed in olive fatigues converged upon him. Guns pointed in his face, they ushered him toward the loading dock, now empty of the guests and security guards who'd brought them down safely. What the fuck was this about?

"Julian Montgomery," a male voice boomed from the shadows of the dock.

A knot tensed in the back of Julian's neck as his mind registered the voice. One from his past. One he'd rather not have to cross paths with again.

"Just a few questions for you if you don't mind." The man emerged from the darkness, stepping onto the wet pavement in the alley. Despite the friendliness of his tone, Julian knew it wasn't a suggestion but a command.

Julian crossed his arms and waited, but said nothing.

"We are trying to assess what happened tonight, and I'd greatly appreciate your cooperation."

"Haven't I always freely given my cooperation to you ... Reggie?" Julian asked.

Iregi "Reggie" Kamau, the leader of the African Special Forces, known as ASF in military circles, glared back at him, unable to hide his disdain and anger over the informal greeting in front of his team.

"Give us a moment," Reggie directed the soldiers.

Julian waited until they were standing alone, out of earshot of the rest of the ASF special agents. Iregi Kamau had been recruited at the inception of the creation of the group. Julian's SEAL team had the displeasure of training the ungrateful and arrogant new agents.

Reggie said, "Are the SEALs encroaching on my territory without following the prescribed protocols? You are supposed to alert me if you are active in any area under ASF jurisdiction."

"You mean the protocols I *taught you* when you were first recruited to lead the group? No protocols were broken. I'm not here on a SEAL mission," Julian responded.

"You expect me to believe that?" Reggie spat the words through gritted teeth, keeping his voice low and out of earshot of his men. "How did you know that the boy had a bomb strapped to his body underneath his coat? My team interviewed all the guests. No one noticed anything out of order. You were the first to go after him even though no one else recognized the waiter as a threat. You must have had some intel."

"I don't need intel. I'm a SEAL trained, ex-special ops soldier. The signs were all there," Julian said.

"Ex-soldier?" Reggie asked.

"Look, the kid was nervous, younger than the other wait staff. His clothes were too bulky on his skinny frame. He'd been sweating the entire night, soaking through his clothes, but only the sleeves of his jacket were damp. Why wasn't his entire jacket drenched with sweat? I decided to find out, so I moved in on him," Julian explained.

Reggie asked, "If you're not in the SEALs anymore, then why are you here?"

"I work private security for Timothy Irungu. Are we done?" Julian asked.

Glaring, Reggie pushed past him and walked toward the agents loitering near the intersection of the alley and the main thoroughfare.

"Julian! Julian!" Mena's words floated from behind him.

"Miss, you cannot be back here!" a special agent yelled.

Julian turned in time to see Mena being forced backward by one of the ASF agents. Pulse jumping, Julian rushed toward the road, jerking the agent away from Mena. Julian glared at Reggie. The leader of the ASF gave a quick nod, and the agent backed away, leaving Julian standing alone in front of Mena.

"You're shaking," Julian whispered into her hair as he pulled her into a tight embrace.

"Don't worry about me," Mena said, then slapped her hands against his chest. "And don't pull anything like that ever again!"

"Ouch, that hurt," Julian said, smiling at Mena as she tried hard to look stern at him. He looked down at her beautiful face. Wisps of her black hair had come loose from the side ponytail and danced in the breeze.

"I'm serious, Julian. You need to let somebody else be the hero next time," Mena said, her eyes pleading with him.

"How about ... there won't be a next time," Julian said.

Mena gave him a brilliant smile. "I like that even better."

"Come on, let's go home," Julian said. He placed his arm around Mena, holding her close as they walked along the sidewalk, past the police barricades. Most of the remaining guests had left the scene. Julian steered Mena around the corner toward the front of the museum.

Blinding flashes popped in his face as a throng of reporters converged on him. Julian gripped Mena's hand tighter as she looked at him. Her stunned expression matched the emotions rifling through him. Microphones jutted toward him as dozens of reporters shouted questions. A male journalist forced his way forward, "How does it feel to be the hero of the night, Julian Montgomery?"

Chapter Fourteen

The warmth of Julian's hand clutching hers as he opened the door to their condo was the only thing keeping Mena sane. His touch brought a semblance of normalcy and familiarity in the midst of a night that was most likely going to change their lives forever. The Kenyan journalists had quickly dug up information on Julian from his heroic acts in St. Basil, and the news had hit the internet faster than either of them expected. Her phone hadn't stopped ringing. Her father, a journalist himself, as well as other family and friends, kept sending text messages, demanding details about the terrorist attack Julian had prevented.

Mena didn't want to be in the public eye. After Pricilla Dumay had tried to kill her, to protect the case the PIIB and St. Basil police were building against her former boss, Mena had been shielded from much of the media scrutiny. Julian hadn't been as lucky. Now he was faced with avoiding the press again.

"You okay?" Julian asked as he closed the door behind them, his hand still gripping hers tightly.

Mena shrugged, not trusting herself to talk. Julian had shielded her from the journalists, nearly carrying her through the throng as he dismissed their questions with a concise, "no comment." The Nairobi police had provided an escort to their condo in the Westlands, where more reporters were camped outside. Mena thanked God they'd chosen a location with top-notch security to protect the residents from unwanted visitors. Slipping into the building through the secured garage, they'd avoided any further interactions with the media. Mena knew that wouldn't last long.

"It'll blow over soon. In a day or two, no one will remember me," Julian said, a hint of hopefulness in his tone.

Mena's knees buckled as she stared into the soulful brown eyes looking back at her. She inhaled sharply, one thought slamming through her mind over and over. Her breath quickened as panic flooded through her.

Julian could have died tonight.

Died. Gone. Forever.

Taking a step toward him, Mena slipped her hands around his neck and buried her head in his chest. A flood of emotions rocked through her body as tears slid down her cheeks, wetting his dark shirt.

Julian lifted her into his arms, squeezing her tightly. As he buried his head in her hair, she felt his muscles relaxing.

Lacing her fingers within his, Mena raised his hands to her lips and kissed them, loving the masculine scent wafting from his skin. One wrong move and she could have been holding these hands in the morgue or worse, not holding them at all.

Would the police have given her any information about him?

She wasn't his wife.

There was nothing to connect them, no proof of how much they loved each other, or how committed they were to each other. Would she have been left wondering and waiting for his parents to give her information?

Mena shuddered. She had to push the gruesome thoughts from her mind.

Julian eased his hands from her grip and slipped an arm around her, pulling her to him. Mena looked up into his eyes, moved by the love and desire reflected there.

Julian leaned down, brushing his lips against hers, softly at first, before his tongue parted her lips and slipped inside her mouth. She savored the feel of his tongue against hers as she pressed her body into his awakening erection.

The heat of their kisses hit a crescendo as Mena grinded her hips against Julian, eliciting a low moan as their bodies rocked against each other. She wanted to consume him and be consumed by him. Merging their bodies into one and never lose the feeling of being with him. She wanted the memories of his touch and his presence to be tattooed on the canvas of her heart for eternity. Mena hadn't realized how much she loved Julian until his life was on the line tonight. How much she couldn't imagine living a life without him.

Her hands found the buttons of his shirt, and she quickly forced each one through the holes, then pushed the shirt from his body.

Leaning back, she savored the view of his sculpted chest and abs, watching his pecs rise and fall with each breath. Mena pressed her hands against his warm skin, allowing her fingertips to trail downward, tracing the grooves of his muscles.

Julian slid his hands along her back until his hands cupped her butt, gently massaging as the intensity in his eyes grew stronger. Mena pushed away all thoughts, allowing her mind to go blank. She didn't want to think or worry. The man she loved was standing in front of her … alive.

Slipping her hands lower along Julian's abdomen, she rested her eyes on the growing bulge in his pants. An insatiable desire and passion ripped through her body as she grabbed the waistband, unbuttoning them in one fluid motion. She reached her hand inside his boxer briefs, sliding against his skin until she felt his rock hard penis throbbing in her hand.

Massaging the shaft, Mena leaned toward Julian and whispered, "Make love to me."

Julian's eyes smoldered as he pushed her backward, pinning her between the wall and his body. Mena wiggled out of her dress, revealing her bare breasts and lacy thong. She lifted a leg, wrapping it around his waist. Reaching his hand between her legs, he pushed her lace underwear to the side and stroked her. His fingers glided easily across her arousal.

She was more than ready for him. She ached for him, needing him to fill her and push away the thoughts of losing him.

Julian lifted her higher, and Mena wrapped both legs around him as he pressed her back against the wall. Ravaging her with a blistering kiss, he removed his fingers and entered her with force. Mena let out an uncontrollable whimper as she stretched to fit him. One hand pressed against her hip to keep her steady and the other on her breast, Julian squeezed and fondled her nipple in perfect concert with his penetrating thrusts. Mena savored the feel of the friction mounting between her legs as he slid back and forth within her, possessing her, staking his claim on her.

The intoxicating fragrance of hot lust and desire lingered in the air. Waves of pleasure undulated through her body, building in intensity, sending her into a manic frenzy. Julian trailed a blaze of kisses down the side of her neck as she gripped his shoulders tightly, gyrating against him and pushing herself to the brink of ecstasy as he thrust deeper, reaching her most sensitive spot.

Mena cried out Julian's name, panting and breathless, as she squeezed her thighs tighter around him, forcing his penis deeper within her. Julian let out a husky groan, then clamped his hands around her wrists, jerking them from around his neck and pressing them against the wall above her head. His thrusts came faster and frenetic as he expanded inside her reaching the verge of climax. A flurry of sensations washed over Mena as she let out a primal moan with her orgasm. A second later, Julian reached a climax, pulling her tightly into his arms as his love flooded within her.

Slowly, Mena unwrapped her legs from his body and placed her feet on the floor.

"Don't move. Not yet, let me hold you," Julian whispered, his face nuzzled into the side of her hair, his embrace melting from tight to tender.

The warmth of his love enveloped Mena. She allowed herself to be present in the moment with him, sharing the intimate space without a thought of anything else. Nothing mattered more than being with Julian.

Intertwining her hands in his, she pulled away, leading him down the short hallway to the bedroom. He followed her without resisting, pressing against her back, unwilling to allow any distance to come between them.

Tonight had been a close call.

Too close.

Mena knew it, and so did Julian. In a flash, they could have been separated forever, wondering what could have been if the suicide bomb had detonated. Sadness welled within Mena's chest, but she pushed it away. She couldn't let her thoughts take her down the grim path of the disaster that could have been. They had survived. They were together. There was nothing but the future ahead of them.

Turning slowly, Mena faced Julian. He lifted her arm toward him, his fingers caressing the rose gold charm bracelet on her wrist. The symbol of their love.

"I know I scared you tonight," Julian said, his eyes expressing regret. "It's hard for me not to help when I know I can. But I realize it's not just my life on the line anymore. For the first time since Broman ... somebody other than my mom gives a damn if I live or die."

Mena swallowed hard, fighting back the tears. She hadn't realized how alone Julian had felt after the attack on the SEAL team. He'd always been so strong and fearless, but he was also an island waiting for her to find his shores.

"It's not fair of me to ask you to be anything other than the man I know you are. But I won't lie. I don't know if I can handle going through something like that again. Watching you risk your life for everyone else, knowing there was nothing I could do to save you," Mena admitted.

"Just knowing that I had you to come home to was all I needed. There was no way I was dying on that rooftop and leaving you alone for some other man to comfort," Julian said, kissing her wrist. A tingle of excitement flooded through her at his touch.

"Really? That's what you're worried about? Some other guy swooping in to take your place when I'm mourning you?" Mena said, a laugh escaping her lips.

Julian nodded, giving her the sexy smile that drove her wild.

"Well, you better stay alive so you won't have to worry about that,"

Mena teased, then pushed Julian down onto the mattress. Straddling him, she leaned down to kiss him fully on the mouth as he entered her once more. A jolt of ecstasy simmered through her body as round two began.

Hours later, Mena laid in the bed, her arms cradling Julian as he snored softly. They'd made love repeatedly through the night, devouring each other with an intense passion Mena had never felt before. She wanted to remember every moment of being with him—the heavy weight of his body resting against hers, the slight brush of his breath against her skin, the intoxicating brown eyes she could stare into forever. Everything she could have lost tonight.

Chapter Fifteen

"Come back to bed," Julian said, reaching his arms toward her.

Steam billowed from the bathroom as Mena stepped out onto the cool tiled floor of the bedroom. She tucked the towel around her damp body tighter. "You know I have to go to work."

Mena side-stepped away from Julian's grasp. One more caress, one more touch, and she knew he'd convince her to stay home. As tempted as she was, Mena was ready to get back to her normal life. She was still working on the complex restoration of the ivory bracelet, and she didn't want to lose momentum. "Wangari said the police have completed their investigation and the museum is open to the public again. She wants the staff to come in today."

"What if the reporters are still down there? They know we're together. I think you should wait a few days to make sure they don't harass you," Julian said.

A dozen or so reporters had staked out their condo building over the weekend, forced to stand across the street by the security guards as they hoped for a chance to catch Julian leaving. The attempted suicide bombing and the American ex-Navy SEAL who'd saved more than a hundred guests had dominated the news.

"Already checked with Fred downstairs. It's all clear," Mena said.

The news coverage of the attempted bombing had died down to a trickle by Sunday. The police had yet to determine who was behind the attack.

"Sounds like you're eager to get out of here. I thought you liked being locked up with me," Julian said, pouting.

"I loved it, you know that," Mena said, trying to ignore his emotional blackmail.

Avoiding the paparazzi outside their condo, she and Julian had ordered grocery delivery and stayed happily holed up away from the world for the weekend. They'd binge-watched movies, cooked up favorites from back home, and spent hours making love. A perfect weekend after what they'd gone through Friday night.

What Mena had loved most was Julian opening up more to her about his past. His early days in the Navy, training for the SEALs, and his first few missions. She'd watched him come alive as he told her about the hijinks he and Broman had gotten into over the years. She was surprised they hadn't been booted from their boat crew.

Mena couldn't help but notice the absence of Sunny Tate from his stories, and she'd resisted the urge to bring up the dark beauty. Hadn't Julian proven to her over and over again that she was the only woman who mattered to him? She knew there had been women in his past just as she had men in her past, but none of that mattered anymore now that they'd found each other.

"What am I supposed to do without you here?" Julian asked, propping himself up on his elbows.

The covers shifted off his naked body, revealing smooth tanned skin, perfectly sculpted muscles of his chest and washboard abs. The dark blue sheets, draped low across his waist, barely covered the part of him she adored most.

Mena didn't respond, but she hoped Julian wasn't planning to go back to work with the TIDES team. She knew he could handle himself in any situation, but she didn't want him working private security.

"Try relaxing. Do something fun that you love to do," Mena suggested.

"Fucking you is fun. I love to do that," Julian said. The crinkle in his forehead was irresistibly sexy. Mena had to resist the urge to touch him, or she would never make it out of the apartment.

"Try something that doesn't involve me, since I will be at work," Mena said, shaking her head at him. He was incorrigible.

Julian laughed, leaning back onto the pillows of the bed. Mena saw a hint of his penis, stirring with desire. His eyes were smoldering, burning her skin with passion from a distance. She had to resist.

"You need a cold shower," Mena teased.

"I need you. Drop your towel, I want to watch you get ready for work," Julian demanded.

"One condition," Mena said.

"What's that?" Julian asked, his voice husky with desire.

"You can't move from that bed, and you can't touch me," Mena said, playing with the edge of her towel.

"Can you touch me?" Julian asked.

Mena contemplated for a minute. "No, I can't touch you either. No touching allowed."

"Can I jack off while I watch you?" Julian asked, shifting into a more comfortable position.

Mena bit her lip. She wasn't sure she had the willpower to watch him jacking off at the sight of her and not want to straddle him and push him over the edge. He knew he was testing the limits of his willpower and hers. "Go for it."

"Let the show begin," Julian said, a sly smile spreading across his face. He pushed the covers from his body.

Mena dropped the towel to the floor and watched as Julian's cock grew hard instantly. The sense of power surging through her at the impact she had on him filled her with desire. Opening the closet, she pulled down a box of red Louboutins and slipped them on her feet.

"You ... are ... so ... fucking ... sexy ... and ... beautiful ... and perfect," Julian said, his hand moving slowly up and down his shaft.

Mena felt her heart slamming into her chest. She was wet as her body craved him. She wanted to feel him inside her, sliding and thrusting, bringing her to climax as he had numerous times over the weekend. Licking her lips, she resolved to resist him and tease him a bit. She could do this.

Reaching over to the drawer, Mena removed a lacy thong and swung it around her fingers, the charms of her bracelet tinkling as she moved her arm.

Julian panted faster.

Mena took a step toward the bed.

"That's cheating," Julian managed to force out of his mouth. "You're torturing me right now, you know that, don't you?"

Mena gave him a dazzling smile, then turned around and bent at the waist as she slipped the thong on. Swerving her body seductively to the music in her head, she turned around and squatted low, bouncing twice before standing again.

"Damn it," Julian muttered, his hand moving quicker, his breath in short, intense bursts speeding up. "Not going to last much longer."

Mena was pleased. She lifted the matching lace bra from the drawer. Raising her arms above her head, she swiveled her hips in smooth circles, giving him a full view of her breasts lifting with each movement. Slipping her arm into one strap of the bra, Mena caressed her breasts, squeezing her taut nipples with her fingers as she let out a low moan.

"Fuck," Julian whispered as his body tensed, then arched. His hand wet with the evidence of his orgasm, spewing from his cock.

"Really? You couldn't hold out much longer?" Mena teased.

"Get over here," Julian said.

Mena walked over to the bed and leaned down, pressing her lips to his. Julian parted her mouth with his tongue, sliding inside, swirling with intense passion, all the while respecting her rules of not touching her anywhere else. Damn, she loved this man.

After a few moments, Mena reluctantly broke the kiss, then turned her attention back to her wardrobe.

"What do you think? Gray pants and red shirt or black pants, white shirt, and red scarf?" Mena asked, pulling the two ensembles from the closet.

Julian sat up, resting his head on his hand as he stared at her two options, looking from one to the other. She loved how he was taking this decision seriously.

"Depends. What do you have going on today?" Julian asked.

"Wangari wants me to give a behind the scenes tour to a prominent group of European collectors this afternoon. They're looking for a place to house some magnificent African art they've acquired over the years, and Wangari wants them to select the Tribal Museum. That's why I need to go to work. I don't want to let her down," Mena said.

"Go more traditional for the investors. Black pants, white shirt with a dash of color from the scarf and the shoes," Julian said, looking pleased with himself.

"Good choice," Mena said, giving him a smile.

Chapter Sixteen

Five hours later, Mena limped off the elevator onto the sixth floor of the Irungu Center. Her feet cried in agony from the heels she'd had on for too long. The tour had been a huge success. The European group had decided to allow the museum to house their collection and had canceled meetings with the other museums they had planned to visit. Mena winced. Just a few more feet and she'd be in the Conservators Room, where her Chanel flats waited underneath her workstation.

Voices grew louder as Mena neared the room. The unmistakable sound of Grace Kadenge and Isaac Gatobu engaging in yet another spirited debate. What were the two arguing about this time? Slipping through the doors, Mena headed toward her workstation.

"All I'm saying is that you are living in the city now. There is no need to limit yourself to Meru women. We are all Kenyans. Who cares what tribe the woman is from. If you don't expand your horizons, you might not ever get married," Grace said, her voice rising.

Mena rolled her eyes as she slipped into her chair. The last thing she wanted to listen to was a debate about marriage.

"Why don't you understand that for me, finding a wife of my same tribe, with my same values and beliefs and history, is the only thing that matters. If other people want to date from other tribes, I don't have a problem with that. It's just not for me," Isaac roared back, his voice shaking with indignation.

Mena dropped her purse in the desk drawer then turned her focus to the ivory bracelet. Anything was better than listening to Grace and Isaac arguing over their tribal differences. Mena had gotten a crash course shortly after she'd arrived. Many Kenyans still held deep attachment to their tribes, which led to divisions within politics, ideals, relationships, and neighborhoods, not unlike how some areas of America were still divided along racial lines.

Grace and Isaac were from different tribes. From what Mena had witnessed, their views on everything in life were diametrically opposed. Although, it wasn't clear to Mena if their differences were fueled by tribal traditions or an underlying sexual tension that seemed to course between the two.

"Take Mena, for instance. She obviously didn't sit around being single just because she couldn't find a black man to date. She embraced racial and cultural differences by dating a white man, not worrying about what the world or tradition thought about her choices," Grace said.

Mena's head jerked up, and she turned back to face the dueling duo.

"Yes, but if you notice, she has not married that white man. Dating, shacking up, whatever, but marriage is a serious union, and even Mena realizes that becoming yoked with a man of a different race is not something to be entered into lightly. I'm guessing that's why Julian is still her boyfriend and not her husband," Isaac countered.

Were they using her private life as fuel for their debate? Or had she entered the twilight zone?

Grace continued, "Time, my dear Isaac, not race is why they aren't married ... yet. The relationship is new, and I understand Mena's desire to get to know Julian more before she lets him put a ring on it. Do you want to keep being this miserable, lonely single guy because you can't find a Meru woman or do you want to be happy in a relationship with a Kenyan woman without worrying about what tribe she's in?"

"How about the two of you leave my relationship out of your

debates," Mena said, disturbed by how much of her private life had become fodder for office gossip.

Grace walked over to Mena and gave her a condescending squeeze around the shoulders. "I'm sorry. We shouldn't have brought you into this."

"I'm sorry too," Isaac said, but Mena doubted his sincerity. "How are you and Julian doing after the craziness of the fundraising dinner? I'm so happy I decided to pass on attending."

"I'm fine, and so is Julian," Mena said.

"I didn't realize he was an ex-Navy SEAL and had worked missions in Africa in the past," Isaac said.

"Wangari said he's part of her private security team, and her family is thrilled to have a bonafide hero protecting her. She said her father is planning to sign TIDES to a long-term contract because of their efforts at the event and give Julian a big fat bonus," Grace said.

Mena forced herself to smile. Wangari had shared the same news with her, but it didn't make her feel any better. The idea of Julian putting his life on the line to save her boss wasn't sitting well with her, but there was nothing she could do to stop it.

"My father met with the TIDES team earlier this afternoon. I can't thank Julian enough for everything he did to save lives and protect the museum," Wangari said, floating into the room, holding a bouquet of flowers.

"Who are those for?" Grace asked, rushing toward the Director of the Irungu Center.

"Not you, this time," Wangari said. "These are for Mena."

"You got me flowers for closing the deal with the European investors?" Mena asked. "You really shouldn't have."

"Closed the deal?" Isaac asked, tension in his voice. "They agreed to let us house their collection of African art?"

"They did," Wangari confirmed. "Lawyers are drawing up the paperwork and should have it signed within the week. But no, I didn't get these flowers for you, Mena. Someone else sent them."

"Maybe, Julian?" Grace asked.

"He's not the flower type," Mena said, a sickening feeling pooling in her stomach.

"Beautiful coral peonies. We don't get many orders for these in Africa. It was a rare request, but my company aims to please," Wangari said.

Mena's throat constricted as she tried to swallow past the anger bubbling within her.

The text messages from a week ago made her shudder.

Need to see you

This could not be happening. Why now?

"Don't just sit there, read the card," Isaac said. He lifted the small card nestled inside the flowers and handed it to her.

Mena plastered on a fake smile, hiding her growing ire, and pulled the card from the envelope.

A single date, written in handwriting she thought she'd forgotten years ago, was scrawled on the card.

January 13th.

Today's date.

For the first time in forever, she hadn't thought of what this day represented. She'd been focused on Julian and her new life. Not her past.

Mena slipped the card back into the envelope as her cell phone vibrated on the table. The text message flashed on the screen.

Meet me in Uhuru Park to celebrate.

Blood rushed through her head as heat radiated on her skin. Her hands trembled as she lifted her purse from the desk drawer.

The coral peonies glowed beautifully in the sunlight flooding the room from the windows. Disgusted, Mena threw the card on the floor, then grabbed the flowers with her fists, crushing them within her fingers and threw them into the trashcan.

"Mena? What's wrong?" Wangari asked, concern etched across her face. Isaac and Grace stared at her as if she'd lost her mind.

"I'm sorry, I have to go," Mena said as she sprinted across the room.

Chapter Seventeen

"Who knew you would be my good luck charm?" Sunny's voice whispered in his ear, her hands resting on his shoulders as her hair brushed against his neck.

Julian lifted the coffee mug to his lips and sipped the bitter black brew. Earlier that morning, Timothy Irungu had wired him a six-figure bonus for saving his daughter's life. But with the payment came a new expectation. One he knew Mena wasn't going to be happy about.

"I hate it when you make me worry," Sunny said, then signaled for the waiter as she took the seat across from him. "Why are you so quiet? What's wrong?"

"Mena's not going to be happy about this," Julian admitted.

Sunny raised both eyebrows as the waiter greeted her at the table. She ordered a plate of nyama na irio, a flavorful dish of mashed green peas and potatoes with stewed meat, and a glass of water then sent the waiter away.

"You talked to her? What did she say exactly?" Sunny asked.

Julian shook his head. "No, I haven't talked to her about any of this, but I know how she was feeling this weekend. Watching me do what I've done hundreds of times as a SEAL scared her. It was different than what happened to us in St. Basil."

"How so?" Sunny asked, a skeptical look crossing her face.

"I was trapped just like she was. I had to save my life and hers," Julian said.

"But you went into a dangerous situation on purpose to save her when you were otherwise safe," Sunny countered.

"Because I love her," Julian whispered.

Sunny shrunk back, the weight of his words affecting her in ways he didn't want to comprehend.

"You think because you risked your life for a bunch of strangers, that makes it different for her? She knows you did countless missions as a SEAL, most of them infinitely more dangerous than what happened Friday night. You are a highly trained, special operative. You don't lose those skills after being a SEAL for as long as you were. It's in your DNA now," Sunny said.

"I know that. You know that. But I think Mena just realized that and she doesn't like it. She didn't say this at all, but I know she wants me to quit working at TIDES," Julian said.

The waiter returned, placing a steaming plate in front of Sunny. She thanked him, then grabbed the empty plate in front of Julian, pushing half the food onto it and then sat it back in front of him. "And what do you want, Montgomery?"

Lifting a fork, Julian took a bite of the food, but couldn't enjoy the intense flavors.

"You can't deny it, can you? Being on the rooftop doing the things you were trained to do felt right. You miss it and you want to do more of it. It's what you love to do and that's nothing wrong with that. Why do you think I created TIDES in the first place?" Sunny asked. "I needed that rush, that intensity of helping others without the restrictions of government protocol. That's what you have working with my team."

"You didn't see the look in her eyes. The fundraising event was supposed to be low key, babysitting a bunch of rich people as they fawned over the President of Kenya. Nothing was supposed to happen Friday night. Enzo and I should have collected a big ass check for very little work. But instead—"

"A hundred guests' lives were saved because you were in the right place at the right time," Sunny said.

"Mena's going to wonder and stress and worry every time I go out on another assignment if it's more dangerous than what it seems. If I'll be in a life or death situation again. If she'll get a phone call telling her I'm dead because I risked my life to save some stranger. I can't put her through that," Julian said. He needed to walk away from TIDES for Mena, but he didn't want to. He needed Mena to understand that being a special operative was all he ever wanted. He missed the thrill and the danger and the excitement.

"If you quit, how are you going to stop yourself from resenting her?" Sunny asked

"What are you talking about?" Julian dropped his fork onto the table. "I'd never resent her for wanting me to be safe."

"You don't think so? What are you going to do with yourself? Go back to being Mena's house boyfriend, taking care of her honey-do list, and being the eye candy on her arm as you escort her to different dinners. How long is that going to keep you happy? A month? Maybe two? It's too late for you Montgomery. The itch is back and you can't help but scratch it," Sunny said.

Julian clenched his jaw, hating how her words resonated within him. Could he walk away from the opportunity to work with the TIDES team? Did he want to throw away a chance to protect the world from terrorists and criminals?

"I'm sure Timothy Irungu won't cancel his contract with you if I'm not leading the team. He'll allow you to swap me out with one of your other team members," Julian said, pushing the words out of his mouth before he said something different. Something he would regret.

"So, that's it?" Sunny asked, looking disappointed. "You're going to walk away."

"I am," Julian said. He was going to put Mena first, show her that she was more important to him than anything else in his life.

"I hope she's worth it," Sunny said, taking a sip of her water.

A wail erupted from a woman at the bar to the left of their table. Julian turned to look at her, an anguished expression etched on her face as she stared at the television screen.

"Turn up the television," a man shouted as patrons of the restaurant stood from their tables and clustered around the bar where a series of flat-screen televisions displayed a gruesome scene.

Julian felt the hair on the back of his neck stand up as his brain struggled to process what was happening.

The newscaster's voice filled the air. "There has been another attack on the Tribal Museum near downtown. Witnesses say bombs exploded at the museum building and gunmen stormed inside, shooting indiscriminately at patrons. There are reports that more than two dozen tourists and workers in the area have sustained severe wounds from shattered glass that rained down to the street below. We have reporters headed to the scene to bring you more details on this tragedy."

Julian jumped up from the table and rushed out of the restaurant.

Chapter Eighteen

Strategically placed bombs planted around the perimeter of the Tribal Museum detonated on cue as Tubeec, and his men exited the truck parked in the alley at the Irungu Center loading dock. Yasir, Liban, and Zahi sprinted around to the front entrance of the museum. The sound of scattered pops from assault rifles marred the air as they shot indiscriminately at tourists and museum patrons. Tubeec hoped they remembered to minimize damage to the artwork inside. He didn't want to senselessly destroy cultural and artistic treasures of African history if it could be avoided.

He watched his extraction team sprint inside the Irungu Center, then turn into an inner stairwell. Their feet pounded the metal steps as they ascended to the top floor. The security cameras had been hacked to show a loop of the same time from the day before. Anyone monitoring the video feed would be oblivious to their entrance. Tubeec stepped over two dead men, unarmed security attendants.

Tubeec followed his men, taking the stairs two at a time. Pushing through the oversized door, he watched as the men cornered the four hostages, capturing them easily. Crying and wailing, the targets lost their motor function, collapsing in terror into the arms of his men, unable to resist being taken.

Glancing at his watch, Tubeec was pleased that they were ahead of schedule. He nodded to the men as they forced the hostages out of the Conservators Room and headed back down the stairwell.

He glanced into the now empty space, eyes drawn to an overturned trash can with crushed and torn coral flowers scattered across the floor. His curiosity piqued, he wondered if he should have gotten more details on the flower delivery. He hadn't asked who the flowers were being delivered to or who had sent them. The intel on deliveries from the flower shop to the Irungu Center had saved him the trouble of placing a fake order. The flowers had apparently found the intended recipient and were not a welcomed gift.

He suspected the flowers had been for Mena Nix. She showed the most signs of exposure, her muscles limp and barely responsive as Rahim had carried her down the stairs. Wangari had been sluggish, indicating a minor level of exposure, while Grace and Isaac had walked mostly under their own power with rifles pointed at their heads.

Drawn toward the flowers, Tubeec walked slowly into the room until his foot rested against the crushed petals. He reached down, careful not to touch any and picked up the card from the floor. The logo of Wangari's famous flower shop was emblazoned in the corner.

Clenching his jaw, he stared at the date scrawled on the card. Was this a hidden message for him? Had someone learned of his plan? Was this some kind of warning?

A beep emitted from his watch.

Tubeec slipped the envelope and the card into his pocket and exited the Conservators Room. He raced down the six flights of stairs until he reached the loading dock. A shaft of light illuminated the masked men, dressed in dark green from head-to-toe, toting rifles and maneuvering the hostages toward the back of the truck. The stench of exhaust wafted from the sleek black vehicle, painted with the recognizable logo of the most prominent flower growers in Kenya, the East African Flower Company. The trucks were common sights, not just on the streets of Nairobi but all across Kenya. No one would take a second glance at them as the trucks exited the alleyway behind the Irungu Center.

Sharp beeps of the truck reversing screeched as Tubeec reached the bottom floor. One of the men rolled the trailer door up with a loud bang. Two other men carried Mena Nix and Wangari Irungu inside. Neither woman struggled, terror in their eyes as they were helplessly dragged into the dark opening of the truck.

The patriarch of the Irungu Family would be desperate to get his sole heir back. Offering Tubeec piles of money for her safe return. But money was useless for this mission. The ransom would be for something more important than cash.

"Help us!" Grace cried, pushing away from Assad, moving quickly, running out of her heels as she staggered toward the street.

"Grace, don't!" Isaac screamed, trying to jerk away from Rahim and Nadifa, who restrained him.

Assad raised the assault rifle, aiming it toward Grace.

Two shots rang out.

Blood spread across the back of the pale yellow dress Grace wore as she stumbled to the ground, collapsing in a heap along the curb in the alley.

"No!!!" Isaac screamed, his voice loud and hoarse, tears clouding his eyes as he bucked against the men holding him back.

Tubeec nodded at Geesi.

A swift blow to the back of Isaac's head with the butt of the assault rifle knocked Isaac out, and he was dragged into the back of the truck.

"What about Grace Kadenge?" Assad asked, stepping onto the concrete landing next to Tubeec.

"Leave her. She's no use to us now." Tubeec headed toward the front cab of the truck.

Grabbing the handle, Tubeec opened the door and nodded to Cangrejos.

Cangrejos lifted his cell phone, speaking quickly, "Exiting in twenty seconds. Coordinate and deploy to your routes now."

Tubeec grabbed the seat belt and clicked it into place.

Five identical East African Flower Company trucks were strategically located within one mile of the museum. The strike team and the bombers were to evacuate to the designated areas, each driving one of the trucks around the downtown area for five minutes until

Cangrejos made it to the highway. The trucks would then take their pre-planned routes along the same highway to different destinations.

"Law enforcement on the ground, but all of our men have vacated the museum premises," Cangrejos said.

As the truck pulled out of the docking area, passing through the narrow alley, Tubeec looked down at Grace's bloody body lying limp on the ground. He could see the slight movement of her torso. She wasn't dead ... yet.

As Cangrejos steered the truck to the left, onto the main thoroughfare, Tubeec put his earpods in his ears, cranking up the American hip-hop music he loved. Reaching into his pocket, he grabbed his cell phone and entered the six-digit code.

Seconds later, a giant burst of flames shot through the air.

Chapter Nineteen

Fumbling with his cell phone, Julian ran faster, pushing and shoving through hoards of screaming tourists and locals fleeing the museum and corporate buildings. Women clutched their purses, running barefoot down the crowded street. Men sprinted past, knocking over slower pedestrians. Panic and fear etched on their faces as they passed him.

The ringing in his ear continued until he heard Mena's voice message ... again.

Damn it!

Why wasn't she answering her phone?

Two more blocks and he'd be at the museum. The acrid smell of gas and gunpowder intensified as he approached the last block.

Police officers, swinging their arms like windmills, ushered the crowds to safety far away from the museum.

While everyone was fleeing danger, Julian surged toward it. The heat brushed hot waves against his skin as he bumped and maneuvered through the bodies pressing past him.

Julian slowed his pace as he reached the end of the street. The Tribal Museum loomed ahead. The modern building, acclaimed as a museum of the future, was engulfed in flames. Shattered glass from the ground floor windows littered the road. Bushes, flowers, and trees disintegrated as orange flames danced across the sculptures adorning the front lawn of the museum, burning everything in sight. The air was thick with plumes of black smoke, choking his lungs.

A warzone stretched before him. Julian shielded his eyes, air pumping heavily in and out of his lungs. His mouth went dry as he tried to swallow past the smoke scratching his throat.

Would he ever see Mena's stunning smile again?

Could he be left with nothing but memories of the woman he loved more than anything in this world?

Shaking the thoughts away, Julian skirted around the barricades and ran along the sidewalk across from the museum. Heavily armed Kenyan Police officers darted back and forth, trying to create a trail to evacuate people away from the museum as the front facade burned into the late evening sky. Sirens could be heard in the distance, battling the sounds of popping glass, crackling scorched earth, and twisting molten metal.

Julian couldn't fathom what life would be like without Mena.

He would gladly sacrifice everything to know she was safe and—

A second explosion ripped through the air.

The wave of the blast slammed into Julian's chest, knocking him backward, banging his head against the concrete street. Julian struggled to get his bearings as piercing screams erupted around him. Dozens of feet trampled past. He rolled over, shaking the dizziness from his head, his eyes drawn to a severed leg less than ten feet away. The street was bloodstained. Broken glass and metal littered the road as people ignored the directions of the police officers trying to maintain order.

The smell of burning gas smothered him as the truck parked in front of the museum ignited with fresh flames, the charred metal crumpling in the heat, leaving an ashy white hollow shell.

The Irungu Center extended out from the side of the museum, seemingly unaffected by the blasts burning the museum next to it.

Could Mena still be inside?

Her offices were in the Irungu Center, not in the museum. She could have heard the commotion and evacuated the building. He needed to make sure the people in the Irungu Center had gotten out safely.

Julian rose, checking the back of his head for any blood. A round knot was developing, but he was otherwise unharmed. Uniformed Kenyan police officers stood outside the revolving glass doors of the Irungu Center. Julian jogged across the street toward the officers.

"Is anyone still inside the Irungu Center, or were they all evacuated?" Julian demanded.

"This area is off-limits. You have to leave sir. Please follow the instructions of the police and exit the museum complex." One of the officers responded, pointing across the street.

"You need to leave this area now," another officer commanded.

"My girlfriend works in this building. I'm trying to find out if she's okay. Can you at least tell me that?" Julian asked, growing frustrated.

"We can't give any details. I'd suggest you call the police hotline that was set up to connect families with loved ones working in the area. You will be able to get the information you are looking for there," the first officer said.

"It's too dangerous for you to be in this area, please cross the street and follow the directions of the officers over there," the second officer added, slipping a hand on his gun.

The last thing Julian needed was to make a scene and get hauled off to jail before he could find Mena. Julian turned and walked along the length of the Center toward the back alley. He knew he could get inside and search himself if the police hadn't locked down the building. Reaching the entrance to the alley, Julian watched as a group of paramedics emerged. A woman lay on the gurney being pushed by two of the EMTs, her yellow dress soaked in dark red blood. Julian focused on her face, recognizing her instantly. It was Mena's co-worker from the fundraising dinner. He couldn't remember her name.

Julian ran over to one of the EMTs, trailing the other paramedics.

"Are there any other casualties from inside the Irungu Center? I'm looking for my girlfriend," Julian said, the words rushing from his mouth as his heart pounded in his chest.

The guy looked up at him, sympathy in his eyes as he shook his head. "Building was empty. We found her in the alley suffering from multiple gunshots. No other victims. I hope you find your girl. This massacre is one of the worst we've experienced in a hell of a long time."

"Thanks," Julian said, but he wasn't sure if he meant it. He still had no idea where Mena was or if she was safe or lying somewhere with bullets riddling her body like the lady on the gurney.

"Montgomery!"

Julian spun around to see Sunny waving at him from across the street. A black Mercedes idled behind her as she ran toward him.

Sunny grabbed his arm and pulled him toward the parked car. "You have to come with me. While the bombs were going off outside the museum, a group of terrorists entered the Irungu Center and kidnapped Wangari Irungu. Her family wants us involved in the search."

"I can't. I have to find Mena. Once I know she's okay, I'll join you," Julian said, pushing away from Sunny's tight grip.

"Montgomery! Mena isn't in there," Sunny said.

"How do you know? Where is she?" Julian demanded.

"The terrorists detonated two bombs outside the museum and sent four gunmen inside to shoot at innocent people—"

"I know all of that. Where is Mena?"

"That's what I'm trying to tell you. All of that was done to cover up the fact that another smaller team of terrorists entered the Irungu Center and kidnapped Wangari Irungu … you have to come with me. We need to start the search to find her," Sunny insisted.

"I'm sorry that Wangari was kidnapped," Julian said, and he meant it. The lengths this group had gone through to abduct one of the richest heiresses in Africa was mind-boggling. But Wangari couldn't be his priority right now. "I'll do whatever I can to help you in the search for her, but not until I find Mena. Do you know where she is?"

Sunny took a deep breath. "That's what I'm trying to explain to you. They didn't just kidnap Wangari …"

"They took Mena?" Julian asked, gripping Sunny's shoulders. "The fuckers took Mena, too?"

Sunny nodded slowly. "You help us save Wangari Irungu's life and you'll also save Mena's."

Chapter Twenty

Easing back against the soft leather of the Mercedes, Julian pondered the assessment of the report completed by the Irungu Family's security team. He was convinced the attack on the museum was related to the botched suicide bombing he'd thwarted three days ago, even though no terrorist group had claimed responsibility for it.

The report indicated skepticism that terrorists were behind the kidnapping of the Irungu Center employees. It presented a different conclusion, one Julian hadn't anticipated or considered.

Non-terrorist conspired kidnapping with political revenge motive.

Summoned to the corporate headquarters of the Irungu horticultural conglomerate, Julian had spent the past hour with Sunny and the rest of the TIDES team. In a large conference room, they were debriefed on the latest news about the shooting and bombing at the museum and the kidnapping of Wangari and her team of conservators. The family was keen to get TIDES involved in the search. Sunny would remain at the Irungu's sprawling estate in Runda, working side-by-side with the head of their security team. Timothy Irungu had specifically asked Julian to lead the field teams and liaise with the African Special Forces on behalf of the family.

Julian had accepted without hesitation.

There was no subtlety in the patriarch's urgent request. Timothy Irungu knew Julian had as much to lose as he did, which was why he wanted Julian on the ground leading the search and rescue efforts with the ASF. In addition to Mena and Wangari, a third conservator, Isaac Gatobu, was also kidnapped. The fourth conservator, Grace Kadenge, was the woman the EMTs had placed into the back of an ambulance. Her injuries were serious, but initial reports from the hospital indicated that she would survive.

Flipping through the report, Julian re-read the section on Wangari's husband, Okeyo Lagat. The scathing assessment of the current Director of Public Prosecutions and his unintended role in the kidnapping was alarming. Lagat was credited for his aggressive efforts to get rid of the financial corruption that had crippled the Kenyan government for decades, but the assessment also blamed him. Over the past four years, Lagat had prosecuted many high ranking members of government and local business leaders—any one of whom might be seeking revenge for their loss of status, money, and in certain cases, freedom. The Irungu security team had concluded that Wangari's kidnapping was likely orchestrated by an enemy of her husband.

Julian exhaled.

If revenge really was the motive, the kidnappers wouldn't be swayed by money. They'd be hell-bent on making Lagat pay.

Focusing on the report again, Julian considered another disturbing detail. The kidnappers had taken extra hostages. Expendables. Mena and the other conservator, Isaac, might be killed if the kidnappers wanted to prove a point. The point being that they were serious and not to be fucked with.

Julian wasn't going to let Mena be an unwitting victim of a political fight that had nothing to do with her. He couldn't let her suffer the consequences of being caught in the wrong place at the wrong time. Not again.

As the car slowed near a gated parking garage, Julian scanned the area around the building. The United Nations Complex and the U.S. embassy loomed in the distance. The metal gate lifted, and the driver turned the car into the garage, descending down the ramp of the darkened structure. Slowly proceeding past rows of dark luxury vehicles with black tinted windows, neatly parked in the center of the spaces, the Mercedes descended two more levels before stopping in front of a set of glass doors.

Sliding across the leather seats, Julian left the report on the floorboard of the backseat and exited the sedan.

A soldier dressed in gray military fatigues greeted him. "This way."

Julian followed him through the glass doors and down a short hallway to an open elevator. Stepping inside, Julian stood between two armed guards in the oversized compartment. The metal doors slid together silently, and the elevator began its descent. Surrounded by the three ASF agents, Julian located the infrared camera in the corner of the elevator, which was undetectable to the untrained eye. There were no buttons on the side panels of the elevator car. The elevator was remotely controlled by agents from ComCentral. The entire compartment was pristine and clean. No smudges or fingerprints on the walls. The floor free of dust, dirt, and debris.

The soft metallic hum of cables moving the elevator lower ended abruptly, and the doors opened.

The unarmed soldier exited first, beckoning Julian to follow him. The armed soldiers followed close behind, the ends of their assault rifles grazing Julian's back as they proceeded down the brightly lit hallway. Julian rested his arms behind him, touching the Beretta M9 tucked in his waistband, ready to grab it if needed. Following the soldier, twisting and turning through several corridors, they finally approached a single wooden door.

"Search him," the unarmed soldier demanded.

Julian turned, holding up his hand to stop the soldiers. He removed the Beretta from his waistband and lifted the leg of his pants to dislodge the butterfly knife. "That's all I got fellas."

Now was not the time to be cagey about weaponry. Finding Mena was more important than keeping equipment he didn't need. He could take out the ASF agents with or without weapons.

One of the soldiers grabbed the weapons, then looked past him at the unarmed soldier.

The unarmed soldier nodded his approval, then opened the door and motioned for Julian to enter. Stepping into the small conference room, Julian's eyes were drawn to the warrior masks that adorned the left and right walls. Near the door, a widescreen television covered most of the width of the wall.

Across the room toward the far end was an oblong table surrounded with six chairs. A built-in bookshelf filled with tactical guides lined the back wall, surrounding a cutout space where the seal of the African Special Forces rested in the middle.

Julian rolled his eyes at the pretentiousness of the organization. The ASF was far from being on the same caliber as the elite special operative organizations of some of the world's greatest militaries.

Iregi Kamau, Chief Special Agent in Charge, sat at the table. A phone glued to his ear as he nodded absently, he scribbled on a notepad. Julian turned to see the door closing behind him. Once again, he'd be one on one with Reggie, and he didn't expect the conversation to be amicable.

Play nice.

Focus on what was important—bringing Mena home safely. He couldn't let the past interfere with his present goal.

Reggie ended his call, then rested the phone on the table. He focused on Julian, not bothering to hide his distrust. "What are you doing here? Where is Sunny?"

"I'm leading the field team assisting ASF on behalf of the Irungu Family," Julian said, walking over to the table. He eased a chair from underneath, sliding it against the expensive carpet, then sat down.

"I'm not working with you. Tell Sunny to get down here now." Reggie turned his back to Julian and begin to shuffle through file folders haphazardly strewn on one of the shelves.

Julian took a deep breath. "Timothy Irungu insisted that Sunny stay with him to oversee the Irungu Security Team while the kidnapping is being investigated. He placed me in charge of his field team."

Reggie turned back to face Julian. "You should return to the Irungu mansion. I will keep Tim apprised of our efforts to rescue his daughter."

"Why are we wasting time here?" Julian asked as he leaned forward, resting his elbows on the table. "We both know you're stuck with me. The faster we can find Wangari and the other hostages and rescue them, the faster we can get the hell out of each other's lives."

Swiveling around in the chair, Reggie folded his arms across his chest and leaned back. "I'm surprised Tim picked you."

Julian scoffed. "You know better than anybody that I'm the best at finding people others don't want to be found. I found you when al-Harakat ambushed your team in Somalia, didn't I?"

A steely coldness infected Reggie's gaze as he stiffened in his chair. Julian hadn't wanted to play that card, but he needed to level the playing field and force Reggie to work with him.

"What has the Irungu security team told you so far?" Reggie asked.

Julian recounted the results of the preliminary assessment. "Ultimately, the ransom request will indicate which is the more likely scenario. If the request is for money, the family is liquidating assets as we speak. Fifty million will be available in unmarked bills within the next hour. If the request is for something ... different, we'll have to assess the plan of action at that time. Is any of this different from what your team determined?"

Reggie shook his head. "We agree, but we don't think the kidnapping is politically motivated. Taking extra hostages is the calling card of al-Harakat and other rebel groups in Kenya. More hostages mean more families to demand ransom money from."

"Al-Harakat meticulously researches the people they intend to target. Neither of the other two targets has families that could pay what the jihadist group would demand for their release," Julian countered. "What evidence did your team find at the location of the attack? I need to review all your reports."

Reggie raised an eyebrow.

"Mr. Irungu expects me and the field team to participate in the investigation with the ASF. It's up to you if you're going to comply or not. But I doubt he'd be pleased to hear that cooperation was being withheld from the representative you agreed to allow to be part of the case," Julian said.

Reggie inhaled sharply. "You are enjoying this, aren't you?"

Julian leaned back in his chair. Under different circumstances, ruffling Reggie's feathers would be fun for him, but not now. Not when

Mena's life hung in the balance. Any delay, any restriction on his ability to help or review evidence could hinder the rescue efforts.

Julian didn't trust Reggie or his team to locate and rescue the hostages without help from the TIDES team. Since their creation over a decade ago, the ASF had made improvements, but they still weren't an elite operative group. Prone to mistakes, they had an embarrassing failure rate.

"When lives are at stake, there's nothing to enjoy. I'm here to help you find Wangari and the other hostages. I mean that," Julian said, and he did. Mena's safe return was directly related to Wangari's rescue. He would do whatever it took to make that happen, even playing nice with Reggie Kamau.

Reggie opened a drawer at the end of the table and extracted a single folder. Sliding it across the table toward Julian, he said, "We've determined a loose timeline of events and potential suspects. I think you'll find there may be holes in the Irungu security team's assessment."

Flipping through the folder, Julian skimmed the contents. Looking for anything to help him determine where Mena was being held, he stared at a note on the report.

Julian looked up at Reggie. "You think a member of the Irungu Family could have orchestrated all of this?"

"If Wangari Irungu is killed, the family's fortune will be divided among dozens of siblings and cousins, any of whom also have incentive to get rid of the child no one expected the Irungu's to have, given their age when she was born," Reggie said.

Julian considered the information but thought it was less likely since Wangari's parents were still alive. If their only child died, they could easily change their will and allow their fortune to be managed by a trust or donate it all to a not-for-profit organization. There would be no guarantee that anyone in the family would become the beneficiaries.

"What about the flower delivery? Any idea who sent them or who they were sent to?" Julian asked, noticing the scrutiny placed on the crushed coral peonies found on the floor of the Conservators Room within the report.

"Not yet, but the team is working on it. We did identify something curious about the peonies, which our lab technicians are analyzing. A strange scent, unlike what you'd expect from flowers," Reggie explained.

A chill slid down Julian's spine as memories assaulted him. "A faint smell, almost citrus-like?"

"How did you know that?" Reggie asked.

"The results will show the flowers had been sprayed with the chemical nerve agent, lazirprene," Julian said.

"Lazirprene. Are you sure?" Reggie asked.

Julian wished he wasn't, but the method of attack and the technique used to facilitate the kidnapping was beginning to fit the distinct style of an enemy he'd faced before.

"Lazirprene attacks the musculoskeletal system, temporarily rendering its victims numb or paralyzed for a period of minutes to hours, depending on the amount of exposure. If that's the chemical on the flowers, then there's no way anyone who came in contact with the peonies would be able to fight back or scream for help. The kidnappers would face no resistance extracting them from the building. That chemical is extremely rare ... so how did it end up being used today? Who could be behind this?" Reggie asked.

Julian pinched the bridge of his nose, tension clawing at his muscles. The search for Mena had become extremely complicated. Bringing her and the other hostages home safely would be harder than any of them expected.

Taking a deep breath, Julian said, "I know exactly who's behind this, and you're not going to like it."

Chapter Twenty-One

A high-pitched wail pierced the air as Mena's eyes flew open. She leaned back against the concrete floor covered in dirt and debris. Her body shook involuntarily as electric shocks pricked her muscles. Leaning forward, she gripped her stomach, realizing the horrifying sound was coming from her own mouth. The pain was paralyzing as her body reawakened. She wiggled her toes, sending another jolt of pain coursing through her body. Despite the sharp discomfort, Mena breathed heavily through each successive convulsion, thankful that she was regaining the feeling in her body.

What had they given her? How had they reduced her body to numb, paralyzed state? She'd panicked when she lost her motor function in the middle of the Conservators Room, falling and banging the side of her skull against the hard floor. Gunmen had appeared at the entrance, storming into the room. She'd watched Wangari struggle to walk before collapsing on the ground. Isaac and Grace had been less effected, stumbling but still able to move, trying to get away, though their attempts had proved futile.

Mena looked around the darkened room. A bright light shone from the hallway, casting a bright rectangle on the grimy floor. The rough grit scratched against her palms as she shifted backward and leaned her body against the wall, hoping to gather enough strength to stand. Her eyes adjusted to the darkness.

Across the room, Wangari was tied to a chair, her mouth gagged with a rag. Isaac lay on the floor, several feet away from her. He was face down in a pool of vomit, his hands tied behind his back and his feet bound with thick ropes. Mena glanced at her own legs, bound tightly together. She wouldn't be standing any time soon.

"Last one is finally coming around," a male voice said from outside the room. "Rahim, get in there and secure her now that she's regaining her muscle function."

Mena looked toward the door as a large figure filled the space, blocking the light. Her eyes followed the man closely as he entered the room. He was dressed in the same dark green trousers and matching button-down shirt she remembered the gunmen wearing from the attack on the Irungu Center. His scarf hung loosely around his neck as he closed the distance between them.

Avoiding eye contact with the rebel, Mena searched for a weapon, something she could use to fight him off. She swiped her hands against the floor. Another painful series of electric shocks racked her arm muscles, and she paused, sucking in a sharp breath.

The man squatted low, forcing her to meet his gaze. He stared back at her without blinking, an unreadable emotion in his eyes. Softly, his hands caressed her arms as he brought her hands together in front of her body. He reached into his pocket and pulled out a strand of coarse, thin rope. Wrapping her wrists tightly, he secured the ends, then stood. Mena tried to move her hands but quickly abandoned that idea as the rope scratched and scraped her skin.

Standing, the man went to the corner of the room and lifted a small pitcher of water. Returning to her side, he looked over his shoulder toward the door for a long moment, then turned his attention back to her.

"Drink," he whispered.

Aware of the harsh dryness of her throat, Mena gratefully accepted the warm liquid, sipping quickly to quench her thirst. He allowed her several seconds of gulping the water until he removed the pitcher and sat it back in the corner.

Mena kept her eyes on the man they called Rahim as he exited the room and disappeared from her view.

"Mena, are you okay?" Isaac managed to turn his head to face her, the dried excrement coating his cheek and chin.

"I think so. I can move, but it's painful. Is Wangari okay? What did they do to her?"

"My guess is the same thing they did to you. She woke up a few hours ago and cried out in pain, but she wouldn't stop screaming. It was horrible. They finally gagged her so they wouldn't hear her, and she passed out about an hour ago," Isaac explained.

"Did they say what they wanted?" Mena asked, wondering if a ransom request had been made while she was still knocked out.

Kidnapping had become an unfortunate risk of life for wealthy Africans. Terrorists had an endless supply of human capital to mine from and demand money to fund their activities. And there weren't too many Kenyans wealthier than Wangari and her family. What she couldn't understand was why the gunmen had taken her and Isaac?

"Not yet. They seem to be waiting for their leader to arrive and give them instructions, but I'm guessing they want a big payout from Wangari's family. I think we were in the wrong place at the wrong time," Isaac lamented.

In the past year, Mena had had more than her fair share of being in the wrong place at the wrong time. She'd walked into the middle of Ella Sapphire's escape from the Genesis Gallery and been forced at gunpoint to drive the pregnant woman to an unknown location, only to end up delivering her baby on the side of the road. Stumbling upon the truth of Priscilla Dumay's immoral enterprise had landed her in the trunk of Zak Webber's car, kidnapped to stop her from going to the police about what she'd overheard. Then being trapped in the basement of Dumay's mansion, desperate to escape before a bomb detonated. Each time, though, she'd had one glimmer of hope. A chance to get out of the situation, unscathed and unharmed ... because of Julian.

Mena's eyes focused on the charm bracelet Julian had given her.

Would she ever see him again?

Or would these moments with Wangari and Isaac be her last?

Footsteps pounded into the room, jolting Mena from her thoughts. Three armed gunmen pointed rifles, one trained on each of them as three others surrounded them.

A rough hand reached under Mena's arm, jerking her to a standing position. Her legs wobbled, still partially numb from whatever they'd done to her earlier. Head swimming from the abrupt movement, Mena leaned against the wall. A sharp blow rocked the back of her head as the man punched her.

"Stand the fuck up!" he shouted in her ear, the stench of cush on his breath, assaulting her nostrils.

Mena stifled a cry as she balanced herself on shaky legs.

"Let's go," another said, as the three of them were led out of the room and into a larger, open space drowned in harsh bright lights. Taking short, choppy steps due to the ropes binding her legs, Mena tried not to fall as one of the gunmen directed her to the furthest chair perched against the wall. The gunman gave her a rough shove. Mena slipped down, banging against the chair with a loud thud.

Wangari was forced into the chair next to her. The gag was removed from her mouth, and she looked ahead with frightened and erratic eyes. Isaac sat down on his own in the chair next to Wangari's.

Mena tore her eyes away from Wangari to look ahead at the man standing in the center of the room, appraising them. He was dressed differently than the others, in black trousers and a tailored white shirt, with diamond cuff links that glittered under the bright lights. His hands, clasped tightly in front of him, were severely scarred.

"Do you know who I am?" the man asked, his question directed at none of them in particular.

Wangari shook her head. Tears slipped down her face as her shoulders hunched forward.

"I am your worst nightmare come true," the man said. "My name is Tubeec Hirad. It is important that you know who has put you in this horrific situation. Please, confirm that you are aware and repeat my name. Go ahead, each of you, say my name," Tubeec instructed.

He pointed at Isaac first. Mena listened as Isaac, then Wangari repeated the man's name. Then it was her turn.

"Tubeec Hirad," Mena said, swallowing past the lump in her throat.

"If you survive this ordeal, I want to ensure that when you tell your tale of woe, you have attributed the source of your pain correctly. Now, I will deal with you first," Tubeec said, pointing to Wangari.

"What do you want? Money?" Wangari asked, her voice quivering.

"Tsk. Tsk." Tubeec shook his head. "Your father has already offered a handsome sum for your return. Unfortunately, this is not about dollars or cents."

"What is it about? Why did you take us?" Wangari asked.

"Your husband has something of value to me. I asked him for a simple exchange. Your life for that item, but he refused. Why would he do that?" Tubeec asked. "Does he value your life so little?"

"My husband is an honorable man. He is a principled man. He has received threats from men like you during his entire time in office and survived them all. He will not hastily put Kenyans in harm's way by succumbing to the whims of terrorists like you," Wangari said.

"That is good news for Kenyans, but not so good news for you and Ms. Nix and Mr. Gatobu, is it?" Tubeec asked, walking over to stand in front of Isaac. "Mr. Gatobu, are you ready to die for your country?"

Isaac squeezed his eyes shut as his body trembled in the chair.

Tubeec Hirad stepped past Wangari and stopped directly in front of Mena.

"And you? The lovely Mena Nix. Are you prepared to die for a country that isn't your own?" Tubeec asked.

Mena looked away. She had never considered that this freak would want something other than money. Money in exchange for the release of a captive was how she thought these kidnappings worked. Obviously, Tubeec Hirad had something different in mind. What Mena couldn't understand was why Okeyo Lagat had refused to meet the terrorist's demands? What could be so important that he'd risk his wife's life to protect?

Mena choked back a sob as the stark reality of her predicament rocked through her body.

"Please! Just let them go! They are innocent in all of this. Keep me, but let them go!" Wangari said.

One of the gunmen approached Tubeec, handing him a cell phone.

Tubeec glanced at the screen, then looked at Mena and smiled, sending a chill coursing down her spine. Turning toward Wangari, Tubeec said, "Breathe easy, Wangari. I'm going to give your husband a second chance to make the right decision."

Chapter Twenty-Two

"Tubeec Hirad is behind the kidnapping. He's the man you need to be looking for."

The weight of Julian's words settled within the room.

The man on every African country's most-wanted list had staged one of the most daring kidnappings in Kenyan history.

The leader of a dedicated network of for-profit killers, kidnappers, terrorists, and thieves, Tubeec Hirad personally cultivated, groomed and indoctrinated each member, growing his militia over the past decade. Unhindered by politics, religion, or special causes, the mercenaries specialized in mayhem and carnage, carrying out surgical strikes at the request of clients all over the world. The specially trained group accepted any request, no matter how heinous, as long as the price paid matched the risks. This distinction had garnered them more members on Interpol's list of red notices than any other terrorist organization in Africa, even more than al-Harakat.

"What makes you think Tubeec Hirad is involved in this? He hasn't been on the radar in East Africa for over a year," Reggie demanded, challenging Julian's conclusion.

"Lazirprene was developed by Tubeec and his wife, Axado. They refined and cultivated the dangerous compound until it was perfected, then started a bidding war with several governments and criminal organizations for the formula. That didn't sit well with many of the groups. The Navy suspected that one of the groups tried to extract the formula by force, brutally attacking Axado and her twin boys, killing all of them. Tubeec refused to give up the formula and was burned alive, but somehow he escaped. Rumor has it that the formula only exists in his head. He produces it from memory, whenever he wants to sell small batches or when he needs it to carry out an attack."

Reggie rubbed his hands down his face, then turned toward one of the agents. "Validate this information. If Tubeec Hirad is the kidnapper, then this whole hostage situation has become infinitely more dangerous."

"Chief Kamau," said a tan-skinned woman with a soft babyface. She stood near a control panel stationed in the center of ComCentral, typing feverishly.

"What do you have?" Reggie asked.

"The footage from the museum was tampered with, replaced with an identical copy of the footage from the day before. It's useless. So, I started scouring cell phone videos and photos taken by citizens and tourists, reconstructing scenes from the time of the attack until now," the woman, whose name badge read BETTS, said in a monotone voice. "There is some footage from the Global Exchange building across the street. It's distant, but helps to construct a dire picture."

The ASF emblem on the monitors around the room dissipated and was replaced by a picture of a group of men dressed in all green, with ammunition vests draped across their chests, holding M4 Carbines.

"These men were seen at various points exiting the Global Exchange building," Agent Betts said, directing their attention to a series of still shots on the monitors. "Here you can barely make out two of the men in the front cab of an East African Flower Company truck. The truck is exiting the alley from the loading dock behind the museum and the Irungu Center. Time of departure coincides with the timing of the second bomb blast."

"Anything else?" Reggie asked.

"Across the alley from the museum, an electronics company is housed on the second floor with windows overlooking the loading dock. That was by design as the Irungu's allowed the company to share the dock for their deliveries. From that view, we were able to capture these images."

The still shot of Wangari Irungu showed the heiress looking disoriented, no doubt from the effects of the Lazirprene. Another picture showed a man with tears in his eyes, his mouth caught in a grimaced cry. Two of the rebels held his arms tightly, while another pointing a gun to the man's head. In the lower left-hand corner, Julian's eyes were drawn to the face he'd fallen in love with months ago. His fingers slid across Mena's blank face. She was being carried into the van, her arms and legs limp, but her eyes alert.

"Where did the truck go?" Reggie asked.

"That's where things get tricky. The truck merged onto the A104, and within minutes, five other identical trucks with identical license plates entered as well. The trucks maneuvered in a virtual shell game along the freeway and then exited at different points, where our intel ends. It's impossible for us to know which of the trucks contained the hostages based on the video footage we currently have," Agent Betts explained.

"Analyze close-ups of the photos and see if you can ID Tubeec Hirad or any militants known to work with him," Reggie directed.

Julian shook his head. "Don't bother."

Reggie's penchant for over-analyzing information would cost them valuable time. Two hours had passed since the attack. Tubeec could have hidden the hostages in Kenya or any number of the surrounding countries by now.

Reggie scowled. "Excuse me?"

Julian said, "You need to find out if Tubeec made contact with anyone in Kenya. Search the dark web for communications anywhere from a week before the attack up until now."

"An attack of this magnitude would take careful planning, but Tubeec Hirad wouldn't be so kind as to leave a trail of breadcrumbs for us to follow through the dark web," Reggie said, dismissing Julian's request.

"Every attack has a fingerprint, a modus operandi, that can be identified if you look carefully. Even Tubeec Hirad can't pull something like this off without leaving some shred of evidence behind. In fact, I'd start with the suicide bombing that I stopped last Friday," Julian said.

"No one has claimed responsibility for that attack," Reggie said.

"My point exactly," Julian said.

The agents hesitated, their gazes shifting toward Reggie.

The special agent in charge gave a quick nod. Several agents scurried toward their computers to start the search.

"That won't be necessary," a deep, sensual female voice interrupted.

Julian turned to see Sunny walking into ComCentral, her gun trained at the back of Okeyo Lagat's head. Three secret service agents followed her, their guns pointed at her as they barked orders, demanding that she release DPP Lagat, which she ignored.

Reggie screamed at the agents, "Put your weapons down!"

Julian walked to Lagat. "Has Tubeec Hirad made contact with you?"

Lagat glared back at Julian, refusing to answer.

Sunny took the butt of her gun and slammed it against his head, sending Lagat down to one knee. "Answer him! Tell him and all of these wonderful ASF agents how you received a direct request from Tubeec Hirad to spare your wife's life that you decided to ignore!"

Chapter Twenty-Three

"What did he say?" Julian asked, stepping in front of the chief special agent.

Reggie gave him a cursory glance, then pushed past him into ComCentral. Julian watched as Reggie looked around the room, searching, then turned back toward him.

"Where's Sunny? I need to speak to her," Reggie said.

"Tim Irungu summoned her back at the family compound in Runda. Did Okeyo tell you what Tubeec Hirad wants from him?" Julian asked. For the last hour, Reggie and a team of agents had been locked in the conference room, questioning Okeyo Lagat about his communications with Tubeec Hirad.

Sunny had admitted that the proof the Irungu security team had gathered indicating a point of contact between Okeyo and Tubeec was circumstantial at best. But once she'd heard that Lazirprene was used in the kidnapping, she'd been convinced that the unknown calls to Okeyo Lagat's phone earlier that morning were from Hirad.

Julian wasn't convinced ... yet.

Reggie turned and walked toward his office in the corner of the command room, with Julian on his heels.

Julian continued, "I didn't create this fucked up situation. Your organization got in bed with the one percent to get off the ground, which means you have to deal with me."

ASF had been the brainchild of a small group of the wealthiest Africans working in concert with the governments of several nations to create an elite special operatives group to protect the continent from the growing presence of terrorism. This legacy made the group beholden to two interests—those of the countries they served and those of the wealthy families who'd made their existence possible.

Reggie crossed his arms over his chest. "Sunny was wrong. DPP Lagat doesn't know anything that can help with our investigation. The phone calls he took this morning were official governmental business and not from Hirad. He was on a plane when the attack occurred, and he didn't learn about it until he landed."

"You believe Sunny was wrong about him?" Julian asked.

"It's no secret that Tim Irungu is not fond of his son-in-law, despite his prestigious position in the Kenyan government. Okeyo Lagat has breathed life into the Office of the Department of Public Prosecutions. He was the first in his role to actually go after corrupt officials and put them in jail. He is one of the good guys. While I understand the family's need to suspect and blame him, suspicion and flimsy evidence doesn't make it true."

"What kind of proof did Lagat give that the calls were government business?" Julian asked.

Reggie ignored the question and walked into his office, sinking down into his leather chair as his eyes focused on the computer monitors.

Julian stepped inside, leaning against the doorframe. "I can do a whole hell of a lot to help if you just drop the grudge and bring me into the fold."

"I'm well aware that you believe your skill set is superior to mine and my team's, but I can assure you that we don't need a former SEAL who hasn't seen action in the past four years," Reggie said.

"Even one who taught you everything you know," Julian countered.

"The Navy's assistance to our organization is much appreciated, but we've moved past those early days. Whether you want to acknowledge it or not, my team is recognized as one of the top operative groups in the world. We've continued to refine and improve on the foundation we were given and are not inferior to other comparable groups," Reggie said. "I will keep you informed of our progress, but I advise you to stay out of our way. I don't need your help."

"Tell that to your team. They were floundering, trying to triangulate the locations of the six East Africa Flower Company trucks on the A104. With my help, we located the two trucks most likely to have contained Tubeec and the hostages and tracked them to a rarely used airstrip outside of Nairobi," Julian said.

"If Tubeec had access to a plane, they could be anywhere right now," Reggie said, pushing up from his chair.

"Which is why I told them to search all the flight plans filed for that airstrip and review radar maps for any non-commercial planes flying within a 50-mile radius of the area," Julian said.

Reggie paced. "The search area needs to be expanded, and media blackout extended to neighboring countries."

"Media blackout?" Julian asked.

"The media hasn't been told about the kidnapping of Wangari Irungu or her staff, and I plan to keep it that way. We secured an executive order to ban the release of that information to the press, giving us a bigger advantage in locating Tubeec Hirad and negotiating the release of the hostages," Reggie said.

The hostages.

Another group of innocent victims ASF was charged with rescuing, like so many before and so many that would come after. No different from the civilians that Julian had vowed to protect from terrorist forces as a SEAL. The nameless civilians who were an amalgamation of an ideal, but not real to him. Even when he'd been pulling them from danger, feeling the warmth of their skin against his, seeing the tears streaming down their faces as they effusively thanked him for his protection. They still hadn't been human to him. They couldn't be. If he'd taken a moment to think about who they were, that they were people with friends and family and hopes and dreams, he would have lost all semblance of the laser focus needed to complete his missions.

Rage raced up the back of Julian's neck.

He wasn't a SEAL on a mission.

He was a man in love with a woman who'd been taken due to no fault of her own. Caught in the wrong place at the wrong time ... again. Just like she had been with Ella ... and Zak Webber ... and Priscilla Dumay.

Negotiating with Tubeec Hirad was pointless. The man was unstable and unpredictable, his actions motivated equally by a whim as they were by a rational strategic approach. Three hours had passed since the kidnapping. Mena could be anywhere, and they didn't have the slightest clue of where to start looking.

Julian had to switch tactics. He couldn't afford to push Reggie's buttons. He needed ASF operating at their best, gathering intel that could lead him to Mena.

Raising his hands in the air as a sign of mock surrender, Julian stepped out of Reggie's office. "I'm going to respect your authority and stay out of the way. But know this—I am available if you need my expertise."

Reggie looked skeptical as he stood, then brushed past Julian and walked back out onto the main floor of ComCentral.

Turning around, Julian watched as Reggie barked orders to his team. Julian took a quick glance around. Each agent in the room hurried to complete their assigned tasks, preoccupied with their own investigations.

An idea struck Julian, one he couldn't resist. One that could get him the answers that Reggie and the ASF had failed to get.

Satisfied that no one was paying attention to him, Julian walked slowly around the perimeter of ComCentral. Exiting through to the hall, he glanced swiftly left and then right. Empty. Picking up the pace, he walked toward the conference room and opened the door, slipping inside.

Chapter Twenty-Four

Okeyo glanced up, pausing the feverish texting on his cell phone. "Julian, right? You're part of the additional security detail that Tim hired to protect us at the fundraising dinner."

"That's right. Mr. Irungu has requested that I assist ASF in the investigation of the kidnapping of his daughter," Julian said, sitting next to Okeyo.

Slipping the cell phone into the inner pocket of his jacket, Okeyo said, "I don't understand how this could have happened."

"Did Agent Kamau brief you on the method used in the attack?" Julian asked.

The DPP nodded. "He mentioned that a chemical nerve agent was used that rendered Wangari and her team paralyzed, making it easy for the men to capture them."

"Lazirprene is a dangerous compound. Only one man is known to have the formula to produce it—Tubeec Hirad," Julian said.

"Tubeec is one of the most dangerous criminals in Africa. I can't imagine why he would target my wife," Okeyo said.

"Really?" Julian asked, turning his chair and leaning forward, closing the space between Okeyo and himself.

A puzzled look settled on Okeyo's face. "What do you mean?"

"You don't seem like a man who is surprised that his wife was kidnapped by one of Africa's most wanted," Julian said.

"I assure you that my heart is breaking, but like you, I've been trained to manage my emotions since they are not useful in solving anything. Similar to the lessons you must have learned as a former Navy SEAL, I presume," Okeyo said.

"Being a SEAL taught me a lot of things that are proving to be useful right now, like how to spot a liar," Julian responded, scrutinizing Okeyo for the reaction he expected—a flash of anger that disappeared as quickly as it appeared.

"Are you implying that I had something to do with this kidnapping?" Okeyo asked, his voice calm and curious. He stood, took his jacket off, and laid it across the arm of the chair, then walked toward the opposite corner of the room.

Julian knew he was getting to the DPP. He was nervous, desperate to increase the distance between them to possibly shield himself from further scrutiny.

"No, you're too smart for that. If you were behind the kidnapping, you'd need the media to know, wouldn't you? You'd need all of Kenya on their hands and knees praying that the wife of their dear Director of Public Prosecutions was found quickly and safely. But there is no news coverage. President Thairu and ASF have made sure of that," Julian said.

"What exactly do you think I'm lying about?" Okeyo challenged.

"I've encountered Tubeec Hirad a few times in my missions as a SEAL. If this was about money, he would have sent the ransom request immediately. But the Irungus haven't heard anything from Hirad, despite sending him messages through channels he is known to monitor. I have no doubt that Tubeec knows they're willing to pay fifty million for the return of their daughter, but he hasn't taken the offer," Julian explained.

Julian stood and leaned against the chair vacated by Okeyo, staring across the room at the lying asshole.

"I don't understand how that equates to me telling lies."

"When Tubeec wants something other than money, he adopts a particular style. He has a target, but he doesn't attack. Instead, he prefers to weaken the resolve of the target by attacking loved ones, using them as bait to get what he wants. So, the way I see it, Wangari is the bait, and you are the target," Julian said.

"While your theory may prove to be true, I can assure you that if I had any information that would help ASF find my wife, I would have freely given it to Chief Special Agent Kamau. You are wasting precious time thinking I know anything that could be useful," Okeyo responded.

"What did Tubeec Hirad ask for when he called you?" Julian asked, growing impatient.

"I don't know what you're talking about." Okeyo looked away, toward the door, then back at Julian. "No one has contacted me."

Julian jerked up from his seat, his feet slamming to the ground in a thunderous bang as he towered over Okeyo.

Okeyo stiffened, his breath quickening as he grabbed the armrests of the chair.

"Tubeec presents an offer before every attack. He called you before you got on the plane this morning. He wanted something from you in exchange for your wife's life. How are you going to feel if we find her body riddled with bullets because you didn't want to tell us what was really going on? How heartbroken will you be then? Or is whatever he wants from you worth her dying?" Julian demanded.

"No! It's not worth her dying at all! I love my wife dearly. I never meant for any of this to happen," Okeyo said, pushing away from Julian.

"What the fuck did he want from you?" Julian asked through gritted teeth, disgusted by the confirmation that Okeyo had lied to Reggie and the ASF.

"From the moment I was appointed as DPP, I have been the subject of bribes, extortion, and death threats ... on my life and that of my family. After four years of living under the constant threat of harm, you become somewhat immune. I was born to be a civil servant, and I'm committed to serving the people of Kenya. Nothing means more to me, so I live with the risks knowing that there are dedicated men and women who will keep my family and me safe," Okeyo said.

Julian leaned over, bringing his face mere inches away from

Okeyo's. "You think that justifies you withholding information from the ASF? You allowed Tubeec to blow up the Tribal Museum, killing innocent people today! You allowed your wife to be kidnapped! All because you presumed it was another empty threat on your life. How the hell are you going to sleep tonight knowing that you could have prevented all of this from happening?"

Okeyo flinched at Julian's words, his shoulders slumping as he glanced off into the distance. "I get threats monthly, sometimes weekly. Why would I have believed that this time would be different? Why would I have ever thought that this crazy bastard would actually follow through on the threat?"

"Because this time, you were talking to Tubeec Hirad," Julian said.

"If I had realized that, I would have done everything in my power to protect Wangari and her staff. I would do anything to save her!"

"Anything?" Julian sat back down in the leather chair, pressing his hands against the table to prevent himself from squeezing them around Okeyo's neck. "What did Tubeec ask for?"

Okeyo was silent.

Julian kept his eyes focused on the man, who shifted uncomfortably under the scrutiny.

Seconds ticked by loudly from the clock hanging on the wall. Julian was prepared to wait as long as necessary to get Okeyo to reveal what Tubeec wanted.

Ten minutes passed before Okeyo finally succumbed to Julian's withering glare.

"It was an impossible request. A betrayal of my country, my people. Something that I could never—"

The door to the conference room opened.

"Tubeec Hirad has made contact," Reggie said, beckoning for them to come forward. "He's insisting on speaking with you, DPP Lagat."

Chapter Twenty-Five

The pungent odor of sweat was stagnant in the room as the gunmen moved about, connecting wires and plugs to extension cords that stretched out of a window at the front of the house and presumably connected to the generator outside.

Mena took a deep breath. Now that they'd found Okeyo Lagat, maybe she would find out why they'd been kidnapped and when they would be released. Not knowing was torture. What did the leader, Tubeec Hirad, want? What would he do if Okeyo couldn't or wouldn't comply with his demands?

A pale guard with a long matted beard stalked toward them. Xirsi, they'd called him. Snatching Isaac to a standing position, Xirsi dragged him across the room toward a sidewall. His wrists and ankles still bound with the coarse ropes, Isaac stumbled and almost fell. Xirsi returned, yanking Wangari from the chair. Her shriek drew the attention of two other guards as she demanded to know what was happening. Her questions were ignored as she was lined up along the wall next to Isaac.

A different gunman approached Mena. The one from before, Rahim. Reaching down, he gently lifted her to her feet, then walked slowly with her, matching the pace of her hindered steps until she was standing next to Wangari. He swiped a stray strand of her hair from her face, then turned and walked away.

Mena watched as Rahim and Xirsi connected more wires to the generator, then assisted another armed guard with connecting the wires to several small silver boxes arranged on a table in the corner of the opposite side of the room.

Mena stole a glance at Wangari and received a look clouded with concern. None of them knew what was about to happen. Mena could only hope that by some miraculous turn of events, they would be freed soon. Despite Wangari's insistence that Okeyo wouldn't compromise his integrity, she couldn't imagine that he wouldn't do whatever it took to save his wife. And by saving Wangari, she and Isaac would also be saved.

Xirsi walked in front of them, a tablet in his hand. Mena stole a quick glance at the surface, noticing the camera app was displayed. Were they going to be recorded? Was Tubeec going to send a video to Okeyo?

"We've made contact. Are you ready?" Xirsi asked.

Grabbing the tablet, Tubeec tapped against the screen several times, then handed it back to Xirsi.

Turning to face them, Tubeec made a point to look at each of them in the eyes. Stopping to her right, Tubeec straightened his shirt and swiped dust from his pants, before looking directly into the camera of the tablet.

Xirsi mouthed a countdown, and then Tubeec spoke. "Mr. Lagat, I am disappointed that we could not reach an agreement. I gave you a simple request, which you have ignored, and now your wife and two of her staff are in a very uncomfortable situation."

Wangari stepped closer to Mena, leaning into her. Mena was grateful for the reassuring touch. A sign of solidarity. They were in this together, and they'd hopefully get out of this together soon. Mena gave Wangari a small smile, then looked over at Isaac. His expression was haunted and stoic, a sadness gripping his features.

Tubeec continued, "Mr. Lagat, there are consequences to your actions. Consequences that will forever be on your conscious. Blood that will forever be on your hands."

Xirsi walked away from Tubeec and pointed the tablet toward Mena. She looked into the tiny round camera lens and tried to convey courage and bravery, despite the tremor in her legs. She reached her hands around her wrist to feel the charm on the bracelet Julian had given her. Willing herself to be strong, she maneuvered the rose gold loops until she could feel the heart-shaped charm between her fingertips. The guard lingered in front of her for a minute before sidestepping to stand in front of Wangari.

Repeating the same action, he allowed the camera to pause on Wangari's tear-stained face several minutes longer.

Then he moved to Isaac. Shoulders slumped, his eyes downcast, Isaac refused to look into the camera.

A loud gunshot rang through the air.

Mena watched in horror as Isaac's head exploded in slow motion, sending a spray of blood across her face. Blood and brain matter coated the back wall as his body fell.

Wangari stumbled backward into Mena, screaming as they toppled to the ground. Dizzy from shock, Mena couldn't take her eyes off Isaac's headless body. He'd been alive, and now he was gone. Her mind was blank, unable to process, or comprehend what was happening.

She focused on the words of Tubeec, growing faint as Rahim lifted her, half carrying her out of the room, away from the death and devastation.

Tubeec said, "You have eight hours to reconsider the simple request that we discussed earlier today and meet me at the location we discussed this morning. If you choose to ignore me for a second time, more blood will be shed, and you will know that another death is on your hands."

Chapter Twenty-Six

Staring into the deep brown eyes of Mena Nix, Julian's heart almost stopped. Her thick lashes were damp with unshed tears as she looked defiantly into the camera.

Her hair was disheveled and dirt-stained the white button-down shirt she wore. The camera moved back, revealing her bound hands. Coarse, thin ropes locked her wrists together, but she could still move her fingers. He watched as she slowly turned her charm bracelet around and around until she found the heart, her fingertips holding on to the small piece.

She didn't know he was watching, staring into her stunning eyes, prepared to move heaven and earth to get her out of Tubeec's clutches. He wanted her to feel the full strength of his love through the camera, giving her hope until he could rescue her.

Julian was jolted from his thoughts as the camera cut away from Mena and focused on Wangari Irungu. A slow burn of yearning settled within him. He was desperate to see Mena again. Julian's eyes drifted across the background of the room where the hostages were, searching for clues or any sign of their location. The plain walls behind them and an open entryway to the side suggested an abandoned house or compound. Tubeec was smart. Keeping the camera view tight from head to waist, ensured that the hostages' location wouldn't be compromised.

Tracing the video feed would give the ASF the best chance of finding the hostages. Julian could help the ASF narrow down Tubeec's location, as long as the video feed continued for several more minutes. Julian took a step toward the IT specialists—

A gunshot reverberated through the air.

Julian stopped in his tracks, staring as Isaac's head exploded live on camera, staining the wall with chunks of skull, brain matter, and blood. His headless form slid down, out of view. Screams and cries could be heard as the camera focused on Tubeec, issuing new instructions and a warning to Okeyo Lagat.

Honing in on the terrorist's words, Julian looked at Okeyo.

The video feed ended, leaving the room in an eerie silence.

Okeyo shook visibly, a trembling hand raised to his mouth. "I never meant for any of this to happen. I never thought so many lives would be lost ..."

"We need the truth if we are going to have any chance of rescuing your wife. It would be unwise of you to withhold any information you have," Reggie's voice was calm, but his hands clenched in tight fists near his side.

Nodding, Okeyo stumbled across the room, slumping down into an empty chair. His head partially obscured in his hands, he said, "Do you recall a leak of highly classified documents that occurred about a year ago?"

Reggie said, "Those documents were thought to contain proof of illegal activities perpetrated by Deputy President Kipsang Rono. Your office conducted an investigation that proved inconclusive."

"It was in my best interest to dissuade powerful forces from knowing what we'd uncovered. My office has been quietly gathering damning evidence against Rono. Evidence that will lead to an indictment on charges of election tampering, conspiracy, and murder. I have definitive proof of Rono's involvement in organizing and funding attacks on election sites in the last presidential election," Okeyo explained.

"Hundreds of Kenyans died in those attacks," Reggie said.

"And I fear that Rono is planning to do the same this year, leading to hundreds of deaths of innocent Kenyans before this election cycle is over," Okeyo said.

Julian interrupted, "Is that what Tubeec Hirad wants from you?"

"I believe that Rono hired Tubeec Hirad to get the evidence from me. With access to it, he can create a new narrative," Okeyo said.

Reggie nodded. "One that points the blame away from Rono and onto someone else. Someone they've paid to take the fall."

"That would allow a diabolical criminal to remain in the second-highest post in the Kenyan government. A travesty to the Kenyan people," Okeyo insisted.

"We've already detected plans for more violence at the polls in the upcoming elections, but we hadn't been able to figure out who is behind it," Reggie admitted.

"Rono wants to bolster his position and make another run at the presidency. I can't hand over the one thing that could finally put an end to his tyranny. I never thought my refusal would lead to this," Okeyo said, breaking down into tears.

One of the IT specialists interrupted. "Chief Kamau, we were unsuccessful in securing the location of the video feed. The encryption and complexity of pathways used made it impossible for us to trace before it was disconnected. I'm sorry."

"Damn it," Reggie said, slamming a fist onto the table.

Julian glared at the technician, realizing he should have been working with them to trace the feed. Prior to becoming a SEAL, he'd been a cryptology technician in the Navy and still possessed an advanced set of skills in deciphering encrypted communications and monitoring electronic networks.

Julian turned and headed toward the hallway. Staying at ComCentral was limiting the work he could be doing to find Mena's location. He had to get the hell out of here and back to TIDES HQ.

Footsteps grew louder behind him. He felt an arm clamp down on his shoulder. Julian turned.

"Where are you going?" Reggie asked, stepping into the hallway with Julian.

"I'm going to debrief Tim Irungu and his family on the latest information," Julian said, which wasn't exactly a lie. He was going to need access to all of the Irungu's technology to track Tubeec Hirad, starting with the disturbing video he'd watched.

Reggie stood in front of him, pushing a hand against his chest.

Julian looked down, knocking his hand away. "You should be glad I'm leaving."

"Who is Mena Nix to you? Why are you really here?" Reggie asked.

The question was a sucker punch to Julian's chest, disorienting him for a second.

"What are you talking about?" Julian asked, not sure if he should reveal the truth to Reggie or keep his relationship with Mena a secret.

"I saw the way you looked at Mena Nix when she was on the video. I saw your concern and love for her. You have another reason to care about this case. One that has nothing to do with Wangari Irungu," Reggie said.

"Mena and I are in a relationship, and I'm going to do whatever it takes to rescue her from Tubeec Hirad."

"Even if that means impeding my investigation?" Reggie countered. "You need to back off and let us handle this."

"From what I can tell, your hackers are getting their asses kicked by Tubeec's encrypted technology. Now, I can stay here and try to find what your team missed, or you can let me go. It's up to you," Julian said, glaring at Reggie.

"There's no way you can find something that my agents can't," Reggie insisted.

"Watch me," Julian said, pushing past the chief special agent.

"If I find out that you've compromised our rescue mission in any way, I will have you arrested," Reggie yelled.

The elevator doors opened, and he stepped inside.

"Do what you have to do," Julian said as the doors closed.

Chapter Twenty-Seven

"Did you get everything set up?" Julian barked, bursting through the doors of the war room at TIDES HQ.

"Hell yeah, motherfucker. We ain't about to let you down," Enzo said, slapping a hand against Julian's shoulder as he walked by.

Sunny said, "Tim Irungu gave us access to his company's servers, so we have all the computing and bandwidth power needed to figure out where the hell Tubeec is."

Zale stood up, holding a clipboard. "Simon is performing forensic auditing on the Irungu Shipping Company to figure out how the hell Tubeec stole six of their delivery trucks without being noticed. None of the trucks have been found, which means Tubeec and his crew could still be using them. Shiloh searched the flight manifests to the airstrip and came up empty. Now she's focused on the radar images for all planes taking off and landing within twenty-four hours of the museum attack. Hakeem is monitoring chatter on the dark web, focused on known members of Tubeec's militia and allies Tubeec has in al-Harakat."

Julian nodded his approval, then walked over to Glaze. "Did you get a copy of Tubeec's video call from the ASF systems?"

"Got it before they detected I was scraping their data and enacted the extra security on their systems. I'm tracing it now. It's one of the most complex traces I've ever had to do, but I'm going to crack it. I will figure out where Tubeec is with Mena," Glaze said.

"How much time do we have?" Enzo asked, standing over a pile of weapons and equipment littering a side table.

"Eight hours is when Tubeec expects Okeyo to meet him with the evidence against Rono," Julian said, angling toward a computer monitor in the corner. "Maybe less than that."

"Let's make the most of it. We don't have nearly enough weapons for an attack on Tubeec's militia. I'm going to have to make a trip to Paul's warehouse to get what we need," Enzo said.

"Call it in before you head out so he can have it pulled and ready for you," Sunny said, following behind Julian.

He glanced over his shoulder, then pulled the cell phone from his pocket.

"What do you have there?" Sunny asked.

Julian twisted the cell phone in the air. "Okeyo Lagat's cell phone."

"Clever. I'm not going to ask how you got that," Sunny said.

Julian connected the small electronic device to several wires extending from the computer. "Tubeec made at least one call to Okeyo this morning and maybe more. I'm going to figure out where those calls were coming from and the last known location of that device."

"Well, if anybody can do it, I know you can," Sunny said, squeezing his shoulder.

"No way Tubeec kept the phone he used to call Okeyo. It's a burner," Hakeem said, swiveling around in his chair.

"Burners tend to have more clues than people realized," Julian said, not in the mood to give Sunny's second-in-command a lesson on how to find those who didn't want to be found.

"You think you can find Tubeec from the calls made to Okeyo's phone?" Hakeem asked.

"I know I can. Question is whether Glaze over there will crack the code to the video faster than I can crack the code on this phone. Either way, it's a win-win situation," Julian said, although his certainty waned.

"I'm impressed," Hakeem said.

Julian accessed the phone, noticing two cryptic text messages sent to Okeyo's phone minutes before the phone call was made and one more sent about an hour after Okeyo had arrived at the ASF ComCentral. Had the bastard been texting Tubeec Hirad when Julian had questioned him?

Checking the messenger app, Julian recognized it as one he'd had little trouble hacking in the past. This was the breakthrough he needed. Wouldn't be long before he narrowed down possible locations to search for Mena.

"About fucking time! Get in here," Enzo said, toppling his chair as he stood.

Taye walked through the door, holding two stuffed bags from a local gourmet hamburger joint. The smell of burgers, fries, and onion rings filled the air. Scrutinizing the stickers on each brown bag, Taye called out names and tossed the bags around the room.

Sunny walked to Julian and handed him a brown bag. "I ordered for you."

Burger, plain/dry, onion rings was scribbled on the outside. She knew what he'd want, even though he had no appetite. He'd have to force himself to eat. It was going to be a long night, and he had to make sure he gave his body fuel for whatever could come next.

He didn't bother saying thanks, turning to focus on the computer monitors. His fingers tapped quickly against the keyboard as he entered code to get past the defenses of the messenger app.

After an hour, Julian hadn't found anything on the phone or the messenger app that could give him definitive information on the location of Tubeec Hirad or the hostages.

"Dead end," Julian said, hurling the cell phone across the room.

"What the fuck!" Enzo screamed, ducking as the phone crashed into the back wall and landed on the floor.

Julian drug his hands down his face, fighting the helplessness threatening to suck him in.

"Relax, man, we're going to find Mena," Enzo said, then turned to Sunny. "Can you call your fiancé and get an update?"

Sunny glared at Enzo as the rest of the TIDES team snickered under their breaths.

Julian looked up. "Fiancé?"

"I do not have a fiancé," Sunny said, through gritted teeth. "Stop spreading lies and stay focused on the work to find Wangari and Mena."

"Ain't no lie. You see, Julian, Sunny, and Reggie were a thing for almost a year until the douchebag fucked it all up by proposing. He wanted to force Sunny to exchange her Beretta for a baby bonnet and be a happy little housewife," Enzo said.

Julian tensed. "Are you serious? You and Reggie?"

"None of this matters right now," Sunny said, pinching the bridge of her nose.

"You said no?" Julian asked, an uneasiness settling within him.

"Of course, I did," Sunny said. "I told Reggie over, and over that, I didn't want to be a wife. I was fine with things the way they were. We were happy. Why the hell did we need a piece of paper to validate our relationship?"

Julian bristled at her outburst, words he'd heard before ... from Mena.

Hakeem walked over and squeezed the back of Sunny's neck, then said, "Reggie kept pushing, and he ended up losing the woman he loved. Should be a lesson to anyone. When someone says they don't want something. Believe them."

"I remember a time when you would have been thrilled to get married ... to be a wife. What changed?" Julian asked.

"Don't," Sunny warned, anger flashing in her eyes. "You of all people know exactly what changed."

Instantly, Julian regretted pushing Sunny. He knew he'd gone too far, and apologizing wouldn't make her feel any better. Saying anything more would only hurt her, and he was done inflicting pain on people he cared about.

The air was thick with recriminations, pain, and guilt. Silence blanketed the room as the members of TIDES ate, returning to their assignments.

"Hey," Glaze said after several minutes. "I think I'm close to getting a hit on the location."

The phone in the war room rang.

Sunny leaned over, pushing the speaker button.

"Hey," Sunny said.

"Are you alone?" Reggie asked.

"Yeah," Sunny said, pressing the volume up on the speakerphone.

Reggie's disembodied voice emitted from the device in the center of the round table. "I'm headed to Uganda to rescue Wangari. I have to go. I just wanted you to hear it from me."

"Uganda? Are you sure?" Sunny frowned.

Julian reached over, pressing mute on the phone. "Ask him where in Uganda."

Sunny nodded and unmuted the phone. "Where in Uganda?"

"Who wants to know?"

"What do you mean?" Sunny asked, swiping a stray strand of her curly black hair from her eyes.

"Am I talking to the new head of Timothy Irungu's security team or the woman who loves me?" Reggie asked.

Sunny hesitated.

"Doesn't matter. I'm not going to give you that information. I'll have a team deployed in less than an hour. You can tell Timothy Irungu that ASF will be bringing his daughter home," Reggie said.

The line disconnected. Julian watched as Sunny scratched the back of her neck absently. Something was wrong.

"Are we going to Uganda?" Hakeem asked, standing.

"No, we're not," Sunny said, her eyes locked onto Julian's. "Glaze, keep working on getting that location. Julian, I need to talk to you outside ... now."

Chapter Twenty-Eight

Tubeec Hirad entered the room, shining a flashlight onto her face. Mena covered her eyes from the harsh light. She could still see the pool of Isaac's blood spreading across the tile. His limp arm was visible from the door opening, a reminder of what could happen to her next. The gunmen hadn't bothered to move his body or cover it out of respect. Stepping through the blood, they'd spread bloody footprints from the open area to the hallway and into her room as they watched her.

She'd been separated from Wangari and hadn't seen her since Isaac was killed. Mena hoped her friend was okay and hadn't been harmed. The terrorist wanted something from Wangari's husband, something he'd refused to give Tubeec. Mena had spent the last few hours praying that Okeyo Lagat would comply with the demands, and she and Wangari would be released soon.

Tubeec walked over and squatted down in front of her, stroking a finger under her chin, lifting her face.

Mena didn't want to provoke the terrorist leader. She'd witnessed firsthand how easily he decided that a life should end. Survival was all that mattered now, doing whatever it took to last another minute, another hour, another day until Wangari's husband paid the ransom for their release.

Tubeec reached behind his back. Mena shivered in the stifling warm air of the room, bracing herself.

As his arm emerged, Mena's eyes settled on the item in his hand. Stunned, she stared as he sprinkled crushed coral peonies petals onto her lap.

Sliding his hands along her bound legs, he caressed her skin underneath the hem of her trousers. The roughness of his scarred skin against her ankles sent a tremor through her body.

"Don't worry. I'm not allowed to harm you," Tubeec said, tightening the knots, then turned his focus toward her wrists, bound by ropes.

"Not allowed?" Mena blurted out before she could stop herself.

"That's right. Did you think you were just an innocent victim, swept up in the kidnapping of the flower heiress?" Tubeec asked, a curve of a smile on his lips. "You were the primary target. Luckily, your relationship with the wife of Okeyo Lagat presented an opportunity for me to get something that I wanted. I wondered, though, what an art conservator could have done to make someone request my assistance."

Mena shook her head. "I don't know why anyone would want you to kidnap me."

Although, that wasn't exactly true.

But could he be that desperate to get her back? Did he have the resources to fund her abduction? She didn't believe that was possible. It couldn't be.

"The peonies were sent to you," Tubeec said.

"Yes," Mena admitted.

"And you destroyed them."

"Yes." When the flowers had arrived, she'd known they weren't from Julian as her co-workers had suspected. She knew exactly who they were from, and the message on the card had confirmed her suspicions.

"My men attempted to find the person who sent the flowers, but they were purchased in cash by someone who obviously didn't want to be identified. But I did find the card on the floor in the midst of the crushed petals. Imagine my surprise when I saw what it said," Tubeec's eyes grew wide.

"You have the card?" Mena asked, her breathing growing labored.

"January 13th," Tubeec said.

Mena looked away. The reminder of the handwritten note and the subsequent text to her phone seemed like a lifetime ago. A threat that paled in comparison to the one standing before her.

"What does that date mean to you, Ms. Nix?" Tubeec asked, his voice growing cold and menacing.

Head spinning, Mena leaned back against the wall, trying to sift through the chaotic memories assaulting her mind. The last thing she wanted to do was talk about how the events of January 13th had changed her life. She wished she could erase everything she'd done that day and the months before it.

Mena gasped as Tubeec's rough hand clamped around her throat. She struggled to breathe as he squeezed tighter.

"When I ask a question, I expect an answer immediately!" Tubeec screamed in her face.

Whimpering, Mena jerked from side to side, trying to loosen the vise Tubeec had around her neck. As quickly as he'd attacked, the terrorist released his grip.

Mena looked into his eyes, knowing she had to answer, or her silence would be the last act of her life. Inhaling deeply, she said, "Worse day of my life."

Tubeec's eyes softened in a moment, pain and hurt reflected back at her. "It appears we have something in common."

Chapter Twenty-Nine

Sunny slammed the back door of the warehouse open and stomped onto the damp concrete of the alley behind the TIDES office.

"I know I was wrong for what I said to you. I didn't want you to find out about Reggie and me, and I damn sure didn't expect you to throw my past in my face. But, I would never, ever do anything to stand in the way of your happiness. You have to believe that I'm not that petty or jealous to stop you from going to Uganda—"

Julian stepped over broken wooden pallets and a rat scurrying toward the garbage bin. He placed his hands on Sunny's arms, stopping her. "I believe you."

"Do you? Because I have no proof of what I'm about to tell you. It's just my word. You'll have to decide whether to trust it or not," Sunny said.

"You don't have to explain what happened back then. I don't need to know the details," Julian said.

Sunny jerked away from him, retreating into the shadows of the garbage bin, overflowing with crumpled food wrappers, empty liquor bottles, and large stuffed garbage bags. Swatting at the flies, she stared into the distance. The hollowness in her gaze tore his heart out.

"I've made my peace with what I went through. The months with

Tubeec when I fought every day to stay alive, not knowing if he would ever let me go," Sunny whispered.

"But, he did, and that's all behind you now," Julian said. She never shared with him the heinous things she'd witnessed as a captive of Tubeec Hirad and his militia. The acts she must have been subjected to month after month. Things that still haunted her.

A gust of wind rushed through the tight space, sending empty plastic water bottles skittering across the surface. The smell of rotting garbage faded from his senses as he stared at Sunny.

"It's not behind me, can't you see? Every time I think I've freed myself from him, he comes back into my life one way or another. I don't know if I'll ever be free of him. But I do know that the time I spent with him, the things I learned can be used for good," Sunny said.

"If you say he's not in Uganda, I believe you," Julian said. Despite what happened between them in the past, Julian knew without a doubt that Sunny would never manipulate him or lie to him. She wouldn't risk Mena's life over the past. Whether it was from direct knowledge or a gut feeling, he'd trust Sunny's instincts over any intel provided by the ASF.

Sunny rubbed her arms, then turned toward him. "He's not there. He'd never go back there."

"Okay," Julian said. Reaching a hand toward her, he took one of her hands in his. "That's all I need to know. We'll keep working to get a new lead on where he could be. Let's go back inside."

"I need you to know that I'm not making this up," Sunny insisted, her eyes searching his as if pleading for confirmation of his belief in her.

Julian nodded. "I know that."

"I did horrible things back then. Things no one knows. I ... did things that I never thought I would, that I will never, ever forgive myself for ... but it also gave me information on Tubeec. I know things about him that I shouldn't—"

"Shh," Julian said, lifting a finger to her lips. "We've all done things we regret. Actions that we hope no one will ever find out about and decisions we made that we'll take to our graves, hoping that the truth will die with us."

The mission in Central Sulawesi raced to his mind, the worst mistake of his life. The moment that had riddled him with guilt and regret, robbing him of a future he didn't believe he deserved. Until he met Mena. He'd opened up to her about his secret. Instead of the repulsion he'd expected, Mena had shown him compassion. Her understanding and acceptance of him, along with the letter Broman had written, helped him to move past the pain and forgive himself for the mistakes he'd made. He hoped Sunny would find a way to forgive herself for whatever she'd been forced to do while Tubeec Hirad held her captive.

"Everyone thinks he and his family were attacked in Somalia, but it didn't happen there. He brought them to Somalia to bury them in their homeland. They were attacked in Uganda. Tubeec saw his family killed before his eyes in that country, and he's never been back since. That's how I know he wouldn't take Wangari and Mena there," Sunny said.

Julian's mind raced. The insight into the terrorist's behavior was shocking, something he never would have expected.

The back door of the TIDES office flung open.

"ASF got it wrong," Glaze said, his eyes wild with excitement.

"Where is Tubeec?" Julian asked, following Glaze back into the war room. Enzo moved quickly, snatching weapons, bulletproof vests, and infrared goggles from the cabinets and arranging them in piles on the conference room table.

"He's actually still in Kenya, in Tarbaj, at a registered CSL for USAFRICOM," said Glaze.

Cooperative security locations, or CSLs, were not official US military bases or outposts. They were locations that could be used by the US military to support a wide range of unspecified contingencies, with the permission of the local government. CSLs could go untapped for years, leaving them dormant hiding places for rebel and militant groups.

"Cagey bastard is hiding in plain sight, knowing that anyone monitoring the area would think it's a secret training run for the US military and not a terrorist who'd kidnapped three innocent people," Glaze said. "Take a look here."

Julian leaned over the monitors, scanning the work Glaze had performed to trace the video call. A sense of dread spread through his limbs as he recognized the combination of patterns.

In an instant, he was back in the small room of base camp in Central Sulawesi, hunting down El Mago, tracing the location of the shadow facilitator through communications he'd intercepted. The pattern had been there, but he'd interpreted it wrong. It wasn't until he returned to the camp to find his SEAL Team slaughtered that he realized the scripts had concealed El Mago's men retracing the communications back to him.

"A concealer script," Julian whispered. "ASF didn't recognize that Tubeec was leading them in the opposite direction of where he was actually located."

"Bingo," Glaze said.

Julian asked, "How far is Tarbaj from here?"

"Northeast Kenya. We could get to Wajir County in ninety minutes, maybe less, but it's an hour or so drive to Tarbaj," Sunny said.

"What's the plan?" Hakeem asked, grabbing one of the bullet-proof vests.

Zale came over with a tablet, placing it on the table between them. "Here's a satellite image of the CSL. Looks like three guards on the perimeter of the four or five room structure. No way of knowing how many of Tubeec's men are on the inside."

"I need two men to go in with me and an explosive expert to create a diversion. That'll provide the cover we need get inside while Sunny operates the drone to be our eyes and ears overhead," Julian said to Sunny.

"I'm in," Enzo said.

"Me too," Hakeem added.

"Not you," Sunny said, snatching the infrared goggles from Hakeem's hand. "You have to stay behind and run the operations from here."

"You're joking," Hakeem said, his voice laced with anger.

"You wanted to be my number two in command. When I'm not here, you have to be," Sunny said.

"Then get Taye to fly us out to Wajir, and you stay behind," Hakeem insisted.

"Don't argue with me. You're staying here." Sunny turned to Julian. "Glaze will go with you and Enzo. I already have two explosive experts who can be ready to go in thirty minutes."

"That will put us in Wajir in about three hours after we pick up the rest of the equipment from Paul DeFloria," Enzo said.

A spike of adrenaline flooded Julian's body. In three hours, he would be with Mena again. He needed her to stay strong and brave a little while longer. He'd have her home and in his arms where she belonged by sunrise.

Chapter Thirty

Tubeec Hirad stood in the doorway, a menacing presence as he spoke a tribal language to one of the gunmen. Mena pressed her head against the wall, sucking in a deep breath as her heart pounded against her rib cage.

Her abduction had been on purpose.

Did you think you were just an innocent victim, swept up in the kidnapping of the flower heiress?

You were the primary target.

What the hell had happened to her life? How had she gotten caught up with horrible criminals, targeted for a reason she didn't know? How would she ever make it out of this situation alive?

She might never see her parents again, or her brothers or Regina and Omar. She might never see Julian again. Never get to tell the people she loved so dearly how much they meant to her and how sorry she was for not being a better daughter and friend to them when she could have been. She'd never get to tell Julian how much joy loving him had brought into her life.

Clutching her hands together, Mena prayed for a way out. She didn't want her life to end like this. She didn't want her last moments to be alone in a dirty, rundown building with a group of gunmen ready to blow her brains out at the whim of their crazed leader.

Tubeec continued to speak to the gunman, Rahim. The only one who'd shown her any semblance of kindness earlier. Tubeec spoke quickly as Rahim nodded.

After several more minutes of discussion, Tubeec exited the room, disappearing down the hallway.

Rahim stepped inside, staring at her with cold, hard eyes. The gentleness and kindness she'd seen before were gone. The man standing before her was the dutiful soldier of Tubeec Hirad, ready to carry out the wishes of his leader with swift efficiency and little regard to her feelings.

Brandishing a large knife, he came closer to her.

Hyperventilating, Mena scurried backward, trying to increase the distance between her and Rahim. Pain seized her chest as she squeezed her eyes shut, tears spilling down her cheeks. Curling her body into a fetal position, she turned from Rahim, hoping and praying he would spare her life. Allow her to survive the kidnapping. If Tubeec had been truthful with her, she wouldn't be killed or harmed. Not until Tubeec delivered her to the person who'd hired him to kidnap her. But could Tubeec be trusted? Would he just as easily have Rahim stab her to death if she was more trouble than she was worth to him?

Rahim grabbed her ankles and jerked her forward. Her eyes flew open as she whimpered, afraid of what punishment screaming or crying out would elicit. Rahim had dropped to one knee, brandishing the knife near her ankles. With a quick motion, he sliced the ropes binding her. A gasp escaped Mena's lips as Rahim yanked her to her feet. The strong, tight grip of Rahim's large hand clamped on her arm sent a jolt of sharp pain through her body. Mena gritted her teeth, refusing to cry out despite the pain radiating through her limb.

His touch was rough as he pushed her forward. Mena struggled to keep up with his long strides. He forced her into the hallway, then slammed her against the wall as two other guards appeared, surrounding Wangari.

Mena looked ahead into the large open room where she'd been earlier. Isaac's dead body was gone. A dark red stain of blood pooled near the wall where he'd been shot. Mena's eyes followed the smears of blood from that room to the cracked and broken concrete of the hallway.

She turned her head to the right. Xirsi carried Isaac's headless body down the hallway and into a room at the end of the hall. Seconds later, Xirsi emerged, wiping his bloody hands against the dark green trousers as he shut the door behind him.

Mena turned back toward Wangari. Her clothes were torn and covered in dirt and blood. She stumbled between the two men, both twice her size as they steered her into a room next to the one Mena had been held in.

Rahim stepped closer to Mena. The musky scent of his sweat assaulted her as he forced her to walk along the hall toward a door leading outside. Mena tried to slow her movements, terrified of what might happen to her. Rahim was too strong to resist. In mere seconds, the warm, brisk night air raked across her skin, sending a spray of fine dirt into her eyes.

Rahim forced her against the sidewall of the building, then walked back to the door and slammed it closed. Mena looked around the deserted yard, trying to focus her eyes in the darkness. To her right, toward the front of the fenced-in compound, a few trees dotted the barren landscape. A lone light shone from the front of the building, casting the rest of the property into a dark abyss. To her left, less than ten feet away from the back of the compound, was a crumbling stone wall. Mena could see no other guards on this part of the property, but that didn't mean they weren't there. The pitch-black darkness obscured her view. She could hear voices in the distance, but she wasn't sure if they were wafting through the breeze from the front of the building or from behind.

Rahim stepped in front of her. His fingers brushed against her face. Mena flinched, squeezing her eyes shut. His rough fingers dragged against her skin, wiping away the dirt until the wind stopped.

"Beautiful. Should not be here," Rahim said.

Mena opened her eyes and stared at the gunman. The softness in his dark eyes had returned. There was no hint of malice in his gaze or his touch and despite the danger of being alone with him, she didn't believe he was going to hurt her.

A rush of emotions hit Mena as her body grew limp. Slipping down into the dirt, she cried uncontrollably. She should not be here. She should be back at her condo in the Westlands with Julian. She should be having her nightly phone call to her mom telling her about all the exciting things she'd learned about Kenyans that day and how her work had progressed. She should be reading her online version of the *Palmchat Gazette*, searching for her Dad's latest article buried on some obscure page of the website. She should be texting her half-brothers, checking up on their lives and looking at pictures of the antics of her nieces and nephews. That's what she should be doing. Not crying into the dirt in some unknown deserted area in Africa, being held hostage by a gang of terrorists.

"No cry," Rahim said, squatting down on the ground next to her. He didn't make eye contact as he gripped the ropes that bound her hands. Slipping his fingers between the knots, he wiggled the tight ropes. The pain of the ropes against her skin eased away, loosening.

Wangari's screams pierced the air. "No! No! Please don't! No! Oh God No!!!"

Rahim stopped as shouts erupted from the building. Dropping her wrists from his hands, he stood and rushed back inside, leaving her alone against the outer wall.

Fear gripped Mena. What were they doing to Wangari? Why would they hurt her now when Okeyo still had time to meet their ransom demand?

The shouts in the tribal language grew more intense and loud. The dull thuds of fists banging flesh grew louder as Wangari's cries hit a crescendo. There was a loud bang, then an eerie silence settled in the night air.

Mena's breathing roared in her ears. Leaning over, she pressed her hands to the ground, trying to stand. She stopped, watching as the rope shifted downward on her forearms, toward her elbow.

Wiggling her hand, she pulled backward forcefully against the ropes. The abrasive braids gave way, slackening with each pull. Mena jerked harder as muffled footsteps pounded the ground. She pushed her arm backward with increasing force. The single heart shaped charm clinked softly against her bracelet.

With one more forceful pull, her right arm was free. The ropes dangled loosely against her left arm. Mena sat still, listening for sounds. The jostled movements continued from the front of the building, but there was no sign of Wangari, no sounds from the woman who'd mentored her and become a dear friend.

If Wangari had been murdered, Mena knew there was no hope for her.

Mena glanced at the stone wall less than ten feet away from the back of the property. It loomed toward the sky, challenging her.

Tempting her.

Chapter Thirty-One

Two minutes past 5 a.m. and the darkness of night was beginning to fade. When the sun rose, any surprise attack would be damn near impossible. Julian shifted the night vision goggles to a more comfortable position as he walked briskly across the dirt road lined with shrubs and brushes. Their movements were quick but silent. An outcropping of trees, about three hundred feet away from the CSL, concealed their presence.

Maneuvering toward a sliver of an opening between the trees, Julian raised his binoculars and focused on the CSL in the distance. The cracked and stained stone one-story compound matched the flattened step pyramid structure they'd studied from the satellite photos back at TIDES HQ. Zale's intel had located the right spot and detected militia movement around the structure. But were the hostages inside? Or had Tubeec pulled one over on TIDES as well?

Turning the binoculars for a sharper focus, Julian scanned the side of the compound.

The front of the building was the width of one room, a tight entry way that opened up into the middle section. From what Zale had been able to research, the middle was twice the size of the entry way and housed a small kitchen area and a large open space. This was believed to be the area where the terrorists had killed Isaac Gatobu. The back section of the building was the widest. It had five windows, each denoting a different room. A second door was on the west side of the compound. Zale estimated that it led to a long hallway that traversed the structure separating the middle and back sections. If their calculations were right, Mena and Wangari were being held in one of those five rooms at the back of the building.

Julian dropped the binoculars, glancing over his shoulder at the four men taking on this mission with him. Dressed in camo fatigues, Enzo and Glaze were outfitted with bullet proof vests, head gear, night vision goggles, and M16 assault rifles. The explosive experts, Wes and Kemp, stood a few paces away. Short and lean, both men carried an M16 and backpacks containing the necessary ingredients to blow up three sections of the stonewall in front of the compound. The diversionary tactics would draw the militia from the structure, giving Julian, Enzo and Glaze a chance to get inside and rescue Wangari and Mena.

The low hum of a drone grew louder. Julian glanced up into the sky, but couldn't see the device cloaked in the early morning darkness.

"Move out in three minutes." Sunny's voice crackled in their ears. She was thirty miles away at an airstrip in Wajir, monitoring their every movement through camera equipped drones. "Montgomery, Enzo and Glaze, break off and head toward the southeast end of the property. Go slow as molasses so you won't be heard. I don't detect any movement back there, but rebel guards could be hiding. It's dark and I can't get a good visual. Kemp and Wes, move along the wall to the front of the compound. Gate is open with one guard sighted inside. He's pacing. Try to avoid being seen as you head to the northwest corner, but shoot him if you need to. Stay low. Set the explosives, then get the hell out of there. Ninety second delay after the explosion, then Julian, Enzo and Glaze can scale the stone wall near the back of the house and enter. Shoot first and ask questions later."

They each gave confirmation of the instructions, then Julian scrambled down low and sprinted toward the stone wall in the distance, with Enzo and Glaze following him. Reaching the wall, Julian dropped to the ground, then crawled until he was at about the halfway mark of the wall that lined the back of the property. Glaze remained at the corner, near the eastern side of the structure and Enzo was halfway between them. Once the bombs detonated, they wouldn't have much time to get over the wall and into the compound to find Mena and Wangari. Each of them would attack the compound from a different entry point to maximize the chance of finding the women quickly.

A warm breeze rushed toward them, peppering his skin with sand. Fingers gripping the M16, he stroked the trigger as his heart beat slowed. The slow metronomic thuds lulling him into the meditative state he remembered from so many missions long ago. Once Wes and Kemp set the explosions, Tubeec's militia would think they were under attack from the front of the compound. Pouring out of the structure, only a skeletal crew should be left behind to guard Mena and Wangari. Two, maybe three, rebels that he, Enzo, and Glaze could easily overpower.

Julian closed his eyes and imagined seeing Mena again. Wrapping his arms around her, feeling her body next to his. He was so close to getting her back safe, but he couldn't focus on that. He had to think one step at a time, one move at a time, subdue one captor at a time.

"Explosives set. Detonation in ten," the words came through Julian's earpiece.

Ten seconds later, a deafening blast and huge fireball burst into the early morning sky. Chaotic shouts filled the air.

"Two squirters coming out of the front door. A light on in room nearest to Glaze on the east side of the compound, no other movement detected. Wes and Kemp, get the hell out of there," Sunny said.

A rapid-fire succession of bullets thundered from the front of the CSL.

"We got a problem. They have night vision goggles. Can see us just as clear as we can see them. We're under fire," the response came from Wes.

Julian stared at Enzo and Glaze several feet away from him. Gun blasts popped like firecrackers in the night sky. The smoky scent of gunpowder hung in the air.

"Should we go in? Provide backup?" Enzo shouted into the comms.

"No! Stay in your locations!" Sunny said. "Sixty more seconds, then move in."

Julian pressed his back against the stone wall, his mind chaotic, fighting the urge to ignore Sunny's orders and take out the rebels attacking Wes and Kemp. But this was the plan. Everything was unfolding as they'd designed. He had to stay and play his part or Mena might not make it out of this situation alive.

Rapid-fire continued from the front of the property.

"I'm hit!"

"Kemp down. Shot in the hip. Two rebels taken out. Gunfire still coming from the front of the house!"

"Get Kemp out of there! I'm coming to get you! Montgomery, Enzo, and Glaze go in now! Do not, I repeat, do not go toward the front of the house," Sunny said.

"Need headshots gentlemen," Julian said into the mouthpiece. "We're fighting a crew built like us."

"No shit!" Enzo responded.

"Let's spill some rebel brains," Glaze added.

"On three. One. Two. Three."

Julian heaved his body over the stone wall in unison with Enzo and Glaze. In his periphery, he saw the men racing to their designated points of entry.

Julian rounded the corner of the house and stalked slowly toward the side door. Easing toward the door, he dropped to the ground pressing his back against the dirt. He pressed his feet into the side of the house and estimated he was one complete body roll away from being in front of the side door.

The air had gone quiet. In the distance, a bird chirped.

Julian trained his ears for any sound coming from the house.

Raspy breathing grew louder as the soft thud of footsteps cautiously approached. Moving his head from side to side, he saw no threat from the outside. The footsteps were coming from within the building.

As the side door creaked open slowly, Julian rolled his body over stopping when he was on his back again. The bearded rebel, with night vision goggles on his face, scanned the empty yard beyond Julian. The rebel's M4 Carbine was trained toward the distance, moving slowly. Pressing his feet against the bottom foundation of the house, Julian unloaded two quick shots to the center of the rebel's head.

The rebel's gun erupted, spraying bullets wildly as his body dropped backward to the floor. Julian stood to his feet, crouching low, and entered the dark hallway. Passing the first door, he peered inside, eyes sweeping over a disheveled bed mat and abandoned covers. There were five rooms along the hallway and room one confirmed empty.

Julian advanced down the hallway. A figure emerged from the doorway of room two and glanced in his direction. The man wasn't wearing night-vision goggles and likely couldn't see Julian standing in the darkness.

The militant went back inside the room. Julian raised his weapon and waited for the man to come out again. Minutes that felt like hours passed. The rebel still hadn't come back into the hallway. Had he escaped through the window? Was he coming—

A sharp blow struck Julian on the back of the head sending a lightning bolt of pain through his brain. Julian stumbled forward, dropping his gun. A man fell on his back, unloading punches to the side of Julian's head, back and sides. Each blow sent a series of pain radiating and rocking through his body. Pushing up from the ground, Julian managed to land an elbow to the man's arm, knocking him off kilter. Flipping over to his back, Julian reached for his knife as the man grabbed for Julian's fallen gun. Slipping the butterfly knife from his ankle holster, Julian jerked his arm in a wide arc, slicing the rebel across the throat.

Blood spewed from the man's neck, spraying across Julian's face. The man grabbed at this throat. An awful gurgling noise emitting from his mouth as he tried to breathe, stumbling backward down the hallway toward the open side door. Julian reached for his gun and took one shot, hitting the man in the center of his chest.

Wiping blood from his goggles, Julian stood and turned, glancing into room two. Empty.

His steps cautious, Julian approached room three. Enzo should have entered the compound through the window of room three, but Julian hadn't seen or heard his friend yet. To his left, across from the open door of room three, the wall ended, revealing an opening into the large room in the middle section of the structure. Rebels might be hiding in that room, waiting to ambush him. Inching slowly to the edge of the wall, Julian—

Gunfire sliced out of room three. Julian dropped to the floor. Return gunfire blasted from the large open room back toward room three. Julian couldn't see the shooters. He stayed low, hoping Enzo was alive inside room three and would win the shootout.

Further down the hall, Glaze emerged from room five, squatting low against the back wall, waiting for the battle to end. Neither of them could risk surprising Enzo or join in the shootout without being able to positively ID which blasts were coming from their friend.

After several more rounds, the shooting ended. Julian held his breath, his weapon extended, waiting to see who would emerge. At the other end of the hall, Glaze did the same. They had to be careful. One wrong move and they could end up killing Enzo instead of a rebel.

A hand extended from room three, then clenched into a thumbs up sign. Standing to his feet, Julian approached room three as Enzo stepped into the hallway.

"Any sign of the hostages?" Enzo asked.

"Rooms one and two were empty," Julian responded.

"My room was empty. No sign of them in there either," Enzo said, pointing toward the large open room of the middle section of the compound.

"Male dead in room five. Isaac Gatobu. Only room four left, but I don't hear any sounds coming from there," said Glaze.

Julian moved forward, motioning for Enzo to follow. He knew what the men were thinking. One last chance to find Mena and Wangari. One last chance to find out if the intel had been accurate or if Tubeec Hirad had made a fool of them as well.

Glaze held back, holding position to provide cover fire in the hallway if any militants showed up. Walking along the side wall, Julian dropped low before swinging around to face the opening.

Wangari Irungu cowered in a corner, her eyes wide with fear as tears streamed down her face. A rebel stood behind her with hands raised. The man nodded toward a gun laying on the floor a few feet from where Julian stood.

"No gun," the rebel said. "I give up."

Julian stood and beckoned for Enzo and Glaze to follow. He entered the room, gun trained on the rebel.

"Julian? Is that you?" Wangari asked. Relief spread across her face.

Julian saw no sign of Mena.

Glaze moved past him and reached a hand toward Wangari, helping her to stand. Enzo picked up the discarded gun from the floor and placed it at the temple of the rebel.

"The other woman you kidnapped. Where is she?" Julian demanded, raising his gun toward the man's face. His heart pounding, he stroked the trigger with his finger.

"I don't know. She escaped."

Chapter Thirty-Two

Inhaling deeply, Tubeec savored the pungent scent of urine filling the air as the soft trickle of liquid pattered against the metal floor of the hollowed-out van. He slid his thumb against the hard ridge of the laryngeal prominence and pressed his fingers into the neck of the hacker who went by the name, Garbo.

Tubeec had contemplated paying the arrogant fool for his services, but had realized quickly that money, as usual, was not the best motivator. Power and fear could incite and compel far better than currency. Undetectable precision and excellence was needed for this delicate task and the fear of being tortured for days before dying was creating an intense focus within Garbo.

Minutes ago, Tubeec had completed the exchange with a contrite Okeyo Lagat. Every piece of evidence the DPP had on Deputy President Kipsang Rono was copied onto a flash drive. Okeyo had followed his instructions perfectly, ditching the ASF Agents assigned to accompany him and delivered exactly what Tubeec wanted.

The consequence of any double-cross was clear.

"If this flash drive does not contain the evidence, you will watch your beautiful wife being murdered live on the morning news," Tubeec had warned Okeyo.

Okeyo assured him that he'd handed over everything they had on Rono. The only thing left was for Tubeec to implement extra insurance in case Okeyo was lying. Even if Tubeec didn't end up with the evidence against Rono, he needed to make sure that the Office of the Department of Public Prosecutions, ODPP, didn't have it either.

Garbo had set up shop across the street from the ODPP House on Ragati Road waiting patiently for Tubeec to return. The van was obscured toward the back of a nearby parking lot, with a direct view of the building surrounded by ivy-covered brick walls and barb wire.

"Why is the virus taking so long?" Tubeec asked, scraping the edge of the syringe along Garbo's face. A debilitating dose of a modified version of lazirprene would render Garbo's body unresponsive to brain cues. Yet, he would still be able to feel the pain of his skin being sliced thousands of times with a razor blade, Tubeec's current weapon of choice.

Garbo glanced up toward Tubeec, then looked away.

"I expanded the attack to ensure that all evidence against Rono would disappear. That means evidence gathered on others might also be erased, but I didn't think you'd care about that," explained Garbo.

Garbo could obliterate all traces of electronic documents from the world with his Venom virus. IT experts and law enforcement agencies would bet their lives that the outcomes of Venom were impossible. An ignorance that worked to Garbo's advantage as he made possible what no one could fathom. A virus that could creep undetected through the networks and servers around the world, strategically deleting targeted information was beyond comprehension. Complete and utter destruction of undesirable information could be attained in mere hours, with no proof the information had ever existed. Venom singlehandedly caused identities and data to vanish. Garbo's virus had made it possible for Tubeec to avoid capture for the past decade.

"I don't. Make it run faster," Tubeec ordered, releasing the man's neck.

Garbo nodded, ignoring his soiled pants as he sat back down and turned his attention to the computers lining one side of the old van.

Tubeec took a step back, easing down onto the worn brocade

covered bench seat lining the opposite wall. He twirled the syringe between his fingers.

Tubeec ran a finger along the flash drive. The contents would give him the ammunition he needed to assert his influence over Deputy President Rono. And if Rono was successful in knocking Noah Thairu out of the top spot, Tubeec would have secured a president under his control. He would owe his success to the man who'd paid him handsomely to abduct Mena Nix. With the money and Mena's close ties to Wangari Irungu, Tubeec had been inspired to grab the top-secret evidence he'd heard DPP Lagat was gathering against Rono.

As lines of texts and strange graphics crowded the computer screens, Tubeec focused on the low symphony of the hacker's fingers moving across the keyboard.

The cell phone buzzed. Reaching down, Tubeec pressed the talk button and placed it against his ear. This was the call he'd been waiting for. Mena Nix should be secured at the airstrip, awaiting the arrival of the man his second team had been sent to deliver back to Kenya.

"Mena Nix is ... gone."

"What did you say?" Jolted, Tubeec clutched the phone tight.

"She escaped. Bashiir, Dalmar and Harbi are out looking for her now," Cangrejos said, a slight tremor in his voice.

"Who was assigned to her? Who was supposed to take her to Mandera?" Tubeec asked, forcing his words through clenched jaws.

"Rahim. He's usually so good, I don't know—"

"Make him feel the consequences of his incompetence," Tubeec said.

"He's missing, too. And there's more bad news."

Tubeec sucked in a breath, then let it out slowly.

A three-dimensional depiction of a globe appeared on the computer monitors across from him. Bright green lines lit up the globe as it turned, darting from city to city throughout Africa, Europe, and North America.

"We lost five men at the compound about an hour ago in an attack."

"There should have been no attack. I paid al-Harakat handsomely to allow us passage in their territory," Tubeec said, feeling his blood boiling.

"It wasn't al-Harakat. A team was sent to rescue the hostages. They got Wangari Irungu," Cangrejos said, his words slow and measured. "But, Assad, Liban, and Suleymaan are with me."

"It couldn't be ASF. Who was behind the attack?" Tubeec asked. Tubeec's reputation would take a hit for this. He'd expected the ASF to be fumbling through the carefully crafted maze of confusion in Uganda, not orchestrating a sneak attack on the compound where he was holding Mena Nix and Wangari Irungu.

"We think it was ..." Cangrejos hesitated.

"Tell me," Tubeec demanded.

"TIDES."

Tubeec almost dropped the phone, then regained his composure.

Tactical and Intelligence Defense Executive Services.

Created with money and resources he'd supplied.

Owned and operated by Sunny Tate.

A flash of the dark-skinned beauty assaulted his memories. Her legs straddling his scarred body, she'd writhed in ecstasy as he pumped hard into her, erupting in an explosive orgasm. She'd reached climax seconds after he did, satisfaction on her face as sweat ran down her neck and flowed between her ample breasts. Sunny hadn't been repulsed by his disfigurement. Her hands caressed his rough, burned skin as if he was the man he'd once been before his life had been destroyed. The man his wife had loved.

"Was Sunny there? Did she lead the attack?" Tubeec asked, his breath quickening as he stifled the erection threatening to grow from the memory of her.

"I can't be sure, but the coordination of the attack was definitely her handiwork. Calculating and methodical, executed with minimal errors," Cangrejos responded.

More like his handiwork. Sunny Tate had learned a lot in her year of captivity with him. More than he'd expected to share, but she'd beguiled him. And when she'd worked off the debt owed to him, he'd kept his word and released her.

Tubeec rested his head against the warm metal of the side of the van. He didn't need Wangari any longer. But Mena Nix was a different story. She'd made a fool of him by escaping his well-trained team. A fact that could never be known. Tubeec had to send the right message for this unfortunate turn of events.

Garbo turned and gave him the thumbs-up sign. The destruction of evidence against Deputy President Rono was complete.

Tubeec said, "How long have Assad and the others been searching for Mena Nix?"

"Not very long, but she will be easy to find. The terrain is harsh, and she's inexperienced."

"When you find her ... encourage the men to ... enjoy her. Make sure she won't think about escaping again."

Chapter Thirty-Three

Squinting, Julian peered through the opened front door. The burned and charred remains of the compound's stone wall still smoldered. Smoke tendrils danced toward the lightening morning sky. The heady stench of gun powder and rancid blood was strong.

Julian stepped over the crumpled dead body of one of the kidnappers. Bullet holes riddled the wall where Julian and Enzo had eliminated each threat inside. Rounding the corner back into the hallway, he watched as Enzo secured the only gunman who'd surrendered. The man had stopped talking, refusing to divulge any further information about the motive for the kidnapping or what Tubeec had planned for the hostages. The only information the bastard had given about Mena was that she'd escaped. A small contingent of mercenaries had been sent out to find her shortly before the TIDES team arrived.

Mena had been right here, in this compound.

And now she was gone. He was too late.

Julian watched as Glaze wrapped an arm around Wangari Irungu, leading her toward the front rooms of the compound. The heiress to the horticultural dynasty was overcome with emotion, crying as she leaned into Glaze, taking shaky steps forward. Deep purple bruises covered her neck and arms, marring her tan skin. Crusted dried blood trailed down the left side of her face from a cut on her eyebrow. Her eyes were disoriented and dazed.

Julian turned away and walked down the hall. Where the hell had Mena gone? How could he find out? He had to track her down. Had to find her before Tubeec's men did.

Pushing through the door leading to the side of the property, Julian stepped out into the brisk humid morning air. Scanning the yard in the dim light of dawn, Julian saw something trampled in the dirt. He squatted down, lifting the object from the ground. Batches of thin ropes darkened red from what he suspected was blood. Had Mena been outside when she got away from Tubeec's men? Were these the ropes that had bound her? Had she found a way to free herself from the ropes and escape?

"Coming in low for pick-up with ETA of three and a half minutes," Sunny's voice crackled through the earbud communications. "Reggie and his team have been alerted, and he's diverting teams to Wajir County. Estimated arrival in one hour. They're picking up the search for Mena. Julian, they're going to find her."

Mena didn't have an hour. They'd already lost too much time. She was out there alone, with trained killers hunting her. He didn't know how many of Tubeec's men had left to search for Mena, but there was no way any of them wanted to report back to their leader that they'd lost one of the hostages. From what he remembered, Tubeec considered any type of failure by a member of his team to be a one-way ticket to the grave.

"Copy that," Glaze spoke into his headset.

Julian asked, "Sunny, what's the closest town to the compound? How far away would Mena need to go to reach people?"

"Pretty far ... over thirty miles in any direction. Given how close we are to the Somalian border, let's hope she didn't head that way," Sunny responded.

Tubeec's men, al-Harakat, and marauding bands of rebels from Somalia weren't Mena's only concerns. As day replaced night, she'd get hit with the brutal heat of the desert. Even if she could hide from the men tracking her, she wouldn't last long without food and water. Two days. Maybe three. His biggest fear was that she would get lost, roaming in circles and heading nowhere, increasing the likelihood that she'd succumb to dehydration, exhaustion, and heatstroke. Too many ways for her to lose her life out here. He couldn't let that happen. He was going to find her. Now.

From the horizon, the helicopter came into view, dipped low, and landed about a hundred yards away. Blades whipped the wind into a frenzy, sending plumes of red sand swirling in the air.

Glaze ran ahead, half-carrying Wangari toward the helo. Enzo followed close behind, his gun trained on the member of Tubeec's team they'd captured.

Jumping inside the helicopter first, Glaze turned and easily lifted Wangari inside, disappearing into the cabin. Enzo poked the captive in the back. The man fell forward then struggled to scramble into the helicopter with his hands and legs bound by ropes. Enzo turned and stared at Julian, waving an arm for him to come.

The dark bloodstains of the ropes in his hand convicted him. He knew what he had to do. He'd known from the first moment he met Mena, standing outside her workshop at the Genesis Gallery, that she was a fighter. She wouldn't let life knock her down without trying to get back up and survive. He'd marveled at her bravery time and again as they fell in love. He couldn't be upset with her for taking the opportunity to escape from the compound. She hadn't known help was on the way. That he was doing everything in his power to bring her home safe.

"Montgomery!" Sunny said. "Don't do this. Don't go after her alone. Wait for the ASF teams!"

"I can't," Julian said, then turned and walked away from the helicopter. Approaching the stone wall, he picked up his backpack where he'd discarded it. Scaling the wall, he sat on top of it, surveying the land.

Mena was desperate, scared, and alone. The night sky would have been brightening, but still dark enough to provide cover. Which way would she have gone?

Spotting a copse of trees in the distance, Julian jumped down from the wall and ran in that direction.

Chapter Thirty-Four

Raising her shirt over her face, Mena dipped her head low, hoping to avoid swallowing the gritty dust again.

She'd been running for what felt like hours, zigzagging across the arid desert, plunging toward the sparse clusters of dying trees, stumbling over dead livestock carcasses infested with flies, trying to seek refuge. The gunmen hunting her were never far away. Their voices drifted across the wind as they called out to each other in their tribal languages, determined in their pursuit to capture her. Mena knew she would be killed the moment they found her.

Stumbling forward, she raced toward brush clustered along deep ruts in the sand of what seemed to be a makeshift road. Should she follow it? Or would it lead back to danger? Would the gunmen expect her to make that move? A dull ache, throbbing near her temples, disrupted her thoughts. Her desperation to escape had placed her in a worse predicament.

Mena stifled a wail as she squeezed between the brush. Digging her hand into the coarse sand, she smeared it over her shirt to camouflage herself, praying it would prevent the men from seeing her.

Leaving the compound might have been her biggest mistake. But when she'd heard Wangari's gut-wrenching cries laced with pure terror, she'd panicked. The brutal sounds of fists against skin had been enough to convince Mena to take her life into her own hands. She'd acted on instinct, hoping to save herself from suffering the same fate as Isaac and Wangari, either at the hands of Tubeec's men or whoever had hired him to abduct her.

Now, she was alone in the desert with no food, no water, and no idea what to do next.

The sky was brightening. The sun would be rising soon. How much longer could she hide from the gunmen? In the growing daylight, she wouldn't be able to conceal her location for long.

Settling within a divot between a tangle of brittle branches, Mena peered out in the distance. She could still hear the men communicating but couldn't tell which direction they would be coming from. She hoped she was hidden enough by the trees to not be seen. Mena pulled her knees to her chest, wrapping her arms tightly around her legs as her body shook violently from exhaustion and pure fear.

She'd had other occasions to think about her death. Times when she'd been certain she wouldn't make it out alive. Snatches of memories of her life flashing across her mind as she prepared for what she'd expected to be the end.

But each time, she'd skirted death. Saved by the man who loved her.

Julian had risked his own life, time and again to bring her from the brink of danger.

Wangari's family had hired TIDES for security and protection. By now, Julian must know she'd been kidnapped along with Wangari and Isaac. Was he out there somewhere trying to find her and save her from the maniac who'd taken her? Could she dare to believe he would save her once again? Or was all hope gone?

A heavy force pressed down against Mena's back, toppling her into the dirt. She screamed, tasting bitter earth on her tongue as she struggled to identify her attacker. Turning, she stared into the dark, dangerous eyes of one of the kidnappers who'd held her at the compound.

He jerked her from the ground, clamping a damp, dusty hand against her mouth. Mena struggled against the weight pressing against her back, trying to free herself as she was yanked from the brush.

"Shh, shh," the gunman whispered in her ear.

Rahim.

The same man who'd showed her kindness by loosening the ropes on her wrists. The man who'd unwittingly helped orchestrate her escape.

He turned her toward him slowly, then crouched low behind the brush. She saw the same kindness in his eyes she'd witnessed earlier. Was he going to take her back to the compound, or was he here to help her escape?

Rahim pressed his finger to his mouth, then gently brushed dust from her face, his fingers lingering against her lips. Mena sat rigid, unmoving, waiting for his next move. Her chest heaved from her ragged breaths.

With his other arm, he pointed toward the road. Rahim pressed his arms and knees onto the ground, effecting a crawling motion, then pointed again in the direction of the road.

"Safe," Rahim whispered, then pointed again. "Safe."

Mena nodded slowly. She needed to crawl, stay low, and follow the road to safety. She didn't know where it would lead, but she knew she had to trust him.

"Go," Rahim urged, slinging his rifle over his shoulder, pointing frantically toward the road again.

The shouts of tribal words grew louder in the air as the sun begin to peek over the horizon. Rahim looked concerned, peering back through the bushes to the vast canvas of desert behind them.

Scrambling forward, Mena moved past Rahim toward the road. Broken branches and rocks lodged in the dirt scratched her knees and hands, stinging her skin, but she pressed forward. As she reached the edge, she dared to stand and run, putting more distance between herself and the danger following them.

Rushing through the gnarled branches clawing at her clothes, Mena forced her legs to go faster.

Stumbling along the ruts, she cut across the road to another cropping of trees. Her legs burned as the ground sloped upward, then abruptly flattened. Mena stumbled to a stop along a ridge. A gust of wind whipped through her hair, hot and blustering against her dry skin. The road angled downhill toward a small building in the distance, surrounded by a low stone fence a couple hundred yards away.

Did Rahim know about this place? Was this where he wanted her to go for safety?

Small puffs of dust erupted from the sand as the rapid-fire pops of bullets whizzed around Mena, pelting the ground.

Screaming, she didn't dare look behind her as a symphony of gunshots rang out. Ducking low, she tumbled down the hill, barely keeping her footing as she raced toward the small concrete building ahead.

"Go, go, go!" Rahim shouted from behind her as he returned fire at the gunmen chasing them.

The angry shouts grew louder and more insistent as the gunshots continued. Mena ran closer to the low stone fencing, her eyes drawn to a large tree in the corner with tangled branches, curving and broken into a nearly perfect heart-shaped hole near the top. The sun peeked through the heart, casting bright rays on the pale blue painted concrete house looming in front of her. A beacon to safety if she could just make it there.

A deep, guttural moan arrested her movement. Mena turned and watched as Rahim's body shook violently from the force of dozens of bullets. He returned fire, sending his shooter to the ground as he fell, his body jerking and twisting as it rolled down the hill toward the stone fence.

Another gunman rushed past Rahim's body. Arm raised toward her, he pointed the barrel of his semiautomatic rifle toward her head.

Mena froze.

The air became quiet and still as the gunman descended upon her. Mena glanced down at the rose gold charm bracelet on her wrist. Sweat rolled down her face, dripping from her chin onto the red dirt below. The heart-shaped charm bracelet glowed in the sunlight. She took one long slow breath, which would probably be her last.

Gunfire rocked the air.

Mena shut her eyes, squeezing tightly as her body fell to the ground.

Chapter Thirty-Five

Intense gunfire blazed above Mena, sending a flurry of birds skittering across the sky. A brief moment of silence was followed by more rounds of fire. A spattering of blood rained down on her legs as the gunman wobbled and collapsed onto the ground.

"Get up! Go into the house now!"

A man's voice, concerned and insistent, spurred her into action.

Mena stumbled to her feet and rushed toward the sprawling one-story concrete house stained a faded robin's egg blue. White curtains adorned the two small windows on opposite sides of the door. Sprinting up the concrete steps, she stopped short, glancing at the mosaic-tiled cross that hung above the door. Thinking about the disaster that had been averted, Mena said a silent prayer of thanks, then turned the knob.

Struggling to adjust to the darkness, she ran a hand along the smooth concrete walls until she found a light switch. Moments later, the room was bathed in a soft yellow glow. To her left was a neatly furnished living room. A dark brown couch accented with lavender pillows was flanked by matching chairs.

Mena darted across the room and kneeled down behind the couch, pressing her body flat against the thin, threadbare tan rug covering the floor. She wasn't sure what to do. The gunshots had ceased, but she was afraid to go near the windows. The man out there had helped her. He'd saved her life.

Heart pounding in her chest, Mena rubbed her fingertips against her temples, trying to soothe the jackhammers beating against her skull. Exhaustion settled in her like a dead weight, draining her of the adrenaline that had fueled her escape. She craved water and rest.

The door opened.

Mena pressed up from the floor, peering over the edge of the couch.

Time stopped.

Heart racing, she shook her head, unable to comprehend what she was seeing was true and real.

"Is it really you?" Her voice was barely above a whisper as she watched him walk inside and shut the door behind him.

Slipping the helmet from his head, he dropped it on the floor and ran a dusty hand through his dark hair, slick from sweat.

The soulful brown eyes she'd fell in love with stared back at her.

"It's me," Julian said, resting against the door.

A canyon of distance separated them. Mena trembled.

In three strides, he was helping her up from behind the couch. Mena took shaky steps toward Julian, staring at him.

"Did they hurt you? Are you in any pain?" He assessed her for injuries, his hands gentle, his eyes canvassing her body.

"My head hurts, and I'm tired, but I'm okay," Mena said, swallowing past the hot mass in her throat. Now that she was safe, her thoughts drifted to the one she left behind. "I'm fine. I can't say the same about Wangari. When I left, they were beating her ... I think they—"

"She's fine. We rescued her, and she should be at the hospital in Garissa now," Julian said.

"You rescued her?" Mena shook her head, unable to believe it.

"Not just me. The whole TIDES team. We got a read on where Tubeec was from the video call and ambushed the compound to save both of you," Julian explained.

A tear slipped down her cheek. If she had waited, this nightmare could have been over hours ago. Julian and TIDES had been coming for her when she'd escaped.

"At least two of us survived." Mena thought of Grace's bloody body lying in the alley behind the Irungu Center as Tubeec and his men kidnapped them.

Julian grabbed her hands, raising them to his lips. His kiss was gentle, against her skin, leaving a trail of heat in its wake. "Grace survived the shooting. She's in ICU but improving little by little every day. Might take several months, but the doctors believe she'll make a full recovery," Julian said.

Relief surged through Mena's body. Dizzy from the unexpected good news, Mena leaned into Julian, welcoming his strong arms around her. The sheer proximity of him had an instant effect. Her body craved him. Her lips yearned to kiss his. "I can't believe you found me. I can't believe you're here."

"You doubted me?" Julian asked, raising an eyebrow, a grin playing at the corners of his mouth. His hand caressed the side of her face. Mena leaned into his touch as a tear slid down her dirt-streaked skin.

"I'm sorry," Mena choked out.

"Hey, hey, don't say that. I'm an asshole for trying to joke with you at a time like this. You forgive me?" Julian asked, slipping an arm around her.

Mena nodded, unable to speak. Love swelled within her as she stared into Julian's gorgeous face, glistening with sweat.

"Let's get you cleaned up," Julian said.

As Julian lifted her with ease, Mena wrapped her arms around his neck. She buried her head in his shoulder as he carried her into a small bathroom around the corner from the living room. Lowering her gently onto the floor, he stood behind her as they stared at each other through the mirror.

Mena glanced at her own haggard appearance. Her hair was grimy, plastered against her scalp. Her eyes were tired and haunted.

Julian slid his hands along her arms until he reached her palms. "Thought you said you weren't hurt."

Mena glanced at her bloody hands, cut and scraped from crawling across the desert terrain. Her body was numb, unable to feel the pain of her injuries.

"It's no big deal," Mena said.

Julian turned the knob of the faucet. A soft trickle of water flowed into the basin. He gently moved her hands under the stream, massaging them softly as blood colored the water before disappearing down the drain.

"I don't know what I would have done if I lost you," Julian admitted. "If I had made one wrong move, ignored one instinct, hesitated for one more second, I wouldn't have been here to protect you. Instead of standing next to you right now, I could have been too late. I'm not sure I would have been able to go on—"

"Don't say that," Mena said, lacing her wet hands in his.

"Not saying it doesn't stop it from being true," Julian said. "I don't want to know what life is like without you."

"You won't have to," Mena said.

"Can you promise me you won't get kidnapped again? This is the second time. I kinda need you to stay out of trouble," Julian said, winking at her.

Mena let out a laugh, her body relaxing from his attempts to lighten the mood. She was safe because of Julian.

"You're so beautiful," Julian whispered.

Mena smiled, biting her lower lip as she glanced at herself in the mirror. "Liar. I'm a dirty mess, and I stink ... bad."

Julian scrunched his face as he playfully waved a hand in front of his nose. "Yeah, but that doesn't stop you from being the most gorgeous woman in the world."

Julian turned her toward him and kissed her on the lips, his mouth moving tenderly over hers as his tongue swirled against her tongue. A familiar passion built between them. She was grateful to have this intimacy with him again.

Breaking the kiss, Julian leaned his forehead next to hers. Their breaths synchronizing, she ran her fingers through his hair.

Stepping back, Julian took his time unbuttoning her dingy white shirt and pushed it off her shoulders to the floor. His hands slid down her arms softly before he focused his attention on her trousers.

Unbuttoning her pants, Julian slid his hands against her hips, pushing the pants to the floor.

Standing in front of him in her lacy black bra and matching thong, Mena shivered as goosebumps peppered her skin. She loved him completely. What they shared was the purest of unconditional love, bridging the good times to the bad and strong enough to withstand anything that tried to tear them apart. How could she have ever thought she wasn't ready to commit to this man? He was everything she'd ever wanted and all the things she never knew she needed.

"Let's get you in the shower," Julian said, then stepped away from her toward the showerhead. Fiddling with the knobs, he turned them back and forth. Satisfied that he had the water temperature right, Julian sat on the edge of the bathtub and reached his hand toward her. Mena placed her hand in his grasp and walked over to him, stopping in between his open legs. Julian leaned his face against her abdomen. The damp wetness of his tears against her skin startled her as his arms pulled her closer to him.

Leaning down, Mena kissed the top of Julian's head and whispered, "I love you."

Chapter Thirty-Six

Minutes later, Julian stepped out of the bathroom, giving Mena time to wash up.

The home had been empty when he'd arrived. Its inhabitants nowhere to be found. The location was along the route of two dirt roads in a town called Giriftu. Zale had highlighted the home as a place to shelter in case things went sideways during the rescue at the CSL, noting that satellite imagery hadn't detected any movement at the house in several weeks. The owners were unknown.

Julian figured it was the best place for him to set up base while he tried to determine where to look for Mena.

He never expected to see Mena running full speed toward the house, chased by two gunmen. Another gunman was helping her, holding off the fire so she could make it to safety. Julian burst through the front door in time to see the gunman falling in a hail of bullets. In his descent, he'd shot the head off of another gunman and there was only one left. One man stalking Mena over the dry baked earth for Julian to take out.

Lifting his M16 rifle, he'd stumbled upon his comms as it fell from his hip. Focusing on the danger unfolding in front of him, Julian locked onto the militant pointing a gun at Mena's face. Pressing the trigger, he'd unleashed a series of shots to the chest of the assailant.

Watching Mena fall backward, he'd been momentarily stunned. Fear that he'd been too late threatened to overcome him. But he'd seen no sign of blood on the front of her shirt. She was in shock, looking dazed as he'd urged her to get inside the house.

While Mena was inside, Julian had rushed across the rocky landscape to drag the three dead bodies into a ravine with crackled, water-thirsted beds.

It was only a matter of time before another contingent of Tubeec's militia would discover the bodies. The small blue house was like a sitting duck in a sea of danger. They couldn't stay here for long and survive. He needed to get them back to Wajir County.

Julian fiddled with the comms, desperate to get it working again. Twisting the wires and testing the buttons, he managed to get the device to come back to life.

Making contact with someone at TIDES was the only chance he'd have to save Mena and himself. Outside the window, the sun was slowly rising in the sky. A sunray flashed against a broken bottle, sparkling in the desolate terrain. The beeps continued from the comms as Julian tapped his fingers against his thigh, willing a connection to be made.

"Julian. Where the hell are you?" Hakeem asked.

Relief coursed through Julian. Stepping away from the window, he sank down onto the couch and sighed heavily.

"I'm at the house in Giriftu, the backup point in case things went wrong with the rescue," Julian said, remembering the map of the area he'd memorized as they'd planned the attack on the compound. "How close are Sunny and the other guys to here?"

"Not close at all. Kemp was hurt real bad," Hakeem responded. "Bullet nicked a major artery and he was bleeding out. Wangari was in a catatonic state. Timothy Irungu told Sunny to fly them to the hospital in Garissa and not to leave until his private jet could get him there."

"Is Kemp okay?"

"Still in surgery."

"When is Timothy Irungu supposed to arrive in Garissa?"

"Should be there within the hour," Hakeem said. "I take it you didn't find Mena ..."

"If you were a betting man, you would have lost all your money," Julian responded.

"You found her? She's with you now?" Hakeem asked.

"Yeah, she's with me at the house. I got three dead men from Tubeec's militia about to stink up the area. Can you reach Sunny?"

"Look, you need to get out of there soon. Stick to the brush and trees along the main road between Giriftu and Wajir. Don't use your comms pack anymore. We'll need to conserve the battery to track you once Sunny is in the area," Hakeem instructed.

"Got it. How long do you think we have?" Julian asked

"Probably two to three hours. Rest up, eat, then leave before then. I'll call Sunny now," Hakeem said.

Julian turned in time to see Mena walking out of the bathroom, wearing nothing but a skimpy towel around her body, wet and glistening from the shower. Julian felt his erection become rock hard.

"Will do. Thanks, Hakeem," Julian said, then dropped the phone to the floor. Two to three hours. That was more than enough time.

Crossing the distance between him and the woman he loved in mere seconds, he snatched the towel, allowing it to drop to the floor. His eyes feasted on her amazing body, toned and slender, with a delicious curve at the hips.

He took a slow deep breath, trying to calm the fire blazing within him. Stepping toward her, he ran a hand against her dark wet hair, slicked back against her head. The look suited her. Nothing to distract from her face. The luscious lips, the long, curved eyelashes over deep brown eyes.

Cradling the back of her head, Julian breathed in the scent of her before lowering his mouth onto hers. His lips were met with a hot, passionate kiss as Mena dug her nails into his back, holding on to him as if her life depended on it. Julian slid his hands along her naked body, resting against her waist. Savoring the taste of her sweet lips as she gyrated against his erection, sending his temperature through the roof. Slipping a hand against his waistband, he unbuttoned the pants, allowing them to fall to the floor. Easing out of his dust-covered, sweaty shirt, Julian stood still as Mena pushed his boxer briefs from his hips. She lowered her body in front of him, her tongue licking along the length of his cock as she forced the underwear to the floor.

Julian writhed with desire, grabbing Mena's arms as he dropped down to the floor. Mena straddled his waist, stroking him deftly. He grew more rigid, staring at her breasts, as she guided him inside her. Julian feasted on her body, caressing her nipples as she lowered herself onto him.

The low moan escaping her mouth as he filled every inch of her, tipped him over the edge. Mena's back arched as she bounced wildly against him, intensifying the pleasure surging between them. They reached a frenetic rhythm, spurred on by the sound of her calling his name over and over again. Julian watched her, mesmerized as his muscles constricted with powerful force and exploded into a tidal wave of an orgasm. Mena's cry filled the room as she collapsed down on him. Her heavy panting matched his own.

Julian held her tightly in his arms. Placing a kiss on her damp forehead, he whispered against her skin, "I love you."

Chapter Thirty-Seven

Julian awoke with a jolt, blinking quickly as his eyes struggled to focus. Muggy heat boiled within the confined space and clawed at his skin. Morning was transitioning into the blazing warmth of an African afternoon. Shifting to his elbows on the thin rug, he peered through the narrow hallway ahead, ignoring the stiffness of his muscles.

Where the hell was Mena?

Unnerved by the eerie quiet, Julian grabbed his clothes and slipped them back on. Reaching for the Beretta M9 resting underneath the coffee table, Julian secured it into his holster, then headed down the hallway.

He peeked around the corner. Mena sat at the table, peeling overripe bananas and cutting them into thin slices. A towel wrapped around her body. Her long legs crossed, one over the other, revealing the sexiest calves he'd ever seen. A thin sheen of sweat coated her face. She looked up at him and smiled, sending a flurry through his body.

Shaking her head, Mena said, "I was hoping you'd sleep a little longer, but I figured you'd wake up as soon as I left the room."

"How long was I in there by myself?" Julian asked, crossing the small kitchen and sitting next to her at the table. He couldn't bear being apart from her for even a second.

Mena raised an eyebrow and looked up at the ceiling, then replied, "Maybe sixty seconds."

Julian laughed. "Doesn't take me long to miss you, does it?"

"Nope. I love it, though. I found these bananas in the pantry, which is almost empty. Is this some kind of safe house or something?" Mena asked.

"Not exactly," Julian said, feeling guilty about breaking into the home. "I don't know who lives here."

"Are you serious? We just made love in some stranger's home, and they could be back at any time. Julian!" Mena said, dropping the crude knife she was using to slice the bananas.

"It was the only option, and we won't be here when they get back," Julian said.

"Where is here, exactly?" Mena asked.

"Giriftu in northeastern Kenya, about five hundred miles away from Nairobi. Zale, one of the TIDES team members, located this as a meeting point in case the rescue operation hit a snag. All the intel she had on this place indicated that whoever lives here isn't around often," Julian explained.

"And what if Zale is wrong?" Mena asked, pushing several slices of the banana toward him. "These people could come back and find us like goldilocks squatting in their home. What are we going to do?"

"They won't find us because we're leaving soon. Going to head toward Wajir to be picked up by Sunny," Julian said.

"Eat the bananas," Mena implored as she rubbed a hand through his hair, then kissed him on the neck. "We both need strength after everything that happened."

"Definitely need strength after what you just did to me," Julian teased. Reaching for her hand, he kissed it softly, then popped a couple of slices of banana in his mouth. "You wore me out. How am I going to have the strength to protect you now?"

"I don't want you to ever have to protect me again," Mena said, looking away from him.

Julian pulled her close, loving the feel of her arms wrapping around him. "I'll do what's necessary, and right now, that means getting you prepped for a long trek to Wajir County. Sunny should be on her way and she'll call once she's nearby. Until then, we keep moving toward the airstrip in Wajir."

"How nice of Sunny," Mena said, a hint of concern in her voice. "She must really care about you to risk her life to come and get us,"

"Hey, it's not like that at all," Julian said, trying to reassure her. At least it hadn't been like that in several years. "She was a special ops pilot in the Navy. She's actually the person who flew into Central Sulawesi and saved Broman and me after the massacre there. The mission that went to hell because of my mistake."

"A mistake that could have been made by anyone in the same circumstances. A mistake your entire SEAL team, including Broman, would have forgiven you for," Mena reminded him.

Julian was still getting used to not berating himself for his past. Mena was a big part of him moving on from the self-imposed exile he'd sentenced himself to after everyone in his SEAL team had been murdered with him and Broman as the lone survivors.

"You can't help but see the best in me, can you?" Julian smiled at Mena, stroking a finger down her face.

"Kind of hard not to when you keep saving my life," Mena said.

"I'm not doing that for you, I'm doing that for me. Told you I never want to know what it's like to be without you again," Julian said, placing a quick peck on her nose. "Come on, you need to get your clothes back on so we can head out. We've already been here too long."

"Five minutes and I'll be ready to go," Mena said, slipping from his embrace and heading back to the bathroom where her clothes were discarded on the floor.

Julian glanced at his watch.

Two hours since he'd talked to Hakeem.

Shouldn't he have heard back something by now?

A ringing pierced the air. "Speak of the devil."

Julian answered the comms. "Hello."

"You need to get the hell out of that house," Hakeem said, his words rushing out in frantic bursts. "Sunny and ASF are trying to get to you, but they're about twenty minutes out. Some rebel group is heading your way and almost at the house. Julian, they are heavily armed. Get the hell out now!"

Julian ended the call, then forced his body to relax as Mena stepped back into the kitchen, fully dressed.

"Everything okay?" Mena asked, emerging from the bathroom in her dust-covered button-down and dark trousers. Her hair was pulled back into a low ponytail at the back of her head. She looked refreshed and ready for whatever lay ahead.

Julian nodded. "Time to go."

He slung the backpack over one shoulder and picked up the M16 from the kitchen table. Mena followed close behind him as he crossed through the living room and opened the door.

Stepping outside on the porch, Julian stopped. The air was laced with danger, tense and stagnant. He turned back to look at Mena, motioning for her to remain inside.

A sharp blow hurled into his back. Julian pitched forward, the ground approaching his face faster than he could brace himself for the fall. The M16 flew from his hand, bouncing forward out of his reach. As his head hit the hard-packed earth, an explosion of pain ricocheted throughout his skull. Julian blinked, trying to focus as darkness shrouded his eyes. With a last glance, he saw Mena, jerking against the men holding her, crying out as she reached for him.

Then his world went black.

Chapter Thirty-Eight

Disoriented, Julian reached for a cup of water from the table next to
his hospital bed. The plastic cup was out of reach. Stretching his
fingers, he tipped over the water pitcher, sending it careening to the
floor.

"Let me get that for you," Sunny said, rushing to the side of the
bed. "I didn't realize you'd woken up."

Julian didn't respond, trying to swallow past the rough, dryness in
his throat. Sunny squatted next to the bed, setting the pitcher upright
then swiped at the water spreading across the floor with a small towel.
Standing, she shook the container, then poured what was left inside
the cup and handed it to him. Julian took a sip of the lukewarm water
and gagged, but continued to drink until it was gone.

"How long was I out this time?" he asked. He'd regained
consciousness briefly as the helicopter landed at the airstrip, and he
was placed into an ambulance. As the EMTs rushed him to the
hospital, he'd shared pertinent details with Sunny about Mena's second
abduction.

Sunny tilted her head, glancing at her watch. "Almost twenty-four
hours."

"Are you fucking serious?" Julian barked, leaning forward. A dull ache slammed through his head, making him dizzy, and he eased himself back against the pillows.

"You suffered a severe concussion, and considering that you had a fractured skull several months ago, the doctors weren't expecting you to be fully conscious for a while," Sunny said.

"Did you find Mena?" Julian asked.

Sunny shook her head. "Not yet. Glaze and Enzo are back in Wajir County, leading the TIDES search. ASF has two teams in the area as well, searching for Mena."

Frowning, Julian read the name of the hospital on the side of the water pitcher.

"Where the hell am I?" Julian asked, feeling his anger building.

"I brought you back to Nairobi—"

"Why did you do that?" Julian demanded. "I need to be close to the search, so I can join the team and help find Mena!"

"You were in no condition to help anyone, let alone Mena. You need to focus on getting better," Sunny said.

"Flying me 500 miles away was fucking overkill. Any clinic in Wajir or Garissa would have been better than this. I've had concussions plenty of times before," Julian said.

"I didn't know what the fuck was wrong with you!" Sunny screamed at him. "All I knew was it felt like history was fucking repeating itself, and you were unconscious being dragged onto my helo ... again. Excuse me if I wanted to take you to the best hospital, just like I did the last damn time."

Julian took a deep breath. "I'm sorry."

"No, you're not. You're pissed at me, and I'm okay with that. If I had to do it again, I'd do the same damn thing. I think Mena would back me up on that and I know her parents do," Sunny said, slumping down into the chair in the corner.

"Her parents?" Julian asked. "How did they find out what happened to Mena?"

"After the museum explosion, they got concerned that they couldn't reach her. Seems like they have some elite connections. Wangari said they flew over this morning in a private 747 owned by Aurora Nathaniel."

"Who is that?"

"Only the second richest woman in France and the mother of Leo Bronson, who owns the *Palmchat Gazette* where Mena's dad works," Sunny said.

"Where are they now?" Julian asked.

"At Wangari's family estate. They've been fully briefed on the details of what happened. Her mother wanted to come to the hospital to see you, but I told her to wait until we knew more about your condition."

"I need to get out of here, Sunny. Dee and Caleb need me to bring their daughter back to them, safe and sound. You've got to take me back to Wajir County."

"I will, as soon as the doctors release you. Somebody should be here soon to check on you," Sunny said.

Julian drummed his fingers against the mattress as impatience threatened to push him over the edge. He was wasting time lying in this bed when Mena was out there.

"Any idea who ambushed us?"

"No, but if I had to guess, I'd say al-Harakat. Reggie thinks whoever did it was acting on Tubeec's request, which is why they didn't bother killing you," Sunny said.

"Why does Tubeec want Mena? What use could she possibly have to him?" Julian asked.

Sunny shifted in the chair, resting her elbows on the armrests as she stared into the distance. Julian waited, knowing she was going to tell him something he didn't want to hear. But he needed to hear it. He needed to understand what was going on in Tubeec Hirad's sick fucking mind.

After several seconds of silence, Sunny said, "Tubeec is driven by inflicting pain on others. He wants the world to suffer the same pain he went through as he watched his wife and twin boys being tortured and killed. He wants you to suffer like he did. Allowing you to watch Mena being taken away from you, knowing you were helpless to stop it ... he wants that to haunt you for the rest of your life. Just like he's haunted."

"But why me and Mena? What put us on his radar?" Julian asked.

"I'm not sure ..."

"Crazy bastard," Julian muttered under his breath.

"It's even worse than that," Sunny said.

"How can it be worse than that?" Julian asked.

"Okeyo and his office lost all the evidence against Rono. The files were destroyed. All copies on all known servers. No trace of them anywhere," Sunny said.

"That's impossible," Julian said.

"I know. That's what makes this whole thing crazy. Some kind of way, Tubeec made it happen. Rono gets what he wanted. No evidence exists anymore that could be used against him and he's free to run for President without fear of being indicted or convicted for past wrongdoings," Sunny said.

"Now I really don't understand why Tubeec cared that Mena got away. Why try to get her back?"

"Maybe because she made a fool of him and his elite team of mercenaries. Tubeec can't allow that to go unpunished, or it will weaken the fear he wields across the continent. He has to make an example out of Mena by ..."

"What?" Julian said, ice-cold settling in his veins.

"I promise you, we're doing everything we can to find her ... before it's too late," Sunny said.

Jerking the I.V. and wires from his body, Julian threw the hospital covers on the floor and stood up.

"What are you doing?" Sunny said, rushing toward him.

Julian stumbled, then regained his bearings as the room stopped spinning. "Where are my clothes? I'm going back to find Mena."

"We don't even know where she is, and you aren't strong enough yet to be any use to the teams searching for her. Get back in bed," Sunny implored, grabbing at his arm.

Julian pushed her away. "I have to find Mena."

The door to his hospital room opened. Reggie Kamau stepped inside, his face creased with concern.

"Actually, you don't," Reggie said, walking over to Julian. "My team found Mena. She's alive ... barely."

Chapter Thirty-Nine

The sound of the long-hand of the clock ticked loudly.

Only an hour had passed since Reggie had given him the devastating news about Mena. Wangari was flying to the hospital in Wajir with Mena's parents in the Irungu family jet. He'd had offers from Reggie and Sunny to take him there, but Julian had refused to go.

He would join them later. He wasn't ready to go through the torrent of emotions in front of an audience.

The woman he loved, left for dead on a dirt road outside of Wajir, brutally violated. The act had weakened Reggie's resolve that al-Harakat was behind the attack. Rebel groups in the area were more likely the culprit for a kidnapping and violent rape.

Mena was suffering from internal bleeding and undergoing emergency surgery, which might last several hours. Once they'd assessed the extent of her injuries, more surgeries could be needed.

It would be several hours before he could see Mena again.

Touch her.

Hold her.

Stumbling out of the hospital against doctor's orders, Julian had refused Sunny's offer, and instead he'd had hailed a taxi. At first, he didn't know where to go. His mind was a jumbled mess, trying to process the information Reggie had shared. He couldn't think clearly. All he wanted was to be away from Sunny and Reggie, to be away from the truth of what had happened to Mena.

Sitting in the back of the cab, Julian had barked, "Just drive."

The cab driver had obliged, weaving in and out of traffic through the heart of downtown Nairobi until Julian felt a magnetic pull to be in the one place that could help him focus.

"Westlands, Siren Condominiums," Julian had said after twenty minutes. The cab had taken him to the home he shared with Mena in record time. Swiping the key card, he walked inside the apartment and almost crumbled to the floor as Mena's familiar scent of sandalwood and orange hit him like a ton of bricks. Staggering toward the slate-gray couch, he slid down onto the cushions. His eyes drifted to the wall where he'd made love to Mena. Julian reached a hand over and stroked the surface, wishing he could be back in that moment, when Mena was safe and unhurt, before Tubeec Hirad had inflicted this terror upon their lives.

Julian turned and punched his fist into the wall. Pain radiated in his knuckles, but it did nothing to stop the anger and sadness warring within him. He punched the wall more, harder, hands flying against the light gray surface. Splotches of red from his bleeding fists staining the surface.

He'd failed to protect her.

The pain she'd suffered was his fault.

He should have left the house in Giriftu immediately after talking to Hakeem. Sticking around to indulge his own pleasures was foolish. He knew better. His own stupid mistakes had led to the ambush.

Just like in Central Sulawesi.

When would he learn?

How many lives had to be destroyed before he got his shit together?

Panting and sweating, Julian fell backward onto the couch, his hands swollen and bloody. Rage seethed through his body as bloodlust rose within him, fueling a desire for revenge and retribution. Thoughts of hunting down each of the bastards who'd attacked Mena and placing bullets between their eyes consumed him.

A soft knock rapped against the door in quick succession.

"Fuck," Julian shouted at the empty room. The last thing he needed was some nosy neighbor coming to check to see if everything was alright.

Things weren't alright.

They might never be alright again.

Crossing the space, Julian reached the door opening it wide.

"Found you," Sunny said, pushing past him and stepping inside the room.

Julian squeezed his eyes shut, not in the mood to talk.

"Get out," Julian said, as he clutched the edge of the open door.

Sunny crossed through the foyer into the kitchen, opening the pantry and then the cabinet doors.

"What the hell are you doing?"

"I'm looking for your stash of vodka. I'm not going to let this turn out like last time," Sunny said.

Julian pushed the door closed and leaned against it, sliding down to the floor. Sunny had been an eyewitness to the devastating guilt that had consumed Julian as Broman endured multiple surgeries. He'd swallowed a bottle of pain killers and drowned himself in a case of vodka stashed in the trunk of his sedan while sitting in the hospital parking lot. Julian had been listless when Sunny found him.

"I would have died that night, if it weren't for you," Julian whispered.

"I was so pissed at you. We were all at the prayer vigil for Broman and your ass was nowhere in sight. I fully planned to make you pay for missing it until I found you out there, almost dead ... I can't go through that again. I can't be the one who continues to find you when you are broken." Sunny grabbed a towel and turned on the faucet.

"I'm sorry."

"You know, I didn't know it was your SEAL team I was flying the helo to rescue. When I saw Emilio pulling Broman's body inside, my heart stopped. Then I saw your face and it was like you didn't recognize us at all. Like you were looking through us at something only you could see. Then you passed out."

"I thought that was the worse day of my life," Julian said.

"Until today? When you found out what happened to Mena." Sunny sat next to him, took his hands and gently cleaned the blood from his knuckles. "None of this is your fault. You did everything you could to protect Mena."

"I made too many mistakes. I took risks I shouldn't have and she's paying the price for it," Julian said.

"Mena is in this situation because of Tubeec, not you. Don't beat yourself up over something that he did. He kidnapped Mena, sending us all down this horrible path," Sunny said.

"What if she doesn't make it? What if her last moments on earth were being ..." Julian choked on the words, unable to say them out loud.

"Trust me, she's going to make it. Anyone who's loved Julian Montgomery knows how hard it is to walk away from him. She's going to fight and claw her way back to health to be with you. Mark my words," Sunny said.

"I hope you're right," Julian said, looking up at Sunny.

Sunny continued, "Right now, you need to focus on praying for her and loving her and supporting her. She needs to feel that coming from you and her whole family. That's what's going to get her through this nightmare."

"You're right. I need to get to Wajir." Julian wanted Mena to feel his presence and his love and he couldn't do that from five hundred miles away. He was going to wait outside her operating room and remind her of all the reasons why she needed to get better. The life that they shared and the life they still had ahead of them.

"The offer from ASF still stands. Their team could fly you there in a little over an hour," Sunny said. "Come on, I'll drive you."

"Thanks Sunny."

"Anytime Montgomery."

Chapter Forty

The wide steel double doors opened toward Julian, revealing the inner sanctum of the ASF ComCentral. Stepping inside, Julian heard the rants and screams of a man in obvious emotional pain. Several agents stood rigid near the door, rooted to their positions, eyes locked on the man stalking back and forth.

Julian glanced over at Sunny, who gave him a quizzical look back.

Pushing past one of the agents, Julian stepped inside and watched the man berating another agent. A man he recognized.

Caleb Olivier.

What the hell was Mena's father doing here? Why wasn't he at the hospital in Wajir?

Julian spotted Mena's mother, Dee, sitting in a chair near a computer monitor across the room. Her face splotchy and red as tears dripped off the end of her nose. She was the spitting image of her only child with the same mesmerizing brown eyes and stunning smile. Her skin was several shades lighter than Mena's and most would mistake her for Mena's older sister rather than her mother.

"You are incompetent and you are liars!" Caleb screamed at Agent Betts, standing stoic near a row of monitors displaying changing screens of arid desert lands. Caleb stalked over to another agent standing near the path to Reggie's office. He pointed his finger at the man's face as he continued, "That poor woman's family is still clueless about what happened to their child. Dee and I have wasted hours praying over a woman who isn't our daughter! You think 'I'm sorry' is good enough for the hell you've put us through?"

"Sir, we have alerted Chief Agent Kamau and he is on his way back to headquarters to speak to you about this situation. Can I ask you to please calm down and have a seat while we wait for him to return?" Agent Betts asked.

"Calm down? Have a seat? You didn't lose my luggage. You lost my daughter!" Caleb screamed, as he turned slowly, staring daggers at each agent he made eye contact with. "Why are you just sitting around here? Get out there and find Mena!"

"Mr. Olivier. We must wait until Chief Agent Kamau returns to be briefed on these developments before we proceed to reinstitute the search for Mena," Agent Betts tried to explain.

"Reinstitute the search?" Sunny whispered.

Julian's mind was reeling.

The woman at the hospital wasn't Mena.

She was still out there. But where?

"What the hell happened?" Julian asked. He stepped around the agents and walked over to Agent Betts.

Caleb paused mid-sentence and turned to glare at Julian. "It's about damn time you got here! That woman going through all those surgeries at the hospital is not Mena. She's not my daughter. The nurse came over about four hours after we'd arrived acting real nervous, explaining that Mena had lost so much blood and they were running low on her blood type."

Dee stood from her chair and walked over to stand between Agent Betts, Julian, Sunny, and Caleb, then said, "Julian, they wanted us to give blood and of course we were willing to, but then the nurse said that Mena's blood type was so rare, O negative, and the hospital didn't have much of that blood left in inventory."

"Mena's not O negative. She's A like me," Julian said, frowning.

"Like me and her mother! That's how we knew that poor woman was not our daughter!" Caleb exploded.

"What if we don't find her because everybody stopped looking? What if we never find her?" Dee asked, her words soft and haunted by the fears she likely never wanted to express.

"What happened?" Julian asked Agent Betts.

"None of this is making any sense. How did the mix-up occur?" Sunny asked.

"Don't say another word," Reggie's voice boomed as he stormed into the room, flanked by four other agents. Reggie waved a hand, sending the four agents through the room to regain order and issue new directions to the team.

Walking over to Dee and Caleb, Reggie said, "I've been apprised of the mistaken identity of the female patient at the Wajir hospital. I cannot express to you how awful I feel about the stress you've endured today, thinking that Mena was in such a horrible condition. Please accept my deepest regrets and rest assured that my team will be re-evaluating our efforts to find your daughter."

Turning to Sunny, Reggie said, "In my office. Now."

Julian watched as Sunny bristled under the direct command.

Dee looked away, swiping a tear as it fell from her eyes.

Caleb glanced at Dee and his features softened as he looped his arm in hers. Pointing a finger at Julian, he said, "Don't you let them go looking for our daughter without you. These fools couldn't find their nose on their face. You and your team saved Wangari Irungu and you are the only one I trust to get out there and actually bring my daughter back home!"

Dee's hopeful eyes looked up at Julian. Eyes so similar to Mena's staring back at him.

"Trust me, with or without Reggie's team, I will find Mena," Julian said. "Why don't the two of you go wait in the conference room and I'll let you know as soon as we have a plan."

Dee and Caleb agreed, then followed Agent Betts out of the room and down the hallway toward the conference room.

Sunny pulled Julian toward Reggie's office. "Something is off. Reggie's likely going to stall, claiming classified intelligence for his information. But we need to get something, anything to start our own search for Mena. I've already texted Enzo. He and Glaze are back at

TIDES trying to reconstruct everything we know and analyze where Mena could be."

Stepping into Reggie's office, Julian closed the door behind him and walked to the chairs in front of Reggie's desk.

Reggie stiffened, his hands clenching into fists as he leaned against the towering bookcases lining the wall.

"How did your guys miss this?" Sunny asked. "Do you know how much time has been wasted because your team failed to do a proper ID?"

"Why is he in here? Shouldn't you go and console Mena's parents while Sunny and I strategize?" Reggie asked, looking over Julian at Sunny.

"He loves Mena! He deserves to be in here more than I do," Sunny said.

"When did you start caring about a man loving a woman?" Reggie asked, shaking his head in disgust. "It's bad enough the Irungus are wielding their power and forcing my team of highly trained special operatives to deal with your little band of military rejects, but now you are parading your ex-lover in my face? He's making a fool of you, getting you to help him find the woman he really wants to be with. News flash—it's not you."

Julian stood and walked over to Reggie.

"You don't know the first fucking thing about my relationship with Sunny. You don't know the things we've been through, the pain we've shared and the losses we've endured. I'm not going to sit here while you disrespect her. We are here for one reason. To find Mena. So act like a big boy and put your emotions to the side, okay," Julian said.

The force of the blow to his face stunned Julian, the ache emanating across his left jaw. The metallic taste of blood on the tip of his tongue. Another one-two punch slamming into Julian's gut sent him stumbling across the desk. Reggie connected with two more blows to his head, sending lights popping behind his eyes.

"Stop it!" Sunny screamed, rushing over to the desk. "We don't have time for this!"

Julian pushed Reggie off him and rolled onto the floor, sucking in breaths. He turned back to Reggie. "Feel better now? Feel like a man?"

Reggie stalked behind his desk and slumped into his chair, anger wafting from him.

Sunny leaned over and helped Julian stand.

"Are you okay?"

"Trust me, I've gotten my ass kicked worse than this and you know it," Julian said.

Sunny gave him a small smile, no doubt remembering the beat down Julian had suffered when their secret had come out all those long years ago.

"I'm going to say this one time, Reggie, and then you need to get past this. The problems in our relationship have nothing to do with Julian. He isn't the reason why I can't marry you. Now can we get back to what's important here?" Sunny asked.

"ASF has been unable to recover the files on the ODPP server that incriminated Kipsang Rono. It's like they never existed. Now Tubeec is walking around with the only copy of that evidence and President Thairu has ordered that we find it," Reggie said.

Julian's blood boiled. He banged his fists against Reggie's desk. "What does this have to do with Mena?"

"It means that I don't have enough resources to track Tubeec Hirad and try to find your girlfriend. The President has made our directive clear. I believe Tubeec may have Mena and if that is the case, we will rescue her when we capture him."

"And what if she isn't?" Julian asked.

Reggie shrugged. "We have a bigger threat to deal with. Finding Mena is no longer a priority for the ASF."

Chapter Forty-One

"Motherfucking bastard! How the hell did you ever fuck around with him for so long?" Enzo pushed away from the table and stalked to the corner of the conference room inside TIDES HQ.

Julian and Sunny had finished debriefing the team about restarting the search for Mena after the ASF botched the rescue mission, misidentifying another woman found near Wajir as the love of Julian's life.

"My love life, or lack thereof, is irrelevant right now," Sunny said, slipping into the leather chair at the head of the conference room table.

Julian stood near the door, his mind calculating the best way to make up the valuable time they'd lost. Glaze and Enzo flanked Sunny, while Zale, Simon, and Taye sat towards the opposite end. There were two empty seats.

"Where's Hakeem and Shiloh?" Julian asked. They would need the entire team searching for Mena.

Taye said, "Hakeem left for the Ukraine a couple of days ago. He's leading the security detail for a delivery of art to some Ukranian businessman." He raised his fingers in air quotes on the last word. "Not sure when he's due back."

"Shiloh is wrapping up a personal trip in South Africa, but won't be back until tomorrow night," Zale said.

"Going to hurt not having Hakeem and Shiloh here, but we'll have to make do without them," Sunny said, a look of concern crossing her face. "What's the chatter on Tubeec's latest mayhem?"

"Not surprising, he's already spread the word about his attack on the Office of the Director of Public Prosecutions' databases and servers, destroying critical evidence against several criminals awaiting trials. No direct mention of the evidence against Rono that was destroyed, but he was most likely responsible for that, too. It's all over the dark web and spreading like wildfire through the militant groups in East Africa," Glaze explained.

Simon added, "We also have good intel that suggests Tubeec is still in the area of northeastern Kenya or southern Ethiopia. He's staying close for some reason, which helps us narrow the search."

"Any word on Mena?" Julian asked, stepping toward the dark wood table. He pressed his palms on the surface, willing himself to stay calm. Mena needed him at his best, gathering information, paying attention to every detail, so he could find her and bring her home.

"Radio silent on that one, which is odd," Glaze said. "Tubeec is not one to hide his exploits. If he was trying to make an example out of Mena, we'd know by now."

"What could that mean?" Simon asked.

"Fuck if I know. Tubeec is crazy as shit and unpredictable," Enzo said.

"Sunny," Julian said, a heavy knot weighting in his stomach. "What does it mean?"

The TIDES team stared at Julian, confusion crossing their faces, then turned to look at their leader.

Sunny ran her fingers through her dark curly hair, gripping the tresses tightly in her hands as she leaned back in the chair. Her expression worried Julian.

"Good news and bad," Sunny said, after several seconds.

"Start with the good. We need that," Taye said.

"We don't know what happened to Mena Nix because Tubeec doesn't want us to. He's keeping her ... alive, for some reason."

"Well, that gives me something to work with," Glaze said, reaching to the console resting in the center of the table. He tapped on the screen, and the screensaver dancing across the monitors lining the room disappeared. "I'll start with the satellite imagery we have from the time when Julian and Mena were ambushed at the house in Giriftu. From there, I can triangulate the most likely routes taken."

"Yeah, but taken to where?" Enzo blurted out. "How the hell are we supposed to know where that crazy fuck would take Mena?"

"Remote rebel compounds and rural airstrips," Julian said. "Find the most obscure ones near Wajir County. Tubeec needs to hide again and this time, he'll be sure to pick a location that's even harder to be discovered."

"I'll pull up the drone photos Sunny took of northeastern Kenya. We can cycle through those to see if there are places with the infrastructure that his team would need to hideout," Zale said.

Taye, Zale, Simon, and Glaze turned their attention to developing a search and rescue strategy for the team.

"Wait a minute. What's the bad news, Sunny?" Enzo asked, pacing back and forth. He was the least tech-savvy, making him useless for this part of the work, but he was the best on the ground, hand-to-hand combat, member of the team.

"Tubeec lost a lot of men because of us. He's probably paid al-Harakat to provide extra protection to his team from another surprise attack. We were outnumbered before, but now the difference is going to be staggering," Sunny said.

"We'll have to work smarter, not harder." Julian walked over to Sunny and leaned against the edge of the table next to her. His hand dropped next to hers, touching it slightly. "Is there anything else?"

"The reason Tubeec could be keeping Mena alive might be personal," Sunny said, her voice barely above a whisper. "He may have grown fond of her and wants her to stick around."

Sunny had never told him the details of what she'd gone through that year Tubeec had her. But Julian had heard about what happened to women Tubeec staked his claim on. His obsessive determination to capture a woman, and force her to be his mistress, lasted until he grew bored or found another woman to obsess over.

Being Tubeec's forced concubine would inflict a pain he wasn't sure Mena could ever overcome. He would not let that happen to her.

Julian would kill Tubeec Hirad first.

"I need to get her away from him," Julian said, a sickening dread washing over him.

An hour later, Julian huddled around the monitors with the TIDES team and analyzed the likely routes taken by Tubeec's men. Four glowing red circles emerged on the map, all within northeast Kenya.

"Four possible locations where they could be hiding," Glaze said, then pointed at two of them. "Based on everything we know about Tubeec and factoring in his penchant for unpredictable and wild whims, I'm fairly certain these two are the most likely locations where Mena is being kept. I'm waiting on more recent satellite images to confirm recent movements in the area.

Julian pointed at another monitor. "To get in and out of any of these locations, he has to use either this airstrip near Wajir or this one in Mandera, near the Ethiopia and Somalia border. The only other airstrip that could be used is the Irungu Family private strip next to the horticultural center they're building on the outskirts of El Wak," Julian said.

"He'd attract too much attention trying to use that one. Timothy Irungu's team would know immediately if there was a breach at their private airstrip, alerting everyone of his location," Zale said.

"I confirmed no unusual activity at those two airstrips. I'm waiting on a call back from the security team at the Irungu horticultural construction site to determine if they've noticed anything out of the ordinary out there," Taye said.

Staring at the map, Julian calculated the distance between the four locations as over 250 miles. There was no way they could cover all that terrain quickly. Time was not on their side.

"We've got to split up," Julian said. "There's no way we can cover that distance in time."

Sunny agreed. "We won't have to. Timothy Irungu has handed over his entire security team to work with us and Wangari has wired more money than we'd ever need to fund our search."

"When did that happen?" Julian asked, impressed with how quickly

Wangari and her father had stepped in to help after ASF turned their backs on looking for Mena.

"Just a few minutes ago. I called them and they were more than happy and willing to help. Wangari wants nothing more than for Mena to be found and brought home safely, like she was," Sunny explained.

"So, we can narrow down the most likely locations and cover those ourselves. The Irungu security teams can cover the two other areas Zale found and fan out to search the surrounding areas between all the locations," Julian said.

"I'll work on getting a contractor to join me, Zale, and Simon to cover Giriftu, where the ambush occurred," Sunny said.

"Taye, Enzo, Glaze and I will head out now, and investigate the area near Takaba," Julian said.

"Timothy Irungu offered up his private airstrip in El Wak as our muster point after we've finished searching. It's the midpoint of all four spots. Communication is key, so let's all stay connected with regular updates and activated trackers, got it," Sunny said.

"We don't have enough shit to do this right. Sunny, you gotta call Paul Defloria. Get his ass up and ready to hand over the equipment we need before we head to the hangar," Enzo said.

"I'm calling him now," Sunny said, then turned to look up at Julian. "Good luck."

Chapter Forty-Two

"You must be Julian Montgomery. Sorry to hear about your lady. It's a damn shame," Paul Defloria said, stepping away from the door to allow Julian to enter. Paul was a short man, lean and petite with a head full of silver hair contrasting with his tan, leathery skin.

"Where do I sign?" Julian asked, not in the mood for small talk. They had over a hundred miles to search tonight and he was anxious to get back to northeastern Kenya.

Paul shuffled through papers, occasionally placing several of them on a clipboard. "Enzo and Glaze out there with my guys, right? It took some wrangling but I managed to get everything you'll need for the rescue. Damn shame how this happens to women in those rural areas. Terrorists using women for sport or to kill, damaging, and changing their lives with their cruel acts."

Julian scribbled his name next to the large highlighted X's on the five sheets of paper, then handed the clipboard back to Paul. Reaching into his pocket, he pulled the TIDES corporate card out and slid it across the desk.

"Mr. Paul, all the provisions are loaded on the helicopter," a voice Julian recognized floated from behind.

"Uhuru?" Julian stood and walked over to the teenage boy, who a week ago had almost lost his life when he was forced to be a suicide bomber at the private fundraising dinner for the president of Kenya. The kid looked good.

"Julian!" Uhuru said, then flung his arms around Julian.

Patting the boy on the back, Julian returned the hug and got a brief reprieve from the pain weighing on his heart.

"What are you doing here?" Julian asked, casting a glance back at Paul.

"Mr. DeFloria gave me a job. Now I can support myself and my sisters. It is a miracle that the police found them near Kibera. The bad men left them there the same night they sent me to bomb the fundraising dinner," Uhuru explained.

"And they are alright? Both of them?" Julian asked. A happy ending like this was rare and it couldn't have happened to a better kid.

"Yes, they are doing well. I'm so thankful for everything you did for me," Uhuru said, then paused. Concern creasing his forehead, he asked, "Are you part of the team searching for the missing American woman?"

"I am. The missing woman is my girlfriend," Julian said, then paused as his voice cracked with emotion.

"No, no, no," Uhuru said, shaking his head, eyes wide with concern. "I'm so sorry she was taken. If there is anything I can do to help, please tell me. I owe you so much. I owe you my life!"

"Thanks, but we got it under control. My buddies and I are flying out now to start the search," Julian managed to choke out.

"Hey, we're losing valuable time. Need to get the fuck out of here." Enzo barged inside, waving a hand at Julian.

Julian gave Uhuru another quick hug, then walked out of the small box of an office within the corrugated warehouse and made his way toward the back of the property where aircraft hangars lined the road. The helo sat outside the hangar, the blades starting to turn slowly as Taye prepped for take-off.

Walking out into the warm night air, Julian looked up at the stars peppering the sky. He wondered if Mena could see the same sky. Was she looking up, praying that he would come to rescue her soon? Or was she already—

Julian's phone buzzed in his pocket.

Grabbing it quickly, he glanced at the screen. Unknown number.

Answering it, Julian said, "Yeah."

"Julian ... oh, God ... I can't believe I finally got through to you!"

Julian felt his legs go weak as he stopped in the middle of the lot. He closed his eyes, willing himself to stay calm. "Mena? Is that you?"

"Yes! Yes! It's me. I'm fine. Oh God! Julian, I miss you so much! I didn't know if I'd be able to get through to you," Mena said, her voice choked with emotion as she cried on the line.

Heart racing, Julian said, "Mena, listen to me. Tell me where you are. I'm coming to get you. Tell me where you are."

The line was silent.

Julian closed his eyes, focusing on the sound of her ragged breaths as she cried. The connection was faint, but he could still hear her on the line.

Mena sniffed, then said, "I'm sorry. No, don't worry. I'm fine. I'm at the safe house ... signal ... bad ... couldn't get through to you ... finally ... will be driving back ... tomorrow ... Tubeec Hirad still after me ... be back ... morning ..."

Julian could barely make out her answer as the cell phone reception crackled and faded in and out.

"What safe house?" Julian asked, his words slow and measured. Glancing up at the helicopter, he motioned for Glaze and Enzo to come over to where he was. He didn't want to move for fear of losing the signal. "Who is with you?"

"Julian? Julian? Are you there? I can't hear you ..." Mena's voice grew more frantic.

"I'm here. Can you hear me? Mena! Mena!" Julian said.

"I hear you! I love you, Julian. This phone is so bad ... so hard ... spotty ... trying to call ... glad ... "

Julian clenched his fist, fighting frustration as the reception distorted Mena's words.

"Mena, who are you with? Where are you?" Julian asked.

"What? Julian? ... did you ... what? Safe house ... with him ... got me ... out ... he rescued me ... I'm okay ... miss you so much."

"Mena, honey listen to me. Tell me who's there with you," Julian said, his words coming out slowly as the reception grew fainter.

"Stay there ... too dangerous ... Tubeec ... will kill you ... coming home ... stay ... I'm fine ... kept ..."

"Mena?"

" ... leaving in morning ..."

"Who is bringing you back? Let me talk to him," Julian said, changing his tactics. "Mena, I want to talk to who is with you now!"

"Hold on ..." Mena said.

He heard the rustling of movement.

Her words were faint, but he listened intently, straining to hear the name she called.

The line went dead.

"Fuck!" Julian said, glancing at the cell phone.

He couldn't call back.

Had he heard the name correctly? The one Mena had said after he asked to speak to the person with her.

Had she said ... Hakeem?

Chapter Forty-Three

Hakeem's heavy hand slammed like a shackle onto her wrist as he snatched the cell phone from her hand.

Heart pounding, Mena looked at Hakeem. The fading sunlight wasn't enough to mask the anger and annoyance clouding his eyes as he frowned at her.

"Who did you call?" Hakeem demanded, his thumbs flying across the screen of the phone.

"I'm sorry—" Mena stumbled backward on the jagged rocks submerged in the rust-colored sand. The stars popped out in the sky, as the moon emerged, casting an eerie glow.

"Bullshit! You just put your life *and mine* in danger. Don't you know Tubeec Hirad has been waiting for a chance to track this cell phone? And you handed him the opportunity he wanted. Who the fuck was so important for you to call?" Hakeem asked, glaring at her.

Twisting against the vice grip on her wrist, Mena felt a sharp pain shooting up her arm. Hakeem yanked her back toward him.

"The cell phone had a few signal bars, so I called Julian. I just needed to hear his voice," Mena tried to explain, the words tumbling from her mouth as she fought panic. "I didn't think you would mind. You made a few calls to TIDES today."

"I encrypted the phone before I made every call. I told you we needed to lay low and keep communications to a minimum for our own safety. Damn it! Wasn't good enough for you that I finally found a way to get us back to Nairobi without tipping Tubeec off. You had to ruin shit by trying to call your boyfriend? Unbelievable," Hakeem said.

Hakeem's outburst stunned her into silence. She'd been careless. Mena had thought the worst was over. Knowing Julian had survived the ambush by Tubeec's men had been the only thing keeping her going.

For the past two days, she'd hidden out with Hakeem riding on the back of a rusted motorbike, avoiding the main roads and zigzagging across northeastern Kenya trying to avoid capture by the band of rebels who'd been offered top dollar to return her to Tubeec Hirad. As they passed through tribal villages, the warnings had been the same each time. Tubeec wanted her found and brought back to him. Some of the villages had already been threatened and pillaged by militants or members of al-Harakat, trying to see if they were hiding Mena. Others refused to shelter them, fearing they would bring death and mayhem to their settlements.

They'd finally arrived at the safe house, but Hakeem had warned her they couldn't stay long. He needed to get a message back to TIDES headquarters, which hadn't been possible with the spotty cell service in the rural areas. It wasn't until this morning that he'd made contact and secured a plan to get them back to Nairobi in a new vehicle under the cloak of night.

Mena held up her hands. "Hakeem, I'm sorry. I messed up and it won't happen again. I'm beyond grateful that you risked your own life to save me. It's a miracle that you were able to overtake the rebels and I can't thank you enough."

The surprise attack at the small blue house had wrecked Mena. Two men had jumped Julian, knocking him out. Mena was dragged away and shoved into an old, ragged SUV. The ignition roared to life and the vehicle took off down the road, leaving Mena staring through the back window, convinced Julian's life had ended right then and there.

Hours later, when the driver stopped to refuel, she found out the truth. Hakeem Underwood, one of the security guards and rescue agents with Tactical and Intelligence Defense Executive Services, emerged from the store, catching the gunmen off guard. Gun pointed at the men's heads, while their weapons lay on the front seats of the SUV, Hakeem had forced one of the men to tie the other up, then knocked him out and tied him up next to the other.

Mena watched it happen through the side window, but she could do nothing to free herself and run away, which made it all the better when Hakeem slid into the front seat and introduced himself. He was here to rescue her and yes, Julian was alive and being transported back to Nairobi by the rest of the TIDES team.

"I don't need your gratitude or your apologies. What I need is for you to follow my instructions and not do anything that could jeopardize us getting back to Nairobi tomorrow. Think you can do that?" Hakeem asked, slamming the cell phone onto the ground. Lifting his leg, he stomped his army boot on top of the small device, leaving it splintered in the sand.

Mena nodded. "I'm confused because Julian didn't seem to know that I was with you."

"That's because I haven't been talking to Julian. He's in the hospital recovering from the injuries from the attack. I don't know if the rest of the team told him what was going on. Last I heard he was still in and out of consciousness," Hakeem said. "I thought since I saved your life, that would give me a little bit of trust, but I guess I was wrong."

"I'm sorry. I do trust you." Mena covered her face in her hands, trying to ward off the panic building within her. The look on Hakeem's face said everything she hadn't realized. They were still in extreme danger.

Hakeem said, "Let me explain something to you. I made two calls to TIDES today. Each time, I initiated an encryption coding to prevent the cell phone from being traced and I monitored the length of time of each call to prevent an override of the encryption. Ask me why I did that."

Mena looked up at him, but said nothing. She knew she'd screwed up and now, she was about to find out the awful truths Hakeem had been shielding her from.

"Because Tubeec Hirad has top-notch hackers working for him, scouring the calls coming into TIDES in hopes of tracking us and finding us before we can get back to Nairobi. Your call to Julian gave him the opening he's been waiting for, all because you couldn't wait a few more hours to hear Julian's fucking voice? I'm one hundred percent sure that Tubeec is locking in on our location as we speak and dispersing a team of killers to this safe house to recapture you. Guess what he's going to do if he finds you. Come on, now. Guess!"

Trembling, Mena refused to let the tears fall. She hadn't considered that Tubeec could still find her before she and Hakeem made their way back to Nairobi.

"I'll tell you what he's going to do. The same thing he did to my sister. He's going to force you to be his fucking sex slave for daring to try to escape from him. You'll be dragged all across Africa as he kidnaps and kills for money and sometimes just for the sport of it. All your fancy education and art credentials will mean nothing. You'll be reduced to the pussy he fucks when the whim strikes him. If he likes you, he'll keep the others away from you. If he doesn't, he'll let any of the guys on his team fuck you too when they get horny enough. Is that what you want? Is it?" Hakeem screamed at her.

"I'm sorry, I didn't know ... " Mena stammered, fear gripping her heart at the disgusting scenes playing out in her mind. She'd heard the stories of human and sex trafficking, the horrible acts women were subjected to until they were deemed no longer useful and then killed.

"We need to get out of here. Now. I can't wait for the provisions and transportation TIDES was arranging for us. We've got to take a chance and take the most direct route to Nairobi tonight."

"How long is that going to take?" Mena asked.

Hakeem cut his eyes toward her, his jaw clenched. "Fifteen, maybe sixteen hours through al-Harakat territories, driving with no headlights to stay off any radars. Go inside and gather all the food from the safe house and the blankets from the bed. I'm going to get the Jeep from the bushes and I'll meet you out front."

Mena took a deep breath. She was going to do whatever Hakeem told her to do. She wasn't the only one in danger anymore. Hakeem was risking his life to protect her and get her back home safely. Her rash actions had turned his careful plans to reunite her with Julian upside down. All because she couldn't wait a few more hours to let Julian know she was okay.

She couldn't feel sorry for herself. Tubeec and his men hadn't found them yet. If she stuck to Hakeem's instructions, she would be back in her condo safe and sound this time tomorrow.

Placing her hand on the bracelet, Mena twirled it around her wrist until the heart-shaped charm rested on the back of her hand.

I'm coming Julian.

Chapter Forty-Four

The chime on the glass door leading into the TIDES offices clanked loudly as Julian banged the door open, then stalked down the hallway toward the low murmur of voices in the conference room.

Turning the corner, Julian walked inside, dropping his assault rifle onto the table with a loud bang. He ripped off the bulletproof vest, threw it into the corner, then stared at the TIDES team sitting around the table: Sunny, Simon, and Zale.

Sunny frowned, then stood, her eyes locked on his.

Fighting the anger and confusion boiling within him, Julian said, "Hakeem has Mena. Do you know anything about that?"

"That's impossible," Zale said, standing up to walk over toward Julian. "Hakeem is in the Ukraine. I've talked to him myself and logged his updates on the security activities on our logs."

Rigid, Sunny placed her hands palm down on the table. Her eyes darted around the room from Julian to each of the other TIDES team members. After a brief silence, she asked, "Why do you think Hakeem has Mena? What happened?"

"We were about to fly out to the airstrip in Mandera when I got a call on my cell," Julian said, remembering the relief that had coursed through his body at the sound of the voice on the line. "It was Mena.

The signal was shitty, but it was her. Thing was, she wasn't afraid. There was no terror or fear in her tone. She kept saying things like I shouldn't worry, she was fine and that *they* were heading back to Nairobi later and she'd see me soon."

"That's great news, mate. But what does that have to do with Hakeem?" Simon asked. "Like Zale said, there's no way he can be in two places at the same time."

"The phone was breaking up bad, so I couldn't make out her answer when I kept asking where she was and who she was with. But finally, I asked to speak to the person helping her. That's when I heard her calling for him. She called out the name, Hakeem," Julian said.

"But the phone was breaking up. You can't be sure she said Hakeem. It could have been another name that sounded similar," Zale insisted.

"I know what I heard. She said Hakeem. I'm sure of it," Julian said.

Simon interrupted, "That doesn't make any sense. You couldn't have heard right. Maybe she's with an agent from ASF. Sunny, can you check with Reggie to see if one of his guys has found Mena."

"If Reggie had found her, he would have called me immediately. I haven't heard from him since Julian and I left ASF ComCentral," Sunny said.

Taye walked into the conference room. "The signal was bad, Julian. You said Mena was confident that she'd be back in Nairobi tomorrow. Why not wait before we make a move?"

Julian glared at Taye. "You think I'm going to sit on my fucking hands and wait to see if Mena shows up?"

"We're wasting fucking time here. Get that motherfucker on the phone so we can get to the bottom of why Mena thinks she's with Hakeem," Enzo said. "Julian knows what he heard and I believe him."

"If Hakeem is in the Ukraine protecting the art deliveries, then that should be easy to prove. Get Hakeem on a video call now. I want to know everything he's done since I talked to him two days ago," Julian said.

Simon held up a hand, a look of disgust crossing his face. "Wait a minute, mate. You're the new one to this operation, not Hakeem. We all have known him a lot longer than we've known you and there's no need to check up on him. What reason would he have to help Mena but keep it a secret? What you're suggesting doesn't make any sense."

"There's more to it. While we were with Paul, some chatter got picked up about Tubeec Hirad connecting with al-Harakat to bring Mena to him in exchange for a hefty cash reward," Glaze said.

"Which is why we don't have time to be sitting around debating this shit," Enzo added. "If Tubeec still had Mena, then he wouldn't need to put the bounty up."

"With al-Harakat searching for Mena, we need to figure out where she is and rescue her now. Hakeem might be able to tell us where she could be," Julian insisted, growing impatient with the resistance coming from the TIDES team. He knew his accusation wasn't sitting well with most of the team, but he knew what he'd heard.

"Did you ever think that this Hakeem that Mena is with could be from al-Harakat seeking to cash in on the bounty? It's probably not our Hakeem at all," Zale added.

"If that's true, then why hasn't al-Harakat cashed in by now? You think it takes two damn days to alert Tubeec that they have the woman he wants? Trust me, it doesn't," Julian said, then added, "Mena could have heard me talking to Hakeem when we were hiding out at the house in Giriftu. He warned me that a rebel group was approaching the house and we needed to leave right away."

"You see, Hakeem was trying to help you. The bloke would never find Mena and keep us in the dark about it," Simon added.

Sunny, who'd been quiet over the last exchange, turned and said, "Hakeem never told us that he found out about an attack on the house in Giriftu. We didn't hear from him until after I'd already tracked Julian down using the signal from his comms pack. I was minutes from the Giriftu house when Hakeem contacted me and I told him I already knew Julian's location."

"Seriously Sunny? Now you don't trust Hakeem either? You think we need to go behind Hakeem's back to prove that he is where he says he is? Unbelievable," Simon said, glaring at Julian.

"No, that's not what I'm saying. I don't want to waste time doing that. Glaze and Zale, can you trace the call made to Julian's phone?

Enzo, I need you to check in with ASF and see what they'll tell you about their hunt for Tubeec. Julian, I need to talk to you ... outside."

Sunny's confidence didn't match her body language. Julian could tell something was bothering her about the whole scenario. Pieces of the puzzle that didn't fit and didn't exonerate Hakeem Underwood.

Following Sunny out of the conference room, he turned into the narrow hallway and walked behind her as she pushed through the back door and out onto the alley behind the TIDES offices.

A harsh amber glow from the crime prevention light at the corner shone down on them as he stepped in front of her.

Facing Sunny, Julian demanded, "Tell me what's going on. Is Hakeem in the Ukraine or not? Could he have Mena?"

Sunny took a deep breath, then exhaled slowly. "Hakeem has worked damn hard to turn his life around." Pointing at the building, Sunny continued, "The team is his family. The only one he has right now and I can't let you take that away from him."

Turning toward the trash dumpster in the corner, Julian kicked the side of the metal container, once then twice. "Fuck! Why did he do it? What the hell is going on?"

"I'm not sure yet. The first thing we need to do is find out where he's hiding out with her. Hakeem knows exactly how to camouflage calls, make them appear as if they are coming from one location when he's actually at another. Glaze and Zale aren't skilled enough to figure it out. But you are," Sunny said.

"Was this his plan all along? When I called TIDES, did he set me up?" Julian asked, anger swirling through his veins as he paced back and forth along the alley.

"I'm not sure," Sunny admitted.

"Why would he kidnap Mena?" Julian asked.

"It's complicated. Hakeem has a troubled past. One he's been trying to run from, but it keeps coming back to haunt him. He was once part of Tubeec Hirad's elite team of mercenaries until a joint SEAL and ASF mission bombed their training compound and got him out."

"He's a mole? Has he been working with Tubeec this whole time?

Plotting against everything we've been trying to do to save Mena?" Julian asked.

"I don't think so. I honestly don't know for sure. My guess is he's going to hand her over to Tubeec under some misguided sense of loyalty to his former leader and cash in on the bounty. But if we get a lock on that cell call, we can get to him before he does that and I can get him the help he needs. Julian, he's been making good progress with his psychiatrist and this is a minor setback. He is a good person, deep inside," Sunny said, gripping Julian's hands. "Please don't hold this against him."

Julian pushed away from Sunny. "I handed Mena over to him on a silver platter. The man I thought was going to help me arranged an ambush so he could get back into Tubeec's good graces and you expect me to believe he's a good person? Why are you protecting this asshole?"

"Because he's my brother!"

"Brother? You don't have a brother. Sunny, I've met your family, your dad, and your four sisters," Julian said.

Sunny said, "But you never met my mom. Hakeem is the baby my mother had that almost broke up my parent's marriage. She gave him up to his father, a Kenyan man, and my Dad agreed not to get a divorce. After she passed away, I found information about Hakeem in one of her old safe deposit boxes. She knew he'd taken up with militant regimes in Africa and was trying to find him."

Everything was starting to make sense. Julian said, "You had the resources to do what your mother couldn't as part of special ops. You found him."

"I orchestrated the joint mission with Reggie's help to get my brother away from Tubeec. But I paid for it. Tubeec was pissed about losing Hakeem, one of his best-trained disciples. I don't know how Tubeec found out about my connection to Hakeem, but he did. That's why he abducted me. He wanted me to pay off the debt owed to him for taking Hakeem," Sunny explained. "Last time I was with you in Florida, Hakeem called me. He'd finally hit rock bottom and wanted my help. That's why I left and came back to Africa. With TIDES, I gave him an outlet to use his training for good, to help people. He's been in therapy all this time and I know he'll be able to get past what Tubeec did to him."

Rubbing the back of his neck, Julian glanced up at the sky. He understood why Sunny was so committed to Hakeem after everything she'd done to rescue him from Tubeec. But now Hakeem had turned back to his old ways. And he would be damned if he'd let Sunny's brand new fucking brother hurt Mena.

"Julian, I never expected this to happen. I'm not going to lose my brother to that bastard again and you're not going to lose Mena. We have to do this my way," Sunny said, her eyes pleading with him.

Julian turned from Sunny and stalked back towards the door leading into the TIDES offices.

"Get me access to each call Hakeem made into TIDES HQ over the past two days and prep the team for the rescue mission," Julian said, stepping inside the building. His body was numb as he focused on the task at hand. A situation that could have been avoided if he'd known the truth about Hakeem Underwood and his former connection to Tubeec Hirad.

"You'll have them in two minutes."

Turning, Julian looked at Sunny and said, "If Mena gets hurt because of this—"

"I know. I understand. But you should know that I'll do whatever it takes to protect my brother, too," Sunny said, then walked back toward the conference room.

Chapter Forty-Five

A jolt slammed into Mena's back and her body tumbled forward, banging against hard plastic. Stunned, she opened her eyes and struggled to regain her balance. Twisted around her body was a heavy blanket that reeked of gas and mothballs. Hakeem had directed her to hide underneath the dark blanket as he drove them across Kenya, trying to avoid dangerous men who wanted to kidnap her and turn her over to Tubeec Hirad.

The rays of the morning sun felt warm across her cheek as she grabbed the blanket and maneuvered onto the back seat.

"Yes, that's the right account number. I will be notified when the funds are transferred ... Wait ... You're changing locations now? I'm halfway to Wajir ... fine, I'll head east. About a couple hours away from that airstrip." Hakeem spoke in a low, hushed tone.

Mena raised her head. Hakeem had a cell phone pinned between his shoulder and his ear. Where had he gotten another phone? He'd destroyed the phone after she'd made the mistake of trying to call Julian.

"Look, you make sure you have everything ready for a quick exchange. I don't know how much time I have before they figure out what I did," Hakeem said, then was silent for several more minutes.

Mena strained to see if he was still on the call. Hakeem held the cell phone in his hand, shaking his head, then slipped it into a pocket on his shirt.

Propping herself up on an elbow, Mena stretched as if she'd just awoken. She wanted to ask Hakeem about the call, but felt herself hesitating. A strange tension in the air made her uneasy.

"Sorry about the bumps. Didn't mean to wake you, but I need to stay off the main roads," Hakeem said from the driver's seat.

She watched his eyes through the rearview mirror watching her. "It's okay, I'm not complaining."

Her throat was dry and cracked. Mena grabbed the water bottle from the floorboard. Twisting the cap off the top of the bottle, Mena pressed it against her lips and drank the sun-warmed liquid. Leaning her head back, she caught a glimpse outside the side window. The desolate landscape was littered with the occasional shrub brush or tree with mud houses in the distance. They should be close to Nairobi by now, but the landscape was still remote and rural. She was expecting to see highways, neighborhoods, and the tall skyscrapers of the modern city coming into view. It couldn't be much longer before they entered Nairobi. Soon, she would be back with Julian, ready to put this entire nightmare behind her.

"Any sign of threats during the night?" Mena asked.

"A few," Hakeem said, steering the Jeep to the left. "Lucky for me you're a sound sleeper and don't snore. I got stopped a couple of times and questioned by some rebels, had to pay some bribes to pass through, but nothing I couldn't handle."

Mena had never been a sound sleeper and she hadn't expected to sleep at all last night, but at some point she must have drifted to sleep although she didn't remember when.

"There're some pop tarts in the knapsack if you're hungry. Just stay low so you can't be seen through the windows," Hakeem said, pointing behind him.

Mena grabbed the shiny metallic package and tore it open, sliding a cold frosted strawberry pop tart out of the package. She'd much rather be feasting on her mom's chicken and waffles, but at this point she couldn't turn down any type of meal. Her hunger pangs had hunger pangs.

Stuffing a large chunk of the pastry into her mouth, Mena stole another glance out of the window. Her eyes locked on a house in the distance. Shifting to a half-sitting position, she strained to adjust her eyes to the sunlight.

It couldn't be possible. Could it?

Was that the faded blue concrete home where she and Julian had hidden? As they passed the home, Mena's eyes were drawn to the mosaic tile cross that hung above the door. The sunlight shimmered off the tiles, sending a prism of light across the porch.

It was definitely the house.

How could they still be near this place if they were only hours away from Nairobi? Julian had explained that the house was in the northeastern part of Kenya, hundreds of miles from the Kenyan capital. How could Hakeem be driving by the house? If he'd driven all night, like she thought, they would be far away from this house by now. What the hell was going on?

Heart rate skyrocketing, Mena glanced over at Hakeem.

Was Hakeem really who he said he was?

Or had she spent the last three days with a man she should have been running from?

"How much longer?" Mena asked, her voice low as she forced the words from the tightness in her throat.

Hakeem glanced back at her, then looked back at the road. "Just a couple more hours. Cover up."

He was lying, Mena knew.

Hakeem wasn't taking her back to Nairobi.

Mena looked through the window, watching the house grow smaller and smaller from view.

Hakeem had lied to her this whole time.

If he wasn't part of the TIDES team with Julian, then who was he working for? Was he taking her back to that maniac, Tubeec Hirad?

The phone call to Julian flickered through Mena's mind.

Hakeem hadn't been worried about alerting Tubeec's men. He'd been afraid Julian would find them before he had a chance to deliver her to the terrorist. From the sound of the phone call he'd made, Mena suspected Tubeec was paying him one hundred thousand dollars for his trouble.

She'd been a fool, believing Hakeem was trying to help her.

Mena leaned back, closing her eyes, exhaling a shaky breath.

Think. She had one chance to make a move and she couldn't afford to make the wrong one. She had to get away from Hakeem. Any move she made would need to be quick before he suspected what was happening.

Turning over, Mena lifted her hands above her head covering her body with the heavy cloth. She allowed her hands to linger near the door release, hoping the blanket would obscure her attempt to escape. Gripping the handle, Mena pulled it forward. The door didn't budge.

"Child locks. You didn't think it would be that easy, did you?" Hakeem asked, his voice cold and menacing.

Mena looked up at the side of his face. His jaw clenched tight, he gripped the steering wheel with one hand and pointed a gun directly toward her with the other.

"You lied. You're not taking me back to Nairobi. What are you going to do with me? Take me back to Tubeec?"

"That's exactly what I'm going to do," Hakeem said.

"Do you even work for TIDES? Do you know Julian?" Mena asked, sitting up in the back seat.

Hakeem said, "I work for TIDES. Julian is fine. If things go as I plan, then you might get your happy ending after all. If not ..."

"What if I pay you not to take me back? How much to pretend you never found me and drive me back to Nairobi? It would take a few days but I could pay you more than what Tubeec is offering," Mena said, her voice shaking as she tried to calculate in her head how much money she and her family could liquidate in short order. She had her condo back in St. Basil and she was sure her Mom had excess funds that could be accessed. Mena could probably get two hundred, maybe three hundred thousand dollars to Hakeem within a month.

Hakeem raised an eyebrow as he looked at her, then shook his head. "This ain't about money. Not for me."

"Please don't do this to me," Mena barely choked out the words. She'd run out of time. Tears stung her eyes as panic gripped her.

"Save your tears," Hakeem said without a hint of remorse.

Mena felt like the wind had been knocked out of her.

What was she going to do?

The dirt road stretched for miles ahead of them, dotted with a few trees and scrub brush. No structures for as far as the eye could see.

She couldn't let Hakeem take her back.

They were approaching a cluster of trees.

But he wouldn't kill her, would he?

Tubeec wanted her alive.

Not dead.

Hakeem wasn't going to shoot her.

He couldn't.

Heart thudding in her chest, Mena screamed and pushed through the opening between the front seats, fumbling her hands toward the steering wheel. She jerked it hard to the right, sending the Jeep careening into the trees lining the road.

Chapter Forty-Six

The bright sun rose above the horizon, blinding Julian as he drove the Humvee across the rugged desert land. Eyes constricting, he squinted, dipping his head low to keep his eyes on the target looming ahead.

The town of Takaba.

Enzo had uncovered the depths of Hakeem's lies with a single phone call to Emershan Smith, the prominent art dealer Hakeem was supposed to be protecting on a trip to deliver art in the Ukraine. Smith was surprised that Enzo didn't know he'd postponed the trip by a month. The information had been relayed to Hakeem a week ago.

Sunny had remained stoic, insisting that Hakeem had to have a good reason for the subterfuge and the rest of the TIDES team shared her views. Everyone except Julian. He hadn't worked side by side with Hakeem over the past few years like they had. He didn't have the same trust in Hakeem, or any of them, for that matter.

Separating himself from the rest of the team, Julian had gone into Sunny's private office and started tracing Mena's call to his cell phone. After an hour of painstaking analysis through a complex web of towers, Julian had uncovered the calls weren't coming from Kiev. They had come from northeastern Kenya, somewhere in the vicinity of a small town named Takaba.

Getting to Takaba presented its own difficulties. There was no airstrip close by. The only option was to fly into Mandera, northeast of the town, or into Wajir, further south of the town. Both were over a hundred miles away. After some considerable debate, they'd settled on Mandera, where Sunny had a contact that would supply a Humvee to the team once they landed.

Julian had been driving all night, speeding across the rugged terrain and sipping watered down coffee as sleep eluded him. Mena had said they were leaving for Nairobi in the morning. He had to make it to Takaba before Hakeem took off with her. He knew for a fact Hakeem was lying to Mena. He had no plans to take her back to Nairobi. He was going to deliver her to Tubeec Hirad.

"It ain't money," Enzo said, his voice startling Julian in the quiet that had settled within the Humvee over the past six hours. Glaze and Taye were snoring in the back. Enzo had been studying maps and intel on the last calls that had come in from Hakeem, trying to figure out what Hakeem's next move would be.

"What?" Julian asked, confused.

"Hakeem didn't take Mena for the bounty. Sure, he's flashy and likes nice things. Bling bling and all that bullshit. But, he ain't broke. None of us are. That bounty is big enough to make these poor ass rebel groups excited, but it's a drop in the bucket for us. He could do a lot less to earn a lot more," Enzo explained.

Julian contemplated Enzo's conclusion. Money was the easiest motive, but if that was off the table, what were they left with?

"Could Tubeec be forcing him to do it?" Julian pondered the idea. If Tubeec was threatening Sunny, would Hakeem do whatever it took to protect his sister? Possibly. A theory he couldn't share with Enzo as Sunny had sworn him to secrecy about her relationship with Hakeem. None of the TIDES team knew about their sibling bond.

"That's more feasible if you ask me. Won't be long before we find out. If he's in some kind of trouble, we're going to do whatever he needs to help him. Once he sees us, I'm sure he'll come clean about what's going on. Hold on ..." Enzo stopped, glancing down at his cell phone.

"Is that Sunny?" Julian asked, hoping she'd gotten more information from Hakeem.

"No. It's Zale. She thinks Hakeem could be hiding out at a hut that was used by poachers a decade ago. Hakeem would have access to that info from our databases," Enzo said.

"As good a place to start as any." Julian glanced at the map on the cell phone, then at his GPS coordinates. Steering the Humvee toward the right, he drove faster. His body bounced in the seat as the vehicle jostled along the deep ruts in the road.

"Wake up, motherfuckers!" Enzo said, turning to shake Taye and Glaze. As he filled the others in on the intel they had so far, Julian focused on the square hut appearing in the distance.

Julian steered the Humvee near what he hoped was the front of the structure and killed the ignition. The hut looked deserted. A wave of disappointment sliced through him. Had they gotten the location wrong?

"Come with me Taye," Enzo said. "Between me and you, we know enough Swahili and other tribal languages to communicate with any locals in the area. Let's see if we can find someone who may have seen Hakeem or Mena."

Enzo and Taye jogged off toward a group of huts in the distance near a watering hole. Glaze lingered behind Julian.

"If they were here, there's got to be some tracks around. Footsteps, tire prints, something. I'm going to search around the hut and see what I can find," Glaze said.

Julian nodded, then stood still as the warm morning air blazed across his skin. The hut was small, constructed of tree branches, and plastered with mud. Compressed leaves and grass formed the thatched roof. Julian ducked his head, stepped onto the small porch and slipped through an opening. A faint lingering aroma of wood smoke wafted in the air. To the left was a stove built into the floor, embers barely perceptible as the fire died out. Lining the wall on the right were dozens of cowhides stacked one on top of the other forming two separate beds. Squatting low, Julian reached his hand toward shiny metal resting between the two beds.

Squeezing his fingers around the object, he pulled it out and stared at the rose gold bracelet. The single heart-shaped charm engraved with the J and M he'd given to Mena rested in the palm of his hand.

Mena had been here. This was where Hakeem had kept her, but where were they now? Mena had said they were leaving for Nairobi this morning. It was just after sunrise. Why weren't they still here?

"Julian!"

Rising to his feet, Julian stuffed the bracelet into the pocket of his pants and emerged from the hut.

"I found empty food wrappers in the brush and tire tracks of a Jeep leading south from here," Glaze said, pointing to a spot a dozen yards away. "The tracks are fresh, within the last twelve hours or so."

Taye and Enzo came running over.

"Any luck?" Taye asked.

"I found Mena's bracelet. She was here. Glaze found some JEEP tracks we can follow," Julian said.

"Not so fast." Enzo held up a hand as he read something on his phone. "Zale sent another update. ASF was tracking a plane known to be carrying Tubeec Hirad and his team out of Ethiopia. The plane was originally scheduled to land in Wajir, but then it diverted mid-air and is tracking toward El Wak."

"Where is El Wak?" Julian asked.

"It's east of here, on the border. ASF has an outpost there and the Kenyan military uses it as a hub for delivering aid and provisions into Somalia," Taye said.

"That's also where the Irungus are constructing greenhouses. Their private airstrip is right outside of that town," Glaze said.

"That's right," Enzo nodded. "If Hakeem hijacking Mena has anything to do with Tubeec, then I bet he's headed there now."

Sliding his hand into his pocket, Julian gripped Mena's bracelet in his hands, then said, "Let's head to El Wak."

Chapter Forty-Seven

The men kicked Hakeem in the side, once, twice, three times. Hakeem doubled over, vomiting a putrid yellow mass onto the red dirt. Coughing violently, he tried to shield himself from further blows and curled his body into a ball near the overturned Jeep.

Mena laid motionless as the men surrounded her. Two of them leaned over, lifting her from the ground like a rag doll, and dragged her toward the military-grade 4x4 several feet away. She didn't resisted. The malice in the dark eyes watching her sent a chill through her body. These were not men to fight back or disobey. They held none of the undercurrent of kindness she had witnessed with Rahim and even Hakeem. These men wouldn't think twice about killing her if she tried to run away from them. They'd quickly put bullets in her back and leave her dying carcass for the animals to feast on in the hot sun.

Opening the back door to the vehicle, one of the men lifted Mena into the air and rolled her into the rear compartment. Her body tumbled, flipping over and over until she landed with a hard thud against the back of the front seats. There were no side doors, only two rounded, thin rectangle windows near the roof of the vehicle on each side. As the sun began its full ascent into the sky, hot shafts of heated air shone onto the metal of the compartment. The men entered behind her, then slammed the door. The air grew still and quiet as each aimed a pistol directly at her.

Closing her eyes, Mena tried to steady her heartbeat. Her arms and shoulders screamed with pain from being tossed into the vehicle. No doubt bruises were forming, but that was the least of her worries.

She had become a commodity, traded back and forth amongst rebels. These men were her new owners, but who were they? Had Tubeec offered to pay the rebel groups in exchange for returning her to him?

She'd heard Hakeem on the phone before dawn, relaying an account number for a funds transfer. Would her new captors be paid instead?

But what if these men didn't know anything about Tubeec Hirad? Where would they take her? What would they do to her?

Mena closed her eyes and cautioned herself to be calm.

What would Julian tell her to do in this moment?

She could almost hear his voice, encouraging her to stay positive and not lose hope.

Julian was always thoughtful and rational in the most dangerous of circumstances. She never once saw him panic or give up, even when the stakes were high. She had to follow his example right now, doing whatever her abductors told her to do.

Trying to take matters into her own hands hadn't worked last time. Another attempt to overturn a vehicle would likely get her killed. Her unplanned and ill-timed hasty decision had resulted in swapping her previous kidnapper with a group of men who were no doubt more deadly. Hakeem was surely the lesser of these two evils. She should have thought longer and harder before crashing the Jeep.

The temperature inside the vehicle ratcheted higher. Mena watched the men as they drank from canteens, the water dripping along the sides and plopping to the floor. She prayed for a drop to quench her parched throat but they offered her nothing.

Through the small windows, Mena saw the other two gunmen. The front doors of the vehicle opened and the men got inside, yelling instructions in a language Mena didn't understand to the men in the back with her. They responded quickly, then maneuvered into new positions, each lifting a hand to hold onto a bar as the vehicle roared to life. Jerking forward, Mena banged her head against the floorboard as the vehicle took off.

Time passed excruciatingly slow as the vehicle bumped and banged across the rough roads. Mena drifted in and out of sleep, exhaustion racking her body from the fear she'd been battling since she realized Hakeem wasn't going to take her back to Nairobi.

A cell phone rang. Mena peered up over her shoulder and saw the driver hand the phone to the rebel sitting in the passenger seat. The man spoke quickly in another language, his hands gesturing wildly as his voice grew more insistent. Then he was silent for a long moment. The gunmen in the back compartment watched him, waiting for an answer or a reaction.

The man turned to face the others with a bright, toothy grin as he kept the phone pressed against his ear. The conversation had obviously become more satisfactory to him. After several more seconds, the man tossed the cell phone into the center compartment and let out a shout.

The other three men joined in the joyous chorus as they pumped their fists in the air.

A part of her held out hope that the men had contacted Tubeec Hirad, who obviously wanted her alive for some reason. If she was handed over to Tubeec, that would give her another hour, another day to survive. Another chance to find an opening to escape or ... to be found by Julian.

As the minutes ticked by into what felt like hours, Mena closed her eyes and imagined Julian. She fantasized about being back in his arms, laying on the bench of his yacht, staring up into another perfect cloudless Caribbean sky on the island of St. Basil. Her only wish was to be back there with him for good. Leaving behind her fellowship and Africa to return to the place that had become her home. To the man she wanted to spend her life with.

Sweat slid along her face and she swiped at her eyes, then reached for her bracelet.

It was ... gone.

No.

Where was her bracelet?

How could she have lost it?

Mena fought the despair threatening to drown her. Throughout all the mayhem after being kidnapped from the Irungu Center, the bracelet had been her one source of strength, helping her through each harrowing moment of her horrifying ordeal. Now it was gone.

Mena couldn't shake the feeling that the loss of the one connection she still had with Julian meant that he wouldn't be coming to her rescue this time. She was truly on her own, subject to the whims of dangerous terrorists.

Chapter Forty-Eight

Pulling the bandana tighter across his nose and mouth, Tubeec lifted a hand to shield his eyes from the plumes of red dust rising from the ground as the Gulfstream landed deftly on the desolate private airstrip north of El Wak, near the Kenya-Somalia border. The plane taxied slowly, passing the dozen greenhouses in various states of construction. Turning, he headed back inside the oversized hanger and motioned for his men to bring the captive from the small six by six-foot security office tucked away in the back corner.

Tubeec watched as his men brought the man to him. His hands were tied tightly behind his back and a black cloth covered his face. The man was a quick learner, no longer resisting and fighting back after suffering the consequences of his initial attempts. In due time, the man would thank Tubeec for abducting him from Ethiopia and bringing him to Kenya.

The long arduous assignment was finally coming to an end. Tubeec hadn't held up his end of the deal, but partial compliance was better than nothing and he had more important things on his mind now. The primaries were months away, but Kipsang Rono was surging in popularity in the tribes known to support him as well as in urban areas of the country. The contents of the flash drive would serve Tubeec well if Rono continued on this trajectory and stole the presidency from Noah Thairu. Tubeec could see a legitimate military position in his future, one that would equip him with the power to crush the men who'd led the attack on his family a decade ago.

The sleek tan and chrome plane rolled to a stop, as the whirring of the jets slowed to a low purr. Tubeec took a step toward the airplane door and watched as the stairs descended. In the darkness of the cabin, a single figure loomed in the doorway.

An old friend from times long ago.

Tubeec regarded him. He hadn't aged well. His plain face was marred by crevices. But the green eyes were the same as Tubeec remembered, sharp, piercing, and calculating.

The man ducked his head outside the plane, raising a hand at Tubeec, before descending the steps. He held a large steel suitcase in one gloved hand. As they approached each other, a hint of conspiratorial satisfaction rested on the man's face.

"Tubeec, it is good to see you again."

"Same to you, my friend, same to you. How are things going in the witness protection program? Have they given you a new name? I was partial to the old," Tubeec said.

"Still Adam Russell," he said, slapping a hand on Tubeec's shoulder, squeezing it. "For now."

"Let's get the business out of the way," Tubeec said.

Balancing the suitcase in the crook of his arm, Adam pressed a button on the side causing the lid to prop open. Tubeec grabbed a stack at random and thumbing through the one hundred dollar bills. From his quick estimation, the case contained more than the agreed-upon sum. Tubeec was not fond of surprises, not even those that seemed to benefit him. The extra money would come with expectations. Expectations Tubeec might not be inclined to fulfill.

Reaching into his pocket, Tubeec pulled out a small vile and pressed down sharply, spraying a fine mist over a few more stacks of bills. When the color didn't turn black—which would have indicated the money was counterfeit—he nodded in approval. Adam closed the lid and handed it to Tubeec.

"Why so generous, my friend?" Tubeec asked, rubbing a scarred finger against his temple.

Adam gave a short laugh. "Later. Now, it's your turn."

"Of course," Tubeec said, beckoning for Cangrejos to come forward with the small plastic first aid kit. Tubeec grabbed the box, then opened it for Adam to look inside.

"Excellent," Adam responded. "And was there any difficulty extracting the doctor from his captors?"

"None at all. Whoever took him will think long and hard before doing it again," Tubeec responded, then motioned for Cangrejos to bring the hooded man forward, stopping close enough for Adam to observe the man but not near enough for an exchange to occur.

Walking to Cangrejos, Tubeec slipped the cloth off the captive's head. The man's eyes flew open, squinting in the bright morning light shining into the hangar. His dark skin and bald head were drenched in sweat. Rags of clothes hung from his skinny frame. As the man's eyes focused, Tubeec watched pure relief flood through him, loosening his muscles as he recognized Adam Russell standing next to the Gulfstream.

Adam took a step toward the man. Tubeec held up a hand. Assad and Suleymaan emerged from the shadows, pointing M4 Carbines at Adam.

"Not so fast," Tubeec said. He wasn't ready to complete the exchange until he'd found out what the extra funds were for. What exactly did Adam want him to do?

Adam tipped his head at Tubeec, then addressed the man, "You're looking well, Quentin. I hope you don't mind the lengths we had to go through to smuggle you out of Ethiopia."

"I won't lie, I never guessed you were behind all of this. How is Priscilla?" Quentin asked.

"She'll be much better once I get you back to St. Basil," Adam explained. "She was anxious to enact your plan, but then you disappeared. For months, we didn't know what happened until we got the ransom call. But you know Priscilla doesn't take kindly to blackmail. So, I had to be creative to facilitate your release. She'll be happy to have you back to put the plan in motion."

"But ... it won't work without—"

"Mena Nix," Tubeec said, unsure of the cryptic plans being discussed by Adam and Quentin or who Priscilla was. Tubeec was mildly curious, but quickly losing interest. The sooner he made it clear that Mena was likely not going to be a part of the deal, the sooner he could get back to Somalia and plan his next moves.

Tubeec wasn't one to make many mistakes, but he had made a big one trusting his former associate, Hakeem Underwood. The years away from the militia had made Hakeem soft. His former protégé had struggled to secure Mena Nix and deliver her to the hangar at the agreed-upon time. Tubeec had given Hakeem confirmation that the money had been wired into his account, but the incompetent fool still hadn't responded to calls from Cangrejos.

"Where is she? I want to leave soon," Adam said, his mouth drawn into a tight line.

"There has been a delay in the transportation of the American woman. Is she worth waiting for? I could easily prorate the fee if you want to leave without her," Tubeec suggested.

"Adam, we can't do that. Without Mena, we have no leverage. No way to enact the plan. We must have her!" Quentin said, his eyes growing wide. "I will not let Priscilla down again. We can't leave without her."

"What's the estimated time of arrival?" Adam asked, crossing his arms over his chest.

Tubeec wished he knew the answer to that question himself. He looked over at Liban and Cangrejos. The two men were engaged in a heated discussion as they passed a phone back and forth between them. "Hold on a moment and let me confer with my team."

Stepping past Assad and Suleymaan, still maintaining a tight hold on Quentin Tufa, Tubeec approached Liban.

"What's going on? Have you located Hakeem and Mena?" Tubeec whispered.

Liban nodded, then showed Tubeec a photo of Mena Nix surrounded by a group of men from al-Harakat.

"When was this taken?" Tubeec asked.

"Just now. They are willing to make an exchange if the bounty is still being paid," Liban said.

Tubeec contemplated his options, not sure he wanted to continue to deal with Adam. He had other preparations to begin and this assignment was dragging on longer than he expected. "Set up a meeting point and get the Jeep ready. I'll ride out with you."

Turning back around, Tubeec walked to Adam and placed a hand on the man's shoulders. "Good news, my friend. Mena Nix is being delivered to our scheduled drop off point now. My team and I will go out personally to collect her and bring her back to you. Cangrejos will stay behind as a sign of good faith."

Adam smiled, exposing deep dimples. "Good. Before you leave, there's one more person I need you to bring to me. He should be easy to lure here."

Chapter Forty-Nine

"Taye! Slow down!" Julian ordered, leaning forward in the passenger seat of the Humvee. About a hundred yards ahead, near a copse of dying trees, a Jeep lay overturned on the road.

"Looks like that motherfucker flipped his Jeep," Enzo said, from the back seat. "How the fuck did he manage that? Ain't shit out here."

The Humvee slowed to a stop a few yards from the Jeep and Taye put the vehicle in park.

Julian opened the door and jumped out, jogging over to the Jeep, which rested on its side with the passenger side door facing up to the sky.

"Julian, these tracks look familiar," Glaze said, squatting down to peer at the skid marks in the dirt. "Like the ones back at the safe house in Takaba."

Sprinting ahead, Julian stepped on the axel beneath the JEEP's chassis and hoisted himself toward the top of the Jeep. The vehicle rocked as he peered through the window. The cab was empty. Dropping back down, he walked to the other side—

Leaning against the roof of the Jeep was Hakeem Underwood. His breathing was ragged and he held his side, grimacing in pain.

"Where the fuck is Mena, you bastard?" Julian demanded, stepping toward Hakeem. Lifting the man from the ground, he drug him toward a tree.

"Hakeem?" Taye said from behind Julian. "Hey, Hakeem is over here. He looks hurt."

Hakeem looked up at Julian, contrition and shame in his eyes. He exhaled, then said, "Al-Harakat ambushed us. They took Mena. They're going to hand her over to Tubeec Hirad for the bounty."

Julian rammed his forearm under Hakeem's neck.

Gurgling from the force of the blow, Hakeem's eyes grew wide with fear.

"What were you planning to do with Mena? Why did you take her and not tell us?" Julian demanded.

An arm wrapped around Julian's waist. He felt himself being pulled backward.

"Take it easy, man," Enzo said, holding Julian back. "Don't do something you might regret later."

"We're waiting for an answer, Hakeem," Glaze said, rounding the corner. The four of them surrounded Hakeem as he stared at each of them.

"I was never going to hurt her. But I needed to use her as ... bait," Hakeem said.

"Bait? For what? What were you planning to do?" Julian asked.

"Kill that bastard Tubeec Hirad. I knew he was desperate to get Mena back. Tubeec doesn't put out a bounty for anyone, but he did for Mena. If I could deliver her, it would get me a chance to be alone with him. To end that miserable bastard's life," Hakeem said, venom and hatred oozing from every word.

"What beef you got with Tubeec? Where is that coming from?" Enzo asked, releasing Julian.

"He kidnapped my sister and held her for over a year. Forced her to do ... despicable things. I'm going to make him regret what he did," Hakeem said.

Julian closed his eyes. After rescuing Hakeem from the diabolical leader of the militia, Sunny had been kidnapped by Tubeec for masterminding Hakeem's escape. Hakeem knew what his sister had gone through to help him and he wanted Tubeec to pay.

"Julian, I promise you I wasn't going to let Mena get hurt in any of this. I was going to get her back to Nairobi safely after I'd finished gutting Tubeec," Hakeem said, the sincerity in his tone ringing true to Julian.

Julian rubbed a hand down his face. He couldn't be distracted by Hakeem's revenge plot. He needed to find Mena. "How do you know it was al-Harakat that hijacked you and kidnapped Mena?"

"I recognized their gear. The brand new TIGR Jeep they were riding in was supplied by Russian benefactors," Hakeem said.

Glaze asked, "So, where do you think they are taking her? To Tubeec?"

"Yeah, I'm sure it didn't take them long to contact Tubeec, he'll instruct them to take her to El Wak. Wasn't too long ago that they took her. I'm sure you can overtake them," Hakeem said.

"And what are you going to do?" Julian asked.

"What I came here to do. As soon as you help me get this Jeep turned over," Hakeem said.

"You can't go after Tubeec alone," Glaze warned. "He'll kill you for sure."

"No, he won't. He thinks I'm on his side. I've been doing small jobs for him, trying to get close enough to make him pay for what he did to my sister," Hakeem admitted.

"Does Sunny know about this bullshit?" Enzo asked.

"No! And you aren't going to say anything about it to her. Just help me get the Jeep turned over and go find Mena. I'll do this on my own," Hakeem said.

"No, you won't. I'm coming with you," Glaze said. "You're going to need back up."

Turning toward Julian, Glaze asked, "Think you can manage without me?"

"Yeah, I can," Julian said. He could manage to save Mena even if they all abandoned him. "Let's get this Jeep back on four wheels."

Taye, Glaze, and Enzo lined up along the side of the Jeep, then on

Julian's count, they heaved and pushed the vehicle in unison. After several tries, the Jeep creaked and rocked, tipping over onto the tires.

"We need to get going," Julian said to Taye and Enzo. He couldn't keep Mena waiting any longer.

Chapter Fifty

"Based on the terrain and the available routes, al-Harakat will have to cross this road to get to El Wak," Enzo confirmed.

Julian peered through the binoculars, looking for any movement on the horizon. An hour had passed and they'd been in contact with TIDES HQ. Zale had helped navigate them across open desert, showing them the main roads to avoid as they tried to cut off al-Harakat before they reached El Wak. Taye had given them an update about finding Hakeem and his plans to go after Tubeec with Glaze.

Sunny was noticeably absent. Simon and Zale indicated she hadn't come into the offices yet and no one had heard from her. Where the hell could she be? Did she know what was going on with Hakeem and his quest for revenge against Tubeec Hirad for her? Was she out trying to stop him?

Julian pushed the thoughts from his mind. He couldn't worry about Sunny. She could take care of herself. His only concern right now was finding Mena and extracting her from the hands of terrorists hoping to trade her for a big payday.

The radio crackled, and Zale's voice lingered in the air, "Transport spotted, traveling east parallel to Saba Route. Closed convoy, one TIGR, four gunmen, hidden Barbie."

Zale and Simon had been flying drones with mounted cameras over the area, and scouring the live feeds to assist them with locating al-Harakat.

Julian pressed the button to speak through his comms. "How far out?"

"Five minutes."

Hidden Barbie.

No identifiable sign that Mena was actually in the convoy, but there was no other reason for a convoy to be heading in this direction. The heavily armed team in that convoy had to be al-Harakat.

"Look, coming up over there," Taye said, pointing as he shifted the Humvee into gear. The military vehicle propelled forward, sending up a cloud of red dirt as it bumped over the uneven terrain. Visibility was limited through the dust, but Julian could make out the sleek gray TIGR gliding across the desert land.

Julian had kept his memories of Mena in the far corners of his mind, refusing to indulge in the pain of missing her, afraid they would swallow him whole into an abyss of loneliness if he let them run rampant. He'd needed to focus his energy on finding and rescuing her.

Knowing he was within minutes of resting his eyes on her beautiful face again sent a surge of adrenaline through him.

Bouncing over a small hill, he had the TIGR in his sights, leaning out of the window with the M4 Carbine perched on his shoulder. In the periphery, he could see Enzo, mirroring his movements, ready to make a coordinated attack on the tires of the TIGR.

Clutching the steering wheel tighter, Taye barreled ahead, turning the Humvee toward the TIGR in a wide arc to give Julian and Enzo the best vantage to shoot at the vehicle. The Humvee swerved again as Julian and Enzo unleashed a steady stream of shots toward the TIGR. The bullets popped through the air, pelting then bouncing off the bulletproof metal and glass. Julian cursed. His shots had been too high to hit the tires. Readjusting his aim, he unleashed another round of bullets, hitting one of the front tires.

The TIGR careened across the dirt road, jerking back and forth. A door swung open and a gunman leaned out, unleashing a round of shots toward the Humvee.

Enzo rebounded, taking several shots. A body fell out the open door of the TIGR, tumbling across the red dirt before rolling to a stop on the ground. The TIGR sped up, racing away from the Humvee. A rifle emerged from the back window, pelting the Humvee with more bullets that pinged off the surface.

Taye swerved in a wider arc, then floored the vehicle until they were on the other side of the TIGR. The erratic movement of the Humvee was destroying Julian's aim. He had to get the TIGR to slow down. Julian jumped out of the Humvee, gripping the rifle tightly as his body banged against the hard earth, rolling several times before coming to a stop. He kept his eyes trained on the moving tires. Fingering the trigger, he focused on the turning wheels and hit each back tire with successive shots.

The TIGR swerved wildly across the sand, tilting and rocking as the driver struggled to keep control of the vehicle. The TIGR spun in a one-hundred-eighty-degree arc. Julian caught sight of the driver through the window. The man's head was barely above the steering wheel. Time stood still as Julian focused on the cadence of his heart beating, slow and methodical. He inhaled, then pulled the trigger over and over.

The rapid-fire of the rifle thundered in his ears, then fell silent.

The TIGR slowed to a stop.

Julian stared at the hole pierced in the front windshield. The driver's head slumped backward, his face a bloody mess of torn skin and bone, unrecognizable as human.

Julian watched the Humvee slowing to a stop on the other side of the TIGR. Enzo emerged from the passenger door, his gun raised as he approached the back door of the TIGR.

"Enzo! Wait!" Julian screamed as he took off running across the sand.

In an instant, the back door of the TIGR opened and shots rang out, pelting Enzo's body. Julian watched Enzo fall, his body jerking back and forth as the bullets hit him.

Raising his gun, Julian shot the two men leaning out the back of the TIGR, their bodies falling on top of Enzo.

Taye raced over, moving the rebel's bodies. One gripped his ankle and Taye placed a clean shot right between the man's eyes, before leaning down to check on Enzo.

"Is he okay?" Julian asked, panting as he stood over Taye and Enzo.

"Fuck yeah, I'm okay," Enzo said, through shallow breaths. "Bulletproof vest took most of the damage, but this arm is bleeding like a motherfucker!"

"We're going to get you some help!" Taye said, looking at Julian with concern in his eyes.

No doubt, Enzo's injuries were a lot worse than his friend realized.

Julian pressed the comms, "Zale, where is the closest hospital?"

"What happened? Is everything okay?" Zale asked. Julian could hear her typing on the keyboard, likely homing in on their location.

"Enzo got shot, need to get him to the hospital asap," Julian urged as Enzo's blood oozed across the sand, darkening the already rust-colored dirt. Lifting Enzo's body, Julian caught sight of torn muscles and bones, areas where the bulletproof vest hadn't been able to protect his friend. Taye grabbed Enzo from the other side and they carried him to the Humvee, placing him in the back seat.

"Keep heading east to El Wak to the district hospital. I'll arrange for a helicopter to meet you to Medivac Enzo back to Kenyatta National Hospital here in Nairobi," Zale said.

Julian ended the call. "You heard the lady."

"What about you?" Taye asked, hesitating.

"I'll drive the TIGR and follow you to the hospital. It'll be slow on busted tires, but I can get there. If we aren't there by the time the medivac arrives, leave without us," Julian insisted.

Taye nodded, started the Humvee, and drove away from Julian, tires skidding in the red dirt.

An eerie silence filled the air as Julian watched the Humvee grow smaller and smaller into the distance. Stepping over one of the dead militants of al-Harakat, he headed toward the TIGR.

Reaching the back door, Julian took a deep breath. Swinging the door open, Julian crawled into the back, then stopped abruptly.

He felt like he couldn't breathe.

Mena was huddled in a tight ball, wedged against the floorboard, her face splattered with the blood of the dead driver slumped over the back of the seat.

Julian scrambled toward the back of the compartment and pulled Mena into his arms. She clung to him, her body trembling. Kissing the top of her head, he squeezed tighter, loving the feel of her body in his arms. He weaved his fingers through her tangled hair as she wrapped her arms tighter around his waist.

"Did they hurt you?" Julian asked, leaning back to look at her. She looked shell-shocked and confused, suffering from the trauma of being kidnapped multiple times over the past three days.

"No," Mena said, burrowing her head into his chest. "I didn't think you would be able to find me this time."

"Hey, don't start doubting me. Nothing was going to stop me from finding you. I would have searched forever," Julian said, sliding a finger down the side of her face. "You sure they didn't hurt you?"

Mena nodded.

Julian leaned back and grabbed a canteen of water. Opening the top, he handed it to Mena. "Drink this."

Grabbing the bottle, Mena gulped the water. Lowering it, she wiped the back of her palm against her mouth.

"Can we go home now?" Mena asked, leaning back against the seat.

"TIDES is sending a plane to El Wak and I can have you back in Nairobi within the hour," Julian reassured her.

"No ... not Nairobi," Mena said. "I want to go back to St. Basil. I don't want to be in Kenya anymore."

Julian rubbed her arms. "Okay, we'll go home ... tonight."

Mena's eyes drifted behind him, her face frowning.

"What's wrong?" Julian asked.

A sigh escaped her lips. "We won't be going home after all."

Chapter Fifty-One

Mena stared into the cold, lifeless eyes of Tubeec Hirad. Three heavily armed gunmen dressed in dark green were jogging up behind him, flanking the militant leader on the left and right sides. Bandanas shielded their noses and mouths from the swirling red sand blowing across the desert.

"Look at me," Julian said.

Mena averted her gaze from the gunmen storming toward them across the flat, desolate terrain.

"We've been in worse situations before and we got out of them alive. We're going to get out of this one too," Julian said, grabbing her hands. "You trust me?"

Mena searched his soulful brown eyes, but couldn't force herself to respond. Her trust in him wasn't the issue.

"Three gunmen behind me, right?" Julian asked.

"Yes," Mena whispered.

"Big guns or small ones?"

"Really big." Mena watched as the men approached and stopped next to Tubeec at the back door of the vehicle.

"No sudden movements and follow their instructions. Okay?"

Julian said, then reached into his pocket and held his hand in front of her.

Mena glanced down at her bracelet resting in the palm of his hand. Tears sprung to her eyes as she grabbed it and slipped it back on her wrist.

"I love you," Julian said.

Mena nodded, "I love you, too."

Julian turned around and faced Tubeec.

A bullet whizzed through the air, slamming into the back of the seat with a loud bang, mere inches away from Mena's head.

Mena shrieked, jumping closer to Julian.

"We will do whatever you want," Julian said, waving his empty hands in the air. Mena's eyes drifted down his back toward the bulge in his waistband.

"Get out," Tubeec said, stepping backward. "Both of you."

Mena watched Julian climb out of the jeep, then he turned and reached for her. Grasping his hand, Mena crawled out and stood next to Julian. The bright harsh warmth of the sun burned her skin as she stared at the assault rifles pointed at them.

Julian stepped in front of her, his muscles tensing. His hand reached backward toward the gun tucked into his waistband. Trying to outshoot three heavily armed men at this close range was foolish. She couldn't let him do it. She couldn't let him continue to put his life on the line for her.

"Kill him and grab the woman," Tubeec said, then turned to walk away. The gunmen raised their rifles, locking in on Julian.

"Wait! No, please don't!" Mena screamed, pushing Julian and rushing forward toward the men. She held up her hands. "I will go with you! You don't have to hurt him."

Tubeec turned around, a confused look crossing his face. The gunmen looked back toward the leader.

Tubeec flicked his wrist downward and the men responded by lowering their weapons. Walking to Mena, Tubeec stopped. "You must love this man very much."

Julian rushed in front of her. "You don't have to do this."

The gunmen raised their rifles, pointing them at Julian as he approached Tubeec, stopping within mere feet of the rebel leader.

"One more step and she will watch you die. Is that what you want?" Tubeec asked.

Julian stood still, his eyes focused on Tubeec. He was calm, unfazed by the danger that surrounded them.

"Go and wait by the TIGR," Tubeec commanded.

Julian didn't budge.

Tubeec shrugged, then turned.

"No!!!" Mena held up her hands, then turned to Julian. "Please, do what they are telling you to do."

"Don't do this," Julian said, reaching for her arm. "These men are dangerous and if you go with them, I might not be able to track you. I might not be able to find you again. There's got to be another way."

"There is no other way. No one else will be coming to save us anytime soon. You can't fight three gunmen by yourself," Mena said.

Julian reached for the Beretta tucked in the back of his pants, a dangerous glint in his eye. "Watch me."

"I won't watch you die," Mena said, gripping his wrist tightly.

"Mena, please—"

"Since we met I've been nothing but trouble for you. You've risked your life too many times to save mine and I can't let you do it again," Mena said, then paused, fighting back tears as her hand trembled in his. "Remember when I stood on the deck of your boat in the middle of the Caribbean screaming at the top of my lungs how much I love you?"

"I can't lose you, not like this," Julian said. "Do not give up! Do you hear me? I can get us out of this, I promise!"

Mena shook her head, "That's how I want you to remember me. To remember us. Just remember that one perfect night on your boat in the middle of Crescent Moon Bay. Just me and you, perfect with our perfect love."

"Mena, I can't do what you're asking me," Julian said, his voice fraught with emotion, his eyes pleading.

"You need to let me do this for you this time. Nobody is after you, but for some reason I keep getting into these awful situations. It stops now. Knowing you are safe is all that matters. Please tell my mom and dad, my brothers, Omar and Regina, all of them, that I love them so much," Mena said. A tear rolled slowly down her face.

Yanking her arm from his grasp, Mena pushed past him and walked over to the men huddled with guns pointing at them.

"I will go with you of my own free will, but you need to let Julian go. Let him live ... please," Mena said. "Tie him up or something so he won't come after us, but don't kill him. That's all I ask. Please."

"I knew a woman once who loved fiercely, dangerously, recklessly ... like you," Tubeec said. He walked toward her and caressed her face. "She didn't hesitate to risk her own life to save those she loved. It is an admirable trait."

Heart pounding, Mena focused on the gunmen in her periphery, their rifles trained on Julian. Even if he was quick enough to get a couple of shots off, he wouldn't be able to kill them all. He would die in a blaze of bullets in the middle of the desert for her. She would not let that happen.

"Do we have a deal?" Mena asked, infusing confidence in her voice. She knew Tubeec wanted her alive. If she could save Julian now, there could be a chance that maybe she could be with him again.

Tubeec smiled at her, then looped his arm in hers, walking her away from the vehicle. "Handcuff the man to the TIGR, but do not harm him."

Chapter Fifty-Two

Shifting against the sand, Julian rolled over, beneath the cover of the Jeep. Pain detonated throughout his body, but he needed to get out of the harsh rays of the sun if he had any chance to survive. For minutes that felt like hours, his body had been a human pinata, absorbing the blows of Tubeec's thugs, pummeling him to the ground. When he'd been unable to fight back any longer, they'd handcuffed him to the axel of the Jeep.

Julian thought they were going to turn the ignition on the bullet-ridden vehicle and drag him a few miles across the red desert land. Lucky for him, the bastards had been summoned by Tubeec to return to El Wak.

Inhaling, Julian felt a sharp pain slice through his lungs. He could have a broken rib, maybe two. Something he could deal with ... after he'd hunted Tubeec down and killed him for taking Mena hostage.

The ground rumbled under his body as a vehicle approached. Julian cowered under the Jeep, peering out into the distance. He couldn't be sure if that was help arriving, a good Samaritan, or someone sent by Tubeec or al-Harakat to kill him. One thing he knew for sure, they were military-grade vehicles.

A man squatted low, his eyes resting on Julian.

"Thought you were dead," Reggie said.

"Don't look so disappointed," Julian responded, from the shadows of the TIGR. "Can you get these off me?"

"What happened out here?" Reggie asked, working a small knife blade back and forth against the cuffs until Julian heard the familiar click.

Yanking his hands down, Julian massaged his swollen wrists, then inched his body from under the Jeep.

Reggie reached a hand down to help him up.

"Al-Harakat had Mena and they were taking her to Tubeec to exchange for the bounty money, but Enzo, Taye, and I got to her first," Julian explained. "Taye took Enzo to the hospital. He was shot up pretty bad and I stayed behind with Mena ... until Tubeec arrived."

"He took Mena?" Reggie asked.

"She agreed to go with him if he spared my life," Julian said, frowning. "For some reason the son of a bitch did, but his guys gave me a good beating before they took off. They're headed to El Wak."

"My team was en route to the airstrip in El Wak, but our planes were downed by anti-aircraft missiles shot from Somalia. My bet is Tubeec called in some favors to buy more time. We have an outpost near here and we were able to scramble and get a ground team together to continue our search for him," Reggie explained.

"Any idea why he wants Mena? Why is she so valuable to him?" Julian asked, taking a sip from the canteen one of the ASF agents gave him.

"Ask Sunny," Reggie said, his shoulders slumping. "She was paid to kidnap Mena. I thought I knew her so well, better than anyone, but this blindsided me. We have evidence that a hundred thousand dollars was wired into her account from a Swiss account linked to Tubeec Hirad."

"The money wasn't sent to Sunny, it was sent to Hakeem," Julian said, then relayed his conversation with Hakeem to Reggie and the secret that Sunny had shared with him a day ago about her sibling.

"Hakeem is her brother," Reggie repeated. "Why am I not surprised she shared her secret with you and not me."

"Whatever you're thinking Sunny and I had in the past, you're wrong," Julian said.

"I'm wrong that you and Sunny were in a relationship, then she dumped you for your best friend and you never got over her, going as far as to blow up her relationship with Broman so she wouldn't be happy with him? Is that wrong?" Reggie asked.

"It wasn't ... like that," Julian said, stumbling over his words. Sunny had told Reggie more than he'd expected.

Did Sunny really think he'd sabotaged her relationship with Broman because he couldn't take losing her? He'd kept his feelings a secret for almost their entire relationship because he wanted Broman to be happy. He would have sacrificed anything for Broman, but the problem was Broman felt the same way about him. Julian had begged Broman not to end the relationship with Sunny, reassuring him that he wouldn't stand in the way of their love. In the end, Broman had chosen him over Sunny and walked away, refusing to love the same woman that Julian had.

But Julian knew now that what he'd felt for Sunny wasn't love. He'd been infatuated and then he'd had his ego bruised. No woman had ever walked away from him for another man. He was the one who did the walking. Yet, Sunny had fallen for Broman and despite finding out later that they were best friends, she had begged Julian to keep their former relationship a secret. A relationship that meant nothing.

Back then it had stung.

Now, he knew she was right. A one-sided infatuation didn't equal love. Mena Nix had shown him what it was like to love someone, truly and unconditionally, and to be loved the same way. The type of love that endured beyond the pain of disappointment and heartache. The type of love that drove him to search all of Kenya until he found Mena again.

"Since you got to Nairobi, she's been putting more distance between us. You've become her priority and I'm on the back burner. Doesn't seem like you're just friends to me," Reggie said.

An agent interrupted, "Chief Agent Kamau, we received intel from Timothy Irungu. An unauthorized Gulfstream landed at the family's private airfield near the construction of the greenhouses early this morning. The Irungu security team isn't responding to any communications and he fears they are all dead. Satellite images have captured three unidentified vehicles, all heading in that direction."

"How far away are we from that airstrip?"

"About an hour," the agent replied.

"One of those vehicles has got to be Tubeec with Mena," Julian insisted.

"Is the Gulfstream still there?" Reggie asked.

"Yes, we've confirmed it's still in the hangar at the airstrip," the agent replied.

Reggie nodded, "Coordinate a three-point entry to the Irungu property near the airstrip. Four-man teams in two of the Jeeps. I will lead the way, using the most direct route in the third Jeep ... with Julian."

Chapter Fifty-Three

The hollow click of a pistol resonated near the side of Mena's face and she grew still. A chill slithered down her spine as she turned her head toward the sound.

To her left, Hakeem rested the barrel of a gun next to the ear of Tubeec's henchman, who kept a tight hold on her arm. His gun, connected to a strap wrapped around his chest, was near his side, out of reach.

Another quick glance to her right and she saw another man, pale with ice blue eyes. In front of her, Tubeec Hirad walked briskly down the middle of the runway toward the opening of the corrugated airplane hangar. The nose of a sleek private jet was barely discernable inside the cavernous space.

"Assad, move away from Mena now," Hakeem barked the order.

Assad released his grip on her arm, pushing her down to the ground. Mena landed with a hard thud on the concrete, crying out from the pain detonating in her hip.

Tubeec stopped at the sound of Hakeem's voice, turned, and watched the ambush unfold. A sly smile crossed his face as he walked toward Hakeem.

"The prodigal protégé has returned," Tubeec said, his arms opened wide as if to hug Hakeem.

A gun blast ricocheted through the air. Assad's body slumped to the ground. Mena held back a scream as she watched blood spewing from the man's neck, his eyes vacant and blank as his body lay lifeless on the ground.

"Hakeem, did you really need to kill a man that was like a brother to you?" Tubeec asked, his arms falling to his side. "Come with me, let's talk."

"I have nothing left to say to you," Hakeem said. Dropping the gun on the ground, he approached Tubeec and extended his arms. The two men embraced, holding each other for a long moment.

The pale man with ice blue eyes approached her slowly, squatting down next to her. "Hey, Mena. I'm Glaze. I work with Julian. I'm going to get you out of here. Don't worry."

Mena nodded, but she couldn't take her eyes off of Hakeem and Tubeec. They were engaged in a congenial conversation, their arms wrapped around each other's shoulders as they stood mere feet away.

"What's going on?" Mena asked.

"Don't worry about Hakeem. He's not going to hurt you," Glaze said, helping her to her feet. "Stay behind me. I need to provide backup for Hakeem. As soon as he's done, we'll get you out of here."

Stepping behind the man, Mena took in her surroundings. The land was void and empty. Nothing but rows of partially constructed greenhouses in the distance. She couldn't see how Hakeem and Glaze planned to escape with her.

"My friend, the exchange is complete. The money has already been delivered to your account. Our arrangement is settled," Tubeec said, walking Hakeem back toward Glaze and Mena. "But I do need you to let me have Ms. Mena Nix. She is critical to a service that I'm providing to a client."

"Can't do that, Tubeec," Hakeem said, an eerie smile on his face. "You won't be harming anyone else ever again."

"What can you do?" Tubeec asked, a challenge in his tone. "It is only by the mercy I am extending to you right now that you haven't been shot dead by my snipers hiding in the hangar. You couldn't possibly believe that I am alone out here."

Mena watched as Cangrejos emerged from the hangar, heavily armed. She remembered him clearly from her captivity with Wangari and Isaac. The man hadn't hesitated to put a bullet in Isaac's head. Would he do the same to Hakeem? Glancing around, Mena looked for a place to provide cover, but the only option was to run into the hangar where she suspected more danger awaited.

Glaze tensed at the sight of Cangrejos, his gun moving between Tubeec and his henchman, ready to shoot either of them if necessary. Hakeem was oblivious to the new threat emerging behind him and Tubeec.

Hakeem laughed. "You once told me that you weren't afraid to die. Well, neither am I."

"But you have so much to live for. A thriving business that has proven to be immensely lucrative. A beautiful sister who risked her own life to save yours. Why should you throw that all away?" Tubeec asked.

Hakeem flinched at the mention of his sister, his eyes growing dark and cold.

Tubeec continued, "Let's remain cordial to each other. Give me Mena and go on your way. No hard feelings."

"You should have told your men to kill me," Hakeem said. With one swift move, his hand released a knife from his waistband and moved in an arc, plunging into Tubeec's chest.

Tubeec's eyes bulged in his face, his hand flying to his chest as he gripped the hilt of the knife. Blood seeped from the wound in a thin line, staining his shirt as he stumbled backward, crashing to the ground. A smile creased his lips.

"Too bad you won't get to see your wife and kids in hell!" Hakeem said, then stomped on Tubeec's chest with his foot. Blood darkened the front of Tubeec's shirt as he grunted in pain, his facial muscles taut in a gruesome grimace.

Glaze screamed, "Get down!"

Mena dropped to the concrete as a blaze of bullets erupted from the hangar. Hakeem scrambled toward them, ducking low to avoid being shot.

Returning fire, Glaze squatted to the ground next to Mena, pressing his body against the warm cement as he tried to take out the hidden gunmen.

"Damn it!" Glaze screamed as his gun stopped responding. His finger flexed against the trigger, but nothing happened. "Out of bullets."

Covering her head with her arms, Mena remained still on the ground, afraid to move. After several seconds, the popping sounds ceased.

Mena peeked above her arm and watched as Hakeem crawled to a large military vehicle hidden between two of the partially completed greenhouses. A quick glance over her shoulder revealed two men emerging from the hangar, carrying rifles pointed at her and Glaze.

The men stomped across the wide concrete, pointing guns at Glaze's head.

"Go. We have no use for you," a man said with a heavy French accent to Glaze. The man then turned to Mena. "You, get up."

Glaze glanced at her, his eyes full of regret as he stood and walked backward toward the greenhouses where Hakeem awaited in the military vehicle. Would they try to help her? Or were they abandoning her to save themselves? She couldn't blame them.

Mena stared down at Tubeec Hirad. A fitting end for the man who'd terrorized her and Wangari and killed Isaac and Grace. She hoped he rotted in hell.

Mena raised her hands in surrender as the men surrounded her, pushing her forward into the hangar. Her footsteps echoed as she entered the towering structure. Across from the private jet, guns, and ammunition littered tables lined against the hangar wall. Her eyes adjusted to the dimness inside the covered area.

A man stood near the plane.

One, unfortunately, very familiar to her.

Her heart pounded in her chest as dread seeped through her veins. Watching the man approach, Mena couldn't breathe. She'd thought she was in danger before, but Tubeec was a minor nuisance compared to what this man from her past represented.

"Adam Russell," Mena whispered, confusion wracking her brain.

"Tie her up and get her on the plane," Adam commanded.

"No, wait! Why are you doing this? What do you want from me?" Mena screamed, trying to resist the men. Her efforts were wasted as they secured her arms and legs with zip ties and lifted her off the ground.

"I don't want anything from you. But Priscilla Dumay does."

Chapter Fifty-Four

"No movement in the hangar. Gulfstream still inside, engines off. No sign of anyone inside or outside," the report from the ASF Agent in the team on the south side of the property crackled in Julian's ear. Julian and Reggie remained still, eyes focused on the open door to the hangar, waiting for further updates. Two agents were snaking their way toward the back of the Irungu's private hangar next to the greenhouse construction project.

Julian and Reggie had driven to the site from the west, parking the jeep behind the furthest greenhouse from the hangar, next to a series of irrigation ditches dug to provide much-needed water to the area. Satisfied that they were obscured from view, they'd been waiting for the other three ASF teams to arrive. Two showed up shortly after they had. One team was positioned along the south of the property behind the hangar while the other had headed around to the east side. The third team had yet to arrive.

"Found the Irungu security team. Three men dead, dumped on the southeast side halfway between the hangar and the security lookout tower. They were shot multiple times in the back with a high-powered assault rifle," another agent reported.

Lifting the binoculars to his eyes, Julian leaned forward past the corner of one of the greenhouses and focused the lenses. He could barely make out the outline of tables and chairs lining the wall of the hangar, but no sign of any people inside. The sun was at an apex as noon approached. The roof of the hangar cast a looming, dark shadow across the interior of the structure. Trailing the binoculars along the front of the hangar, the edge of a bloody body came into view. Twisting the lenses to zoom in closer, Julian recognized the dead man bleeding out on the tarmac. He lowered the binoculars and turned to Reggie.

"Tubeec was stabbed. He's dying over there," Julian said, handing Reggie the binoculars.

"What? Are you sure?" Reggie asked.

"See for yourself," Julian said. He ignored the pain roaring through his muscles and the sharp stabbing in his lungs with each breath he took. On the ride toward El Wak, Julian had availed himself of the medical supplies in Reggie's jeep, wrapping his chest tightly to reduce the pressure from what the ASF had confirmed were a couple of cracked ribs.

Squinting into the distance, Julian could barely make out another body lying listless on the ground, not too far from Tubeec.

If Tubeec Hirad had gotten himself and his team killed, did that mean Hakeem had been successful in exacting his revenge? Had Sunny's brother rescued Mena in the process? Was that why there was no activity in the hangar?

"Good riddance to one of Africa's most wanted," Reggie lowered the binoculars and handed them back to Julian. A smug smile of satisfaction spread across his face.

"We need to get into the hangar," Julian said.

"Hold on. Team three is approaching in the next couple of minutes. When they arrive, we'll join them and drive into the hangar. Just because Tubeec may be dead doesn't mean there isn't an ambush waiting inside," Reggie warned.

Julian wished like hell he had a way to communicate to the TIDES team. Glaze and Hakeem had likely arrived at the hangar long before he had with Reggie and the other ASF agents, but there was no sign of them anywhere.

Pressing the button on the comms, Julian spoke, "Any sign of TIDES?"

Waiting for a response, Julian wasn't surprised when two negatives were returned.

"Team three is here," Reggie said, pointing behind him.

Julian turned to see a military vehicle, machine guns mounted on its roof, approaching slowly, the rust color blending in with the terrain of northeast Kenya.

Reggie turned and walked toward the vehicle as it approached, waving a hand in the air. Lowering the binoculars, Julian followed.

"What took you so long?" Reggie demanded as he approached the driver's door.

"Picked up an extra passenger," the agent replied. The back door swung open and Sunny Tate emerged, dressed in full tactical gear toting an AR-15.

"What are you doing here?" Reggie asked, walking over to Sunny.

"We don't have much time. Taye got Enzo to a hospital in Wajir, he's going to be fine. Hakeem and Glaze made their way to the military airstrip in El Wak and they are safe," Sunny said, then turned to Julian. "But somebody else wants Mena. They let Glaze go, but tied Mena up and took her and put her on the plane."

Julian thought Tubeec wanted Mena as his mistress, not because someone else wanted her.

"Do you know anyone who has a grudge against Mena or would want her kidnapped?" Sunny asked.

"No," Julian said, grappling with this unexpected turn of events.

"Well, somebody wants her. We're lucky that we got here in time before the Gulfstream took off, but who knows what they're waiting on and how much time we have to get in there and rescue her," Sunny explained.

"Did Hakeem and Glaze tell you how many men are with this other group? What are we up against?" Julian asked.

"They didn't know how many were still in the hangar, but every rebel that came out of there was heavily armed and looked local, possibly trained by Tubeec or part of al-Harakat," Sunny said.

"We're wasting time," Julian insisted. Slipping the M4-Carbine over his arm, he walked over to the vehicle and eased inside. Sunny and Reggie followed behind, entering the tank. Each of them found a position where they could secure their weapons and shoot if gunmen were waiting to ambush them.

"We'll enter the hangar in twenty seconds. Wait for my command," Reggie instructed.

Julian focused his eyes on the hangar. The vehicle jerked forward, speeding ahead. An agent sitting next to Julian handed him a vest of bullets.

"You might need this," the agent said, then turned to look through the front windows of the vehicle.

Reggie shouted over the loud engine of the truck. "Be alert and vigilant before firing to ensure we don't take out anyone we should be trying to save."

The truck blazed forward. Julian could see the Gulfstream inside the hangar. The loud hum of the plane's engines started, whirring as it prepared to taxi out onto the runway.

As they neared the entrance, Julian jumped from the moving truck followed by Reggie, Sunny, and the other agents and stormed through the hangar, with guns raised.

Shots rang out from the plane.

The agents scattered, seeking cover and returning fire. Julian pulled the trigger of the M4 Carbine, pelting the side of the plane with bullets as he rushed toward the airplane door. He scanned the windows. Mena's face stared at him in shock. Julian unloaded on the plane's door, riddling it with bullets that bounced back toward him, making small dents in the surface.

Bulletproof?

The door shifted open. Julian pointed the rifle at the figure hovering in the crack.

"Open the damn door! Now!" Julian screamed, squeezing the trigger. A blaze of bullets clattered against the plane. Reggie and his men had taken out the snipers and had the aircraft surrounded.

The door opened wider. The steps, unfolding slowly, descended toward the floor of the hangar. A man stood in the gap.

Adam Russell?

Adam was supposed to be in witness protection, waiting to testify. What was he doing here? Why did he want Mena?

Realization struck Julian. Fuck!

Adam didn't want Mena, but Priscilla Dumay sure as hell did.

Julian aimed his gun at Adam as the man hurled a container down to the ground. The glass crashed onto the concrete floor as Adam disappeared back into the cabin of the plane.

A dense fog of gas filled the hangar, burning and clawing at Julian's eyes. The fumes filled the space with a vengeance, the harsh chemicals assaulting his nose, and burning his lungs. Julian stumbled backward, dizzy, and disoriented. The ASF agents were disarmed, vomiting, and crawling away from the hangar, trying to get out to fresh air.

Julian couldn't go back. He had to get to Mena. Pressing forward, he reached the bottom step of the ladder leading up to the opening of the Gulfstream. His eyes glued to Adam Russell's face peering at him through the window. Vomit and bile wretched in his abdomen. Julian stopped as the liquid spewed from his mouth, leaving a sour after taste. His vision was blurred, eyes watering and burning, but he couldn't give up. He needed to get Mena off that plane. A fit of coughing launched out of his body, rocking him as he struggled to breathe. He could barely move, his muscles seizing and constricting, growing numb. The agents had all collapsed, unmoving in the hangar. Reggie Kamau lay on his back, a stream of vomit bubbling out of his mouth. Sunny was staggering out of the hangar, crawling on her hands and knees.

Julian tried to move his arms and legs, but they weren't responding. Closing his eyes, he inhaled a deep breath, then coughed violently, seizing internally from the fumes.

A coldness infected his body, despair settling within him. He wouldn't save her this time. He wouldn't be her hero. Mena would be delivered to Priscilla Dumay and there was nothing he could do to stop it.

Julian coughed again, the metallic taste of blood spreading in his mouth.

He wanted to see Mena one last time. The woman he loved more than he'd thought was ever possible.

He needed to lift his eyelids, to see her face one more time.

Struggling to open his eyes, he gazed toward the window he'd seen Mena looking out of, her mouth was moving as she banged against the window. Tears streaming down her face. She was so beautiful. She'd blessed him with a gift he'd never thought he'd have after all the damage he'd done. She was strong. She'd escaped before and he prayed she would again. Even if he wouldn't be around to be with her after it was all over.

Chapter Fifty-Five

A bright light filled his vision.

A blank canvas of white, warm, and inviting pulling him forward like a moth to a flame.

"Come ..."

A woman's voice, low and sweet whispered in his ear.

"Julian ... come ..."

He felt wetness against his face. He wanted to touch it, to feel something, anything, but he couldn't.

"Please ... Julian ..." her comforting words grew louder. He couldn't see who she was.

An angel?

Was this heaven?

"Julian ... come ... please ... come ... back ..."

The voice.

A sharp pang rocked the side of his face.

He sucked in a deep breath, filling his lungs with air as his body revolted in agony. Deep, coarse coughs wracked his body, sending spasms of discomfort through his chest.

The fog in his mind cleared. Julian forced his eyes open and stared up into the most beautiful face in the world.

"Am I dreaming?" Julian whispered, his hands reaching up for her, but grasping nothing but air.

Mena sat on the floor near his head, her body twisted at an awkward angle from the zip ties that bound her wrists and her ankles. She stared down at him, a warm smile spreading across her lips. "Thank God you came back to me."

"How did I get here?" Julian asked, trying to remember what happened before he succumbed to the darkness. Squeezing his eyes shut, Julian cycled through his fuzzy memories. The targeted attack on the private hangar owned by the Irungu Family, with Reggie and Sunny close behind him. Adam Russell standing in the open doorway of the plane.

"Two of Adam Russell's men carried you onboard," Mena said, leaning back.

"What happened to the others?" Julian asked, concern growing for Reggie, Sunny, and the ASF agents who'd charged into the hangar with him. Had they survived the ambush?

"I don't know. After they got you on board, the plane taxied and took off. I think they were left behind, passed out from the gas," Mena said.

Concentrating, Julian tried to move his legs, but they didn't respond. Not yet. He sucked in a sharp breath from the excruciating, electric currents assaulting every muscle in his body as his nerve endings slowly came to life. In a few more minutes, he should have full mobility. "How long have we been in the air?"

"Feels like hours, but I can't be sure," Mena said, a look of concern spreading across her face. "Adam is behind all of this. He told the pilots not to take off until you got to the hangar."

"You know that for sure?" Julian asked, stunned.

"Priscilla Dumay wants both of us brought back to St. Basil. I don't know what she plans to do to us, but this was all her doing. She paid Tubeec to kidnap me. I'm not sure why he took Wangari, Isaac and Grace as well."

"Tubeec got greedy and saw a way to use your friendship with Wangari Irungu to orchestrate a personal mission of his own," Julian said.

"He wanted something from Okeyo Lagat," Mena said. "Do you know what it was?"

"Evidence that could land Deputy President Kipsang Rono in prison. Tubeec arranged for the evidence to be destroyed. Either Rono paid him to do it or Tubeec was hoping to have the Deputy President owe him a big favor," Julian said, no longer concerned with the nuances of Kenyan politics. Not when he needed to figure out why Adam Russell wasn't in witness protection right now and what Dumay wanted with him and Mena.

"How many gunmen are on board with us?" Julian asked.

"Only two from what I could see," Mena said.

"Two guards, Adam, and two pilots," Julian muttered out loud, trying to formulate a plan of attack once he was able to break the lock that he was sure had them trapped in the bedroom compartment.

"And Dr. Quentin Tufa," Mena said. "He's on the plane as well."

"So Dumay has us with her beloved adopted brother." Julian thought about the ramifications of that information. With Adam on board, he was fairly certain they wouldn't be harmed before the plane landed. But with Quentin as one of the passengers, he knew Dumay wouldn't take any chances that her brother wouldn't arrive back safely. He could use this to their advantage.

Mena said, "Once we land, I think we'll find out exactly what Dumay has in store for us."

"We're not going to give her that chance," Julian said, pumping air into his lungs as the shooting pangs leveled off into minor aches in his muscles. Trying again, he was able to bend his legs and wiggle his toes within his boots.

"What are you going to do?" Mena asked.

"Get control of this plane from Adam," Julian said. "But first, I got to get you out of those zip ties."

Chapter Fifty-Six

Sliding the door open, Julian peered out into the compartment. Two large sofas lined the walls of the plane. Dr. Quentin Tufa lay asleep on one of the sofas, snoring with his mouth slack. No sign of a weapon nearby him.

Across from Quentin stood two African guys, their backs to Julian, engaged in a heated discussion in what sounded like French. Both were shorter and leaner than Julian. Two AR-15s rested against the sofa near the men, a couple of arms lengths away.

Likely, they had expected Julian to be knocked out for much longer, which was why they hadn't tied him up or restrained him in the room with Mena. They also had been careless in their search of his body for weapons, discovering the Berettas, but missing the butterfly knife secured in his calf holster. The knife had come in handy to get Mena out of the zip ties used to restrain her and to open the locked door.

Closing the door, Julian rested the butterfly knife on the table next to the bed and assessed his options. With the element of surprise, he could easily take them out as long as Quentin didn't wake up.

Adam Russell was conspicuously absent from the room, likely in the front compartment of the Gulfstream, separated from the other men. Julian wasn't naive enough to think Adam wasn't heavily armed and ready to blow his head off if he discovered what he was doing.

"Shouldn't we wait until we land. It would be much safer to try to get away then, wouldn't it?" Mena asked.

Julian turned to look at the love of his life. She was wringing her hands as she stared back at him, fear and worry etched on her face. He didn't want to do anything that could get her hurt, but not making a move on Adam and his men until they landed was the worst of all of their options.

"We won't get a better chance than the one we have right now. I can get the jump on the two gunmen, and then Quentin and Adam will be a lot easier to deal with," Julian said.

"It's too dangerous!" Mena whispered, pulling Julian's arm. He stepped away from the door and placed his hands on her hips, facing her.

Mena continued, "I don't want you to go out there. Whatever Priscilla Dumay wants from us, it's not to see us dead. She needs us alive for some reason or she would have paid Tubeec Hirad to murder us instead. We should wait this out, see what she wants and then decide what to do then. Please, Julian."

Her idea wasn't bad. But, his experience had taught him that going on the offensive was the best way of getting the upper hand on an enemy. Allowing Dumay to further embroil them in whatever web she was spinning could leave them trapped, with few options. Julian wasn't going to let that happen.

"We can't play this game with Dumay. Right now, we have a chance to take the advantage and do something she wouldn't expect," Julian said.

"I don't have a good feeling about this," Mena said, tears welling in her eyes as she pulled him into her arms.

Julian pressed his lips against her forehead, wrapping his arms tighter around her waist. "Thought you trusted me."

"It's not you I'm worried about. Adam has gone through a lot of trouble and dealt with some dangerous men to make sure he could kidnap us and take us back to St. Basil. He's not going to let Priscilla down," Mena insisted, as she rested her head against his chest.

"And I'm not going to let you down. Priscilla's days of terrorizing you are over. I promise you that," Julian said. Hearing the fear and concern in Mena's voice further solidified his resolve to end things with Dumay now. Once they got back to St. Basil, he didn't want Mena worrying about being attacked or abducted. Forget testifying at Dumay's trial. Julian was going to make sure that bitch never got the chance to hurt Mena again.

"Fine. What do you need me to do?" Mena asked.

Julian smiled at his fearless beauty. She had all the confidence and boldness in the world when he was at her side. But this battle he was going to fight on his own.

"I need you to hide in the bathroom while I take care of things out there. It's going to get ... messy. I want you protected as much as I can," Julian said.

"You'll need back up," Mena said. "I know how to shoot a gun now."

"You got one hidden in there," Julian asked, pulling her shirt open as he stared down at her amazing breasts.

"Stop it!" Mena laughed. "Be serious. No, I don't have a gun on me."

"Then I guess you'll have to hide in the bathroom, Annie Oakley. Seriously, I don't want to worry about you while I'm out there. Once I'm done, I'll be back to get you," Julian said.

Mena caressed the sides of his face with her hands, leaning in to give him the most passionate kiss. Savoring the taste of her, Julian allowed himself a moment to indulge, swirling his tongue next to hers as his hands slipped down and rubbed her ass.

Too soon, Mena pulled away from him. "You better come back alive or I will never forgive you."

Julian watched as Mena walked backward toward the bathroom. She blew him a kiss, then stepped inside and closed the door behind her.

Turning back toward the door leading out of the bedroom, Julian slid it open and watched the gunmen. They were still arguing. One of the men held a tablet between them as their heated exchange continued. Julian focused on the screen. Video of a soccer match being played, maybe from the World Cup.

The guns were still on the couch. The man closest to Julian pointed at the video, vigorously trying to make some point to the other gunman who was looking off into the distance as if contemplating the man's perspective.

Julian felt the familiar anticipation of combat settling through his body, adrenaline pumping as he focused on the slow metronomic beats thudding in his chest. His hand gripped the butterfly knife and he slipped out of the room, easing the door closed behind him.

In two steps, he reached down and swiped one of the guns from the couch with his left hand while plunging the blade of the butterfly knife into one of the men's throat, twisting then jerking it forward. The rebel dropped the tablet, his hands flying to his throat as his body fell to the ground. Julian pushed the man forward toppling him into the other rebel, who let out a frantic cry. Julian pointed the gun at his chest and pulled the trigger, silencing his wails.

"The lazy fools didn't tie you up like they should have," Dr. Quentin Tufa said, rising from the couch. He stretched and yawned, then settled back against the sofa. "I swear if we don't give specific instructions, things never come out right."

Julian sat down on the couch across from Quentin, securing the second AR-15 on his body with the shoulder strap. He pointed the gun at Dumay's co-conspirator in crime and adopted brother.

Quentin taunted, "Go ahead. Kill me. You can't stop what we've already put in motion."

Chapter Fifty-Seven

A loud shot sent a jolt through Mena. She screamed, unable to stop the sound from erupting from her mouth.

Grasping for the silver handle of the bathroom door, she squeezed it tight, turned, and pushed the door open. Had Julian been shot? What was happening out there?

Against the warning bells going off in her head, Mena rushed forward through the bedroom and slid open the door, stepping into the middle compartment of the plane.

The smell of death gagged her. The sickening and overpowering sweet metallic scent mixed with smoke from the rifle lingered in the air.

Scanning the room, her eyes were drawn to two dead men, their bodies crossing each other in a heap on the floor. One man's neck was mangled and open revealing tissue and muscle as blood continued to ooze from the wound. The other man's eyes were wide open, staring at the ceiling in shock. His neck, chest, and arms covered in dark blood.

Gasping, Mena fought to resist vomiting as she stumbled backward.

"Mena!"

Startled away from the gruesome scene, Mena looked toward the sound and saw Julian standing near one of the couches. Concern clouded his face as he stared at her.

"You shouldn't be out here. Go back inside the bedroom," Julian said.

Mena rushed toward him, flinging her arms around him. "I thought you'd been shot. I had to come out and make sure you were okay."

"I'm fine, but you need to go back where you're safe. I still need to find Adam Russell," Julian said. He rested one arm around her while he pointed the large assault rifle toward someone behind her.

She looked over her shoulder. Dr. Quentin Tufa was on the couch, his head propped up on his hands as he stared back at them.

"No need to worry about Adam Russell. He won't be ambushing anyone," Quentin said.

"You're lying," Julian said, stepping in front of Mena shielding her from the view of the two dead bodies and Quentin. Mena peered around Julian's massive frame, her hand gripping one of his arms.

"Check the luggage closet for yourself. Adam thought he could redeem himself for agreeing to testify against my sister by getting me out of Africa undetected," Quentin said, shifting his feet to the floor as he sat upright. "My sister is more forgiving than I am."

Julian turned and placed the assault rifle in Mena's hands.

"I'm going to tie Quentin up while you hold the gun on him. If he makes a crazy move, you shoot him, center mass. Don't worry about me. I'll make sure I give you enough room to make the shot," Julian said.

"I've never shot a rifle before," Mena said. The rifle weighed a ton as it rested against her forearm.

"Like riding a bicycle, you've ridden one, you've rode them all. Trust your instincts, okay," Julian said, then gave her a quick peck on the cheek.

Mena held the gun outward, lacing her finger on the trigger and directed it toward Quentin's chest. Julian snatched tactical ties from the pocket of one of the dead gunmen and used them to secure Quentin's hands and feet. He didn't resist being restrained, allowing Julian to immobilize him without a fight.

Lifting Quentin from the couch, Julian dragged the man past Mena and into the bedroom where they'd been kept for most of the flight. She stood alone in the middle of the compartment, unsure of what to do next. Had Quentin killed Adam Russell? Was the danger over?

The door to the bedroom closed with a loud bang. Mena jumped and turned, pointing the rifle at Julian's head. He was calm, reaching for the barrel as he lowered it to her side, then slipped the weapon from her hand.

"You're okay," Julian said, squeezing her hand. "I'm going to check the luggage closet and see if Tufa was telling us the truth."

Mena stepped back, her mind swirling with confusion and terror as she held her breath. Julian gripped the gun tightly as he approached the door near the back of the compartment. Lifting the latch to open the closet door, he tugged at it and the door swung open. Inside, Mena could see Adam Russell, bound and gagged. His body twisted at an awkward angle to fit into the space. A gash with dried blood was on his head, above the temple.

Julian squatted low and pressed his fingers against Adam's neck. "He's still breathing."

Standing, Julian stood up and closed the door. "We'll leave him in there for now."

Mena walked over to Julian.

"What's our next move?" Mena asked.

"We wait until the pilot lands the plane in St. Basil and we make a run for it there—"

A gunshot blast rang through the air.

Hot searing pain sliced through Mena's arm. She looked down at the blood oozing from her bicep as she fell backward onto the floor, her landing softened by the body of one of the dead gunmen.

Julian spun around.

Mena screamed as bullets whizzed through the cabin.

Chapter Fifty-Eight

Julian looked at the man with two gunshot wounds to the chest wedged between the open cockpit door.

Bastard must have been one of the pilots. Would the other one come out firing too? Julian weighed the risks, standing his ground as he pointed the rifle toward the open door.

Leaning slightly, he looked for any signs of another threat from the cockpit. The Gulfstream likely had an auto-pilot function, but he was gambling that the lead pilot wouldn't leave his post to join the fray, especially with his co-pilot bleeding out in the doorway next to him. Keeping the plane steady and headed to its destination without crashing probably was his greater concern.

Turning around, Julian rushed over to Mena. She was sweating profusely, her face a mask of pain as she gripped her bloody arm with her left hand.

"It hurts like hell," Mena said, through shaky breaths. The dark red blood staining her fingers as it coursed down the length of her arm. Her body was propped against one of the dead gunmen sprawled on the floor near the center of the cabin.

Julian scrambled down to the floor and wrapped his arms around

Mena. Rising to his feet, he carried her to the couch. Her body trembled as she struggled to deal with the pain.

"Can you move your hand away? Let me take a look," Julian said.

Leaning her head back against the cushion of the couch, she slowly uncurled her fingers from her bloodied arm. The wound was nasty, skin and muscles ripped to shreds but luckily, he detected an exit wound. Julian suspected the bullet had damaged her muscles and not hit her humerus bone. Dealing with a gunshot wound would be tough enough. He didn't want her dealing with a broken bone on top of that.

"How bad is it?" Mena asked, her eyes clenched tight.

"You really want the answer to that?" Julian asked, scanning the room for materials to stop the bleeding. The blood was gushing at a rate faster than Julian would have preferred. A sign that the major brachial artery in her arm could have been hit. He had to make sure she didn't bleed out before the plane landed and he could get her to the hospital.

"Good question. The less I know until I get to the hospital, the better. Nothing we can do until we land anyway," Mena said.

"Have you forgotten that you're dating a highly trained ex-special forces veteran of the military?" Julian said, giving her a wink.

A laugh erupted from Mena, then she winced in pain. "Don't make me laugh."

"I love your laugh. It's good to hear, despite this fucked up situation," Julian said.

Moving toward the cabinet next to the couch, Julian opened the door and pulled out the first aid kit. Inside, a row of four clear medical vials were secured to the lid. Julian removed one of the vials and peered at the clear contents. No label or markings to indicate what was inside. He'd hoped it was an antibiotic, but couldn't take a chance of giving it to Mena without knowing for sure. Julian slipped the vial into his pocket just in case, then turned his focus to the other contents. Grabbing a handful of triangular bandages, roller gauze, scissors, and the bottle of pain relievers, he headed back to Mena.

"Take four of these," Julian said, opening the bottle and shaking the pills out onto her hand. He wrapped her arm in bandages secured by roller gauze to staunch the bleeding.

Mena popped the pills in her mouth and swallowed, looking up at him. "Is it over?"

Glancing around at the gruesome scene, Julian paused. He'd killed three men on the plane to protect Mena, tied up Quentin Tufa, and left Adam Russell in an unknown state, but alive, bound and gagged in a luggage closet.

He didn't want to think about what Mena thought of him right now. The quickness to which he resorted to taking out the threats, without any hesitation. The quickness he planned to unleash to eliminate the last threat against them.

But the look on her face eased away any concern that was building. He saw pure love in her eyes and a desperate hope that the challenges they'd faced were now behind them. He would do anything to protect her and keep her safe.

Julian leaned over and placed his lips against hers, savoring the soft sweetness of her mouth as he kissed her fully.

"Yeah, it's over. When we land, we'll call Kendrick and get the police to round up Quentin and Adam—"

Turbulence shook the plane, jolting Julian. He stumbled backward, struggling to maintain his balance.

"Julian, what's happening?" Mena asked, reaching for him.

"Just stay here," Julian said, picking up the assault rifle. "I'm going to go check on the pilot."

Julian took a step toward the flight deck, then dropped to his knees as the plane lurched forward into a dangerously steep descent. What the hell was wrong with the pilot? Was he trying to crash the plane ... on purpose? Glancing out the window, Julian could see land in the distance. Tropical islands dotting the water.

Struggling to stand, Julian rushed toward the cockpit, stepping over the dead co-pilot in the doorway and peered inside, his gun pointed toward the pilot seat.

Empty.

A surge of adrenaline spiked through his veins as he scanned the cockpit. Lights flashed across the instrument board and the control wheel shook wildly as the altimeter registered falling altitude.

Dropping the gun, Julian slid into the pilot's seat and placed the headset on his head. He had to do something, anything to get the plane not to crash.

"There's no other pilot?" Mena's voice wafted from behind.

"Looks like I took out the one guy who was flying this plane," Julian said, annoyed that he hadn't checked earlier after he shot the pilot. He'd assumed that the Gulfstream was manned by two pilots like protocol. But this was far from a typical situation. Maniacs like Adam Russell and Quentin Tufa followed rules of their own design and weren't concerned with safety standards.

Mena slid into the co-pilot chair, fumbling with the straps of the seat belt before locking herself in. "Have you ever flown a plane?"

"Never," Julian said, a wisp of sadness in his tone that he hadn't wanted to let out.

Mena grimaced, then reached her hand out toward his. "I love you, Julian. Thank you for—"

"Stop it. We're not dying. Not today," Julian said, squeezing her hand then bringing it to his lips for a quick kiss.

Julian pressed the VHF radio button and flipped the talk switch on the communication panel.

"Mayday, mayday, mayday," Julian spoke into the headset.

The radio was silent.

"Are you sure it's on?" Mena asked.

Julian checked the lights and switch again. "Can't say for sure, but it looks like it."

"Try again," Mena encouraged.

"Mayday, mayday, mayday, we need immediate help to avoid a crash. Mayday, mayday, mayday," Julian said, blood rushing in his ears as he waited for a response.

The radio crackled, then a voice filled the air. "N303GA St. Killian go ahead."

"Pilot is incapacitated. Need help to land safely."

"N303GA say last known location."

"I don't know. Took off from El Wak in Kenya," Julian said, shifting in his seat. "Losing altitude steadily. Kind of nose-diving. How do I get level?"

"Squawk 7700 if you have a transponder."

"I don't know what that means," Julian said. "Plane is falling! How do I get it level?"

"N303GA have you flown a plane before?"

"No," Julian responded.

A brief silence, then a voice he'd recognize anywhere came on the line.

"Lucky you have friends in high places, N303GA," a woman's voice filled the air.

"Damn it, Sunny! Get me out of this fucking mess," Julian said, relief coursing through his body.

"I'm in an ASF military jet with Reggie. We've been following your plane this whole time. No way I was letting you get kidnapped. Now pay close attention because this is going to sound like Greek. I will describe what stuff looks like and just do exactly what I say," Sunny said.

"You're going to enjoy bossing me around, aren't you?" Julian quipped.

Julian tightened his seat belt, then followed the instructions from Sunny on the radio. Within minutes, he'd brought the plane to level and re-engaged the autopilot.

"We'll have you landed in about ten minutes," Sunny said.

A loud beep filled the air.

"What was that?" Mena asked, straining forward.

Julian scanned the instrument panel, his eyes drawn to the flashing alert.

"Got a problem," Julian spoke into the headset.

"What's wrong?" Sunny asked.

"Fuel level low error message," Julian said. An eerie quiet settled in the cockpit as the engines stopped. Mena glanced at him, terror in her eyes.

"Damn. You're not close enough. Power on the fuel pumps and go full throttle," Sunny barked in his ear.

Julian followed her directions, but the engines wouldn't start.

The plane was going down.

Fast.

"Julian, listen to me. You're going to have to land the plane on the water. It's the best chance you have," Sunny said. "The angles will be important. Too steep and the force of the collision will kill you. Out of balance and the plane could cartwheel and tear the aircraft to pieces."

"You're scaring the shit out of me, right now," Julian said.

"I know you. You operate better when you know all the risks," Sunny responded. "Water is no different from land. Just pretend that's glass down there and you have to land this baby soft and gentle."

Julian ignored the ocean looming closer through the window, focusing on the details of Sunny's instructions instead. Muscles aching with tension, he held onto the control wheel as the plane dove closer and closer to the water. An island loomed straight ahead as the plane rocked back and forth. Julian glanced at Mena, her eyes squeezed shut as she braced for impact.

"Pull back on the yoke. Slowly!" Sunny directed.

Seconds later the plane struck the surface of the Caribbean Sea. The impact was deafening, shuddering the aircraft as water sprayed across the windshield. Julian fought to retain control of the wheel. His body bounced and jerked back and forth until the plane slammed to a stop, hurling him into the tight harness of the seat belt. Pain detonated across his chest, aggravating his cracked ribs and knocking the wind out of him. He fought to inhale, but the pain was searing and he almost blacked out from the effort.

"Good job, Montgomery," Sunny's voice crackled in the headset. "We have a visual of your location. Palmchat Islands Coast Guard has been alerted. Help is on the way."

"Couldn't have done it without you. I owe you Sunny," Julian said.

"Damn right, you do."

Leaning backward, he fumbled for the release of the seatbelt, then turned toward Mena.

"You okay?" Mena asked.

"I am now," Julian said, unhooking her seatbelt and pulling her into his arms.

"Good. Let's get off this damn plane," Mena said.

Leading the way, Julian stepped over the dead bodies piled up on the cabin floor and activated the emergency window exit. Pushing it open, the side of the plane was tilted, partially submerged in the beach, with about a three foot drop to the ground.

Jumping down, he turned and lifted Mena off the plane. The sounds of sirens filled the air. Coast guard and police boats raced across the waves, making their way to the wreckage.

"Julian ... look behind you," Mena said, a frown piercing her beautiful face.

Julian turned around and winced.

A mansion, burned and in ruins loomed in front of him. The same mansion he and Mena had escaped from a year ago. He'd landed the plane on Dumay's private island. The place where all the mayhem had begun.

Chapter Fifty-Nine

"Was that Sunny? What did she say?" Mena asked.

Julian closed the hotel door behind him, then tossed his phone on the bedside table, before sliding across the bed and placing a decadent kiss on her mouth.

She savored the sweetness of his lips, the sexy scent he exuded. A feeling she thought she might not ever have again, yet here he was in bed next to her, put up in the Queen Palm Hotel in St. Killian, courtesy of Caleb's boss at the *Palmchat Gazette*, Leo Bronson.

"Yeah, it was her. Enzo is back home and expected to make a full recovery," Julian said, then stretched out on the bed next to Mena. "Tubeec Hirad survived being stabbed by Hakeem. He claims to have a copy of the evidence Okeyo Lagat had against Deputy President Rono and is trying to use it as a bargaining chip for his release."

"Do they believe him? He has to be lying," Mena said, flinching as she readjusted the sling on her arm.

"Maybe. Maybe not. ASF is taking his claims seriously and considering brokering a deal to see what he has," Julian said.

"I can't believe they would consider negotiating with a terrorist," Mena said, shaking her head in disbelief.

"Why don't we let Reggie figure out that mess." Julian pulled her into his arms. "Is that okay? I'm not hurting your arm, am I?"

"It's fine. I'm too doped up to feel any pain," Mena lied, looking down at her heavily bandaged swollen right arm. The bullet had entered near the middle of her bicep and came out above her elbow without hitting bone or a major artery. It was the best prognosis considering the situation. The doctors at St. Killian General had cleaned the wound, stitched her up, bandaged and splinted her arm, and then sent her home with sobering warnings about the difficult recovery period and potential loss of normal use even with months of physical therapy she had ahead of her.

"Good, well not good that you're a dope head right now, but I'm glad you're not in pain," Julian teased.

Mena slapped the back of his head.

"Ouch!" Julian said, then leaned over and kissed her again.

"Maybe ASF can get the evidence against Rono without having to set Tubeec free. Then, Rono can finally be held accountable for the countless attacks he orchestrated on innocent Kenyans who supported his political rivals," Mena said.

"Arresting Rono would be a slam dunk. Conviction could be a lot tougher, given Rono's well-connected friends, but his political career would be D.O.A. That's if Tubeec actually has the evidence against him," Julian said, twirling a strand of her dark hair around his finger. "But I'm sure Okeyo Lagat will do everything in his power to put Rono in jail, with or without Tubeec Hirad. It may take some time, but he should be able to gather the evidence he had before. Speaking of Okeyo, did you get a chance to talk to Wangari while I was out?"

Mena stroked his arm, lost in the memories of her conversation with the Director of the museum. "She was disappointed and offered a lot of concessions to entice me to finish out the fellowship. Private residence with a driver and a private TIDES bodyguard."

"You already have a private TIDES bodyguard," Julian said.

"I think she feels a lot of guilt about what happened and wants to make amends, but she doesn't know the real truth behind it all. Dumay set all of this in motion and that had nothing to do with Wangari or Okeyo. None of this was her fault," Mena said.

"Having second thoughts?" Julian asked.

"No. Even knowing that Priscilla wants us back in St. Basil for some reason, I can't see myself going back to Nairobi to finish out the fellowship," Mena admitted. After everything Priscilla had put her through, hiring an African terrorist to abduct her and bring her back to the Palmchat Islands, Mena was more convicted than ever to ensure Priscilla was found guilty of all of her crimes.

"If we're not going back to Nairobi, then where to next? Do you want to stay here and be close to your dad?" Julian asked, a curious look in his eyes.

Mena cringed. Not that she didn't love her father but being on the same island with him was going to be tough. She had a few more hours before her parents landed in the Bronson private jet. While she couldn't wait to see them again, she was also dreading the smothering and overprotectiveness she knew was coming.

"I think going back to St. Basil is what I want," Mena said. "Regina and Omar are both there. They say 'hi' by the way and thanks for saving my life ... again."

Julian laughed, then kissed her on the forehead. "Did they really think I wouldn't?"

Mena paused, emotions choking her throat as she worked to push past them.

"Julian, I don't know how to thank you for everything you did in Africa. You risked your life over and over again to find me. To save me from getting killed."

Julian was quiet. His soulful brown eyes expressed an infinite wave of love, filling her to the brim and threatening to take her under. She hoped he felt how much she loved him in return.

Mena continued, "You were my relentless hero, not letting anything stop you from rescuing me. I will never forget what you did and I will never take you for granted again. I promise you that I will do anything and everything to protect our love. I'm all in ... with you."

Chapter Sixty

The door to the elevator dinged, opening into the opulent lobby of the
Queen Palm Hotel.

Mena glanced left and right, then stepped outside into the fray of
tourists milling about the grand establishment. She'd been lucky that
Julian had already left the hotel to run errands when she got the text
message. Glancing down at her phone, she checked the location of the
private cabana again. Number 15 near the waterfall pool and closest to
the beach.

She didn't have much time to get rid of him.

Julian would be back in a few hours and then they had dinner with
her parents tonight at Caleb's house. She was determined to not let
this meeting ruin her day. Everything had changed for her after facing
down death over and over again in the desert of northeastern Kenya.
Mena knew without a doubt that she wanted nothing more than to be
with Julian forever. A commitment she cherished. She never thought
she'd get married again, but now that was all she wanted.

Julian had been giddy and secretive about his outing today. She had
a feeling they were on the same page and by dinner tonight, they would
be engaged. The last thing she needed was her past coming back to
ruin this day for her.

Taking the winding path past the Olympic sized pool, through the jungle enclave and out toward the outer pool decks, Mena scanned the numbers on the cabanas until she saw 15. It was discreet, the opening partially hidden from the view of anyone walking by and the furthest from the hotel. At least he gave her that courtesy.

As she stepped toward the cabana, the fabric curtain opened and she went inside. Her breath caught in her throat as she looked at the man she'd married four years ago. Dr. Michael Marsh. He hadn't changed one bit, still the same handsome doctor she'd made the mistake of falling in love with.

"What took you so long?" Michael asked, walking toward her, his hazel eyes concerned as he stopped mere feet from her. The kind eyes that she'd fallen for so many years ago. "I've been worried sick since the bombing at the museum. When you didn't show up to meet me, I knew something was wrong. I kept trying to find you, but the Kenyan police didn't know anything. Then I heard you were on that private plane that crashed landed on one of the outer Palmchat Islands. I got here as fast as I could."

"You shouldn't have followed me to Kenya, and you shouldn't have come here either," Mena said, remembering the coral peonies that had arrived at the Irungu Center before Tubeec's attack. The exact flowers from her bridal bouquet had arrived on what would have been their fifth anniversary, January 13th.

"Don't say that," Michael said, reaching for her. Mena slipped away from his touch, walking deeper into the cabana.

"What happened to your arm?" Michael asked, closing the space between them. "Let me take a look at it."

"Don't touch me. You're a damn neurologist. That doesn't qualify you to assess a gunshot wound," Mena said, exasperated by the proximity of him.

"Gunshot wound? Who shot you? What the hell happened on that plane?" Michael asked. The genuine concern in his tone rattled Mena, shaking her resolve.

"I'm fine. I've been checked out by the best doctors in St. Killian. I don't need a second opinion," Mena said. "I don't have all day to waste with you. Why have you been trying to get in touch with me? What do you want?"

"You." Michael's eyes twinkled as the words oozed from his mouth.

Her mouth fell open. "What did you just say?"

"You heard me. I want you. I want us back. Somewhere deep inside of you, I know you still love me. You didn't want our marriage to end just like I didn't. We were both blindsided. But now, everything has changed. We belong together and if you could accept the truth of what really happened, we could get back everything we had before. I've never stopped loving you," Michael said.

"You love me so much that you didn't tell me you had not one, not two, but three other wives across three states. Do you know how disgusting it feels to know that you tricked me and lied to me! You were a polygamist, juggling four wives at one time—"

"I was not married to all of those women!" Michael screamed back at her. "The day I met you, I walked away from all of them. I swear to you. When I stood before that minister on the beach in Miami and vowed to love you, I believed I was free of all the mistakes of my past."

"But you weren't! What about Emma and Alexis? When you married me, they both thought you were their husband," Mena said.

"No, they didn't. I hadn't been around them much in years," Michael said.

"Are you serious right now?"

"Yes. Both Emma and Alexis signed affidavits that they were aware of my marriage with Courtney and knew that our unions were not valid," said Michael.

"What are you talking about? When did they do that?"

"During the bigamy trial, it all came out. That's not all. I have proof that divorce papers were drawn up for me and Courtney a month after you and I met. She was supposed to sign the papers and file them with the court, but she didn't. I thought I was divorced before we fell in love and before I proposed to you," Michael said, reaching for Mena's hand.

Mena jerked away from him. "That's not what she told me after she showed up at my doorstep with a gun and a rag doused with chloroform. If she believed her marriage was over, why the hell did she kidnap me and try to kill me for sleeping with her husband?"

"You know better than anyone how unstable Courtney is. She didn't want to accept the fact that we were over. That I'd met you and found true love. She didn't want us to be happy. Don't forget that I was your first hero. I risked my life to save you from that crazy bitch because I love you. Don't you remember how good we were together? How much we meant to each other and the life we were building? We can have that again. It's not too late."

Mena jabbed her fingers into Michael's chest, pushing him backward. "I don't want to be with you! I am in love with someone else. Julian Montgomery. Do you hear me? He's the man I'm going to marry."

"You can't marry him," Michael said, pain in his eyes as he reached for her.

"The hell I can't. I feel nothing for you, Michael. Anything I felt for you died the day Courtney showed up on the doorstep of our home," Mena said.

"Then I guess you'll be the bigamist, not me," Michael said, walking away from her toward the opening of the cabana curtains.

"What does that mean?" Mena asked, stomping after him.

"You can't marry Julian because you're already married. Once I won the case of the criminal charges for bigamy, that means our marriage was valid. You never filed for an annulment or a divorce—"

"That's because our marriage was void based on the statutes of the state of Florida. I didn't have to file anything for a marriage that was never valid in the first place," Mena said, stalking over toward him.

"Except our marriage wasn't void. The court ruled that I wasn't a bigamist and that means ..."

"No, that can't be true," Mena shook her head, her body trembling with anger.

"It is true. Mena, based on the laws of the state of Florida, you are still my wife."

Epilogue

Easing the motorcycle into the curved entrance to the Queen Palm hotel, Julian guided to a stop and stared over at Mena waiting under the expansive portico. The wind whipped through her hair as she absently spun the bracelet around her wrist, smiling back at him.

Mena rushed over to him. His mouth found hers and he parted her lips with his tongue, desperate to taste her after being apart from her for the past eight hours.

Breaking the kiss, Julian said, "Hey beautiful."

"Hey," Mena said, breathless. "So, this was your top-secret errand?"

"I knew it would take all day to get the ferry over to St. Basil, grab the bike from Kendrick's house and return to St. Killian," Julian said. "You like the surprise?"

"I love it," Mena said as Julian pushed his body back along the bike seat.

The small jewelry box secured into the pocket of his cargo pants pressed firmly against his thigh. This wasn't the only surprise he had in store for Mena. He hoped she meant it when she told him she was "all-in." He loved her more than he thought was fathomable and it was time for them to make the ultimate commitment to one another.

"Ladies first," Julian said, allowing her to get in front of him. Mena straddled the bike. He loved the strength and confidence she exuded when she was in command of the Harley Road King. But with one arm in a sling, she wouldn't be able to steer the bike. Slipping his arms underneath hers, Julian gripped the bars and revved the engine.

"It's too early to leave for my Dad's house. What are you up to?" Mena said.

"On the ferry, I heard about this magical place on the island. It's on the way to Caleb's and I thought we could stop there first," Julian said.

"Magic? Seriously?" Mena asked.

"Stop being a skeptic and roll with it," Julian said, kissing her cheek. Adjusting the kickstand on the motorcycle, he peeled out of the driveway and onto the open road.

Twenty minutes later, he brought the bike to a stop along a deserted stretch of tropical road. Julian swung his leg over the bike, then lifted Mena off. Her eyes danced with excitement at the breathtaking view that stretched in front of them.

He was so lucky to have her. The woman who'd made life worth living again with her unconditional love and acceptance of him, his flaws, and all the mistakes he'd made in the past. He'd trusted her with his deepest, darkest secrets and had gotten compassion and understanding in response. A liberating act that had changed his life forever.

"You think that's beautiful," Julian said tipping his head toward the light turquoise waters of the inlet. "Wait til you see what's down there."

Slipping his hand in hers, Julian led Mena down a short trail through a copse of hibiscus bushes until the shrubbery gave way and revealed a thin stretch of black sand beach leading into the water.

"Amazing," Mena said, kneeling to run her hand through the grainy black sand. "I can't believe we have the place all to ourselves."

"It's more popular for sunrises, but the ridge up there blocks the area from the magnificent sunset views that you can get on the other side of the island. So, for right now, this is our own private space," Julian explained.

"And what's so magical about it?" Mena asked. She stood and stepped toward him, wrapping her arm around his waist.

"I was told that this is the only black sand beach in the Palmchat Islands outside of St. Felipe. The locals tell stories that over the decades, hundreds of people have come here and had all their troubles washed away. Floating in the water and drying on the black sand is supposed to cleanse you from all the pain and burdens in life. You emerge with a clean slate, ready to live life again without the challenges you'd faced before," Julian said. "But there's a sort of ritual to get the magic to work."

"A ritual?" Mena giggled, lacing her fingers within his as he pulled her closer.

"Yes and after everything we've been through, I think we should do it. Couldn't hurt, right?"

"I don't know," Mena said, a teasing glint in her eyes. "You haven't told me what this ritual is ..."

"It's simple. First you need to take these off," Julian said, pointing to her clothes.

"You know what happened the last time you lured me to go swimming in my underwear. I'm not sure about this ..." Mena said, hesitating.

"Stop it. All of that is in our past," Julian said, pulling the shirt over his head. Turning, he reached into his pocket and slipped the small box out, concealing it in his fist, then allowed his pants to fall to the sand.

Mena inhaled sharply as her eyes, smoldering with desire, trailed down his body, making him rock hard.

"Your turn," Julian asked.

Mena slowly pulled her tank top over her head, careful not to cause any discomfort to her arm. The smooth brown skin of her flat stomach beckoned him and he dipped low, placing a flurry of kisses around her navel.

"Oooh! That tickles," Mena squirmed, then rested her hand on his shoulder.

Julian unbuttoned her capri pants and pulled them down over her hips to the sand.

Stepping away from their discarded clothes, Julian grabbed Mena's hand and led her to the water's edge.

"Are we going in?" Mena asked, a playful hint in her eyes.

"Your hair might get wet. Don't want you to be mad at me," Julian teased.

"I don't care. Let's wash all our burdens away," Mena said, squealing as she splashed through the water.

Standing alone on the beach, Julian watched her. His heart swelled with love for that woman. Opening the lid, he slipped the ring onto his pinky, then dropped the box onto the sand and chased after her.

"Took you long enough," Mena said, floating over to him.

Julian caressed his hands down the sides of her face, then kissed her gently. Their mouths moved in harmony with each other, sending a blaze of heat straight through his body. The kiss grew hotter with each passing second.

Pulling away, Julian stared into her sensual brown eyes.

"Did you mean it when you said you were all-in with me, with us?" Julian asked, his heart pounding in his chest.

"Of course, I did. I love you," Mena said, blessing him with a thousand-watt smile.

"Good. So, now I have one more little question," Julian said, slipping his hand out of the water. The three-carat round brilliant diamond ring sparkled between his fingers. "Will you marry me?"

Thank you for reading! I hope you loved the continuation of the soul mates love story of Julian and Mena and how Julian fought to rescue Mena from the clutches of Tubeec Hirad. While they one this battle, the war against Priscilla Dumay rages on as she's lured them back to St. Basil for an unknown reason ...

If you enjoyed THE RELENTLESS HERO, then I know you'll love the next book in the series, THE FALLEN HERO.

Julian and Mena are prepared to finally get justice for Ella and themselves by testifying against Priscilla Dumay in the criminal trial.

But disaster strikes when an unforeseen conflict lands Julian on the wrong side of the law.

What happens when this hero falls from grace?

CLICK HERE TO READ THE FALLEN HERO TODAY!

https://bit.ly/thefallenhero

If you enjoyed my novel, I'd appreciate your help in spreading the word, including telling a friend. Reviews help readers find books! I would love it if you left a review of THE RELENTLESS HERO on Amazon, BookBub or your favorite book site.

Angel Vane has been entertaining readers with her brand of crime thrillers for women. Now you can get one of her novellas for FREE, you just need to go to the link and tell her where to send it:

GET MY FREE SHORT STORY NOW
https://BookHip.com/SFTKRK

Also by Angel Vane

HERO IN PARADISE SERIES

Ex-Navy Seal Julian Montgomery fights off threats to the new life he's trying to build with art conservator Mena Nix. A gripping romantic suspense series with diabolical enemies, unpredictable twists and steamy romance!

THE HIDDEN THREAT (Prequel Novella)

THE ACCIDENTAL HERO

THE RELENTLESS HERO

THE FALLEN HERO

THE UNEXPECTED HERO (Coming Soon)

STAND-ALONE NOVELS

Stand-alone romantic mystery novels all set in the fictional Palmchat Islands.

THE UNWORTHY WIFE

THE SILENT ENEMY

About the Author

Angel Vane has a dramatic personality, is prone to exaggeration and is in perpetual pursuit of her creative muse. She loves writing, reading, traveling, spa days and soap operas. Angel resides in Tomball, Texas.

For more information:
angelvaneauthor@gmail.com

About the Publisher

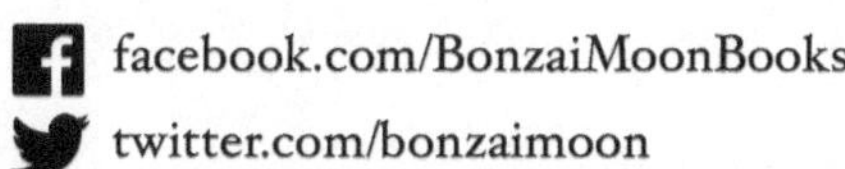

BonzaiMoon Books is a family-run, artisanal publishing company created in the summer of 2014. We publish works of fiction in various genres. Our passion and focus is working with authors who write the books you want to read, and giving those authors the opportunity to have more direct input in the publishing of their work.

For more information:
www.bonzaimoonbooks.com
info@bonzaimoonbooks.com

facebook.com/BonzaiMoonBooks
twitter.com/bonzaimoon

www.ingramcontent.com/pod-product-compliance
Lightning Source LLC
Chambersburg PA
CBHW030400200726
48286CB00015B/1843